WHEN THERE WAS YOU

CALIFORNIA DREAMING

BOOK TWO

K.C LAKE

OPEN BOOK PUBLISHING CO, LLC

Library of Congress Control Number: 2025916997

ISBN: 978-1-959229-12-4 (hardback)

ISBN: 978-1-959229-13-1 (paperback)

ISBN: 978-1-959229-15-5 (illustrated paperback)

ISBN: 978-1-959229-14-8 (digital)

Cover photo (paperback): "Chesapeake Bay Sunset" by Marina Pierce, copyright © 2025 (Bay Creek Beach in Cape Charles, Virginia).

*For those of you who are just a little (or a lot) broken
but used it to become the kickass, magnificent person
you are now... I see you.*

Reading order

Please note you are about to read book two in the California Dreaming series, which is a continuation of book one. If you have not read book one, *When There Was Us*, you are advised to do so now. *When There Was You* is not a standalone.

PREFACE

In California, circa 1982, modern technology was in its infancy, illegal drugs (especially cocaine, marijuana and LSD) were easily accessible and popular, young adults rarely used condoms, tattoos were worn mostly by criminals or hippies, theaters had one screen and played the same movie for weeks or longer, and muscle cars abounded as part of a vast car culture that has long endured in the Golden State. I have vivid, fond, reckless memories of this time in my life—and it provided the perfect backdrop for this story.

"And there I marveled at the forest's trees; my soul rooted to its deep verdant sea. I could no more leave it, than it could walk from me."

— ANGIE WEILAND-CROSBY

PROLOGUE
1989

Despite a restless night plagued by memories better left in the past, I damn near spring out of bed like a released jack-in-the-box when the hotel phone trills. My wake-up call. Through a fog of fatigue, I shuffle into the bathroom and into a hot shower, closing my eyes for a precious minute as water cascades across my skin.

As I reach for the miniature bar of soap, my gaze snags on the diamond sparkling on my ring finger and emotion lodges in my throat. Washing the planes of my body, I soon disappear into another memory...one where Mick caresses every inch with his strong, callused fingers, massaging shampoo into my hair, and whispering *You're perfect* and *I love you* with reverence.

I've got a whole cadre of shower memories with both Mick and Remy, many X-rated. When they attempt to surface in all their glory, I shoot them down with a mental Photon Torpedo from the starship *Enterprise*.

But the echo of their faces persists—their enigmatic smiles, the glint in their eyes, the cigarettes clamped between their sexy lips—and with it, a piercing pain I haven't experienced fully in years. With Mick, it's disappointment. With Remy, lingering anger.

But today isn't about them. It's about the friend we lost before his time. The lesson is stark and jarring: *There but for the grace of God go us*.

A bitter huff escapes me. I turn off the shower, retrieve a bath towel, and haul it back behind the curtain. Clinging to the remaining steamy warmth, I wrap the coarse material around me tightly, a physical attempt to keep the memories from soaking through my skin. Shaking my head, I rub the towel vigorously against my body, the truth refusing to be smothered.

Today is very much about Mick and Remy. And me.

ONE

1984

Mick teases me with a sticky marshmallow he just pulled from the fire. I arc toward his hand as he brings it closer to my lips only to jerk the treat away.

I strike again, and his smile turns mischievous. When I tumble against his legs, he laughs. The next time, victory is mine, and the golden cube of sugary goodness melts on my tongue as I let out a garbled "Ha!"

Those gray pools with the darker outer ring fixate on me, full of mirth, until I grab his fingers and pull them to my mouth. Sucking them clean, I watch the storm brew in those glorious eyes, and a slow smile dances on my lips.

"Fucking heroin," he groans, calling me one of two pet names I never tire of hearing him say.

We're on the private beach beneath the totally cool cottage he rents in Half Moon Bay, the fire warming us on this nippy March evening. The stars blaze a path overhead, the Milky Way visible out here in no man's land, my favorite place on earth—aside from being in Mick Callahan's arms.

Mr. Fine and All Mine flips me onto my back against the blanket, the weight of his sturdy frame pinning me as he kisses me breathless, our tongues tangling in the flickering light and igniting a whole different kind of flame.

I'm putty in his hands, my insides akin to the very marshmallow just consumed.

"I love you," I breathe. *Forever.*

He hovers over me, his long chestnut hair fluttering in the breeze. "I love you, baby."

Mick resettles beside me, spooning my body with his, his signature salty aroma mixing with the ocean's. We're quiet in the easy, organic way we often are, letting the Pacific's crashing waves provide the soundtrack, a hint of woodsmoke and caramelized sugar lingering in the air. The fire emits a loud pop, spitting sparks upward, and when my gaze follows one heavenward, a shooting star performs its swan song in the midnight sky.

It's a beautiful, perfect evening, one that feels like a hit of pure oxygen in my lungs. I'm unsure I could breathe without Mick anymore—or exit his orbit.

His callused hand travels up my arm, the tips of his fingers trailing lightly and sending ripples across my skin. "Remy's not coming until tomorrow around dinnertime," he says. "What do you want to do with our Saturday?"

I'm contemplative at first, but soon my blood races thinking about the three of us together. It's a potent combination—one that will likely feature a delirious, sextastic threesome. Or as my roommate Kit likes to call it, "a sandwich."

It's only happened twice. The first time was last October, on the boat. I thought our trio was capsizing for good, and then everything turned on a dime. We'd all shared our feelings, wants, and needs, and then somehow, agreed to share each other. And share each other we did that day. *Whew.*

The second time was just before Christmas. Suffice it to say, *they* were my best gift. Still are.

Our arrangement has *potentially disastrous* stamped all over it, I know. Yet it's been anything but. I see Mick a lot.

Remy less. Getting the three of us together has proven challenging. We live in different cities around the Bay Area. I'm a junior at San Jose State and in class five days a week, plus work part-time as a hostess for a local restaurant. Remy's still a mechanic at the Chevron in Oakland and has a overbearing mother to placate. Mick works at the boatyard in a supervisory role. His abusive father passed away in January after a prolonged, emotional shitshow surrounding his deteriorating health, which became Mick's responsibility to manage. He hasn't jumped ship or made any noise about moving to Florida—as he planned before his father rerouted his life—and I'm selfishly hopeful he won't.

When the three of us finagle time under one roof, it's a homecoming, since that's how our friendship began. The original Three Musketeers.

Until we complicated it.

I'm impressed with how we've managed. No jealousy or angst or petty bullshit drama. Together or separate, we're sharing the love...literally.

I quell my thrumming pulse and answer Mick's question. "Sailing? Or hiking? I'm game for anything."

"Want a surf lesson?"

With a gasp, I angle my face toward him. "For real?"

He gives me that heart-stopping, one-sided smile, and nods. "I've got an extra wetsuit and board. You mentioned wanting to learn. I already checked the forecast, and the waves should be small."

"I can't believe it. Yes!" I do a full one-eighty and pepper kisses across his face. Pulling back, I gaze into his eyes. "You never cease to amaze me."

Two

The scent of fresh coffee coaxes me awake. Blinking, I spy a bare-chested, tousled-haired Mick holding a steaming cup near my face.

"Rise and surf, sleepyhead."

A yawn emerges as I stretch my limbs then sit up.

Mick hands me the mug. "Here's a splash of coffee to go with your milk and sugar."

"Hilarious." I blow on the liquid and carefully sip. "Not too shabby, Mr. Callahan. Then again, you know what I like."

He grins, that dimple creasing his cheek. "Don't I?"

"God, don't look at me like that or we'll never leave the bed."

"Hmm..." He cocks his head, as if contemplating the merits of that statement.

I smile and flip aside the covers. Apparently, surfing trumps sex. Besides, I know I'll be getting that in spades later...with my *two* gorgeous men. This is going to be a day for the memory books.

After we inhale a quick breakfast of scrambled egg sandwiches, Mick outfits me in a navy neoprene wetsuit, which lays thick and heavy against my skin. He carries his OP shortboard—airbrushed with a sun-rising-over-the-ocean scene—as we navigate the windy, foggy path to the beach. The cool morning breeze blows across my exposed flesh and I'm grateful for the protective layer.

When we get to the bottom, our feet sink into the sand as we trudge toward the surf.

Mick places the board next to his longboard. "There's a lot to learn, so we'll take it at a slow pace and see how it goes. If you progress enough to get in the water, you'll be on the big boy."

Doubt twists in my gut about whether I'm equipped for this. That big-ass board and I won't even register as a snack if the ocean swallows us whole. I'm forty-nine percent petrified and fifty-one percent stoked.

Now's not the time for doomsday prophecies, quips my rational brain.

"Sounds good," I lie.

He explains the benefits of the longboard before demonstrating pop-up form.

When it's my turn, I stretch out on the fiberglass and attempt to rise, using my momentum. I try landing my feet close to the outer edges like he showed me, but one slides off and I fall straight into the sand. I go again. And again. And again. There's so much to remember. Feet flat. Knees bent. Chest forward. Arms out. It takes several tries, but eventually, I get the hang of it, despite lacking grace.

We talk about surfing conditions, wind direction, wave breaks, and the channel, which is the ideal place to paddle out. There's also a proper way to paddle—alternating arms vs. both at once.

It's a lot of information to absorb, but Mick's a good teacher, and a damn handsome one too. Our focus, after learning the pop-up, is paddling out. Then to try catching a wave—either prone, kneeling, or upright like a badass.

His gray eyes zero in on mine. "Most people don't get up

on their first day, or the second or third. It's not about how fast it happens but mastering the different pieces of the puzzle and then practicing them. Eventually," he promises, "it will all come together."

There's a twinge of wanting the glory of standing my first day, but my expectations stay low. It was hard enough getting it right on the sand. At the same time, Mick's so gentle and clear with his explanations, I'm excited to try.

By midday, the fog has evaporated, and sunshine warms us from overhead against cloudless, azure skies. The small waves appear manageable for a rookie like me.

"Ready?" he asks.

"As I'll ever be."

"Want me to grab the longboard or—?"

"I've got it."

Mick gives me an approving gaze, grabs the shortboard, and heads for the surf. I heft the unwieldy surfboard, grappling for a few steps before gaining my bearings.

I wade in, my toes breaching the shockingly icy ocean, followed by the frigid sea slithering into my wetsuit. "Holy mother!"

Mick chuckles. "I should've warned you. It's hella cold when you first get in before the water warms up under your wetsuit."

My lips press into a sardonic smile that evaporates when my teeth chatter.

"Can you see the channel?" he asks.

Welcoming the diversion, I scan the incoming waves, assessing prior to taking a stab, and pointing to what I think is one.

"Right on, Jax. Great job."

Pleased, I follow his lead and climb onto the longboard. As we paddle out together, I swallow any qualms. I've got my safe harbor by my side. His presence gives me a confidence boost.

If not for the adrenaline pumping through my veins, my limbs might quit propelling me. It's work paddling out, the waves undulating beneath us and providing serious resistance.

When we stop, Mick pulls my surfboard next to his and kisses me. It doesn't do much to calm my twitchy nerves, but I try and relax...again. We watch sets roll past, Mick pointing out the merits of each.

"Here comes a good one for you," he says. "Ready?"

My adrenal glands spike. "Yup."

"Paddle!"

My arms glide through the ocean as the wave lifts me. My stomach dips wildly and I cling to the board, gripping the sides like the white-knuckled chicken I am. I remain prone for a few minutes before turning out of it, as Mick suggested. *Total fucking rush!*

"How'd that go?" Mr. Gorgeous asks when I reach him.

"Good! I freaked out a little, so I didn't even try to pop up, but it helped to ride it for a while, get the hang of it, you know?"

"Atta girl."

We spend a couple of hours on the water. I ride waves flat, others kneeling, and some where I finally attempt to stand. I come close a few times but never fully land it, plunging into the ocean without an ounce of finesse.

Not that I care. I'm trying and improving, and that's what counts. Being here with Mick, learning to surf...it's one of the coolest days of my life. Then again, anytime I combine my two oceans—and Mick embodies everything ocean—it's powerful.

And the day's not over, not by a long shot. *The best is yet to come.* A laugh escapes at my own double entendre. I predict we're all coming tonight—and that brings on a full-body shudder of glorious anticipation.

We hike back up the cliff, peel off our wetsuits, and lay them on the deck railing. After showering off the sand and saltwater, we both don our usual, broken-in Levi's on our lower halves. Mick throws on a T-shirt, and I opt for something prettier—a white gauzy top—but I don't bother with a bra, and with the gossamer-thin material, it leaves little to the imagination. I blow-dry my hair and apply a touch of makeup, then rejoin my man, who's loading albums on the turntable.

ZZ Top's *Tres Hombres* plays first, those telltale guitar riffs filling the cottage, followed by their signature bluesy sound. My body responds, and I dance toward my boyfriend, slow and sultry. We both mouth, "Have mercy," when the band sings it, and he grabs my hand and spins me around the floor.

We're buoyant as we make dinner. Mick preps steaks for the grill and I make home fries the way Remy taught me—with fresh garlic and scallions sautéed in olive oil. While those are cooking, I rinse off cherry tomatoes and slice cucumbers for a salad, anticipation pinballing through my system as my thoughts swirl.

Mick encircles me with one arm. "You seem a little keyed up, baby," he murmurs, his breath warm in my ear.

He knows I am.

"Maybe a little," I breathe.

"I was thinking we could try something new tonight," he says, low, his beautiful eyes gleaming.

"What...what do you mean?"

He *tsks* me. "All good things come to those who wait. Besides, I want to run it by Remy first."

Now I'm dying of curiosity, my pulse leaping. "You think he won't go for it?"

Mick scoffs. "Are you kidding? Remy's game for anything. This is right up his alley—and I think yours. It's downright... raunchy."

The tension in my belly grows tighter and wetness seeps through my pink bikini underwear.

"*Fuck*. Now I've got a raging hard-on. I'm going to start the steaks before I bend you over the table."

My lips part, and my fingertips graze the bulge in his jeans. He shakes his head with a smile that says he can't wait to finish what we're starting.

An hour later, when Remy still hasn't showed or called, we sit down and eat without him.

I sip my Cabernet, my irritation growing. "It's not like him not to call. What do you think is going on?"

Mick slices off another hunk of steak. "I don't know."

I chew on my salad with more force than necessary, unable to stop stewing. "Maybe it's his parents. Or just his bitch mother."

"Maybe."

"What if he's in trouble? What if he's in the hospital?"

"Jacqui," he says, waiting until I meet his gaze. "We don't know anything. All we can do is wait for more information. And you know Remy's an irresponsible, reckless dipshit sometimes." He tips his beer to his mouth and takes a long swallow, his Adam's apple bobbing the way I love.

I snort. "*Most* of the time." Sawing into my sirloin, I chew a piece, savoring the bite. "The steak's delicious."

His lips lift in agreement. "So are these potatoes, baby."

As the turntable releases a new record, Mick steers our conversation elsewhere. "Fill me in on how your week went at school. What did you learn?"

I chuckle at the way he asks that last part, like I'm in kindergarten. "Journalism was good."

It's my most time-consuming class at three hours every day. We're more like staff than students. Our newsroom is huge, with a separate advertising department across the hall. Together, we run *The Spartan Daily* school newspaper. We have an advisor, but the entirety of every edition is created by students, then printed by the *San Jose Mercury News.*

It's fascinating to understand the inner workings of a

publication and what drives the number of pages each day, plus see an article I've written make it into the final edition. It's mind-blowing that something of this magnitude is left in the hands of undergrads. And no pressure—the newspaper has never missed a day in school history, so none of us intends to let that happen on *our* watch.

I fill him in on what I hate (hard news articles) and what I want (lifestyle features), and how the editor allowed me to pitch him five suggested features, and he'll green light one. Mick pours me another glass of wine as I rattle them off: how to get the perfect tan, best surfing spots in the region, finding true love on campus, what books students are reading, and advice faculty would tell their younger selves.

"Great ideas, baby. Bet he picks the last one," he says. "It's got a lot of meat to it. I can't wait to read it."

The familiar pride unfurls inside. I'm the plant and he's the water, and with his praise, I bloom.

We finish dinner. While I'm cleaning up, Mick tries calling Remy again, but there's still no answer.

"Should we call his parents?" I ask. "Maybe they know where he is."

"Negative. That will only sound the alarms and piss off Remy."

I sigh, frustrated and annoyed, even though he's right.

Where the fuck is he?

We take our drinks and sit in the lounge chairs out front to watch the sunset. The sky is painted with vivid color over the Pacific, deep oranges and reds with slashes of purple and gold. We soak in the beauty, which almost seems created just for us.

As the sun begins its descent into the depths, my skin chills and I climb between Mick's legs, absorbing his warmth as I lay back against his chest.

"Mick?"

"Hmm?"

"Do you ever have any regrets...about the three of us?"

He's quiet, as if curating his response. "Yes. And no. Here's the thing...if I had to choose between not having you or sharing you with my best friend, there was only one answer."

I digest his words.

"I never meant to fall in love with you," he admits. "I resisted it, but I'm not sure I had a choice. From the first hit, I've been fucked."

"That's why you call me 'heroin'?"

"Exactly why. Those honey eyes, long hair, body that won't quit...fucking irresistible. But that was just initially. You're the whole package, Jax. Your mind, sense of humor, kindness, willingness to go for what you want. Everything about you makes me want to be with you, near you, inside you. And now...I can't see my life without you in it." He caresses my forearm, sending a ripple of tiny bumps across my skin.

That's a confession he's never made. And I swim in it, reaching up to squeeze the other arm he's wrapped around me.

"If I hadn't left, hadn't shut the door, maybe you wouldn't have gone there with Remy. I can't really blame you." Mick scoffs and it's tinged with...bitterness? Sarcasm? "I'm sure it's what *he* wanted from the very beginning. And because Remy can be a total dog, I didn't want him to treat you poorly." He pauses.

"That's bullshit," he admits. "I wanted you for myself even knowing I couldn't expect it, considering..." He trails off. "But I've seen firsthand how Remy feels about you...and it's pretty much how *I* feel about you, so I can't exactly fault the asshole, can I?"

He's right. If Mick had never left, I never would've sought Remy's arms. I'm about to agree, pushing though the discomfiting tightness in my chest, when he continues.

"If I have to share with someone, it could only work with Remy...because I couldn't handle this with anyone else. And I can't imagine choosing this again in my lifetime."

I exhale a big breath at his admission, even as it creates new questions and underlying tensions. "I know it's not *normal*." The word tastes bitter on my tongue. "And I hate that our relationship is like some dirty little secret."

If society saw us openly sharing each other, we'd be ostracized, judged, ridiculed, labeled as deviants, more. Weirdly, it does seem natural. So how can it be wrong? Why are there hangups and unwritten rules about human behavior and appropriate relationship constructs?

Mick doesn't comment but squeezes me reassuringly.

Keeping my rambling thoughts to myself, I ask, "Are you worried about how this will end up?"

"I don't think about it, and I don't have the answers. All I know is I'm fucking crazy about you—so is Remy—and we're just going to ride this thing out."

"I'm crazy about you too," I murmur, lifting my head, my lips, in offering.

Our kiss begins soft, turns to probing, then heated. His hand cups my jaw, his other hand lacing through my hair as he hardens beneath me. We don't even notice when the sun sinks fully below the horizon, plunging us into twilight.

When we part, Mick issues a command in his deep, husky voice. "Now get your sweet ass in my bed so I can show you how much I fucking love and worship you."

THREE

Remy doesn't arrive that night. Or the next morning. When there's still no word by noon, I've traded pissed for distraught. My stomach is either in knots or flipping cartwheels. We hang out indoors in case he calls or shows up—reading, listening to albums, aimlessly watching television. My imagination runs wild with grim scenarios flashing in my mind. Even Mick appears uneasy.

When the phone jangles at five o'clock that afternoon, we both jump, leaping to our feet and racing toward the black wall unit near the kitchen. Mick answers and I hover.

"I'll accept the charges." A collect call. He gives me a nod that it's Remy, and I desperately want to rip the receiver out of his hand.

"*What?*" Pause. "You've got to be shitting me."

It's all agonizing one-sided replies. I shift from one leg to the other, straining to hear.

What happened?

"Fuck," Mick mutters, sliding a hand through his hair. "What can I do, man?"

Something is very, very wrong.

I pace. Patience is *not* one of my strong suits.

"Christ, Remy...whatever you need, you know I'll do it, brother."

What does he need?

"I'm sorry. And I want to give you a ration of shit, but I won't."

Pause.

"Do what you have to...and don't fuck around. This could be good for you."

What could?

"Yeah, man. I will. Keep in touch if you can."

If?

"Later."

Mick hangs up, and I'm dumbfounded he didn't fork over the phone to let me talk with Remy. "Why didn't you—"

Mick's head bows before his gaze swings to mine. "He didn't have time."

"But...but..."

"He risked some shit to make that collect call, Jax," he mutters, one of his hands cupping the back of his neck. "Remy's at the Betty Ford Center in Rancho Mirage."

"What the hell?"

"He got busted with coke, and his parents bailed him out of jail and pulled their magical purse strings to work some deal."

Mick yanks open the fridge, grabs a beer and wastes no time draining half.

I stand, expectant, the ground shifting under my feet as viscerally as an actual earthquake. "How much coke?"

"A crap ton. Enough to charge him with possession and intent to sell, a felony with almost assured prison time."

"*Goddamn* him." I knew the blow had gotten out of hand—the all-nighters, the reckless attitude. "So now he's in rehab?"

"Apparently. But in exchange, Mom and Dad are running

the show, and he's not sure how long he's going to be there. It could be months."

I struggle for what to say. "He...he didn't want to talk to me?"

"He wasn't even supposed to call. Said he has zero phone privileges, but he wanted us to know what happened and that he's sorry."

"He's *sorry?*" I sink into a nearby chair. Remy's just... gone? For however long his parents deem necessary?

A part of me can't help thinking how happy they must be to hold those marionette strings he so readily cut from their grasp. Now, he's back to being their puppet.

And I know exactly where that leaves me.

MICK SPEAKS, BUT IT ALL SOUNDS LIKE BUZZING IN my ears—and no amount of sitting around talking will change matters or stem the tidal wave pulling me under.

"I need to go," I say, standing up from the couch where we've been parked for the last hour. "I've got homework."

Trudging upstairs, I collect my belongings. My movements are stiff as memories flash. The day I met Remy. My first ride in his fast Camaro Z/28. How he called me "New Girl." His charm, flirtatiousness, those mischievous sapphire eyes. The way he welcomed me into the fold like I'd always belonged. How he saved me, cared for me, after the robbery. Our first kiss. More.

Mick pulls me in for a long embrace, plants a kiss on my forehead, and peers into my face, his own creased with worry. "Call me when you get home so I know you're safe."

I nod, chewing on my lower lip.

He walks me to my VW Bug and opens the door. Its condition mirrors my emotional state: dented and scratched, the seams splitting open on the seats. "I love you," he says, those mesmerizing gray eyes fixated on me.

My answer comes out hoarse. "I love you, too. So much."

The driver's seat squeaks when my butt slides onto it. He gently shuts the door, and I crank the ignition, the familiar rattle of the engine resounding. My eyes flick to the rearview as my tires crunch along the lengthy gravel drive. Mick tracks me until I'm out of sight.

Once I'm on the road, the floodgates open in a tidal wave of sorrow and self-pity. Whatever's happening to Remy has shifted our course, placing us firmly in the unknown. I'm no fortuneteller, but this seems like a death knell. It's impossible not to circle back to Mrs. Remington's long game. She wanted me out of the picture, never believing I was good enough for her son. She tried her damnedest to get rid of me by threatening to revoke Remy's trust fund, then set him up on dates with "respectable" women, not *tramps* like me. She must know Remy's bucked her wishes and eschewed her meddling. Now she's got the upper hand, the muscles to flex, the get-out-of-jail-free card. If his mother has her way—which she's now in the position to—it could be months before I see him again.

I don't deny Remy needs help. He's been off the rails too many times. Something terrible was bound to happen. Maybe, hopefully, rehab will straighten him out.

Of course, his wealthy parents placed him in the best rehab in the country, the renowned Betty Ford program. If memory serves, Rancho Mirage is near Palm Springs, playground for the rich and famous. And while treatment anywhere surely isn't a picnic, doing it at a swanky resort facility probably beats slumming it in downtown Oakland.

I vacillate between resentment, selfishness, and the unshakable, foreboding dread I'm losing Remy.

My heart seems altered, like it knows he's already gone from my life.

And maybe he is.

Four

I dial Mick's number, pressing thoughts churning in my mind. He answers on the third ring, and I drag the phone onto my balcony and light a smoke.

"You okay?" he asks.

No. "I've been thinking."

"About Remy?"

"About all of us, really," I murmur. "But one thing specifically. I don't want to do any more drugs."

Mick exhales loudly. "I had the same thought. With everything happening with Remy...if it wasn't clear before now, that shit is poison."

Relief spreads through me. I was unsure how important partying was to Mick, and this confirms it's not. "Watching Remy get hooked liked that...seeing where he is now...scares me. I don't want it to happen to me. Or you."

He hums then I hear his Zippo flick as he lights a cigarette, visualizing just the way his head tilts as he does it. "I think some are prone to it, maybe? Meaning, hardwired. Remy's never had boundaries. He's always been the life of the party, the instigator, the master of ceremonies."

"No brakes." I take a long pull and the cherry burns brightly.

"Exactly," he mutters. "And he was—*is*—a difficult, stubborn motherfucker to rein in."

"Tell me about it." Whenever I tried, he lashed out, blew me off, or worse, made me out to be a nag.

"I figured he'd grow out of it. I assumed we all would."

This is precisely what I've realized in the past twenty-four hours. "It was wearing thin. In hindsight, my attitude about it was stupid. I made those same assumptions...that I'd wake up one day and *boom*, have my shit together, act like a responsible adult. And after watching my father abuse alcohol and my mother become addicted to pills, you'd think I'd have the sense to steer clear."

"You're on your way now, baby."

"Yup. Not looking back. No more drugs."

"No more drugs," Mick agrees. "But I'm hanging onto this bad smoking habit a bit longer," he adds, inhaling another audible drag.

I groan, gazing at the dwindling cigarette still trapped between my two fingers. "Not quite ready for prime time there yet either. But someday."

He chuckles. "Someday."

∼

WEEKS PASS WITHOUT ANOTHER WORD FROM Randolph Remington III. I've never been more grateful for Mick's presence, and we spend every available second together. He's extremely good at distracting me...surf lessons, fires on the beach, dinners at sunset, languid lovemaking.

It's what our relationship would have been like if Remy and I had never gotten romantically involved. Despite the numbing pain the absence of my red-haired, blue-eyed lover brings, I'm okay. More than okay. I'm madly in love with

Mick Callahan and have been from the moment I laid eyes on his perfect lips, haunting eyes, scarred eyebrow, and drool-worthy hardbody.

Mick helped create our powerful connection by letting me in, sharing his painful past, and embracing whatever we are or could be. He once told me I was giving, but in truth, he's the giver. Damn near selfless. He's infused me with pride, confidence, and validity. He believes in me—the most potent aphrodisiac on the planet. I can't imagine loving another human being more than I do him. Ever.

Not that I've written Remy off or don't obsess about him. But what choice do I have except to wait until he's out of rehab to know how to move forward—or even *if* we will? As Mick suggested, I'm waiting for more information instead of drowning in all the *what ifs*.

FIVE

"Meet me at the boatyard. Pack for an overnight," Mick says through the phone.

I squeal, loud enough he probably pulled the receiver away from his ear. "We're going out overnight?"

"Yeah, baby." Bet he's smiling.

"Mick Callahan, you are my favorite human being on the planet."

"Better be."

"And you realize this kind of treatment is why you get blow jobs at the wheel, captain."

He hums. "Another reason I'm addicted to you. I'll pretty much do anything for you now."

I catch my reflection in the bedroom mirror—momentarily transfixed at the happiness radiating from my face.

We hang up and I busy myself getting ready, shoving clothes and toiletries into a backpack. I pull on my bikini, shorts, and a cute tank, and snag warmer stuff for when the fog rolls in and we're out on the bay.

I nearly trip in my haste to get downstairs. My roommates study me from the living room couch in our shared condo. Kit is slumped into the cushions, using the coffee table as a footrest as she watches TV; Jaswinder sits cross-legged reading a *Glamour* magazine.

"Where's the fire, Jax?" Jas says, flipping her gorgeous onyx hair off her face. Her white jeans and peasant top contrast gorgeously with her deep beige skin.

"Let me guess," Kit muses, mischief in her warm whiskey eyes. "Off to see the wizard? Mr. Marvelous? What amazing adventure has he conjured up for you today?"

I laugh, dropping my backpack onto the carpet with a thud. "We're sailing...but he's taking me somewhere overnight!"

Jas drops her head back with a groan. "You're such a lucky bitch."

"We hate you," Kit adds, standing up to adjust her navy sweatpants and oversized T-shirt.

"What about you, Jas? You're dating a total hottie."

She smiles knowingly. "True. And we're dragging Kit out to LA Rocks tonight."

A memory surfaces of my twenty-first birthday. We danced for hours in that club—Remy, his buddy Vinny, my roommates, and me—all drunk off our asses.

I don't want to remember. Not today. It's easier not to think about Remy at all. Even Mick and I agreed to stop talking about him for now.

"Against my will," Kit inserts. "They keep trying to set me up with someone. I'm perfectly fine rolling solo. I don't need a man to be complete. None of us do."

I tilt my head, considering. "But there are perks."

"Says the girl with two men who would slay dragons for her." Kit blanches, realizing she's stepped in it.

My smile fades. Jas shoots Kit a look.

"I'm sorry, Jax. It just...slipped out."

I shake my head. "It's okay."

"No word from Remy, huh?" Jas asks.

"No," I murmur. "He's still in rehab without phone privileges. If he could call, he would." *Right?*

The girls' heads bob in sync.

"Go enjoy Mr. Perfect Man...and your overnight," Jas says.

Kit waves. "Yes, fine, enjoy your man." She raises her brows and pins me with a stare. "Until you don't need his ass anymore."

I smile—wider when I picture my boyfriend's firm ass and those sexy divots at the base of his back. "I can't imagine not ever needing Mick's ass...and every other *ass*-et he has."

We all share a laugh before I snag a soda from the fridge, pick up my stuff, and bid them farewell.

I RACE OUT TO THE MARINA AND INTO MICK'S ARMS. In short order, we're heading for open water on a sleek thirty-footer. The boat's gleaming white hull is offset by teal accents with rich teak flooring and trim, giving it a stately vibe.

In minutes, I've stripped down to my new black bikini. My boyfriend's admiring gaze roves over my body, his smile big enough to bring out that irresistible dimple.

"I was starting to have withdrawal symptoms," he says.

"I've got your hit right here, handsome."

That keeps the grin on his face.

We sail for a few hours, and I revel in Mick doing his whole seafaring gig. He's so at home on every boat, where his combined passion for the sea and outdoors is unmasked and unleashed. My heart lifts as I watch the chestnut hair riffle around my captain's contented face. I love his hair...how soft it is, how it falls in gentle waves, how it's lighter where the sun's kissed it. And I adore how he's always kept it long, past the nape yet not all the way to his shoulders.

He drops anchor and we nibble on hard salami, fontina, grapes, and hunks of fresh baguette. He's drinking beer, me wine. The sun warms us from overhead, light glints off the water, and the wind snaps the sails and flags from slack to attention.

A gust whips my hair horizontally, wayward strands kissing Mick's cheek. "Sorry," I say, trying to wrangle it back.

"You know I dig your hair. In every iteration." He admires my golden locks for a moment then shakes two cigarettes out of his pack, clamps them between his lips, and covers the Zippo's flame with his hand to get them lit. He hands me one while exhaling the acrid smoke.

We're quiet as we smoke, enjoying the rocking of the boat, the sun on our faces, the ease of being in each other's company.

After Mick pitches his cigarette butt overboard, he snags a length of nautical rope and ties a variety of knots in succession.

I'm mesmerized watching him work. "Teach me one."

He glances up, one side of his mouth lifting. "The bowline is an essential sailing knot. Make sure you loop on top, not the bottom, like this," he says, demonstrating. "There's an old Boy Scout saying to help you remember the sequence: The rabbit goes out of the hole, around the tree, and back through the hole."

He pulls the knot tight, and it leaves a loop. "Now you try."

Rope in hand, I mentally repeat the instructions and complete the knot. Satisfaction hums through me as I return the length so he can show me more.

Mick nudges my shoulder with his. "You're a natural." He whips through a clove hitch next like he's done it a hundred times. He probably has. "Hold out your hands and place your palms together."

When I've done as he asked, he winds the cord around my wrist.

"Here's what I like about the slipknot." He binds my wrists and cinches the knot snug. "You're at my mercy."

His gaze is teasing and heated, and just like that, my inner flame ignites.

Mick lifts my arms by the rope. "Up you go, baby."

My eyes widen as he coaxes me to stand.

He tugs, leading me behind the large cockpit wheel, where he secures the tail of the rope over my head, concentration and a small smile etched on his face. He steps back to survey my position. The boat deck dips lower here, the wheel supporting my back and offering a modicum of privacy.

Oh my.

"Mmm," he murmurs, stepping forward. He releases the ties on my string bikini top, and it floats to the slatted teak near my feet. My nipples harden under his gaze and the light wind caressing them. "So beautiful."

His eyes lift to my mouth before he consumes me with one of his devastating kisses—the possessive, claiming, you-will-always-be-mine kind. Heat floods my center and my heart thumps wildly, constricting my breath.

Mick lowers his head and sweeps his tongue across my taut nipple and areola, sending another jolt to my groin. When he finishes with the left, he lavishes attention on the right. My pelvis arches toward him as a low moan escapes my lips.

He drops to his knees, and this sight alone makes me shiver in anticipation...and more wet. He undoes the two strings at my hips and the last of my bikini falls away. Mick spreads my legs and dives between my thighs. I gasp as his tongue plunges into my depths and again when he sucks on the bundle of nerves pulsating from his touch.

I pant his name like a mantra. Mick, Mick, *Miiiiiiiiii-iiiiick.*

His groans of pleasure fuel mine. "God, I love the taste of you."

Our eyes meet when he stares up at me, pupils blown, all but eclipsing the gray. "And the way you look right now, baby? Filthy. I'm never letting you off this boat."

I'd like nothing more than to sail off into the sunset with this man and never look back.

Lust hazes my vision as he works his glorious fingers and tongue in tandem on a body he's mastered. My orgasm rips through me, my legs shaking and buckling in its wake.

Stars appear behind my lids as Mick rides it out. Before my spasms abate, he whips me around, grabs my hips, and steadies me. He glides his tip through my drenched center, and I back toward him, begging for more.

He doesn't make me wait, ramming his hard cock all the way in and stealing my breath. Our moans commingle then dissipate into thin air.

"Goddamn, I love how we fit, how you hug every inch."

"Yes," I pant. "You're perfect." Us together? *Sublime.*

He roars out his satisfaction and then gives me more. And more. And still more, fucking me like it's our last day on earth. I relish the fullness of him, how we connect, the rightness.

The boat rocks underneath us, the sun adding heat as sweat beads on our skin. My moans and his grunts are a porn movie soundtrack, and at his mercy, I'm the sexiest woman alive. Naked. Exposed. Bound. All his to play with, and I like how he's using me, possessing me, claiming me.

God, he's fucking me hard. My lashed wrists wrench with his thrusts. He's not gentle and the rope burns, but I want every ounce of carnal pleasure edged with that delicious sting.

The exquisite tension escalates. He's close.

Give it to me. Give it all to me.

Mick grunts loudly and explodes into me, grinding his hips against my shaking legs and bucking through his release. He collapses over my back, one of his arms snaking down around my torso to stabilize us as our breathing steadies.

"You okay, baby?" he murmurs.

"Yes," I rasp. "God, yes."

Mick reaches up and easily undoes the knot, freeing my hands. Pulling me into his lap on the nearest bench seat, he holds me as we finish coming down, and I savor our connection and the comfort of being in his arms.

He lifts my chin and kisses me deeply, sharing what's left of me on his tongue and infusing so much love with his gentle probing. He inspects my wrists. "You sure you're alright? I didn't hurt you?"

Through a wondrous, post-coital daze, I caress his cheek. "Not even. That was...amazing."

His relief gives way to his one-sided smile. "Good. I've got lots more ideas—and rope. Especially once I get you back to my bed." His eyes gleam, jump-starting my just sated girl parts.

"You can do whatever you want to me. I'm yours." I press my lips against his.

We sunbathe, kiss, and talk more before we sail into a deserted cove for the night. We steer clear of tough topics, and it's not difficult. Being together is effortless, every moment solidifying our love and weaving it into something stronger.

That night, rocked gently by the Pacific, we fall asleep wrapped in each other's arms.

Six

A week later, my heart stutters like it's the first time ever glimpsing Mick Callahan. He's on my doorstep in his typical faded Levi's, a black AC/DC concert tee stretched over his muscular chest. His gray eyes, highlighted by that darker outer rim, etched indelibly in my brain.

His lips are curved into a smile, but there's something weary in his expression. I launch myself at him, our mouths pressing together as his arms bring me closer. His breath holds traces of mint, but it's nothing compared to his faintly salty ocean scent that follows him everywhere. I adore the entire Mick package—and I'm still thoroughly Micknotized.

He grins against my mouth when I make no effort to stop kissing him. "Can I come in or..."

I pull back a few inches. "Or what?"

"Or are we going to give the neighbors a real show?"

Chuckling, I release my hold and step back to allow him entry.

"Are your roommates home?" he asks, trailing me into the living room.

"They went away this weekend. Some annual camping thing."

Mick's eyebrows raise and he scoops me around the waist. "We've got the place to ourselves?" He kisses the hollow of my throat.

"Uh huh," I breathe.

His tongue licks a slow trail up my neck. "What should we do with all this privacy?"

I squirm as his warm breath sears me in the best way. Words evaporate, replaced by jagged panting.

He shifts my hair over my shoulder for better access, licking the shell of my ear and then probing deeper, eliciting a needy whimper from deep within me. "Is that your final answer?"

"Mick..." It's a plea. The man reduces me to rubble—and subsequent begging.

He chuckles and...stops.

My eyes flare open. "You can be such a bastard."

He grins. "Let's get dinner like we planned. Mexican sounds really damn good."

"Fine. I'll be dessert."

He pulls me in for another kiss. "Yes, you will. We'll save the best for last."

After I slip on some sandals, he tucks me into the Mustang, and we head toward downtown San Jose. We roll down the windows and absorb the day's lingering sunlight.

Mick glances over at me. "I talked to Rick."

The admission sends a jolt through me. He has news about Remy...*finally*. My shock is followed by an inner recoil as any mention of Mr. Remington reminds me that he's a lecherous creep and his wife's a high-handed battle-ax.

I want to shout, *Why the hell didn't you lead with this?* but don't. "What did he say?"

"Remy's still in rehab, but they think he'll be coming home in a few weeks. He's supposedly better."

"Meaning?"

"Hell if I know. He's confined with no access to drugs or

alcohol, so he can't exactly fuck up. Maybe he's saying and doing all the right things. If I know Remy…"

"He's playing the game."

Mick nods and lights us both cigarettes.

I take a long pull off mine, appreciating the zing of the tobacco searing my lungs. "Did he say anything else?"

"They got rid of his apartment, cancelled his lease, and they expect Remy to move in with them for the foreseeable future."

My head whips toward Mick. "Wow."

"It's pretty fucked up. And I doubt Remy knows."

"Unfuckingbelievable. Virginia must be in heaven, getting to control her boy's every step." And that doesn't bode well for me. I'm not "welcome" at her house; the memory of her telling me so replays like it happened yesterday instead of months ago. Simmering anger burns through my chest.

"She'd love nothing more."

"I'm screwed. You realize that don't you?"

Mick flicks his butt out the window and reaches for my hand, stroking my knuckles with his thumb. "We don't know anything yet, Jax. Let's just see what happens."

But all I can see is Remy being ripped from my life, which will then put a strain on Mick and me. The three of us work together. As a team. As Musketeers.

Taking a deep breath, I listen to my beautiful man. He's smart, level-headed, logical. Always so calm. Right about most things. I trust he knows what he's talking about.

The alternative is unfathomable.

Seven

Rain pelts comfortingly against the roof of the cottage, louder up here in the loft. It's poured all day, and Mick and I have cocooned inside making love, snacking, and lounging.

It's my last weekend before I hole up for finals, and it's unlikely I'll see Mick for a couple of weeks. Once the semester ends, I'm starting my internship, working part time as a receptionist for a hair salon, and still hostessing at Original Joe's. Between the three, I should be able to cover my expenses.

My father made it perfectly clear months ago that he would not pay my rent or bills while I "lounge around" all summer. His ultimatum: move home or support myself. When I explained my internship was a mandatory class, he met me in the middle, providing half and leaving me to earn the rest.

There's no way in hell I'm ever moving back to my parents' house again. Living free of restrictive parental controls is even better than I'd imagined, and I'm no longer in a front row seat witnessing my mother's deepening slide into depression and Valium therapy. Plus, I love my roommates.

It's unacceptable to abandon them or leave them in a lurch. I'd take on four jobs if it meant keeping my status quo intact.

Until my schedule is settled, it's impossible to know how it affects my time with Mick. He's awesome about making it work, though. The former Mr. Cryptic and Unavailable is now Mr. Easygoing.

My mind is far from at ease, however. Thoughts about Remy getting discharged from rehab and returning to Oakland turn my insides into roiling lava. His return will supposedly occur around the same time as finals. If I think too much about it, I spiral. Too many unanswered questions skitter through my brain. It's impossible not to predict a total doomsday situation for us if Remy remains under his parents' control.

What if. What if. What fucking if.

Mick and I shower together. He washes my hair, massaging my scalp and gently filtering through the long strands—one of the most decadent experiences of my life.

A slow groan escapes. "You spoil me," I say.

"It's my pleasure, believe me." He kisses my shoulder so tenderly, I melt even more.

He finishes, and I repay the favor, soaping him head to foot. My hands glide over every square inch of his chiseled planes and valleys, paying homage to his beautiful physique.

Afterward, we reheat leftover Chinese food and bring it all into the living room to eat while watching *Magnum, P.I.* reruns.

"Don't even think of eating all the Moo Shu Pork. You know it's my favorite," I say.

He feigns outrage. "If you really loved me, you'd let me have it."

I grin, unable to fight Mr. Fucking Gorgeous. "You can have everything of mine."

That brings a sterling smile to his face, that dimple

taunting me like a siren call. He plants a plum-sauce-infused kiss on my mouth and hands over the container. "Fuck me."

My victorious laugh echoes in the space. I wasn't lying, but I happily polish off the rest of the carton all the same.

Sunday dawns clear with no rain, clouds, or fog. Mick dials the weather line and confirms we've got a beautiful day at our disposal. We're both itching to get out after being cooped up yesterday...not that it didn't have its advantages.

"We should hike Mount Tam," he says, arms crossed over his naked chest, his lower half clad in Levi's. With his tousled hair and bulging biceps, all six feet of him are distracting.

I blink, de-Micknotizing myself. "I've never been, even though it's so close." I duck into the fridge and grab ingredients for a scramble. "How high is it?"

"About twenty-five hundred feet to the peak. If it's clear, you get a hell of a payout—a three-hundred-and-sixty-degree view of Marin, SF, the East Bay, Mount Diablo, and our lady the Pacific. This could be one of those days. It'll be fun."

The vegetables sizzle when they hit the hot pan, and I stir, coating them in olive oil. "Fun like learning-to-surf fun, or fun as in this-is-going-to-kill-me fun?"

Mick presses against me in answer, snaking one arm around my waist. "Don't you trust me to show you a good time?" His deep voice shoots straight to command central.

I hum out a chuckle.

"Have I steered you wrong yet?" His breath tickles...and so much more.

"No," I breathe, trying and failing to concentrate on cooking.

He kisses my cheek.

God, this man.

I finish our scramble as Mick butters thick slices of fresh sourdough toast, and we sit down to eat, trading smiles.

We dress in shorts, T-shirts, and sneakers, and I corral my hair into a ponytail. Mick grabs a backpack, stuffing in snacks, a canteen (of course he has one), and a first aid kit. Fucking Boy Scout.

And all mine.

The Mustang engine rumbles its familiar cadence as we drive north up the highway to San Francisco before crossing the majestic Golden Gate Bridge. Barges and boats large and small speckle the deep blue water surrounding us.

My excitement mounts as we enter Mt. Tamalpais State Park, with signs for Muir Woods, Muir Beach, and Stinson Beach. Mick parks in the campground lot and leads the way to the trailhead. It's a gorgeous day, a breezy sixty-eight degrees and climbing.

As I follow in Mick's footsteps, I'm hit with a sudden pang. Does he regret staying? His dream was moving to Florida, getting away from the Bay Area. Yet he's still here. *Because of me.* I question whether I'm worth it. He *is* living his dream of working on the water—and he's made it clear I'm wanted and cherished. Maybe I'm still waiting for the other shoe to drop because of our early days, our back and forth, him so easily...leaving. Now he's worried about Remy, another tether. Are we holding him back?

Mick jars me from my thoughts, glancing back as we make our way up the trail. "Do you know why Mount Tam is called the sleeping lady?"

"Nope."

"It's the shape, the contour of the mountain." He illustrates with his hand. "It looks like the profile of woman lying down. It's based on an old legend, one where a heartbroken Native American woman was abandoned by her lover, laid down, and died."

"That's sad." *Let's hope it's not foreshadowing.*

Why am I on this negative wave? As if the universe is trying to intervene, my shoe snags on a tree root and I lurch ungracefully.

As we climb, Mick points out medicinal plants, helps me avoid poison oak, and describes places he wants to take me camping. I'm happy to let him do most of the talking as I labor behind him, wondering how much smoking has impacted my lungs.

We near the summit and the trail broadens, revealing a breathtaking vista of the Pacific. Grasses flank our dirt path, big rocks jut from the ground, and it only gets better as we continue.

Pausing when we reach a good viewing spot, we crawl out onto a rock cluster. My entire body sighs contentedly when I sit and stretch my legs, especially my feet.

Mick opens the backpack. "Hungry?"

"Starving."

He pulls out the snacks and offers me the canteen. I slug down a few gulps.

"This is incredible," I marvel.

"Mm-hmm," he answers, biting into an apple.

We're silent as the stunning panorama washes over us. It's peaceful up here, basking in the sunlight while cooled by the breeze swirling on the mountaintop.

I gasp and nudge Mick, whispering, *"Bald eagle."* I so rarely see one, and never the condors anymore.

"Those are the bad motherfuckers of the bird world."

It flies by, a badass indeed, scrutinizing us.

After resting a spell, we continue exploring the various sides of the summit—every perspective worth the effort. Experiencing this with Mick—more of his reverence for the great outdoors—it's clear I love it too. It's easy to visualize a lifetime of hiking, camping, canoeing, surfing, sailing... together. And when we pause to gaze toward San Francisco, his arms wrapped around me, the thought cements itself deep: *I want to marry this man.*

I don't know whether he feels the same. And I can't answer the other thought attempting to wiggle its way in: What. About. Remy?

EIGHT

After studying for days, I'm bleary eyed and can't wait to be done with the semester. I've just got to push through the weekend, then my exams next week, and I'll be home free. Sort of. I'm going to be slammed all summer between two part-time jobs and my internship. I'm stoked about the latter, which is for a regional health magazine.

I miss Mick, but he's right to steer clear and let me focus. There is no focusing with Mr. Phenomenal around. As I rotate my stiff neck, it cracks unapologetically. I reposition my bed pillows, get comfortable, and open my hefty Communications Law textbook to review—again—the material aligned with my final.

Hours later, the phone trills. A glance at the clock shows it's 8:14 p.m., still early by cramming standards.

"Hey, baby," Mick's voice croons in my ear.

I push the book off my lap, unhunching my tight shoulders. "Hi."

"How goes the studying?"

I recline, stretching long, and nearly groan with the release. "It's buckets of fun, are you kidding?"

He snorts.

"And I miss you."

When he pauses, my sixth sense jumps into alert mode. "What's wrong?"

Mick lets out an audible breath. "Remy's home."

I lurch upright, my heart banging in my chest like a caged bird as my legs swing off the bed to the floor. "Where?"

"Piedmont." His parent's house.

"When can we see him?"

"I'm heading over there in the morning."

The implication is clear. He's going alone. We both know I'm not welcome at the Remington household. "You...talked to him?"

"Briefly—just long enough to make a plan to see him tomorrow and tell him I'm glad he's alright."

My head hangs, my forehead sinking against my hand. "This sucks." *For me, anyhow.*

"I'm sorry, Jax. I know this hurts. I'll suss things out, see what I can arrange. But don't let it derail your studying."

"Fat chance. It's already blowing up my brain."

"This is why I debated even telling you."

My incredulous huff punctuates the silence. "That's totally messed up, Mick."

"You know I would never keep something of this magnitude from you. But can you hang on to your patience a little while longer...and not allow it to fuck up your finals?"

He's right. "Yeah, sure, whatever," I mutter.

"Good girl."

My throat constricts and a few tears slide down my cheeks. "You'll call me tomorrow?"

"As soon as possible. I promise."

I sniffle. "Tell him I love him?"

"Of course."

"And Mick?"

"Yeah?"

"I love you."

"I know, baby. I love you too."

It's the most interminable, insufferable twenty-two hours of my life. I try my damnedest to study, to ignore the anxiety swirling through me, to not watch the clock. But the longer it takes Mick to check in, the angrier I become, conjuring fantasies of hanging up on him.

When he finally calls, he sounds exhausted. Reticent.

"How is he?" I hold my breath.

"Healthy. And...happy."

Well, that's good. "So, what's the deal?"

Mick doesn't say anything for such a long time that dread gallops up my spine.

"What is it? Something's wrong. Just tell me—"

"Remy's engaged."

I snort at the absurdity of that statement. But Mick doesn't utter a sound.

"Wait. Are you *serious*?"

He sighs, and I picture him raking a hand through his hair. "Unfortunately, yeah, I am."

"Bu...but," I sputter. "How? When? Why?"

"He met her in rehab and...things progressed."

"You've got to be fucking kidding me. This chick is a drug addict? Solid choice." *Not to mention, how the hell could he be in love with someone else...someone other than me?*

"She works there," he clarifies, "and apparently, they fell in love."

It's a knife stab to the heart, the gut, everywhere. Emotions bleed out from every wound. I stop pacing the living room floor and sag against the wall, slumping to the carpet.

"I don't understand," I rasp. "He was only there a couple

of months. How does he come out *engaged*? What about everything we shared?"

"I'm sorry, baby. He's almost a different guy. He claimed he experienced a 'spiritual awakening' and now he's got some...vision or mission or purpose. He never wants to drink or use drugs again. He's in love. He's...excited about life." Mick seems to grapple with explaining what he witnessed.

"And his parents are on board with this engagement?"

"She's from a good family. They're thrilled, gave it their blessing. Thinks she'll help him stay on track."

"Did you meet her?" I whisper.

"No. She's still working at the facility, but she's moving here soon. They plan to get married in six months. They... already set the wedding date."

The finality of it sinks further into my chest. *RIP Remy and Jacqui.*

"He asked you to be his best man." My voice is flat, broken.

"Mm-hmm." It's almost like he doesn't want to admit it.

We're both silent.

"I'm sorry, Jax," he finally says. "For what it's worth, Remy is too."

My sarcastic bark rings hollow. "What bullshit."

Mick sighs. "I don't know what to say. I can barely wrap my head around all this."

"Whatever."

"Don't."

"Don't what?" I spit. "Be hurt? Incensed? Blindsided? Bewildered?"

"Christ. You should feel whatever you need to. But don't take this out on me."

"You know, Mick, right now you aren't exactly topping my list of concerns. If that makes me a selfish bitch, then so be it. You want to know how I feel? After months of waiting— *worrying*—Remy comes out of rehab without a care in the world and a new fiancée. The two best pals are together again, while Jacqui, the whore, is cast aside as if she never mattered."

"That's..." There's a thud. Did he punch a wall? "Although some of that may be true," he grits out, "you know damn well neither of us think of you that way. We fucking loved you. I still love you. Do *not* cheapen what we have with that dramatic bullshit."

His words hit like a slap, but the roar in my ears deafens everything. They don't penetrate. And nothing he says will change how much this burns.

"I have to go," I manage.

"Goddamn it! Don't fucking do this."

But I do.

Through blinding tears, I replace the receiver. My breath sputters and stalls, and my thoughts rage, deluging me like a summer squall.

My roommates find me on the floor, curled against the wall, hiccuping after running out of tears. I never knew a body could stop manufacturing them, but at some point, the torrent stopped, leaving my skin raw, chapped, and tender to the touch after repeatedly squeegeeing my face with my fingers.

Jas and Kit pull me into their arms and hold me, but I'm an empty, limp ghost of myself. Then they ply me with left-over pizza and boxed wine as they force me to relive that phone call.

Mick must be so pissed at me. And worried.

My sullen inner child doesn't care.

That's false...I'm just not ready to deal with it yet.

My roommates are sympathetic, asking questions and treading carefully. I'm grateful they're not probing too deep. My head hurts. My heart's been through a meat grinder. The unknowns loom.

"No more sandwiches," I finally say, unsure how I'm managing to joke. I will miss those Mick and Remy sandwiches.

Kit offers a half-hearted smile. "It was good while it lasted though, right?"

I bite back more tears and nod. It really was. "The realist in me always knew it wouldn't last forever. But I sure never predicted it ending this way."

Jas's head bobs. "I'm shocked—and I'm a reporter. I pride myself on being impossible to surprise, but damn if I ever saw this coming...not from Remy."

The words from the past come tumbling back. Words shared just before I'd moved.

I love you, Rem, I'd said.

I fucking adore you, he'd answered.

I believed it. Now, though...I can't help wondering if Remy had been spewing poetic bullshit. If anything he'd said was honest. How the fuck can he treat me like this? Cast me aside without even a conversation? It doesn't make sense unless he never cared about me in the first place. But that doesn't ring true either. Damn it, I'm *not* feeling sorry for him. I'll walk on glass shards over a bed of fire before that happens.

"You and Mick are still good, right?" Jas asks.

My tear ducts reactivate. "I behaved like a total asshole."

"He'll understand," Kit says.

MICK DOESN'T ANSWER HIS PHONE WHEN I CALL HIM later that night. Not that I blame him. Much. Still on shaky ground, I opt to give him space and try again tomorrow.

The next day comes, and his phone remains unanswered. Is he punishing me? I hardly remember a word I said now. I'm numb and doing my best not to think about any of it. But as the day progresses, my anxiety escalates, panicky flutters whispering, *You're losing him too.* And I can't. He's my fucking world. As much as I need to buck up and keep studying, I need to make things right with Mick more.

The afternoon light wanes. Time to stop waffling. Speeding to Half Moon Bay, I chain smoke while death-gripping the steering wheel.

I'm relieved when I spot his blue Mustang in the driveway, although my heart palpitations ramp up as I step from the car.

Mick stares at me through the big glass windows of the cottage. He's too far away for me to decipher his expression, but winged things flap around my insides like coked-up bees.

When he makes no move my direction, I push open the door. Mick leans against the kitchen counter, arms folded across his chest, gray eyes dark and stormy. His stance fills me with foreboding.

I drop my purse on the couch and approach, meeting his piercing gaze. "Hey," I whisper.

He nods, the movement curt.

"I'm sorry," I blurt. "The way I acted...was really shitty."

He nods again.

Damn it. "Please, can we talk this through?"

"I don't know. Can we? I'm not sure what there is to say."

I'm on unsteady ground. "I don't understand. I was upset, okay?"

He regards me cooly, eyes like steel. "Here's the thing, Jacqui. I've been about as patient as a man can be—more than a man should *have* to be."

"I—"

"Let me finish. You asked a while ago if I had regrets about this whole party of three. I was honest. Yes and no. And I've done my damnedest to make this work, to love you, and fucking share you when I really just want you all to my fucking self."

Sweat trickles down my back as my pulse rapid fires.

"And then this shit goes down with Remy. Surprise, surprise...except it's not. Remy's a fuckup, has been his entire, rich playboy-entitled life. And a part of me wasn't sorry in the slightest. What happened to him was a hundred percent his fault, on the heels of us trying to help him see reality for the past, what...year? And the bonus? Having you all to myself. It's been *a fucking dream*."

Tears prick the back of my eyelids and my throat stings with his admission.

"And then you get angry with *me* about Remy's shit? And shed a tear over Remy *after all this*? How do you think that makes me feel? Am I your consolation prize? Second choice?"

"No—"

"Does all this," he demands, gesturing between us, "mean nothing to you? Think about it for five fucking minutes. See my perspective. Not yours. Not Remy's. *Mine*." His hand bangs against his chest with his last word.

My body sags under an avalanche of guilt. Have I made him think he's second best?

It hits me then. How he's always believed he's not good enough, that he'll never be able to give me what I "deserve," and worse—that he deserves nothing for himself, not even happiness.

I take a tentative step toward him. "Mick." My voice cracks as I swipe away the tears cascading down my cheeks. "I love you more than anyone...ever...in my entire life."

His arms don't loosen across his chest.

I inch forward. "You are my world," I continue, my voice breaking again. "My universe. You give me life, bring light to my dark corners, fill me with purpose and joy. You're imprinted on my soul, own my heart, and you are the most beautiful man I've been lucky to know, inside and out."

Mick's eyes shine with a glossy layer, his throat working as he swallows.

"My life means nothing without you in it." I'm close now.

More tears spill from my eyes. I pause, trying to speak past the thick emotion. "I have treasured every single second with you from the first moment. I never meant to make you think you're less than anyone or anything. Mick...you are my everything."

His gaze softens, a tear sliding down his cheek, and he opens his arms.

I fall into them, gripping him tight as he pulls me into his grasp. We cling to each other as sorrow, regret, and love flow between us.

"I'm so sorry," I murmur, my words muffled by his shirt.

He kisses my forehead. "Me, too."

"I don't want to lose you, Mick."

"You won't," he rasps.

"I love you."

"I love you so fucking much."

Our mouths meet in a raw, earnest kiss, our pain swirling with honesty, our hearts desperate to stay fused.

NINE

I make it through finals, begin my internship, and toggle between my other two jobs. Mick and I steal time where we can. Surfing. Hiking. Sailing. Making love.

We mostly avoid discussions about Remy.

In private, grief and anger hijack my thoughts at random, and I apply fresh bandages to my wounded ego. My emotions fluctuate wildly, sometimes turning self-flagellating for believing Remy was ever a genuine friend. I can't rectify the coldness in which he's discarded me and moved on.

The urge to charge over to the Remington palace-turned-prison and confront Remy pulls with gale-wind force. I deserve answers, respect, and at the very least, a proper, dignified breakup...but I won't stoop to embarrassing myself or allowing Remy's parents to diminish me further. Been there, done that, and nope. The motherfucker should grow a pair and call me.

True confession: I've caved and tried calling. Seven times. Okay, twelve. Mostly answered by his bitch mother, the other few by his sleazy father. I chickened out and hung up every time, swallowing the ugly words poised for release. My heart raced so loudly, my breathing labored—and I probably sounded like a perverted crank caller.

Worse, damn if I also don't *miss* Remy. His affable exuberance, ability to make me laugh, salacious smiles, the affection in his voice when he called me sweetheart. He's one of the Three Musketeers.

Was. Was. Was.

There is no more *us*.

Mick, who's always had a chokehold on my heart, makes it easier to distance whatever portion I'd devoted to Randolph Remington III. And being able to give ourselves to each other fully is potent, heady, and beautiful. I cannot imagine a day I won't be *consumed* with Mick Callahan.

Still, underneath it all lurks questions, unease, trepidation. How *is* this going to play out? Mick and Remy are best friends. The kind who've lived through thick and thin, the kind who watch each other's backs, the kind who will be linked forever. This triad worked when we shared the love, but I'm still the "new girl" in this equation, and Remy has put nuclear distance between himself and me. If Mick, Remy, and I can't ever hang out together—and right now, that sounds like an impossible bridge to cross—how can Mick and I live happily ever after?

It's almost painful watching Mick balance on a teeter-totter weighed on either side by his best friend and girlfriend. It only makes me love him deeper and see the genuine goodness nestled at his core.

While I've done a bang-up job keeping my thoughts internalized, I can't help myself from asking Mick random questions when I reach a tipping point.

What's Remy's fiancée's name? Sherry.

Do you like her? She seems nice.

Is she pretty? Silent reproach.

Where's the wedding: The Claremont. (The most pretentious hotel in the area.)

What are you doing for the bachelor party? I don't know.

Does she know about the three of us? No.

How's his recovery going? He's drinking a lot. His parents believed him when he said alcohol wasn't his problem. He's in a new outpatient program now.

Does he ask about me? No. (Ouch.)

My crazed schedule of working three jobs and spending time with Mick help distract me. I'm thrilled learning and absorbing the inner workings of a magazine, from how they determine their editorial calendar to what happens in the art department to the crucial role of advertising. I gulp it down like iced tea on a blistering day. As an intern, I'm exposed to slivers of each department, and throw myself into every task, even gofering.

The salon gig also yields unexpected dividends. The camaraderie of the stylists lifts my spirits as they take me under their wing and into the fold. They eye my hair like it's spun gold and beg to cut it, add highlights, try new things. Surprising myself, I let them. They take what I thought was already a fabulous asset and turn me into a supermodel.

Mick's tongue practically hangs out of his mouth at each iteration, and he can't stop staring...or keep his hands to himself. That's fine by me. Maybe we've finally leveled the playing field, if that's even possible.

By the end of a hectic summer, I'm clearer about my path in the writing realm and the direction my career can take if I pursue a magazine job. It's massively appealing. I'm also hella better at styling my hair.

The sting dulls over the Three Musketeers fallout, even though tension remains.

TEN

Fall semester begins, heralding my final year in college. The finish line is in sight, and I couldn't be happier about it.

Mick whisks me away for an early birthday celebration over Labor Day. We take four days and drive to the northeast corner of the state to Lassen Volcanic National Park, where we camp, hike to the top of Mt. Lassen, frolic in the unusually warm Bathtub Lake, check out the fumaroles, mud pots, and boiling pools, and bask in each other's company. There is no place I'd rather be than in Mick's orbit, especially when Mr. Nature is in his element.

Remy's November nuptials loom large—the point of no return. Not that I expect anything from that chickenshit, self-absorbed asshole at this juncture. Any thoughts I once harbored of speaking with him—let alone attempting any sort of platonic friendship—evaporated after how callously he's treated me.

Obviously, I won't be Mick's plus-one at the wedding, a fact that both grinds and relieves. He should be free to bring his girlfriend. Even if she formerly banged the groom. And despite that Mrs. Remington would throw me out on my ass.

But how excruciating (and awkward) would it be watching Remy get married...especially with our unfinished business? And how would his new wife take the news if she caught wind of our triad? It's an impossible situation.

Mick provides the barest details when pressed—and morbid curiosity keeps me pressing—even when it leads to petty arguments.

"IT'S JUST UNFAIR YOU DON'T GET A SAY. I'M YOUR girlfriend. I should be your date." Bringing this up post-coitally probably isn't my best timing.

"Jax," Mick groans. "We've been over this."

I roll away from him and light a cigarette, sitting up against his headboard and puffing with ferocity.

"Do you even *want* to be there?" he asks.

No, but I bristle at the exclusion. "It doesn't really matter, does it? Just forget it."

He sighs and guilt washes through me.

"Don't you agree this whole wedding is a sham? Remy's not even able to stay sober. He has no business getting married."

Mick sits up and lights a Marlboro. "I'm surprised it's gone this far, but it's happening, and I hope for both their sakes that it lasts."

"What about us, Mick?" It pops out before I can stop it.

His gaze snaps my direction. "What do you mean?"

"It's just...your time is already spread so thin. Between our schedules, jobs, and you spending time with Remy in Oakland while I'm in San Jose... how long can we keep going like this?"

His eyes burn into mine. "And what, exactly, do you propose? I'm doing my fucking level best to manage this shit situation. Are you saying you want to call it quits?"

"No!" I squeeze my eyes shut take a deep breath. I need to

chill. I'm not helping matters but goddamn it, I'm choking with irritation.

"Then what do you expect me to do?"

Good question. I suck the last of the nicotine into my lungs and smash the embers into the ashtray. "I'm sorry. I'm frustrated."

He threads his hand through mine. "Baby, so am I, but it is what it is. There's no manual for this, so please try and understand."

~

THE WEDDING PROMISES TO BE A GRAND AFFAIR held at the palatial Claremont Hotel in Berkeley. The sprawling, pristine white, Tudor-style hotel reeks of old-school elegance and only the grossly wealthy book it. The Remingtons surely want to broadcast and boast to their friends and enemies alike with this event. Honestly, I have a hard time picturing Remy being alright with it all...he's never been about those kinds of trappings.

Then again, maybe the newly reformed Remy isn't anyone I'd recognize.

Mick's already sporadic companionship becomes sparser as the Big Day nears.

He gets fitted for a tux, a vision I'm desperate to see. Because my guy devastates in Levi's and... well, naked. Envisioning him in a black tuxedo? I can only imagine, but it's a *hell yes, please*.

For the bachelor party, Mick charters a company boat to take Remy and guests out for a night on the bay. His childhood buddies Terry, Vinny, and Jeremy will all be in attendance, along with Remy's brother, cousins, and a handful of other friends.

"Tell me there are no strippers," I demand, only a little serious.

Mick laughs. "Is my baby jealous?"

"Nope." *I just don't want you touching anyone but me.*

"You're cute when you lie."

"You didn't answer my question."

Mick pulls me against him, resting his hands on my hips. "I did not coordinate any strippers coming aboard. I can't vouch for the other guys, however."

Harrumph. "If I know Jeremy..."

He shakes his head, giving me a lopsided smile. "You know I'm in love with you, right? There is no other woman alive who could or will ever top you. You're it for me, baby."

"God, I love you. You can say that to me every day for the rest of our lives." I kiss him, infusing all my love into it, silently hoping one day we'll be the ones getting married.

The warmth of that kiss fades when I don't see Mick for days leading up to the wedding. He's pressed into best man duties, labors over writing his speech, then departs for the rehearsal dinner and wedding itself.

I remind myself once this is behind us, we'll carve out time together, find a new groove, allow our love to persevere.

We just have to get through this first.

ELEVEN

I'm working at the salon and can only be classified as a train wreck. My thoughts are off the rails, my heart virtually in pieces. It's November tenth, the day Remy marries another. A woman I've never met. A wedding to which I'm not invited or welcome.

A lot's changed between three best friends in less than a year.

I haven't spoken to Mick in two days, as he's been inundated with wedding activities and responsibilities. I've been so fucking pleasant. Causing zero waves. Trying to lessen the guilt he lugs around for being trapped in the middle. It's not his fault, and I never want him to feel inferior or *not enough* again.

My chest eases a tad thinking about him. All that he is to me.

This isn't about me not wholly loving Mick. It's about residual angst.

An unsatisfying, unresolved equation. Or a baffling word problem.

If Jacqui has two apples and one rots, how many apples can she technically eat?

Jacqui would like to throw the rotten apple against a wall and watch it get attacked by worms. Or at least examine the apple to understand why it rotted. Maybe talk about the benefits of making applesauce before it's too late.

Jesus. This is why math and I are not friends.

I tap my pen absently against the pages of the appointment book.

No closure.

No closure.

No closure.

How can I get that when one party refuses to provide it?

Then it hits me.

I *can* get closure.

By doing one thing to give it to myself.

Despite agreeing not to.

An inelegant huff leaves my lips. I'm my own woman, and this one is driving to the Claremont Hotel to get her fucking closure.

It's dark when I arrive. The nuptials are long over, uttered in some nearby church, and not something I wanted to witness. No, I just need to lay eyes on Remy with his wife. And yeah, if I'm honest, Mick in his tuxedo. I'm not going to make a scene or even make my presence known...I don't think.

I didn't bother dressing for the occasion.

Glancing at my jeans and sweater, a small smile inches up my lips at how Mrs. Remington would sneer at me, the "tramp", if I were to crash her precious son's wedding. I chuckle, despite the pounding of my heart. *That would be worth the price of admission.*

Unfamiliar as I am with this swanky resort, I don't know how I'll accomplish my task, but there's nothing like false bravado with a shot of venomous anger to help fuel me along.

I steer one direction, but it leads to tennis courts and recreation areas. After doubling back past the main entrance, I discover a parking area flanking another section of the hotel and ease into a spot hidden by plenty of other cars much nicer than mine. Including one 1965 blue Mustang fastback.

Approaching the perimeter, I fight the urge to assume the role of 007 in stealth mode. *The name's Bond. Jax Bond.* Before long, tall windows beaming with light come into view, along with a faint thumping of music. The glass panes showcase the party within.

I sink into the shadows and approach the farthest window. My pulse thunders in my ears. The gigantic ballroom is full of women in chic dresses and men in dark suits. Champagne flutes sit at table settings. Bodies gyrate to the music on the makeshift dance floor.

And then I see Mick and Remy. My chestnut-haired boyfriend steals my breath; he looks like a zillion bucks in a sharp, black tuxedo that hugs his frame. Standing next to him, laughing at something Mick said, is Remy. His copper hair is trimmed and slicked back, those sapphire eyes bright even from this distance, and he is devastating in his all-white tux.

They're both laughing now.

It's a kick to my solar plexus.

Two Musketeers with the third peering through the window like a fucking perv. A loser. A jilted lover. Rotten meat in a sandwich. But I can't even blink, let alone stop staring.

My eyes prick as the bride approaches. Remy's smile widens as he slips an arm around her and they share a kiss. She tugs his hand, urging him toward the dance floor, and the band smartly launches into the tender song, "Oh Sherrie." All eyes are on the newlyweds as they claim the center and Remy twirls her in a circle.

Sherry is resplendent in a white gown. She oozes class, her light brown hair gathered into a neat chignon. Sparkling earrings dangle from her lobes, and even from here, I can make out the massive shiny rock on her ring finger.

As the pair waltz across the floor, it's painfully clear there's love between them. Remy used to look at me like that. With adoration and...more.

I think a part of me doubted it until now.

But there's no unseeing the finality of the scene playing out.

Remy is married.

The band switches gears, launching into Bob Seger's over-played "Old Time Rock & Roll," and to my dismay, my gray-eyed lover joins the fracas. He's smiling. Dancing. Beer in hand.

It's enough to make me want to smash through these floor-to-ceiling ballroom windows and punch him in the mouth. Do I want him to be morose? Missing me? Just a smidge melancholy that the Three Musketeers are officially deceased?

Goddamn right I do.

Mick's gaze darts in my direction, and I flinch into the shadows, sucking in a sharp breath and holding it, paralyzed. He can't see me, can he?

And what if he fucking did? *I don't care.* I exhale with force, my tears flowing as I stalk back to my car.

I got what I came for—in fucking spades—and the weight of it crushes me. My cheeks flood with my visible pain, blurring my vision. Footfalls echo against the pavement, and I scramble to find my keys, which my purse seems to have swallowed whole.

Shit. Shit. Shit.

I use my sleeve to dry my eyes. The footsteps cease, and I know before even turning around that it's Mick.

He's breathing hard, his eyes searching mine. Disbelief. Pain. "Jax."

My head hangs. I can't face him right now.

Part of me wants to jump off a cliff.

Crawl in a hole.

Drive to Montana and start over.

But all I do is stand there and cry.

Mick wraps me in his arms, his ocean scent coating me like a second skin. "Baby, why are you doing this to yourself?"

All that comes out is a strained, pitiful sob. I clutch him back, no longer angry enough to say the spiteful, ugly, jealous comments initially present.

He rubs my back. "You know there's nothing I want more than you to be in there by my side, don't you?"

I nod against his chest.

"But baby, you can't be here. Right or wrong, it doesn't matter. You know the situation."

"It just hurts."

Mick sighs, kissing my temple. "I know. And I'm sorry."

"I needed to see for myself," I whisper, finally brave enough to lift my head and meet his gaze.

He cups my face, thumbing away my tears. "Did it help?"

Biting my lip, I nod meekly.

"Go home, Jax. I'll call you in a few hours."

"Okay."

"On the Remingtons' tab," he adds.

My lips turn up a little.

He kisses me gently, tenderly, as if I'm breakable. *I am.* "I love you, Jacqueline Hall." He's so goddamn sincere it makes me want to cry all over again.

"I love you too."

His fingers intertwine with mine and he gives my hand a squeeze.

My gaze finds his again, my throat still tight. "Maybe don't look like you're having so much fun? Or be so devastatingly handsome?" I wave my hand at his attire. "I may never get over you in this tux."

His gray eyes graze me warmly, his lopsided smile emerging. "I'm glad it's doing something for you, because I'm counting the seconds until I can peel off this fucking monkey suit."

"I'm sure every bridesmaid is also counting the seconds, hoping to be there to witness it."

He rolls his eyes and shakes his head.

Our hands unclasp, and I locate my keys. Wordlessly, Mick unlocks my door and helps me inside. He stoops, gently kissing my lips. "Please drive safe. You're precious cargo."

My head bobs as I gulp down fresh tears.

I crank up the Beetle and begin driving away from this closed chapter of my life. Sparing one last glance at Mick in the rearview, my skin prickles. His expression is unfathomable—but foreboding, like a storm trapped in the clouds.

TWELVE

Something shifts after Remy's wedding day. A trace of desperation now exists where Mick and I are concerned, as if we're on borrowed time, the hourglass flipped with the sand running out.

Mick seems to draw inward. He's quieter, weighed down, like he's wrestling with unseen demons. I tread lightly but am determined to address whatever this is—and fix it—before we break.

The day after Thanksgiving, Mick and I hike down to the private beach at his cottage. We're bundled in sweatshirts and jeans, but blessed with a clear day, the breeze slightly tempered by the towering cliffs surrounding us. We kick off our shoes by the trail and he takes my hand as we walk through the sand, the top layer barely warmed by the noonday sun.

We stop near the water's edge—I know better than to dip my toes in the frigid Pacific this time of year. Mick picks up a flat stone from the assortment scattered ashore. He sidearms the rock with a flick of his wrist, getting five skips before it disappears into the murky depths. I join in and we spend companionable minutes seeing how far out in the ocean our stones travel and how many skips we can get. Mick: seven. Me: five. He has bigger biceps, I rationalize.

I spread our blanket and when we settle on it, our shoulders touch, closing any gap. Lately, we can't bear any distance between us. Gazing into the deep blue expanse, seagulls cascade across the landscape, their harsh cries rising over the waves crashing onshore. I don't want to fight or ruin what precious time we have, but questions gnaw at me. I've practiced saying what I need without accusation and with the hope he won't become defensive.

Mr. Perceptive speaks first. "You're ruminating."

I huff out a startled laugh. "Busted."

"What's on your mind?"

Did his shoulder just tense? *Don't chicken out.* "Can we have what might be a difficult conversation, one that could help clarify a few things?"

Mick taps a couple of cigarettes out of his pack, clamps them in his lips, and cups his hand around the Zippo's flame to get them lit. He hands me one, his expression unreadable. "Sure, baby."

I take a fortifying drag. "Remy's been trying to get clean and sober now for eight months, and he's still struggling."

He nods.

I extend my index finger. "This is after going to the Betty Ford Center, arguably the best rehab facility in the nation." My other fingers keep count. "He's been through a couple of spin-dry cycles at local hospitals. He's been in a few different outpatient programs. And he's been to a whole lot of AA and NA meetings."

He takes another long drag. "Yup."

"I guess what I'm wondering is... maybe Remy's not going to recover, you know? It seems like something he has to want more than he wants to use."

"It's possible he won't get a handle on it. Between the meetings I've gone to with him and reading some of the recovery material, I've learned this is a disease. It's not as simple as wanting to quit. He has a compulsion, something physical he's battling, and it makes him weak and susceptible."

I flick my ash, carefully selecting my words. "I guess what I want to know is...do you plan to help him indefinitely? Do you think he has some personal responsibility here? That maybe he needs to stand on his own two feet?"

Mick scrubs his palm over his face. "I don't have an answer for that. I just know I need to be there for him for as long as it takes."

"But why? I'm honestly not trying to be an asshole here. I want to understand." I stub out my cigarette in the sand.

He stares forward, lost in the enormity of the Pacific, his hair undulating in the wind. "I've never really elaborated on how bad things were growing up, but Remy made a fucked-up situation a hell of a lot better. We became friends in elementary school when he moved across the street. One of those rare, instant connections. It wasn't long before I was showing up with regularity to get away from the shit happening in my house— especially after dark. He'd let me in, ask me if I needed anything, and I'd sleep in his room. His parents didn't even know at first."

I rest my hand on his thigh as images of him as a terrified, broken boy flash in my mind.

"Remy never pushed for details, even when I showed up bloody or bruised. Eventually, his parents caught on, and even they didn't pressure me much. Instead, they opened their house to me, fed me, and once, had some nurse friend of theirs stitch me up."

"Oh, Mick."

"The bullshit with my family went on for years," he mutters. "The Remingtons gave me a safe place to land, and escape to, all the way through high school. They never asked for anything, aside from wanting to report my father. But people covered that shit up then. Probably still do." He pauses. "I'm in their debt. I owe it to Remy to help him, even if it takes time, even if it's inconvenient."

A piercing discomfort builds behind my sternum. "I understand." And god, do I. But the unknown purgatory of our situation stretches as far as the horizon.

"I know it's impacting us...and it sucks."

Tears slide down my cheeks.

"And I don't want it to. But Jax, I don't know what else to fucking do. I'm failing everyone." He shakes out two more cigarettes.

I squeeze his leg. "You're not. You're such a good man."

He lights the smokes, hands mine over, and takes a long pull from his. "My hope is something will take hold, Remy will stay clean, and we'll all go on living our lives."

As I exhale a drag, I try to release the held frustration and my selfish desires with it. If only they could evaporate as easily as this smoke dissipating in the air. "But we're still impacted by Remy and the inability to all be in one place together. That worries me."

Mick places his hand on mine. "That's going to sort itself out over time. I'm sure of it."

I'm less sure. Much less.

We're quiet, trapped in our own thoughts.

"You know what I dream about?" I ask.

"Hmm?"

"Us going to Florida. You, getting the job you want on the water. Me, working for a magazine. Spending our weekends sailing and surfing."

"The surfing's crap in Florida, baby."

"With all that ocean *and* the Gulf? What a waste." I glance at the sets of waves rolling in and wonder what the

Atlantic looks like in comparison. "We'll sail and go to the beach and make love a lot then."

"That's a damn fine dream."

The unspoken what ifs remain. What if Remy never gets clean? What if Mick deigns to help him forever? What if Mick always forsakes himself for everyone else? What if we don't survive this?

THIRTEEN

Three days before Christmas, I load my car, pulsing in anticipation at spending time with Mick prior to heading to Oakland. It's reminiscent of last year, *sans Remy*, and it takes serious fortitude to shove away thoughts of the best Christmas I've ever had—the gifts, the sex, the affection swirling between us.

When some memories resurface, I indulge them. Mick and I hunting for a tree, bringing it back to his place and decorating it. Snuggling on the couch watching holiday classics. We're repeating some of those new traditions, starting with this afternoon, and I'm so ready for it.

Maybe our seasonal spirit will drown the pessimistic whispers following me around.

Mick remains distracted—unless we're making love, eyes locked, our bodies merged in a breathless kind of unity, one so poignant it often brings me to tears. The rest of the time, it's almost as if the boat is leaving the marina without me, forcing me to run and leap, hurling my body onto the deck before it can.

I wish he'd let me comfort him, help him. He's my everything. Not just a VIP but the MIP, the most important person in my life. Nothing he could say or do could change that, but he stays closed—like a book on a shelf too high to reach—giving me little to go on.

The divide widens.

And I'm panicked he's slipping away.

I hug Jas and Kit farewell. We exchanged presents last night over a bottle of wine and stayed up talking late into the night. My roommates are headed to Oakland tomorrow to spend the break at their parents' houses. I try not to think too hard about a few days from now, when I'm trapped in another predictably bleak holiday with Fred and Barbara Hall.

Christmas music serenades me from the radio as I make the familiar drive to Half Moon Bay. I'm instantly comforted when the Pacific—and soon after, Mick's driveway—comes into view.

My gray-eyed ocean struts to my car with a huge grin, and my heart sprints toward all that gorgeousness. He opens my door and pulls me impatiently into his arms. "Hey, baby," he murmurs before sealing his lips over mine.

Every cell in my body awakens with his kiss, his sheer presence, and I love being the focus of his ardor.

We pull apart and my smile broadens. "Merry Christmas."

"Merry Christmas."

"I missed you."

"Guess college finals take precedence over me, eh?"

I snort. "Unfortunately. But I'm trying to forget about those right now."

He pulls me firmly against him. "I've got some ideas how to accomplish that—and I need my fucking fix."

When he presses his lips to mine again, his tongue probing and claiming, my insides liquify and I moan into his mouth, already needy for all things Mick.

Everything else falls away except this man and the way he jumpstarts my heart.

He tugs me by the hand into the house. We only make it to the kitchen.

"What do you—"

His sentence falters as I drop to my knees and rip open his button fly. Our eyes connect before I drag his Levi's and briefs down his hips and wrap my lips around his steadily growing cock. Devouring. My groan resounds as I'm filled with relief. I crave Mick like a vampire craves blood. He moans my name, fisting my hair and thrusting into my mouth. Heat blazes through me. Wetness soaks my underwear. My knees chafe from the linoleum, and I don't care. He tastes so fucking good. Big, veiny, throbbing. I'm voracious. Needy. My palms clutch his firm ass and bring him deeper as I suck him to the back of my throat.

"Fuuuuuuuck..."

His balls tighten. Pace quickens. He's losing control, and an animalistic noise of desire comes straight from my depths.

Mick detonates, shooting his release into my mouth and grinding it out amidst a string of guttural sounds. I collect every drop, waiting until he stills to swallow the evidence of his pleasure. His unfocused gaze finds mine, and a lopsided smile graces his lips as he sags against the counter.

"Goddamn, woman."

I beam up at him, licking my lips, and his eyes turn molten.

He helps me to standing and makes quick work of stripping me naked. I let out a surprised squeak when he swiftly lifts me off my feet and sets me on the tiled countertop. He dispenses with his jeans and shirt, spreads my legs, and stands in between them. Our mouths join and I wrap my arms around his smooth, broad shoulders. He presses my back flush against the cool surface, sending a chill across my torso as my nipples go fully rigid. I soon forget any discomfort as his lips blaze a warm trail down my neck, stopping to nip at my throat, before his hands—then tongue—claim my breasts. A garbled succession of moans escape as I writhe beneath him, my center desperate.

I will never tire of seeing him like this, his beautiful gray eyes so full of desire for me. So present. So potent.

His mouth latches onto my breast as he pushes two of his fingers inside my pussy. He groans around my flesh. I'm soaked...for him. Always for him.

Little noises of pleasure leave my lips. *Ohhhh. Unghh. Ahhhh.* They turn to heavy breaths as he fucks me with his fingers, his teeth grazing over one nipple, the sear of his touch forever ruining me.

I'm mewling, begging, moaning, bracing my heels to spread my legs wider, wanting all of him to have all of me. His mouth travels lower to suck on that vibrating bundle of nerves, alternating with flattening his tongue against my entrance, making everything slicker. In harmonious tandem with his glorious fingers pistoning inside me, Mick brings me to orgasm lightning fast. I wail as the edges of my vision darken, pleasure exploding and rocketing through me.

I'm delirious, my pelvis jerking with reverberations when Mick grips my hips and hauls my feet to the floor. He spins me toward the counter and enters me roughly from behind. I cry out and he growls his approval. Oh. Fuck. Yes. He's so hard. So beautifully hard. This man fills me sublimely. There is nothing better than this. *Nothing.*

"Fuuuck," he breathes. "Your pussy squeezes me like it's never letting go."

I never want to let go.

He thrusts into me with deep strokes, each one a declaration. *Mine. Mine. Mine.*

I'm yours.

"Fuck me, Mick. Fuck me hard."

He answers by driving into me fast and forcefully. *Holy hell.* I brace against the counter, taking every delicious ram and demand he makes. My breasts surge with each drive, my nipples grazing the tile with a pleasurable friction. He owns me—my heart, my body, my soul—and it's all I want.

"Goddamn, you're perfect," he grunts out.

Stars skirt my peripheral vision again. "So...are you," I manage between husky breaths.

Mick's strokes come faster. He quickens, and I cry out as his orgasm erupts, the pleasure between us intense. He stays buried inside me, collapsed over my back, as our breathing normalizes. Our bodies are glued from the sweat coating them. He kisses my back with a tenderness that makes my eyes mist; his love is so palpable...tangible...in this moment.

We break apart, my legs already stiff and my center deliciously used. He swipes a kitchen towel, and we clean ourselves up, all smiles as we dress.

"Merry Christmas," I say with an arched brow.

He grins, his dimple making an appearance. "Christmas came early." Turning serious, he palms my face, tilting my mouth to his. "I love you, Jacqui."

"I don't think words can adequately express how much I love you, Mick."

We repeat last year's inaugural festivities—dinner out followed by finding a beautiful tree smelling of pine and sap. Mick hauls it inside and we adorn it with string lights and decorations. We turn off all the other lights in the house save for our Christmas tree and settle in front of the TV with hot cocoa to watch *It's a Wonderful Life*.

I'm zonked when it's time for bed, but it takes zero coaxing from my gray-eyed lover to make slow, languid love before we drop off to sleep, my body spooned tightly into his.

Shrill ringing barges into my dreams, and I jerk awake.

"This better be good," Mick mutters as he grabs the phone.

My gaze swings to the oversized windows facing the ocean. It's still dark out, but by the wisp of brightness just tinging the sky, dawn is near.

"Slow down," he tells the caller.

My pulse ticks up. Is it an emergency?

Mick shifts into a sitting position, listening intently. "When's the last time you saw him?" he asks.

I'd bet money this is about Remy. I stifle a sigh.

"Yeah, you don't want to do that."

Do what?

"I really don't know. Have you tried Vinny?"

Definitely Remy. And whatever crap is happening with him...*again.*

"I see."

A sharp pain emanates from my jaw, and I realize it's clenched.

Mick rakes a hand through his hair. The sky is light enough now to make out his features, the sun breaking the horizon. "I can try..."

My stomach drops.

"Yup. Not ideal. But I understand."

What's not ideal?

"I'll let you know as soon as I do."

Pause.

"Mm-hmm. Okay."

Mick says goodbye and hangs up. He doesn't meet my gaze.

My voice sticks in my throat. "What?"

"It's Remy. He didn't come home last night and Sherry's freaking out."

"And she wants *you* to track him down?"

He squeezes his eyes shut for a long moment, as if bracing for a fight, and nods.

Goddamn it. "How is this your problem?"

"It shouldn't be, but she doesn't want Remy's parents to

find out, and she's out of her mind with worry. She didn't know who else to turn to."

My eyes tear, and I don't know if it's from anger or hurt. "It's Christmas Eve, Mick. This is our time."

The morning sun casts its glow over his throat and face, highlighting his Adam's apple when he swallows. "I know, baby, and I'm sorry."

"But you're going." My heart stutters and flares. It's sending Morse Code. An SOS message.

He looks away. "I've got to."

I rip off the covers and stalk around the loft, yanking on clothes, seething with thousands of pent-up, unsaid words.

Mick watches silently.

Here we are again. Hostage to Remy's fuckups. Our life in limbo because he can't get his together.

When is it going to end?

Part of me knows it's unfair to take this out on Mick. He's a good man. Of course he's always going to show up for his friend. But *goddamn him.* Today, perhaps selfishly, I want him to choose *me.* This isn't our problem. Resentment ricochets in my head—Remy, first and foremost, but Sherry too. Isn't this her area of expertise? How come she isn't handling it? Helping him? I wonder if she regrets meeting him, falling for him, marrying him. It can't be easy. It sure as fuck is raining on my parade on a regular basis. Ugly thoughts ripple through me as I wallow in the unfairness of it all.

Mick says nothing as he rises from the bed and pulls on his jeans. I clutch my stuff and hurry down the stairs. He stays quiet as he trails after me. Bitterness climbs my throat as I spy the unopened presents under the tree. I'm riveted to the spot, eyes glued to those gifts. Merry fucking Christmas.

I choke back a sob as Mick wraps his arms around me from behind. He buries his head in my hair.

"Don't leave angry," he murmurs. "Please."

A sniffle escapes, along with a trickle of tears. "It's not how I wanted the day to go," I whisper.

He lets out a long breath, the warmth of it seeping into my neck. "Same, baby."

Dropping everything in my arms, I turn and sink into him. We hold each tightly, as if neither of us wants to let go for fear we'll break.

And we feel breakable. Vulnerable.

He shifts, the precursor to leaving, and my hands slide to his hips. He cups my face. Kisses me tenderly. He infuses all the love he has into that kiss, silently begging my forgiveness, my patience, my understanding.

I can deny him nothing. He has all of me.

I'm yours. I'm yours. I'm yours.

We part and he stares at me intently. "I'll call as soon as I can. And I'll bring the gifts. We'll open them in Oakland. Maybe you can come over to Mom's tomorrow? You know she wants to see you."

I nod. And of course I want to see his mom. We've only met twice, but I like and respect her so much. It's hard to think about that right now, knowing the most important person in my life needs to track down Remy, who is God knows where. Hanging with his dealer buddies? Sleeping in the gutter? Worse?

"Be careful, Mick."

He nods, but I'm not reassured. *About anything.*

FOURTEEN

It's a long day of suffering, wondering what's happening with Mick and Remy as I fake happiness for my parents' benefit. They're trying too and it's almost macabre. But at least our interaction is easier now that we aren't living in the same existence-suffocating house.

When my father suggests watching *A Christmas Carol*, I jump at the chance to distract my thoughts. He uncorks a bottle of zinfandel and pours us each a glass as the movie begins. It may only be once a year when the three of us converge for this tradition, but recognition flickers warmly in my chest.

Despite knowing exactly how it ends, inevitable tears fall when Scrooge redeems himself.

We all deserve redemption, don't we? I wonder if I'm charitable enough to believe Remy does too. I want to be.

I'm cleaning the dinner dishes, holiday tunes playing softly in the background, when the phone rings.

"I've got it," I call out to my parents, who lounge in the living room in front of the fire as I dry my hands with a kitchen towel.

"Hello?"

"Hey, baby."

Relief hurtles through me. "Are you alright?"

"Yes." He sounds tense.

"Remy?"

"I found him. Finally. It's not good, Jax."

"What do you mean?"

"He's doing crack."

I sag against the counter. Crack cocaine is sweeping Oakland like a wildfire, and people are falling fast. It's reportedly as addictive as heroin. "Oh, Mick. That's...bad." And *goddamn it*, Remy.

"Yeah. I'll fill you in later."

"Where are you now?"

"The Remingtons' annual Christmas Eve bash," he says ruefully.

That brings on an instantaneous round of flashing memories. "Adult-man-sitting?"

"Something like that. How are things going there?" His Zippo flicks, followed by an exhale.

"Surprisingly okay...even nice at times. But I'm relieved to hear from you. I was worried."

He pauses, like there's so much he could say but isn't. "I know it's difficult with your parents, so 'nice' is high praise."

My eyes well and I gulp down the emotion. "We still on for tomorrow?"

"Yeah, baby. Come up to the house whenever you're ready—after you open presents and can steal away."

Thank god. "I can do that."

"I'm sorry...again."

"Don't," I whisper, wanting him to hear—and believe —me. "Don't ever apologize for being a good person, a good friend, *a good man*. I would never want you to change."

He huffs out a long breath. "I don't deserve you."

I hate it when he says that. It always harpoons a piece of

my heart. "You deserve all of me, Mick Callahan. I'm yours and always will be."

"Spoken like true heroin."

If anyone's a drug, it's him, not me. A thought that fades as we both go quiet, quickly sobered by his comment as we circle back to Remy and his drug problems. Now, even more serious than before.

"Not the best word choice today, is it?" he murmurs.

"No," I whisper.

It effectively ends our conversation after we promise to see each other tomorrow.

The unknowns echo between us, unspoken yet so very loud.

A dreary rain falls Christmas morning, providing a gray backdrop to the modest festivities. Our gifts are opened within an hour, after which I clean up the debris and join my mother in making breakfast. We're having French toast with cinnamon and a sprinkling of powdered sugar, sausage links, and fresh fruit.

All I can think about is escaping to Mick's.

Even though yesterday was bearable, being in this house is stifling, and I'm using every ounce of my tolerance reserves to get through the minutes.

My relationship with my parents is set in a foundation of lies and neglect. They stopped parenting me in elementary school. Well, aside from my father's heavy-handed efforts to keep me in whatever line he draws at his whim—arbitrary lines about things like curfews and grades—all while drinking too much and cheating on my mother. As for dear old mom, she continues fading, spending her days in a drug-addled haze since my older sister drowned. She looks one step closer to death every time I see her.

Over our meal, I alert my parents to my plans to "see

friends," promising to be back in time to help with dinner. Surprisingly, there's no griping or heavy-handed comments. They still have no idea Mick is my boyfriend, let alone the love of my fucking life, and I see no reason to tell them about it after my father made it clear he wasn't good enough for me. He didn't even know Mick when he told him that bullshit. This secret is problematic the longer we stay together. I don't let myself wonder if we won't.

An hour later, I drive to Mick's mom's house.

Mick greets me at the door and pulls me into his arms, murmuring "Merry Christmas," before claiming my lips.

He flashes me a tender smile, but there's no missing his tired eyes and the presence of something heavier. This entire situation with Remy is stressful—and only getting worse—and he's mired in it whether he wants to be or not.

I follow him inside and give his mom an exuberant holiday greeting, handing her a loaf of gingerbread I baked yesterday and a bottle of white wine.

She wraps me in a hug. "So nice to see you, Jacqui."

"You too. Thank you for having me. The house looks lovely," I say, taking in the festive decorations and charming, understated tree. Every item matches her personal aesthetic, which I love. A mixture of seasonal spices perfumes the air, along with the earthy aroma from the fir.

Mick and I claim one sofa and his mom takes the chair across from us. I sip on spiced apple cider as we make small talk. We chat about school and my post-graduation plans—still very undecided—and she offers helpful insights.

"Mom," Mick says, cutting her off thirty minutes later.

She eyes him quizzically.

"If Jacqui doesn't get to open her presents soon, she's going to combust."

I scoff. "Am not."

His eyes find mine, and I'm totally busted. "I know you, remember?"

I purse my lips, then chuckle.

A genuine smile crosses his mom's face as she excuses herself and disappears down the hallway, I think to give us some privacy.

Mick's not wrong. The gift giving is my favorite part of Christmas, and last year was incredible when—

I screech those thoughts to a halt...I *really* don't want to think about how everything's changed since then. Instead, I gaze at Mick, whose grin lights up his face, the one I never tire of looking at, the one my heart responds to with actual palpitations. Goddamn, I love him. More than anyone or anything in my life.

He saunters over to the tree, where our gifts to each other lay scattered, picks one up, and places a weighty box carefully into my lap. Excitement thrums through me as I speculate about what it might be.

I rip through the paper and ribbon with a big grin plastered on my face. Inside are books, and not just any old books, but the kind a writer needs. *The Elements of Style* by Strunk and White. The spiral bound *Associated Press Stylebook*, an essential text for journalists. *The Chicago Manual of Style*, the other must-have for writers. And a special edition of *Writer's Digest* magazine.

My eyes lift to meet his. "Mick...these are perfect. And helpful. How did you even know..."

"I can't take credit. My mom said they would be useful."

I'm touched, the warmth of his never-ending support and encouragement bowling me over once again. "Thank you so much." Bridging the small gap between us, I press my lips to his.

I set the books and magazine on the coffee table and walk over to the tree, getting on all fours to reach what I need.

"That's one hell of a view," Mick says.

I shake my ass for good measure and glance at him over

my shoulder. Grabbing his gifts, I rejoin him on the sofa, totally stoked to watch his reaction.

He's genuinely delighted by the book of nautical knots.

"Not that you aren't already quite proficient with some of these..." We grin at each other as he opens another gift, which is about wooden boat design, something I thought he'd love.

"Oh, cool." He flips the pages, pleased with what he sees. "Baby, this is fantastic. Have I told you how much I think about building my own?"

"No, but it seems right in your wheelhouse, or should I say boathouse?"

He glances back at the book in his hands, his expression delighted. "I can't wait to read this. Thank you." He pulls me closer, grazing my temple with his lips.

Before I can give him one more, he stands and retrieves another package. My breath hitches when I see the size. It's small...ring sized. I don't dare hope. And that's crazy thinking anyway.

I peel away the paper, revealing a black velvet box and my fool heart beats wildly against my ribs. I sneak a quick peek at Mick—his lopsided smile lighting up his face as he watches me—then return my focus to the box. I lift the lid and the air whooshes from my lungs. Inside are delicate, diamond-shaped earrings a nearly translucent shade of aquamarine. Are they stones? Gems? Whatever's hanging from these stainless hooks is *stunning*.

"It's sea glass," he explains. "It's been broken, weathered, and worn smooth by the ocean. It starts out a jagged shard and after years of turbulence and basically, abuse, it becomes beautiful. Like you, baby."

Wow. "Like us," I gently correct, staring into his eyes. We've both suffered at the hands of our parents.

He gives me his lopsided smile. "It's rarer than you might think. The real stuff is old glassware, the kind no one makes anymore, and it takes decades, sometimes even centuries, of tumbling through the sea to buff all the rough edges. It's special—even more so because of what it's been through."

The sentiment is raw and poetic, and once again, he knocks my socks off with the thoughtful, wise, and profound way his mind works. "They're gorgeous, Mick." I swallow to dislodge the knot in my throat. "And capture us completely."

I pluck them from the velvet box and loop them through my earlobes. He shifts my hair to admire them, humming appreciatively when he sees them in place, and I'm treated to another potent version of my ocean and how he looks right now, in this moment. It's breathtaking.

Our gaze collides and holds. "I love them. And you."

Before I'm tempted to chicken out, I hand him my final gift. My nerves tangle as he examines the wrapping. An eternity seems to pass as he carefully opens it, running his finger under each section of tape.

"Jacqui…" He stops speaking.

"It's a short story. It's…about us," I blurt, as I drown in embarrassment, wondering how I ever deemed this worthy of jack shit.

Mick lifts it from the tissue holding it snug in the box. I painstakingly typed it on my typewriter, managing not to blotch it with egregious amounts of Wite-Out, then copied and bound it between two thick covers at Kinko's.

"*Ocean Deep, a Love Story*, by Jacqueline Hall," he murmurs. He flips through it, not saying a goddamned word, and my confidence plummets further.

I'm such an idiot. What was I thinking?

His reverent gaze captures mine. "I'm honored…and speechless. I've never received a more personal, thoughtful gift." He stares back at the story, essentially my heart on a platter, the most vulnerable piece I've ever written. He sets it gingerly back in the box and onto the coffee table. "Come here," he whispers, his voice raspy.

Is he...emotional?

I crawl into his lap, and he holds me tightly. I grip him back, my head landing between his shoulder and neck, lost in his familiar essence, enveloped by everything Mick. We're quiet, saying volumes without uttering a word.

Mick crashes out on the couch, giving me more time with his mom. We nibble on appetizers and talk about her upcoming travels, her work, her favorite projects. I praise her for creating a fine man in Mick and ask about his brothers, what they're like, how their personalities differ, why she chose to name her sons after musicians. She confesses she's never seen her son as smitten with a girl as he is with me. With zero hesitation, I profess him the love of my life, which makes her smile knowingly.

My boyfriend wakes and we share another precious hour together. When I can't put it off any longer, I bid his mom goodbye, and Mick walks me to my car.

"You're headed to San Jose tonight?" he asks.

I nod. "I have work in the morning. What about you?"

He shoves his hands into his pockets. "I've been summoned for a meeting at the Remingtons' tomorrow afternoon, then I plan to head home."

"Any idea what about?"

He shrugs. "Not sure, but I'm guessing it's some kind of intervention."

"Call me?"

"Of course, baby."

We share another forceful hug. But I can't stop the premonition everything is about to go sideways.

My parents are done in by the time I return, their eyes glazed from their drugs of choice. It's a good thing I'm there to make the bulk of our Christmas dinner, or it might go to the wayside. Ditto on cleaning up, which reminds me how nothing changes here; any glimmers of it are phantoms, mirages, wishful thinking. My thoughts churn uneasily over more pressing topics, and it takes genuine effort to join my parental units in faking it—a family hallmark—until it's time to leave.

Relief at getting out of there floods when I settle into the Bug, my breath visible in the cool air. I crank the heater and steer for San Jose, fighting every urge to return to Mick's for one more kiss, hug, and some kind of reassurance that everything is going to be alright.

FIFTEEN

I t's a long, wearisome day—I work eight hours at the salon then head straight to Original Joe's to hostess, arriving in time to scarf a plate of spaghetti and meatballs before starting my shift.

My tasks help keep my thoughts off Mick, Remy, and whatever's going down, but like weeds growing through the cracks, they're pervasive. It's 10:30 p.m. when I clock out, and the sky is a blackish indigo, clouds floating across a nearly full moon. Will Mick call tonight? If not, I'll go out of my mind.

It turns out, my answer is sitting in my driveway in a blue Mustang fastback.

My heart leaps in elation, then sinks with dread.

Calming my whirring insides, I pull alongside Mick and kill the engine. I can't see him well; the streetlight casts us both in shadow. But as we exit our cars and I draw near, I'm startled by his bloodshot eyes. Has he been crying?

What happened?

I wrap him in my arms. He offers no words, but clings to me like a life preserver.

We part and I stare into those gray eyes. "Are you—"

"Let's go inside," he murmurs.

I open the door to the condo, grateful my roommates are still in Oakland for a few more days. Mick throws the deadbolt as I kick off my shoes, drop my purse, and practically bite my tongue waiting for him to speak. I'm in unfamiliar territory, and it physically hurts to see him so plainly hurting.

He slips his arms around my waist from behind and rests his chin on my shoulder, then lets loose an audible breath followed by a hitch. I hear the torment in it.

My head whips. "Mick, what hap—"

"Baby, I'm fucking exhausted, and..." A heavy pause stretches out. "What I need is to hold you close and crash. Can we do that? I know you have questions. I just... tomorrow, I'll tell you everything."

His cheek nestles against mine, rough from not shaving, his ocean scent faintly present, his arms so familiar around my waist. It calms me, settles me.

"Please," he rasps.

"Okay," I whisper, swiveling in his grasp to kiss him tenderly.

I lead him by the hand to my bedroom, and we shrug off our clothes and spoon our naked bodies together underneath the covers. Mick's arm binds me closer. His breathing soon evens out, my distraught prince succumbing to temporary peace. An anxious undercurrent churns through my bloodstream, but before long, exhaustion drags me under.

Sixteen

When my eyes open, Mick's staring at me intently. A canvas of indecipherable emotion swirls in those gray pools. Sharp spikes of adrenaline pump through my veins, yanking me into consciousness.

Mick extends a hand, lightly stroking my face from forehead to chin. His gaze fastens on mine, as if etching this moment into his memory.

"What's happening?" I whisper.

His eyes close, a furrow forming in the valley of his brows, making the scar splitting his right brow more obvious. "It's not good."

He heaves out a frustrated sigh, hoisting himself to sitting. He pulls his jeans off the floor and fishes out his Marlboros. Clamping a cigarette between his lips, he flicks his Zippo twice to ignite it, a stream of smoke following. "But it's bigger than that. This whole shitshow has blown up to epic fucking proportions."

"What happened with the Remingtons?" I fumble for my pack.

Mick's at the ready with his lighter and the burn of nicotine down my throat has never been more welcome.

"Virginia and Rick are at their wits' end, and it's totally understandable." Mick draws one of his knees up to rest his forearm against it. "Remy's in full fuck-up mode, and that affects everyone in his universe."

Don't I know it.

We both take long drags as I wait excruciating seconds to understand why he's so shaken. Why he *cried* the night before.

"They asked me for a big fucking favor," he says low, his head hanging.

"What kind of favor?" It's an effort to keep my voice level.

He takes three more pulls, burning his cigarette down to the filter, then violently stubs it against the ashtray, avoiding my gaze. His throat undulates like he just swallowed a hard-boiled egg. "They want Remy to live with me so I can help him get clean—"

"*WHAT?*"

He chews his lip and nods, swallows again. "Remy and Sherry. A tag-team approach where I drop Remy off at a new outpatient rehab during the day, then Sherry or I take him to meetings in the evenings."

"That's outrageous! And ridiculous!"

Silence.

"You're not thinking of actually doing it, are you?" I take two furious puffs, almost choking, before grounding it out.

He heaves out another lengthy breath, and then I know. *He is.*

I throw off the covers and pace, my thoughts scattering as I grapple with the implications. I fling my hands violently in the air. "What the fuck, Mick? This will consume your entire life. And what about us? We can't possibly navigate that! I mean, how long would this last?"

Mick approaches, his eyes dulled, shoulders hunched.

"Jax," he murmurs, holding my hips as our gaze locks. "He's tried a half dozen ways to get clean already. His parents and wife don't have a clue how to deal with him or this."

"And you do?"

"I don't fucking know, but I can't argue that if he's in Half Moon Bay, he's removed from the people and places that make it easy for him to score drugs. You know how remote my place is—there's no way for him to find that shit out there. And he'll either be at the recovery facility or with me and Sherry."

I glare, astonished he's considering this. Not considering...decided.

"It's not what I want, Jax—you *know* that. But I've wracked my brain to think of another solution, and..." He falters, looking bereft. "I've got nothing."

"But how is this going to work? When will we see each other?"

His eyes glass. He says nothing as his throat bobs.

"Oh my god. We're not going to, are we?"

"I don't see how we can stay together if I do this. And it's not a choice. I have to help Remy."

My knees buckle and he grips me tighter, holding me up. "But why?" I cry. "He's already done rehabs, dry-out stints, meetings. Been to jail. His parents threatened him with his trust fund. *None of it has changed anything.* He's still being a selfish prick."

"I owe a debt," Mick whispers. "And it's time to pay up."

Tears trickle down my cheeks. This again. "That's one hell of a price tag."

"Remy is my best friend. He and his family were there when I needed them. They gave me a safe place to land, a home away from the shitty fucking one I had. Away from abuse that lasted for years." He swallows, meeting my tortured gaze, a tear slipping down his own cheek. "Rem needs me now. I can't abandon him. It's my turn to try and save his life."

"But we love each other. What we have is..." my voice breaks, "everything."

"I know, baby. I know."

My fingers grip his sides. "Then let's talk about how to make it work."

"Jax," he implores, his hand smoothing my hair. "This situation is going to take *months*. Maybe longer. I will *not* put your life on hold or allow you to be shackled just because I am. I will *not* ask you to wait for me when I have no idea how long it's going to take. I will *not* ruin your life at my expense."

Tears streak down my face. "But I will."

Mick squeezes his eyes shut before pinning me with those gray eyes. "I know...and it's not right."

"Yes, it is...because I love you more than I do myself. There is *no one* righter for me than you. You are *everything* to me. I would wait five lifetimes for you if I had to. That's how perfect you are, *we* are."

His eyes flare. "You think I don't feel the same? That I don't love you more than I do myself? I have never loved a soul the way I do you. You are the reason my heart even fucking beats. But I love you *too much* to allow you to waste time hoping for something that now seems impossible. Don't you see, Jax? This situation with Remy isn't about how long this newest BS is going to take... six months, a year, two years...it's *lifelong*. Everything has changed between the three of us, and we can't go back in time to change it. We can't *go back* to being friends. The three of us can't even hang out because there's too much history, way too much intensity, and his wife will never understand any of it, let alone accept it."

It's all my fears realized. The sense of foreboding that's hovered like a cloud finally unleashing its storm.

"This latest predicament is just a catalyst for what I'd hoped, fucking prayed, wasn't happening...but there's no denying the reality. Can't you see? We're trapped in a rip current and can't find our way back to shore."

He knew. Even a part of me did too.

My sobs fill the room. I sink my face into his chest and we cling to each other...and cry.

Mick and I ease into the shower, meeting under the warm spray. He presses his lips gently to mine as we hold one another. Closing my swollen eyes, I lean my head back into the stream and let the water soak my skin.

Injustice and unfairness rage within. I've known somewhere deep inside—maybe even from Remy's phone call from rehab—that this was our inevitable conclusion. I hoped we could overcome the obstacles, that love would triumph and conquer all. Another wave hits, sobs threatening to unleash and drown me. I tamp it down, fortifying the mental dam staving off my total collapse.

I can't think about the end, can't bear it or fathom it. I must stay in the absolute present. Second by second. Or else I'll shatter into so many pieces I will never be whole again.

I give myself permission to cry for months, years, once my ocean walks out the door. Until then, I will bury my self-pity and inhale every moment of him—us—that remains, committing it to memory.

Mick soaps my body. He's so careful, reverent, quiet...is he memorizing me too? He shampoos my hair—one of my favorite things—his hands gentle but thorough. I fight another sob. *This is the last time he will do this.*

He rubs in conditioner then pulls me close to kiss me softly. His tongue finds mine and they glide and swirl together, writing their own love letter in a language they've mastered. He grips me tighter, and I clutch his frame as our kisses speak for us. My fingers rove across his masculine contours, broad shoulders, and down the valley of his back.

His erection hardens between us, sparking desire from my throat to the sweet spot buried in my center.

He breaks the kiss and cups my cheek, his earnest eyes searching mine, his wet lashes making the gray irises even more vivid. "I want to make love to you for hours," he murmurs. It's a question, a plea.

Choking back the emotion threatening to topple the dam, I nod.

Don't cry. Don't cry. Don't cry.

It's an unspoken agreement. We'll make love, not war.

For as long as we can.

TIME IS A TICKING ATOM BOMB, EACH SECOND bringing us closer to our impending demise as a couple. Not just demise...utter destruction.

I call in sick to work and we hole up to make love, eat, and watch TV twined together. It's the first time I've truly understood the meaning of bittersweet.

Now we're naked in my bed, the glow of our aftermath dimmed by Mick's nearing departure. These are our last precious moments, and they're quickly dwindling. I'm due at the restaurant for the dinner shift soon, and he's leaving...

And never returning.

"This fucking sucks," I mumble into his bare chest, my fingers tracing the happy trail on his lower abdomen, the hair a shade darker than the chestnut color framing his face.

Mick kisses my temple. "Yeah, it does. But you and me? We're survivors. So don't you dare let this stop you from kicking ass and taking names. Take the world by storm and show it exactly what I see."

I'm viscerally aware this is my last pep talk from Mick Callahan. My eyes find his. "You're the best man I've ever known. You've given me so much. Love. Acceptance. Guidance. Encouragement. Confidence. Respect." A rueful laugh escapes. "Can't forget orgasms." Nose stinging, I inhale a deep breath and rest my cheek against his chest. "You've done more for me in our time together than I've gotten in a lifetime. You took all my broken parts and made me...whole. Complete."

His arms wrap around me tightly, his voice sincere as he murmurs into my ear. "You are complete without anyone else. Never forget that. The only person in life you need to rely on is you. *You, Jax. You* are the most important ally, friend, and warrior in your own life."

I want to remember this wisdom, let it sink in...but I'm already shattering, splintering, disintegrating...incomplete. I don't know how to be the woman he seems to think I am.

MICK TAKES ME BY THE HAND AND LEADS ME OUT the front door. The sun is lowering in the sky, and my mind flashes to the sunsets we've enjoyed at his place in Half Moon Bay. That only cues a parade of memories we've created that I'll miss.

He opens the door to the Mustang and throws his hoodie inside. A shiver courses through me as the chill outside hits. He presses me against the car, reminiscent of so many other glorious times, and cradles my face. "I'll never regret one second with you."

A tear escapes down one cheek, and he thumbs it away. "Same. I love you, now and forever."

"No more tears, baby. I'm not worth it."

My heart flinches. "Stop saying that, Mick. Stop believing it. How can you think you're unworthy when ours is the most profound connection I've experienced with another human being? You are the planet I orbit. The moon that shifts my tides. The beat to my goddamned heart."

His forehead touches mine. "I'm so fucking sorry. Those words probably sound hollow, but I am, Jax. This is the hardest decision I've ever been forced to make. You mean everything to me."

All I can manage is a wan smile. "You're kicking your heroin habit."

"There's no such thing with you and me."

I nod without understanding, hanging by a tenuous thread.

"I'm doing this for you," he murmurs. "Remember when I said you weren't destined to be caged—you were meant to fly? You were meant to *soar*. That's all I want for you."

My splintering fragile self understands this, but I will never accept it.

He pulls me close and kisses me gently, and our lips say the goodbye neither of us wants to speak out loud. We part and his hand finds mine again. He squeezes it and brings it to his lips for one last kiss.

"I love you, Jax." Then he slides into the driver's seat of his fastback.

My heart hammers in my chest. This is it. *This is really it.*

"I love you so fucking much, Mick."

He cranks up the Mustang and it growls to life before the idle calms to a steady purr. He shuts the door while I stand rooted and immobile. Mick's eyes flash to mine once more, his expression grim, then he guns it down the street.

Seventeen

I stare blankly at my bedroom ceiling. I'm hollow. Drowning. Shattered.

I thought I'd brushed the absolute height of agonizing pain before...but my despair furrows deep, consuming me.

I
am
utterly,
all-consumingly
lost.

EIGHTEEN

My heart beats...how is a mystery. It's broken beyond repair.
Maybe forever.

NINETEEN

I force myself out of bed. Get dressed. Feed my face. Perform required tasks. Go through the tedious motions of life.

It's not a choice.

And it's a crime against humanity to face life on life's terms when I don't feel alive...and question whether I want to be.

Fuck my stomach for rumbling.

Fuck my eyes for opening every morning.

Fuck my brain for dwelling on what cannot be.

And fuck me for trusting Mick Callahan with my heart.

Twenty

Sometime in February, I laugh.

I don't mean to, but Kit lobbed me one of her stupidly clever observations about frat boys. A group of them proudly wearing Greek symbols sits at a table near us in the university's cafeteria, where we're sipping coffees in between morning classes. They're loud and belligerent in a way that screams *assholes*.

My cackle happens naturally, and the sound is so foreign to my ears that I nearly clap a hand over my mouth.

Kit's eyes beam satisfaction. "There she is," she says softly.

My eyes water and I swallow the emotion. "I'm in here somewhere. At least hopefully I still am. Actually...fuck that. I'm never *hoping* again. Hope is dangerous."

Kit looks like she wants to argue, but doesn't, instead giving my hand a squeeze. "I know you're hurting, but you're absolutely in there. No one can take that from you. Especially not men. It's time to rise like a motherfucking Phoenix from the ashes, babycakes."

I blink hard; her tender words have landed right where she meant them.

She glances at the Greeks again when their guffaws echo in the space. "And torch those smug dipshits on the way up, will you? Except for that guy on the end. He's *cute*."

My lips turn up again.

Maybe I *am* going to get through this.

Twenty-One

I n late March, Kit and Jas barge into my room without knocking. Not breaking stride, Jas arrives at my bedside and flings off my comforter. "Get up. We're going out."

"I'm fine right where I am." I pretend to resume reading my paperback.

Kit crosses her arms. "Enough of this shit. You're going clubbing with us."

My face must broadcast my horror. I'm absolutely not ready for something that...*public*—nor remotely interested.

"You have no choice, Jax. We're busting you out of this self-imposed prison cell. Go doll up," Jas says, grabbing the book from my hand and yanking me from my warm bed.

Kit places her hands on my shoulders. "What she said. Your pity party is officially over. Tonight, you will flirt and dance with members of the opposite sex, and be reminded that you are a gorgeous—"

"Catastrophe," I answer.

"Babe," Kit finishes.

"Who needs to get laid by a hot guy," Jas adds.

I cringe. "Have you lost your mind?"

"Nope," she says. "Take a shower. Do your makeup. Kit and I will pick out a cute outfit."

"But—"

"Don't even try to argue, cupcake," Kit says. "This is a hostile takeover."

"A *loving* hostile takeover," Jas amends.

My eyes shift between my two friends, my dear roommates, my only light in this three-month-long eclipse. They're only trying to help. *Again.* Maybe I owe it to them. To myself. I throw my hands up. "Okay, fine, you win."

The girls squeal in victory.

"But I am *not* getting laid."

My roommates take me to a new club named Enigma. Strobe lights pulse, flashing across the dimly lit tables surrounding the dance floor. A smoky haze fills the air. Bodies move to the music, the bass thumping so loud I can't hear much else.

I follow Jas through the crowd, every step reminding me I'm a minnow away from its pond. The whole scene vibrates around me, foreign and intrusive.

We snag a table and a spandex-wearing cocktail waitress with ratted hair and a shirt showing off her pale midriff takes our drink requests. Jas tacks on three shots of peppermint schnapps to our order. Looks like it's going to be one of those nights.

I light a cigarette and adjust to the shock of being somewhere other than our condo in comfy sweats. The blaring music and staccato lights threaten to give me a headache. Everything screams...and not in a welcome, I've really-missed-this way. I'd pay money to be back in my bed immersed in *Lonesome Dove*. I'm halfway through and it's the best book I've ever read. Reading and school are my escapes. My safety nets. If my mind is allowed to wander, it inevitably lands on Mick and all we've lost.

He hasn't called. Written. Crawled back, realizing he can't live without me. He's made zero moves to reverse his decision. And I've honored it, as excruciatingly hard as it's been. I haven't phoned him once, dropped by the marina, or shown up at his house. I've hardly left the sanctity of the condo unless it's for school or work.

I'm a hostage trapped in a fucked-up type of limbo. Even though my captor gave me up, there's a ransom to pay...and it's steep. My crushed heart barely beats, limping along at minimum capacity to keep me alive.

I prefer to stay busy, my brain occupied and my body tired. Avoidance is the name of the game. Mick and Remy still find me in my dreams, but the rest of the time, I actively fight their intrusions while conscious.

Jas waves a hand in front of my face. "You with us?"

I blink. "Yup. Sorry."

Kit scans the nearby tables. "Fine-ass men at nine o'clock."

Jas and I look. Five guys stand around a table. It's hard to see their faces, but a few might be attractive. As if I care.

The waitress arrives with our drinks, and Jas buys the round. We clink our shot glasses together before slamming them back. The schnapps flames a hot trail down my throat, and I follow up with a long pull of my sea breeze.

Kit's actively flirting with the table of guys now, further jangling my nerves. I dread interacting with anyone other than my roommates.

I'm not ready. I'm not ready. I'm not ready.

When Kit saunters over to their table, paralysis grips my chest. *I'm not ready.* I stare into my cocktail, pink from the cranberry juice with a bright segment of lime notched onto the lip of the glass.

"Hey." Jas seeks my gaze. "Just let loose a little. Drink. Dance. Okay? You've got to start somewhere."

The prickling behind my eyelids reminds me how broken I am. Sucking in a breath, I realize she's right. Mick's not coming back. There is no one to save me. There's just me in this equation now, maybe forever. I need to take some baby steps, so I nod at her in silent agreement.

I inhale the rest of my cocktail and get going on another. The tension in my muscles and posture begins to relax.

As I down another shot, Kit returns with the stable of guys trailing her, and we make room at our table. I engage, laugh a little, lower my guard. The stocky blonde—Rick... Ray?—asks me to dance, and I say yes. My body moves of its own volition. It's always responded naturally to music, and soon I'm blissfully unaware of anything aside from my hips and arms swaying, matching the energy on the floor.

Rick-Ray grins, assessing me top to bottom. A pang of sadness washes over me, but it's dulled by alcohol. His appraisal reminds me I'm desirable, and I flash him a smile.

We stay out for a few songs, then return to the table. I long to fling off the hand he rests on my lower back, the weight of it unfamiliar and unwelcome as he ushers me to my seat. But I don't.

A couple of hours later, I'm trashed—and consumed with calling Mick, or better yet, showing up on his doorstep. When I exit the bathroom, Rick-Ray is leaning against the adjacent wall.

"Just making sure you're alright," he slurs.

"Mm-hmm...fine." *I'm so not fine.*

He braces a hand on the wall, maybe to hold himself upright. "What do you say we get outta here, beautiful?"

I balk at the inference and shake my head.

His face registers surprise. "C'mon. You know you like me."

"You seem nice, but I'm not interested," I say, moving past him with a forced smile.

He grabs my hand. "Your number then. Gimme that."

I yank out of his grasp. "I repeat: *not happening*."

"So you're one of those?"

My head jerks, meeting blue eyes that have turned cruel. "One what?"

"Cock tease."

"Fuck you." Unbelievable.

"That's what I'm working on, sweetheart."

I flee. Not only does the *sweetheart* reference nearly take me to the ground for harkening back to Remy, but this creep is about to get kicked in the nads. I'm on the verge of imploding, the dam breaking as I all but run back to my friends.

I just want to go home.

TWENTY-TWO

With two months left of school, it's paramount that I find a job. I graduate in May along with Jas and Kit, and all three of us are figuring out our next steps. Mr. and Mrs. Singh, Jas's parents, plan to keep the condo as an investment, but depending on where we all land, housing is yet another item on the list of unknowns. One fact crystalizes: I sure as hell do not want to move back in with my parents.

I'm certain they don't want that either if the way my father continues pressuring me about my future is any indication. He's always been great at adding to my pressures, and lately, his micromanagement suffocates with laser accuracy, even from sixty miles away. It's been a while since I've had to deal with his bullshit. He largely—blissfully—left me alone once I moved to San Jose, but here we are.

A smart girl would apply to magazines and newspapers in Los Angeles, which is vast and brimming with opportunities, but the thought of smog, fake Hollywood, and high crime doesn't appeal—aside from providing distance from the Bay Area.

My first choice is San Francisco (despite its proximity to

Mr. He Who Decimated My Heart) but I stay openminded about working anywhere in the region.

Every weekend, I drive to the public library and research publications up and down the peninsula, scouring want ads and copying down contact information. Armed with portfolio samples and a letter of recommendation from my advisor, I type personalized cover letters and assemble packages to potential employers, even the loftier ones—aiming high. I've got nothing to lose.

More than anything, the excitement brewing in my chest shows me I'm healing. I'm not whole, but I'm not a sixteenth of the pie anymore either.

Fly—right, Mick?

I'm trying.

~

JAS AND KIT CONTINUE TO PUSH ME OUT OF MY comfort zone. We go to restaurants and bars together. I let myself have fun. Sometimes I flirt or dance with random guys. The days—and nights—get easier. The sting of rejection fades. Genuine smiles cross my face.

Do I want to date anyone? Nope.

Do I want a one-night stand? Nope.

Do I need a man? Nope.

Maybe never again.

~

IN LATE APRIL, I READ A WANT AD FOR *SAN Francisco Life*. The rush washes over me. *This. It's the one.* Even though it's an editorial assistant position—so, not a writer exactly—a foot in the door seems like half the battle. I pounce, desperate for the opportunity to work at this popular

—and beautiful—lifestyle magazine in the heart of down-town. The heavens practically part.

When I share about it with my advisor on Monday, he offers to call the editor, a former colleague-turned-friend, on my behalf. By the time I get home, there's a message on our answering machine granting me an interview. I phone the administrative assistant back and set it up, crowing loudly after hanging up.

Two days later, Jas lands a spot at the *San Jose Mercury News* as a junior reporter—an incredible opportunity—and Kit has applications with advertising agencies along the peninsula, plus two impending interviews. They're both desperate to stay roommates but also pursue their dreams.

Regardless of how it shakes out, there's no question Jas and Kit will always be friends, and I hope we'll all keep in touch. My track record's not stupendous in that area, but for them, I'll do better. My only other real friend remains Kendra, whom I met through Mick, Remy, and their core group of friends. Despite our hectic schedules and physical distance, Kendra and I still squeeze in monthly phone calls. All three of them have solidified permanent alcoves in my battered heart.

~

My appearance for my interview warrants special attention. Thankfully, my parents gave me five hundred dollars to invest in a professional wardrobe.

I pair a crisp black button-down with an ivory pencil skirt, sheer nylons, and low heels. After carefully blow-drying my hair and curling the ends, I scoop the honey-blond swaths framing my face into a tiger-patterned comb and leave my feathered bangs loose, along with the rest. I apply conservative makeup and a coat of gloss. A final glance in the mirror pulls my lips into a smile. I'm almost unrecognizable...in a good way.

Making my way downstairs, all that's left is to collect my chic leather messenger bag containing a notepad, pen and extra portfolio samples, my purse, and the directions I transcribed when we set the appointment.

It's early afternoon when I crank up the VW and head up the peninsula, steeling myself for those mile markers of a love lost. I've got a lineup of cassettes at the ready to keep my mind occupied: Rush's *Grace Under Pressure*, The Pretenders' *Learning to Crawl*, *Purple Rain* (one of the best movie soundtracks ever), and Stevie Ray Vaughan and Double Trouble's live album, which I push into the tape deck first. It's one of my favorites and will amp me up...even though I'm already jumping out of my skin.

When I get to Menlo Park, I sing ridiculously loud...and even more deafeningly as I pass the heart-piercing sign for Half Moon Bay. Shriek-singing is the only way to keep my tears from breaking the dam.

The future is ahead. The future is ahead. The future is ahead.

An hour later I'm in San Francisco, exiting on Market Street and heading toward the Embarcadero Center downtown. It's sensory overload with taxis and cars, bike messengers and BART kiosks, skyscrapers and hotels, and hordes of busy people crowding the streets and crosswalks.

I arrive at the parking garage and steer my car down the ramp and into a vacant visitor space. An elevator whisks me to the twenty-first floor. *Please let this work out. This girl needs a fresh start.* I suck in a fortifying breath as my destination nears. I'm ready to give it my best shot. The bell dings and metal doors open...like an offering to the gods.

Twenty-Three

The official job offer comes seven days later, and I leap into the air after accepting it. In my heart, I'd known. Between acing the interview and my horoscope predicting it (the sun's heating up my tenth house of professional advancement and goals), I'd stayed positive. They had other applicants, and that left room for my insecurities and unknowns to infiltrate my brain, especially over the span of a week—but I got the job.

I'm moving to San Francisco. I'm going to work for a magazine. No more shifts as a gas station attendant or restaurant hostess. This is a career-girl position. One that could lead to being a real writer someday.

My roommates aren't home, and I'm ready to burst, so I call Kendra.

"Guess who you're talking to?" I say.

"Jacqui? Or have aliens abducted you and it just *sounds* like Jacqui?"

"Jacqui Hall, the newest editorial assistant for *San Francisco Life*!" The phone cord stretches taut once I step onto the veranda.

She whoops. "Pumpkin, I'm so proud of you! And wait until you hear this…"

"What?" I ask before sparking up a cigarette.

"I'm headed to the city too!"

I scream. "You got into UC Hastings?"

"Sure did. Law school, here I come."

"Oh my god!" I squeal. "Hold up. Does this mean we can be roommates?"

"You bet your sweet ass. I probably won't be much fun… my social life is about to take an even bigger hit. May it rest in peace."

"This is amazing. Look at the stars aligning to bring us together again." My heart squeezes and my eyelids prick. *Thank you*, I throw toward the heavens.

"Who could have predicted this turn of events?" she says. The warmth in her voice reminds me of many shared moments.

"You're the best imaginary friend ever," I say, flicking my ash. "Wait until I tell my dad."

"Right?" Kendra snorts at my reference to when my father thought I made up her existence to cover for my falsehoods. I lied my pretty little head off with Kendra's blessing to steal overnights with the men in my life.

"Hey, Jacqui?"

"Hmm?"

"You still smoking? Because I need our apartment to be smoke free. It gives me a headache and—"

"Done. I've been meaning to quit. I'm an idiot for ever getting hooked." *And it reminds me of the two motherfuckers I'm trying to forget.* Eying the half-pack sitting on my dresser, I vow it will be my last.

"Just like that?"

How difficult will kicking the habit be? It sure as shit hasn't been easy quitting Mick. This will be child's play in comparison. "It's time."

"I'd say thank you, but you should probably thank *me* instead. After all, I am saving your life."

That makes me chuckle. "I'll get back to you once I'm through my withdrawal symptoms, when I have something nice to say."

We talk a while longer, ironing out plans for our near future.

I phone my parents next and tell them about the job, Kendra, all of it. My father is pleased, which matters—despite me wishing it didn't—and my mother's cheer is apparent even through her medicated haze.

The front door slams and I rush downstairs, eager to celebrate with my girls, who've become my "real" family.

I falter as I reach the hallway...jarred by the realization that I'm *hopeful*. Hope is dangerous. Hope sinks ships—and I've already been on the emotional *Titanic*. Pushing my feet forward, I allow myself to experience the undiluted joy of starting a new chapter—and firmly closing the book on this one. To spread my wings and soar, just like Mick wanted.

I'm ready.

Twenty-Four

Graduation day brings an ultramarine sky dotted with clouds, and I breathe easier knowing our commencement ceremony can be held outdoors as scheduled.

Boston's "Don't Look Back" blares its apropos message throughout the condo as Jas, Kit, and I put the final touches on our appearance. There's no dimming the mile-wide smile on my face.

School's over. Degree? Earned. Employment? Secured. Heart? Intact, even if by a thread.

Kendra and I move into our new apartment in the city next week, and my job starts right after. I've quit smoking—I think—and it hasn't even been so terrible. After the first few days, it was more about fighting the habit of it.

I snag my cap and gown and head downstairs to wait for my roommates. We're carpooling. Our parents are meeting us at the university and we're all going out for a meal afterward. The doorbell rings and my heels echo against the tile foyer as I approach the door.

A wiry, gray-haired man holds a long, rectangular box in

his arms with a clipboard tucked under one. "Delivery for Jacqueline Hall."

"Really? That's me." I'm shocked silent for a moment. Who's sending me flowers?

"I just need your signature," he says.

Once our transaction completes, he hands me the box, and I take it inside.

Kit walks downstairs as I'm setting it on the dining table. She looks lovely in a mulberry dress that's formfitting up top and flowy on the bottom.

"Oooh. Who are they from?" she asks.

I shrug, lifting the lid. I'm momentarily stunned by the dozen long-stemmed red roses tied with an ivory bow.

Then I fish out the card.

My world tilts on its axis. I'm wholly unprepared for what's staring back at me.

I'm so proud of you, Jax. Fly high, baby.

Love,
Mick

My heart thumps wildly. *Holy shit. Holy shit. Holy shit.* Mick sent me flowers. Roses. He communicated. He... what is he doing?

I hold out the note for Kit, then drop into a chair.

"Wow," she murmurs.

"I know."

Except I don't know. But I do. It's nothing...and everything. It's so fucking typical of Mick. A gentleman. My biggest fan. The love of my life. He hasn't forgotten me. It tugs at me, launching a tenuous hope. A sliver of light that maybe he...wants more?

"Why does he have to be such a magnanimous asshole?" Kit remarks.

I snort softly. She's a hundred percent accurate. "Will you put these in water for me? I'm about to go to pieces, and don't want my mascara running."

Kit's gaze spears mine. "You are not shedding one more tear over that man."

I bite my lip and nod, swallowing anything resembling emotion that's trying damn hard to escape.

She swipes the box from view and gets busy in the kitchen filling a vase at the sink. My insides swirl with longing, and a little satisfaction. *He's still thinking about me. He's still rooting for me. He still wants the best for me.* I squeeze my eyes shut and remind myself of the sobering reality. Nothing's changed. He doesn't want to get back together. He's not making any promises. He doesn't really want me. The dam swells, lodging behind my sternum, and I breathe through it.

Jas joins us, stunning in a sapphire blue jumpsuit that contrasts perfectly with her skin tone, dark hair, and onyx eyes. "What's going on? Who got flowers?"

"Later," Kit says, sending Jas a pointed look, probably because she thinks I'm fragile. "We need to motor or we're going to be late."

As I sit through the ceremony, it's easy to zone out. Even though my roommates and I are all part of the School of Mass Communications, we're still seated alphabetically and there are thousands graduating today. Now that speeches are over, students are queuing by schools to walk onstage to receive their degrees and shake hands with the muckety mucks. Thoughts churn as I await my turn. I'm proud of myself for earning a bachelor's degree. After working hard, scoring the magazine job seems like a hell of a payout. Living with Kendra adds icing on an already epic cake.

When they finally announce our school, I'm all smiles as I

inch my way to the stage, up the steps, and collect my diploma. My roommates' obnoxiously loud cheers amidst polite applause make me grin even wider. I totally return the love when it's their moment.

Once all the diplomas are distributed, we're directed to cross our tassels to the opposite side, pronounced graduated, and we launch our caps to the heavens. It's a grand sight, and the symbolism isn't lost on me. Each one of us is taking flight. When the caps fall to the earth, our journey here is officially complete.

Our families congregate, sharing hugs and congratulations while Jas, Kit, and I luxuriate in the attention and our accomplishment.

"You did it!" my mother says, looking remarkably clear-eyed. She's still wafer thin, and her attempt to camouflage it with her A-line dress doesn't fool me. But when we hug, I gasp. She's bony and sharp angled, covered by a nearly translucent layer of flesh...literal skin and bones. Hiding my distress —this isn't the time or place—I don't squeeze her too tightly.

My father steals me next, holding me at arms' length. "I'm proud of you, Jacqueline. You made it to the finish line, and now you're moving to the city and starting a terrific job. You're really on your way." A genuine smile crosses his face, and I can't help my answering grin as he pulls me in for a close hug.

After more congratulations, we disperse and reconvene at Original Joe's. My boss saved us a table and treats us like royalty. I've already worked my last shift, and he had nothing but praise for how much he appreciated me being a part of their close-knit staff. I'll never forget the people or incredible chow.

Our three families mesh well enough. Despite my worry about how my parents will come across to others, they put on a good show, and our dirty laundry stays buried, where it belongs. Jas and Kit's families have known each other for years, and it's my pleasure to finally meet them in person.

It's impossible not to be dazzled by Jas's parents. Mr. Singh sports a ruby turban with his navy suit, and has a pitch-black mustache, long beard, and striking eyebrows. His wife is resplendent in an amethyst sari and flat sandals. Her hair is as dark as her husband's and coasts down her back. I've never seen a woman of her age with hair so long. Jas told me once they don't cut their hair, something to do with their culture. Her parents also had an arranged marriage—and even descend from Indian royalty. It's honestly fascinating. Kit's parents are dressed similar to mine. Mr. Varisano wears a black suit, and I easily see the Italian in his facial features, olive skin tone, and dark brunette hair. His wife is the opposite with fair skin, blue eyes, and brown hair that veers auburn.

Our graduation is celebrated by our collective parents in style, with easy conversation, heaping plates of food, and delicious desserts.

MY ROOMMATES AND I SAY OUR GOODBYES A WEEK later. It's rough. In our own way, we were also the Three Musketeers, and our little band of heathens is breaking up as we begin our next chapter of life. There are tears shed, promises made, and hugs we can't seem to end.

Even so, as I drive to my new home, my heart brims with excitement, anticipation, and the thrill of the unknown.

One thing is certain. I'm desperate for change—anything to take my mind off what I've lost...and show me everything I stand to gain.

Twenty-Five

April 1987, almost two years later

Jay touches a spot on his lower lip. "You've got some ketchup here."

I dab my napkin on the same area on my face, then lift my eyebrows, looking for confirmation.

He nods, a shock of his curly blond locks falling across his pale blue eyes. "Back to your ridiculously gorgeous self."

Before I can respond, his gaze shifts behind me, smoldering, as he finger-combs his hair into place. "Oh. My. Cheese. And. Crackers." His hushed tone is effused with praise, wonder, and the inflection that is decidedly Jay.

I'm going to assume my coworker has spotted yet another man who's stoked the always-burning fires of his libido.

"Who is *that*?" he purrs, mostly to himself.

I pivot and find the object of his desire. He's handsome alright. And Jay's type. The verdict's out on whether he's also gay. "You're drooling."

His eyes snap back to mine. "I could and would do a lot more with that hunk of male virility in the flesh."

"Mm-hmm. How are things with Rory, by the way?"

Jay rolls his eyes. "It's not illegal to look. And he's fine, nosey Parker. What's happening with *your* love life? Are you still dating what's-his-name?"

I fight a sigh, using my straw like a plunger to agitate the sugar pooling on the bottom of my iced tea. "Nope. I'm not sure a guy in finance is ever going to be the right fit for me."

A guffaw erupts from Jay. "Oh honey, was he too small?"

Flashing him a flat look, I prop my elbow on the table and rest my chin in my hand. "We didn't get that far. He bored me to near tears." And I'm not exaggerating. Much. "Why do the numbers guys always want to talk about the nitty-gritty details of their boring-ass jobs? Math is *not* sexy."

"Unless he's nine inches with a girth that would choke a whale." Jay's eyes flare as he checks out the cute guy behind me again.

I stifle a smile. "Is sex all you think about?"

He shrugs. "It's the only thing *worth* thinking about. And you need some good dick more than anyone I know."

"Whatever," I dismiss, trying not to think about the *good dick* I've had...and lost.

I've tried to move on, to *get out there*, as everyone says. No one ever comes close to doing it for me. Mick and Remy ruined me for life. The longest I've stayed interested in a man is under four weeks, and the one time I caved on sex... I shudder remembering that disappointing debacle.

I glance at my watch. "You about ready? I need to get back to the office."

"Me too. I've got an art department meeting in twenty."

We stand and clean up our mess, dumping everything into the trash. As we pass the nice-looking male my colleague ogled, the guy does a double take, appraising me top to bottom.

"Bitch," Jay mutters when we emerge onto the bustling streets of San Francisco.

I laugh. "When you're hot, you're hot..."

"The worst part is you won't even sample that gloriousness."

"He's not a slab of meat."

"And that's where you're wrong—and why you're single, Jacqui."

"You're incorrigible."

"But right," he singsongs.

I'm elbows deep proofreading the June issue of the magazine when my phone beeps, one of the squares lighting up with an incoming call. "Jacqui," I answer, eyes glued to the spread showcasing where to find the best sushi in the city.

"Need you in my office," Eleanor says, all-business.

When I began working here, my no-nonsense boss freaked me out a tad. Fresh out of college, I had zero professional experience and barely interacted with the few employers I'd had. She intimidated me until I understood her better and found my rhythm as her assistant.

"On my way."

I snag a notepad and pen and walk to her corner office. She's focused on writing in a thick tome she calls her "work bible."

When I rap my knuckles on the dense door, Eleanor waves me in. "Close the door."

My insides twinge. Have I done something wrong?

"Have a seat, Jacqui."

Nervous flutters amplify as I drop into one of her contemporary lime chairs. Through her window, a slice of the deep blue bay cuts through the skyscrapers.

She steeples her hands, elbows resting on her black metal desk. "I have an opportunity for you." A small smile plays at her lips.

Maybe I'm getting another story. I've had a dozen so far while balancing my editorial assistant responsibilities.

"One of the five publications in our group, *Virginia Now*, has an opening, and it's an editorial position for the Travel & Culture section. As much as I hate to lose you, I think you'd be perfect for it."

My heart trips so hard, a thud reverberates in my chest. My mouth forms a silent O as my thoughts riot. Virginia. Writing. The *travel section*. "Wow, th-that's...amazing," I finally sputter.

She acknowledges with a terse nod. "Had a hunch you'd like it. You'll have to fly out for a formal interview, but with our endorsement, you should be a front runner. And if you get the job, they'll pay a stipend for relocation costs."

This is a dream come true, and it's not like I'm tied to California. Even though...it's my home, embedded in my cells, containing some of my favorite people.

"Thank you, Eleanor. Your faith in me means a lot. I love working at *San Francisco Life*."

"It shows. You're eager and talented. And it's probably unfair I've kept you straddling two positions all this time, but people like you are tough to find—or replace."

I'm still technically her assistant, but also write for the various sections, which is Eleanor's way of keeping me incentivized. It's worked, and in my dual role, I've had my fingers in all slices of the magazine pie. I've thoroughly enjoyed it.

I grin. "I'm almost speechless."

"I'm going to set this in motion, but please keep it between us for now."

"I will."

"How far are you through the June issue?"

"Over halfway. I'll have it on your desk by close of business." That term is a misnomer. We may shut the doors at 5 p.m., but that rarely means our workday's over. Publishing is a living, breathing animal, one where deadlines and emergencies rule the landscape.

"Great."

I stand, beaming. "Thank you again."

My boss nods, returning an uncharacteristically sentimental smile.

Stealing outside, I grant myself ten minutes to absorb this revelation. My hands press against my cheeks and that consuming smile, then I walk down the block, letting out an unbridled whoop and not caring who stares. I'm dying to tell someone. My friends and Mrs. Callahan, whose job in this very niche inspired me from the minute Mick told me she wrote for a travel publication.

Mick would be proud of me, too. Really fucking proud. But how would he feel about me moving across the country? Taking that step seals the deal for us, solidly shuts that door.

It's shut, girl. *And locked.*

We've had no contact since our breakup—other than his graduation bouquet—and it's clear we're not going to. I have no clue what's happening in his life and whether he's still beholden to Remy or if the former Three Musketeers could ever share friendship again now that everything's so convoluted. But Mick knows where I stand. I would have waited for him. I would have given him anything he needed—and all of me.

I've got to move on.

And this is a damned good way to do so.

TWENTY-SIX

One week later, I'm exiting through the rotating glass doors of the skyscraper housing *Virginia Now* magazine and resisting the urge to leap into the air. Excess energy ping-pongs through my system, a rightful smile belying my exhilaration. Not to jinx my luck, but that couldn't have gone any better.

I met with Maureen, another no-nonsense managing editor (confident and fortyish), and Tyler, the Travel & Culture editor (a twenty-something dressed like he reads *GQ*). Our rapport was easy and effortless. Answers to their questions slid confidently from my mouth, and my enthusiasm was obvious. They praised my portfolio, which aside from *San Francisco Life* pieces, consists of pieces from *The Spartan Daily*, the San Jose wellness publication during my internship, and a smattering of personal work.

Trees in spring bloom brighten the sidewalk in shades of deep-to-light pinks, and the sun's rays bathe me in warmth. When I pass by an attractive bar—its plate glass windows showcasing an airy, bright interior—my legs propel me through the front door almost of their own volition. My responsibilities are done for the day, and this calls for a celebration. Knock on wood, I'll get the job.

I claim a stool at the long wooden bar. A sunbeam casts a glow against the tiered liquor bottles lined up in neat rows. I'm lost in their colorful hues until a cocktail napkin placed before me ushers me back to the present. A slender woman asks for my order. She's got a spiky pixie haircut and is clad in all-black fitted clothing. It's not a look I could get away with, but one I strongly admire.

When my drink arrives, I take a welcome swallow of the cool Tequila Sunrise and close my eyes. *Heaven.* My neck is so stiff, I lean my head back, shaking my long hair off my shoulders and working out the kinks. Better. A few more sips in, I'm replaying the interview. In my heart, I know it's right. I *want* that job. My high heel taps against the metal footrest under the bar, and I debate ducking into the bathroom to take off these infernal nylons. That is one aspect of wearing professional attire I'm not stoked about, but it seems expected.

"You're sending Morse Code up my leg with all that tapping."

My head swivels to the guy three stools down. He's staring at me with the greenest damn eyes I've ever seen. His eyebrows raise, and his gaze pins me before shifting to my foot.

"Oh. Sorry." I place a hand on my thigh and stop. Offering up a sheepish smile, I make the mistake of meeting his gaze again. With his rich brunette hair and sun-kissed skin as a backdrop to those ridiculous eyes, he's handsome as hell. Heart-stoppingly so, even for this jaded, headed-for-spinsterhood gal. A thin coat of stubble accentuates his chin and jawline.

He skewers me with an incredulous stare. "Are you the kind of person who can't sit still?

I realize my foot is back at it, and I bring it to a halt. A zing of irritation permeates. This guy's being a grumpy dick —immediately making him less gorgeous. *Ha.* "No. I'm just happy, something I have a feeling you never experience."

His head drops, but one side of his mouth twitches as if he's fighting a grin.

I return to my cocktail.

He mutters something indiscernible.

When I glance his way, he's cuffing the back of his head and staring straight ahead. Perhaps he's having a bad day.

"Can I buy you a drink? Help fuel your"—his hand swirls in the air, his brows lifting my way again—"happiness?"

I decide to cut him some slack. "Sure. Maybe some of it will rub off on you."

He tips his head at the bartender. "We'll take two more when you have a minute, please," he says, motioning to our drinks.

My eyes slide down his body while he's occupied. He's a full-on man, with muscular arms straining a black button-down rolled halfway up his forearms, blue jeans that are dark but broken in, and scuffed work boots that remind me of two mechanics I'm still trying to forget. It's enough to get my heart skipping a beat.

And it's been a really, *really* long time since there's been any of that nonsense.

The barkeep places a fresh cocktail on my napkin, and I murmur a thanks. "And thank you...?"

"Butch." He lifts his beer.

"Hmm. Never met a Butch before."

"Today's the day, apparently."

"Apparently."

"And you are?"

I can't help myself. "Sundance."

He shakes his head, once again fighting a smile, and I realize how much I want to see him unleash a genuine one. "Although..."

"What?"

His gaze drags over me from top to bottom. "It fits."

My cheeks burn, and I'm left tongue-tied.

He tips his beer, the liquid making his Adam's apple undulate in a way I can't help but watch. His shirt is open a few buttons and my eyes zero in on the golden skin peeking through. *God, stop checking him out already.*

"You live around here?" I ask.

"Not really. You?"

Another cryptic motherfucker. "Not even close."

His eyebrows lift again. "Where you from, Sundance?"

"California."

Butch snorts. "Figures."

"Why? Because my hair's blond? Give me a break."

"Like, totally, I'm sure," he deadpans, attempting—and failing at—the proper inflection.

I toss him a glare and sip more of my drink. I want to shoot every Valley girl *and* Frank Zappa, whose stupid song broadcasted their existence to the entire world.

He raises his hands in surrender. "Just teasing. You here on vacation?"

"Job interview."

"That's the reason for the good mood?"

My smile says it all.

"So, the California girl's leaving the sunshine state and coming over here to give the mid-Atlantic a spin?"

The pain surrounding that statement envelops me like a blanket, smothering me for a long moment, and I can only nod. Leaving is the only way to create the fresh start I desperately need, but I refrain from saying it out loud. That's way too intimate for a stranger at a bar.

He leaves it alone, maybe sensing my discomfort. When I glance at him again, his lifted expression is a silent question about whether he can move closer. My head dips in assent. What the hell. It's not like he's proposing marriage. I nearly snort...I can't even muster interest in a man longer than three dates. And I'm here for a split second of time, so yeah...what the hell.

His height towers as he moves to the stool next to mine. Damn, he's tall, like well over six feet. He fills out those jeans nicely too...and everything else. He's also older than me, but it's hard to tell by how much.

"Virginia's got a lot going for it," he says softly.

My eyes meet his, which this close are going to be my downfall. He has bedroom eyes, fuck-me-into-oblivion eyes, maybe even fall-in-love-with-me eyes. They're stunning.

Before I can control my mouth, I blurt it out. "You have incredible eyes."

"So do you." He studies me closer. "Amber—with a hint of fire," he decides, and my skin prickles from his proximity and scrutiny. "Have you ever seen the real thing?"

I shake my head dumbly, like I've forgotten English.

"It's fossilized sap from conifer trees, which probably doesn't sound very glamorous, but it's beautiful, coming in shades of yellow, orange, and sometimes green. People make jewelry with it nowadays, which is a far sight better than these fossils sitting around collecting dust in archeology labs." He stares hard, examining me. "Unusual."

"Unusual *good*?" Now it sounds like I'm fishing for a compliment.

He mutters under his breath as he faces his beer, those corded forearms snagging my attention. "Yeah, Sundance. Everything about you is unusual good."

Warmth spreads through me like butter on hot toast, and my stomach swoops. "So, where are you from if you're 'not really' from here?"

"Further south. I'm here for...legal bullshit." He grimaces, but only for a split second.

"Bummer. Do you want to talk about it—or am I being too intrusive?"

Butch sighs, giving me a sideways glance. "It's a long, sad story I won't trouble you with, but suffice it to say, I'm not a fan of lawyers or the court system or utter strangers making decisions that affect my life."

"I'm sorry." He seems dejected.

He rolls his head back and to the sides, his neck cracking. "Actually, I'm sorry. I was rude earlier and shouldn't..." He pauses. "I'm just tired."

It's hard not to study him, to wonder what's really going on in his life. "If you have so far to drive, why are you drinking?"

Something akin to grief or frustration or despair flickers in his expression...all guesses on my part as I mine his face for clues.

After a weighty pause, he says, "I won't have another. Two's my limit." There's something indecipherable in that admission. Is he an alcoholic? Or maybe one of his parents? Or...Jesus, why am I guessing? He drains the remainder of his beer and my gaze flicks to his left hand. No ring.

"What are you doing with the rest of your night?" I utter before my brain can corral my words.

I've got his full attention now. His green eyes laser focus on me then dip down to my mouth. "Yet to be determined."

What am I doing? He's a fucking stranger.

A gorgeous stranger.

I don't know why, but I'm feeling reckless. Wild. Happy-go-lucky.

My smile unfurls. "I've got a hotel room."

TWENTY-SEVEN

Butch and I eye-fuck each other in the glass elevator that rises from the hotel atrium toward the sky. My nerve endings crackle when he stands close enough that his distinctive scent practically assaults me. He smells damn good. His fingers lift and trace my jaw. Heat blasts through me, incinerating my panties.

I clear my throat and gaze up at him. He's ridiculously tall; he probably has seven inches on me. "Uh, just to be straightforward, this is a no-strings-attached, one-time offer."

He grins—the panty-dropping kind, except mine are already wrecked.

His mouth lowers to my ear. "So you just want a man... who knows how to pleasure a woman...to make you come so hard you see stars? Fuck you slow, deep, senseless? As many times as you can take it?"

Oh my god.

My heart hammers alarmingly fast. When his fingertips trail brazenly down my neck and over my breast, tiny chill-bumps erupt across my skin. I'm tingling all the way to my toes.

"Got it," he murmurs.

I'm in major trouble.

That low-pitched voice. That sexy confidence. And that goddamn scent...what is it? Woodsy and a hint of something sweeter, like maple. I swear this guy's a lumberjack dripping syrup on his abs with eyes like a verdant forest.

Get it together.

The elevator dings and Butch drops his roving hand as two women enter, immersed in conversation as one depresses the button for her desired floor. Butch's eyes never leave mine, a wicked grin dancing on his lips as the women continue debating some beauty pageant rule and how unfair it is to their daughters.

My pulse lowers for five seconds. I can barely look at him. Those eyes. Such a deep emerald green. What woman can survive his penetrating stare wrapped in *that* package? I'm entranced, like I've joined a cult and he's the leader. *What is happening here?*

The elevator chimes for our floor.

"Pardon me, ladies," Butch says, and they part like the Red Sea.

Like how my thighs are about to.

He touches the small of my back and I coax my unstable legs to move. It's embarrassing how weak-kneed I am. We make it to my room, but the card key refuses to cooperate no matter how much I swipe it. I'm entirely flustered.

"May I?" he offers.

"Please."

One try and it opens effortlessly for Butch. *Of course.* Pushing the door with his giant arm, he holds it open for me. It closes behind us with a deafening clang. My nerves rage, and I'm suddenly acutely aware of being out of my depth. For all my bravado, this isn't exactly my thing. I've just invited a stranger to have sex.

He approaches with those forest-green, cult daddy eyes

fastened on me. "I'm going to kiss the hell out of you now," he purrs in that bass timbre.

The satchel clutched in my hand drops to the floor. My mouth goes dry, and I swallow with difficulty.

He cups the back of my head and corrals my waist with those sure hands. My heart thuds harder as he guides us together.

Mr. Lumberjack presses his lips to mine and sparks *fly*, igniting a wildfire engulfing me from head to toe.

Holy shit.

We devour each other, mouths opening, tongues intertwining, exploring, probing, seeking. My arms wrap around his strapping shoulders, taut muscles evident under his button-down. The hungry sounds emanating from us only fuel the fire, and I'm grateful this man has a sure grip because my knees gave out five minutes ago.

Eager to see and touch every inch of him, I reach between us and fumble to unbutton this infernal barrier called a shirt. Equally impatient, he takes over, whipping it off and chucking it onto a nearby chair. How I love watching those muscles flex. My gaze traces his broad shoulders, spectacular build, manly chest hair, and that tapered V diving into his jeans. Our lips collide again, hungry and exploratory. My hands rove greedily across his contoured planes. His huge hands chart a path down my back to my ass. His fingers travel the length of my skirt, then he hikes the material and his palms cup my cheeks.

His claiming grip, even through my sheer nylons, further soaks my lace underwear. Those thick fingers—which were impossible to miss at the bar—knead my flesh, and goddamn if I'm not ready to sell my soul to have one of them inside me right now. His hands traverse upwards, untucking my blouse before diving underneath. His calluses scratch gently against my naked skin in the most deliciously welcome way.

Lumberjack or not, this is a man who works with his hands, and something about that turns me on even more.

He carefully lifts the blouse over my head, my nipples hardening further at the way he devours me with his eyes. My stomach dips dramatically...and I'm a trembling, needy mess. His fingers graze over my breasts, ensconced in an ivory bra, and I moan. Loudly. Heat courses through my blood, the fire blazing out of control now.

I need this. I need *him*. Rightfully interpreting my signals, he deftly unclasps my bra, which falls to my feet.

"Goddamn, you're gorgeous," he murmurs before lowering to suck one of my nipples. Then *he* groans, a sexy vibration that rocks me to my core.

My gasp fuels him as his warm tongue takes me to dizzying heights. I'm launched into another dimension. *Yes. Yes. A thousand times yessssssssss.* Butch showers attention on both breasts, squeezing and sucking until the pulsing between my thighs intensifies to DEFCON 3. There's no question I'm going to fuck this strange and beautiful man. Hopefully several times.

I don't know who I am right now.

And I don't care.

This man knows what the hell he's doing.

And I want it.

Badly.

I search blindly for his belt and unbuckle it. My eyes catch his, then shift to his smirking mouth. God, his lips. They're magical all on their own, with a meaty lower lip I've already sucked on and a sharply defined cupid's bow. Those seem to be my downfall, my catnip, my fetish.

"Sundance."

I meet his gaze, freezing. He's not stopping this train, is he? Having second thoughts?

"I think we're on the same page," he says, moving strands of hair from my eyes, "but don't want to assume."

"Okay," I breathe.

"I want to kiss, lick, suck, touch, and fuck all of you."

Oh my. "Yes...me too...all those things." I return to unbuttoning his jeans.

He chuckles, grabbing my hand and holding it still. "Do we need protection?"

"I'm on the Pill. And I haven't slept with anyone since... for a while. I'm good if you are." This registers as both stupid and reckless, but the thought leaves as quickly as it comes.

"Better than good." He grins wide, releasing my hand. His hard-on strains through the denim, and I salivate. I've missed the male apparatus.

Damn...Jay was right. I *did* need some dick.

Butch unlaces his boots and kicks them off, giving me time to appreciate how his jeans strain against those long, burly legs.

"Your turn," he says, voice husky. "But allow me." He kneels before me, and something about it seems so...tender and beautiful and dirty all at the same time. He deftly removes my high heel, then follows suit with the other. He shimmies off my pencil skirt and carefully rolls down my nylons.

He's now mere inches over eye level with my soaked panties. He leans in, grabs my hips, presses his face to that now-useless garment...and inhales. His nose furrows *right there*, and I whimper. His growl is low and damn-near feral. His tongue laps at the material, his hot breath breaching it, and I clutch his shoulders, my whimpers intensifying.

"So ready, so wet..." he murmurs as he continues pressing his mouth against the fabric.

I watch through heavy lids as he wiggles his index finger under my panties, barely grazing across my entrance. My stance widens, the anticipation halting my breath. He pulls the fabric aside and plunges into me without pretense. I cry out, breathing hard as he works it in and out, slowly, purposefully, his eyes fixated.

His finger is *so big,* filling me in the best way. The intensity rocks me head to toe.

"Fuuuuuck," he marvels. "You feel incredible."

"So, so good," I rasp.

He removes that wonderful instrument and licks it. I nearly fall to the ground.

Butch stands and flips off the bedcovers. He spins me onto the bed and drags my underwear down my legs, smelling them for good measure when he's holding the scrap of lace in his giant hand. "Your smell is addicting," he says.

I'd be embarrassed if lust weren't obliterating rational thought.

The sheets are soft under my naked body as he spreads my thighs, and his mouth and tongue begin exploring my most sacred space.

We're both vocal, Butch's groans reverberating straight up my center. "Talk to me. Tell me what you want," he murmurs.

His stubble scrapes my tender flesh as we adjust to this journey of discovery. He doesn't require many navigational cues—and when he lands on the bullseye with the perfect pressure, I quiver and my moans intensify.

"Like that. Just like that. Oh god. Don't stop," I plead.

My orgasm builds, tension mounting through my core as my legs go taut, breath ceasing as release roars through my body, a flash flood annihilating everything in its path. I ride the wave of delirium through the most unrecognizable scream I've ever emitted, one that leaves me gasping for air and wondering if I've just serenaded the entire hotel.

Through it all, I register Butch pushing my thighs further apart—against my body's natural inclination to press them closed. He's still spreading me wide as the last spasms shudder through my vagina, and I realize he's...

watching. Intently. And something about that is super fucking hot.

I lift my head and our eyes connect. I'm struck again by the beautiful forest in his, visible even now through his blown pupils. "You're...really good at that," I say hoarsely.

Butch chuckles, his breath tickling my sensitive bits. "You make it easy."

He releases my thighs and stands, swiftly stripping off the rest of his clothes. My gaze snaps to his erection. The lumberjack is packing—like a fucking redwood—thick, straining, and *well* above average. I'm slack jawed. And desperate for carnal knowledge.

He looks pleased. Maybe even a little smug.

"Butch," I purr.

"Hmm," he murmurs, stroking his impressive dick. "This what you want?"

I nod, speechless.

He positions himself, leaning forward on his arms to kiss me languidly, as if we have nothing but time. His lips trail to my ear. "I can't wait to be inside of you too, Sundance," he whispers, his warm breath adding more heat to the inferno roiling through my body.

He rubs the tip along my entrance, testing. No need. I'm soaked, beyond ready, open for business. Our moans converge as my legs widen, and he pushes in further. Holy hell. It's a good thing I'm primed, because his girth steals my air straight from my lungs.

"Relax, beautiful. Breathe."

I take a few inhalations and force myself to calm. He eases in another inch.

"You're so big," I marvel.

"And you're so fucking tight I'm about to lose my shit."

"Relax, Butch. *Breathe*," I joke through more staggered breaths.

Our eyes meet, smiles matching. This man is a heady

sight. Gorgeous. Strong. And totally focused on me. My mouth falls open as he thrusts deeper, pleasure zinging through my system.

When he's all the way home, his eyes close, and I watch him raptly. His brunette locks are damp from perspiration, curling slightly at the ends. His neck and arm muscles strain. His weight fills me with a comfort I don't understand.

His eyes open and we share another languid smile. "You okay?"

This man. If it wasn't a one-nighter, bet I could fall for him. "Never better."

Slowly, he moves his hips, working us into a rhythm. My legs lift, allowing him in deeper, and the friction...and sheer volume of Mr. Lumberjack blows my mind. He quickens his tempo, ramming into me with deliberate strokes, our moans and heavy breaths filling the room. I'm delirious from the pleasure, clawing at his back like a crazed woman. I wrap my limbs around him, my fingernails digging in, wanting him closer, closer, closer as our centers meet again and again.

His pace turns even more vigorous, and the momentum edges my delirium as he nears climax. My exclamations intensify. The sensations are extreme enough that my eyes prick unexpectedly. Our gazes clash in the final moments, and my euphoria is mirrored in his expression. He explodes and I cry out, overwhelmed with...all of it. His maple scent mixed with salty sweat. His hard muscles against my soft skin. How he clutches me to him as he grinds out every drop. The soundtrack of our ragged breaths punctuating the quiet space.

I pull him in tighter, and he collapses into me, both of us basking in the spoils of this unexpected, incredible, and damn-near perfect liaison.

Minutes later, I'm wrapped around one side of Butch with his fingers lightly tracing over my hip and down one leg. It's surprising intimate for two strangers, but after what just went down, maybe not.

Waning light filters in the hotel window, the sky is a dusky shade of blue, and sounds of distant sirens permeate the silence.

"Hungry?" I ask.

"For more of you? Yes."

I chuckle. "How about food? We could order room service."

"Also yes...as long as you remain naked."

A warmth spreads at his words. *He wants me.* And being wanted has always fueled and filled me. I'm acutely aware I can't go there. I'm not looking for love anymore. Either is my battered heart. This is why a one-night stand works. The unspoken rules are clear: this is all it is and ever will be.

Reluctantly, I pry myself from his incredible body, scoot off the mattress, and snag the hotel menu. Standing near the edge of the bed, I clear my throat and read our choices.

"Appetizers include..." I study the list.

"I already had an appetizer, and nothing's topping that." Butch props himself on one elbow with the sheet barely covering his...main course...and looking every bit the *Playgirl* centerfold.

I grin, scanning the array of options. "How about a 'King-Size Hamburger' or 'Two Grilled Frankfurters with Sweet Relish'? We can score 'Cheese Gold Fish' for a buck. This verbiage cracks me up...it's so old fashioned. Get this: We can order 'stuffed celery with creamed Roquefort cheese'! And, oh my god, 'Iced Vichyssoise.' How very—"

"I like you narrating the menu, Sundance. It's getting me hard."

My eyes shoot right to the burgeoning sheet, and I bite my lip. "Mmm...perhaps we don't need canapés after all." Tossing the menu into the air, I climb Mr. Lumberjack like, ahem, a tree.

We've done just about everything...given each other head (that sixty-nine was especially memorable), screwed in a variety of positions and places in this hotel suite, taken a shower together, shared multiple orgasms. I've only vetoed one request—the one where his fingers lightly caressed my back entrance and he asked, *Is this up for grabs?* in his sexy voice. I shook my head, trying to hide my surprise. His only response was a murmured, *Shame.*

We finally ordered room service (a "King-Size Cheese-burger" for him and BLT for me). I fork another bite of "Cheese Cake" into his mouth. Watching him lick the creamy dessert from his lower lip—chest bare, sheet covering him from the waist down—is a vision likely burned into my memory forever.

Ditching the plate, I seek his lips. Again. We both groan, inhaling each other and the sweetness from the cake, as our tongues commingle.

"You are insatiable," he murmurs.

He's right. I'm like a depraved, sex-starved machine. "For you."

And we go another round.

After midnight, Butch leaves me—sated, exhausted, and big-dick sore—with one last lingering kiss.

"See you, gorgeous," he whispers, tenderly stroking my hair.

I gaze into those glorious emerald eyes one final time. "Back atcha, handsome."

He hesitates, as if wanting to say more. It's the same for me...but what do you say after a night like that? *Thanks for a good time? Have a nice life? Wanna get married and do this forever?*

Instead, he presses a tender kiss to my forehead and mutters something I can't discern on his way out.

The hotel door snicks closed behind him, leaving me alone in this bed we fully utilized. One where our fused musky scent deliciously lingers.

I sense we both carry shards of regret. We're good together. Not just the sex, either. We were comfortable in a way strangers typically aren't. And when we talked, even sharing a few confessions, it seemed natural. Maybe the intense sex also says something about us. *So. Good.* Butch was attentive, experienced, and focused on my pleasure. It rocked my world in the best, toe-curling way.

But let's be realistic. I don't even know his full name, age, or zip code—and I certainly never offered up of *my* details. We're just Butch and Sundance, two outlaws who carved out a perfect night of debauchery like it was our last night alive.

The likelihood of ever seeing him again? One in a million.

Twenty-Eight

On the flight home, I plug in the complimentary headphones and find an easy-listening music channel. Staring out the small oval window next to my seat, I replay my trip, from the interview to all things Butch. The potent combination of the two forces me to acknowledge blunt reality.

I need to move on...not just *on*, but forward.

And this job is my ticket. Moving across the country gives me distance, a fresh perspective, and a clean slate. I'll no longer be haunted by memories forty miles down the peninsula. Rather, I'll be stimulated by a new environment to explore, inspired to tell stories of the people and places I find.

There's an undeniable spark and genuine excitement pumping through my system...and I've missed this innate inner joy. I'm disappointed it's taken so long to admit I've been going through the motions.

Butch also awakened something dormant. My desires. My sexuality. My body and its connection when intimate with another. It shocked the hell out of me. I didn't go looking for a hookup, it just happened...but damn if it didn't switch the light back on. I'm not ready to risk getting my heart broken any time soon. I may never be. But I'm willing to own that I'm not dead yet, either, and if it's not hurting me or anyone else, I'm staying open to...opportunities. I pray there are more guys like Butch out there.

I shiver in remembrance of his greedy hands, spectacular mouth, and ginormous dick. Those gorgeous eyes. His dominating height. His sultry smell. Butch was *all* man. *Lumberjack Man.*

Shaking off the memory, I squeeze my thighs together and retrieve my paperback before I orgasm in my seat. Although reading Sidney Sheldon won't help matters. He packs the heat in his novels (and the dudes are always hung), but it's all I've got.

~

KENDRA'S HUGE BROWN EYES LIGHT AS I REGALE her with the details of my trip. I can't contain my enthusiasm about my potential new job, obvious swooning over my dalliance with Butch, and renewed motivation to stop sulking, waiting, *existing,* and start living.

She wraps me in a hug. "This makes me so happy, pumpkin." She pulls back, still holding my arms. "Your spark is back."

I smile at her tenderly, my eyes stinging. Because now I know, after finally seeing it for myself.

Kendra purses her lips in her signature way. "Even if it means you moving across the damn country."

We share a laugh.

"It would be major," I say. "But a good thing."

She nods, fighting her own tears. "I know, Jacqui, and I sincerely hope it works out for you."

My grin broadens.

"And who knows? Maybe you'll run into this Butch character again." She gives me a devilish smile.

I wish.

The intercom buzzes with our Chinese food delivery. Kendra grants the person entry and waits at the door. I switch on the TV, landing on a Pirates vs. Cubs game and scouring the screen for our friend Terry, who was drafted by Pittsburgh after college.

Kendra returns, pulling out white cartons filled with steaming, aromatic dishes and setting them on the coffee table.

"This okay?" I ask, knowing her breakup with Terry still hurts, even years later. She loved him deeply...and if anyone understands, it's me.

She nods, and we settle in to watch Terrence Walker play Major League Baseball.

I snag two pork dumplings and put a heaping spoonful of rice topped with Szechuan chicken on my plate.

Terry comes up to bat with two outs and no men on base. The Pirates are behind by one run. He takes a strike, narrowly avoids getting pegged by a wayward pitch, ignores a ball, then hits a fastball, sending that sucker into left field near the foul line. We squeal as he makes it to second.

There's nothing more beautiful than watching Terry steal bases. I chant, *"Get a hit, get a hit, get a hit"* under my breath as the next player steps into the batter's box.

He singles, advancing our boy to third.

Tension's high now, and I can't eat one bite until this inning plays out.

"Damn that man for looking so good," Kendra murmurs as Terry crosses home plate.

I chuckle. "Always was a handsome motherfucker."

She rubs her palms against her thighs with a forceful exhalation. "I miss him. *Still.* Which is just stupid. I doubt he gives me a second's thought, and he's probably been with a thousand women by now. Being a baseball star as fine as *that"*—

she waves her hand at the TV—"has surely opened a lot of legs."

She's right, but I don't confirm it aloud, settling for giving her forearm a squeeze.

"I really thought we'd get married," she whispers, her eyes glassing.

"Your grand love story has yet to be revealed, my friend. You're not only a stunningly gorgeous woman, but you are the kindest soul I've ever met. Fuck Terry for squandering that. He doesn't deserve you."

Just like Mick Callahan doesn't deserve me.

Kendra casts me a grateful glance.

We both may understand the heavy toll of loving our respective men, but it's another matter for the heart to let them go.

TWENTY-NINE

When I'm offered—and accept—the job, there's little time to celebrate. I have two weeks to exit the life I've made in California and report for work in Virginia.

My veins pump a cocktail of exhilaration with a twist of anxiety as I nail down the many details. I find a studio apartment from three thousand miles away, sight unseen, thanks to some help from the magazine's human resources coordinator. It even comes furnished—beyond helpful until I can afford to buy some furniture. As for my current abode, Kendra luckily knows another law student who needs a place and can move in once I exit.

According to my father (and I don't disagree), my Beetle is too old and dilapidated to drive across the country and lacks the cargo space to haul my stuff. He helps me shop for a car and generously makes the down payment on a brand new red Toyota, and I leave the lot with my first new ride...one that comes with five years of monthly payments. It's boxy and economical—nothing remotely sexy like American muscle—but earns points for the "sports package" adding a spoiler and pinstriping.

My parents agree to store some of my belongings so I can focus on taking necessities. The same day I drop off storage items, my father and I map out my trip using the newest road atlas, including likely motel stops. It's almost a straight shot from California to Virginia, so I'm allowing four days, although it could take less. The moving expenses stipend from the magazine will cover those costs and then some.

Then it's time for goodbyes.

First on my list—and the easiest to leave—are my parents. Even though we're on better footing since I left home, it doesn't erase years of neglect.

The hard part is knowing my mother has one foot in the grave, and she's the one killing herself a little more each minute. "Suicide Is Painless" isn't only the theme song from *M*A*S*H*, it's hers. Severely underweight, popping Valium and drinking wine every day, she's so sickly she's unemployable—and stubbornly refuses to seek help or change. I despise her for it on top of a pile of anger and disrespect.

My father drinks himself into nightly comas, surely continues cheating on her, and seems to remain blissfully in denial about his wife...or he's given up like I have. I'm unable to deal with their problems, and deep inside, I want to distance myself as fast as possible. Three thousand miles will do that in spades.

Our goodbyes are quick.

I hug my mother first. "Please take care of yourself, Mom." *She won't.*

"You too, honey. Go show those Virginians how amazing you are."

"I will."

She squeezes me—as best she can in her frail state. "Don't forget about us."

My grip stays loose, worried her birdlike bones will snap under pressure. It's a relief to let her go and shift to my father.

"Be careful driving to Virginia. Stop if you get tired, but

don't linger at rest stops. Err on the side of caution, okay? As a young woman, you're vulnerable traveling alone. And don't forget to call when you get there...and from time to time." He gives me a firm squeeze and releases me.

I glance from one parent to the other. We're not big on verbal pronouncements and sentiments, but it seems right, considering it's a significant moment. "Love you guys."

"We love you too," they echo, and my chest loosens, relieved they said it back. I could probably count the number of times they've told me they love me on two hands. Maybe one.

Opening the door to the Toyota, I settle into the driver's seat and roll down my window. Giving them a final wave, I take off, watching their figures recede through the side mirror until they're two dots...and then gone.

I release a shuddering breath. Fear of the unknown looms —along with elation. And I'm one step closer to meeting both head-on.

After I make it back to San Francisco, Kendra and I talk past midnight, not really wanting our last night together to end. We laugh, cry, and pledge to stay in touch and kick ass at our respective professions.

The following morning, I pack my remaining belongings. My gaze lingers on the earrings and anklet Mick gave me, then I resolutely place my jewelry case in a duffel bag with my clothes. I'm leaving the big furniture for Kendra's next roommate, which makes my life easier.

After stuffing everything into my car, I take the apartment key off my ring and leave it with a final note to Kendra.

I absorb one last look as I drive through the city, not knowing when I'll return, then I accelerate onto the freeway and cruise down to San Jose.

Upon my arrival, Jas, Kit, and I stand in a group hug for five minutes. It's been too long since I've seen my old roomies, and a sharp pang lodges behind my sternum as we reunite.

These girls have been there for me through some of my brightest—and hardest—days the past few years. Leaving them fills me with a sudden, unexpected grief. They are two of the kindest, funniest, and best human beings I know—and volunteer life rafts during my stormiest time. Will the distance sink our friendship?

"There goes the mascara," I choke out.

Jas sniffles. "Mine too."

Kit huffs out a big breath. "No crying!" she pronounces.

"El Torito's for old times' sake?" Jas asks.

I nod and we trade smiles, each wiping our cheeks.

"No tequila," I warn. "I have to drive tomorrow."

Kit emits an evil laugh. "Sure thing, Jax."

At the restaurant, we share a pitcher of margaritas and nachos. And a few rounds of tequila shots. We reminisce, catch up on the latest in our lives, and soak in our last meal together...for a while.

We return to their apartment and stay up way too late. I crash on their couch, the same one from our condo that has comforted us all at one time or another. The one Mick slept on when Remy, Mick, and I were trying to remember how to be the Three Musketeers. The one Jas and I needed when we were recovering from our car accident. The one the three of us sat on watching *Cheers* and *Taxi* and nursing hangovers. It's full of memories that seep into my mind as I sleep, fueling restless dreams.

IN THE MORNING, I SHARE A RUSHED, FIERCE goodbye with the girls as they head to their respective jobs and leave me to shower and lock up.

I have one more stop on my way out of California, and I haven't told a soul I'm making it.

My insides thrash as if a school of minnows swims in my

bloodstream, darting one direction then another, the closer I get to Half Moon Bay.

When I pull up at the marina and spot Mick's blue Mustang, my pulse pounds. I glance into the rearview mirror for vanity's sake and apply a quick coat of lip gloss, then walk into the office.

A young woman greets me. She's pretty in a modest, underdone way. Not a lot of makeup, no flashy clothes. Her curly beige hair is pulled into a ponytail and held by a ruffled pink scrunchie. The place looks the same as I remember—borderline cluttered, with brochures in racks to my left, advertisements for boat trips and rentals plastered along the wall behind the long counter.

"Can I help you?" she asks.

"I'm looking for Mick Callahan. Is he available?"

She glances at the open calendar on her desk, then to me again. "Did you book a rental or charter? I'm sorry, but it's not listed."

"No, it's...personal. I'm an old friend." *That's under-stating things a tad.*

Her face falls before she catches herself, and her gaze turns assessing. "Sure, well, yes. Let me tell him you're here."

"Actually, if he's in the marina and not with a customer, can I just walk out there to meet him? You can point me in the right direction. I, uh, know my way around."

"Oh." Pause. "I guess." She appears to grapple with my request—maybe my whole presence.

"Thanks. So...where can I find him?"

She points me to the dock on the far left and I leave her, likely watching my every move. A twinge of jealousy spikes. If I were a betting woman, I'd say she's dating my former lover.

I spot Mick working on a large sailboat, and drink him in. His muscles flex under his T-shirt, his hair's shorter, and a circle beard hugs his face. It suits him. Mr. Incredible is only better looking, if that's even possible. Shouldn't there be a law of physics against that?

"Hey, stranger," I say.

Mick glances up, surprise registering before he tilts his head and offers me a genuine smile, one that lights up his spectacular face. "Jax." His eyes scour me quickly, then he leaps from the bow of the sailboat onto the pier.

My heart pounds like the traitor she is, despite all the pain, anger, and angst Mick left in his tsunami wake. He moves closer until we're standing at arm's length. His skin is weathered from the sun, the lines at the corner of his lips slightly more pronounced in his smile.

"I'm leaving. California, I mean."

"Yeah?" His hand rakes through his hair, distracting me. There's a flicker of pain in his eyes but when he blinks, it's erased.

"I just wanted to say goodbye. We didn't..." My gaze shifts to the horizon, then back to him. "I didn't want to split without letting you know."

His gray eyes warm, filling me with a rush of emotion so strong that my heart jolts. "Where you headed?"

"East coast. I'm going to work for a magazine in Virginia. The Travel & Culture section, if you can believe it."

His eyes shine with something like admiration—or knowing him, satisfaction. "That's great, Jax. Good for you."

I nod, offering up a small smile. "As a wise man once told me, I should be proud of myself. And I am."

Mick smiles broadly enough to show me that dimple I love.

"Will you tell your mom, and say goodbye to her for me? She inspired me so much."

He nods, still beaming. "She'll be stoked to hear the news."

"How's Remy?" I force out.

He pauses, stroking his bearded jaw, and I wonder if the

hair is brittle or soft. My fingers itch to touch it. "He's clean... but struggling. He slips sometimes. His wife is a fucking saint and sticking by him. So am I. He's trying."

That guts like a machete. I truly want Remy to recover. It's just...we haven't spoken since he unceremoniously jilted me, as if I was an extra twelve-pack that accidentally fell off his beer truck. The shot of adrenaline rocketing through me is one hell of an indicator that I'm still pissed.

I jerk my head toward the office. "Not that it's any of my business, but are you seeing her? Her stare's boring a hole into my back." I can't help my impish smile.

He cuffs the back of his neck. Why is everything he does still so ridiculously attractive? His silence deafens. And is answer enough.

Pang. Pang. Panggggggggg. Fuck, that cuts deep. "Do you love her?"

He looks at me incredulously. "No." And I can tell he's not lying. *Poor girl.*

"Are you happy, Mick?"

"And we're back to your favorite question. You know what I think about that one." Those gray pools fill with mirth, and his lip curls on one side.

My eyes well suddenly and I stare at the ground... anywhere to avoid looking at him. His proximity is a visceral reminder of all we were, all we lost—and the finality slams into me. He's dating. I'm moving across the country.

"Hey," he says softly, stepping close enough that I smell his familiar ocean scent mixing with the salt of the Pacific.

It's irritating that I'm so transparent. So much for playing it cool.

He gently lifts my chin and just one touch from him makes me choke back a sob. "I'm glad you stopped by. Jax... I'm sorry. About everything. If I could go back in time and change our circumstances, fix this, I would. I care about you. Still. *Always.*"

He doesn't say "but" even though it hangs in the air between us. We both know nothing's changed. He's on Team Remy. And he should be. That's his best friend. Someone who was there for Mick during his hardest years. He's returning the favor. Not only can't the former Three Musketeers hang out anymore, but Mick made it clear he wouldn't clip my wingspan. And he's never believed himself worthy of happiness. Probably not even love. The entire situation remains a convoluted mess that's no closer to resolving, and maybe that's partly why I came to say goodbye.

"I loved you with my whole heart," I admit. "You'll always have a piece of it."

His gray eyes clash with my amber, and he runs a hand through his chestnut hair again. He's still devastating, but I rather miss the longer version of those waves.

"Same, heroin."

That volume of emotion lifts and falls, shuddering in my chest. It's time to go. I got what I needed—and wanted—from this farewell.

"Goodbye, Mick." I risk touching him, taking his hand and trying hard to ignore the charge it sets off in me from head to toe.

He surprises me by pulling me into his arms...and nothing in me resists. Sinking into him, I revel one last time in his familiar embrace.

"Be happy," I murmur against his neck, and he squeezes me tighter.

"Good luck, Jax." He pulls away with a smile, nothing but sincerity on his stupidly gorgeous face. "Go kick some ass."

Chasing away any sadness, I flash him a grin. "You know it."

My bravado lasts all of ten minutes. Before making my way back to the highway, I'm fucking spiraling. Seeing Mick shakes old memories loose, placing them front and center for the first time in months. And my heart seems plenty eager to relive the rollercoaster ride of the Three Musketeers.

Mick and Remy gave me something I've never had. Their friendship—and love—completed me, made me whole.

They starred in the most important episodes of my life.

What if my show's over? Cancelled? And that's all I get? One great love. One broken heart. One and done.

What if they were the only men who could fulfill that destiny?

Half of me is missing and will never be replaced. I'm hollow. Like a shell without a crab. There's no life here...just walls holding in my organs, lungs breathing on their own. I'm here, yet not here at all.

Fuck love.

Fuck giving your whole heart to someone—or two someones.

Fuck taking risks when these are the repercussions.

Fuck Mick for throwing away something so special neither of us may ever see it again in our lifetimes.

And fuck Alfred Tennyson for his oft-quoted bullshit, "'Tis better to have loved and lost than never to have loved at all."

What a crock.

An image appears in my mind: my heart, riddled with holes—bullet-shaped wounds and the resulting shrapnel. Maybe it can't hold love anymore.

Hours pass as I ruminate. I scarcely notice the landscape or register what song comes on the radio as I drive on autopilot across California.

Finally, my anger crystalizes and wakes me the hell up. *Get your head out of your ass. The Three Musketeers are dead...but you're not. This is your time to shine.*

After crossing the state line into Arizona, I exit into the visitor station rest stop. I use the bathroom and splash cold water on my face, then dab a towel from the dispenser to dry it.

Getting back into my Toyota, my resolve hardens. I plug in a Led Zeppelin tape, crank it, and hit the gas. I'm leaving all my angst in California.

The rear view.

The past.

My next chapter begins now, and it stars *me*. I don't need a man—or anyone else—to fucking complete my story.

I'm writing it.

THIRTY

I arrive in Virginia exhausted and with little time to spare. Navigating to my apartment building in the sprawling city of Richmond, I find my designated parking spot in the underground lot, haul my belongings inside, and call my parents as promised.

My studio is tiny but adorable—a perfect size for one—and comes with a view since I'm on the tenth floor. The furnishings are sufficient, neither grand nor eyesores. Once I add my personal touches, the space will become homier.

After unpacking, I'm too zonked to do anything but track down some food. Fortunately, I live in a section of the city that's walking distance to restaurants and shops, and I venture out to weigh my options.

The cool air refreshes me as I stroll the neighborhood, and it's not long before a pizza joint lures me in with its aromatic promises. The modest décor doesn't worry me... especially when a pizza whizzes past and I get a glimpse. Yes, please. I order a medium pie with extra cheese and a Coke, then sit at a table and whip out my worn copy of *The Great Santini*, falling into its pages to distract my growling stomach.

It arrives and I abandon my book and inhale four heavenly slices.

Despite my intention to explore the neighborhood further, exhaustion coaxes me home. The reality startles me.

I live in Virginia now.

THE FOLLOWING MORNING, I HIT UP THE GROCERY store. It's not a chain I recognize, but neither is anything else I've seen, aside from fast food and gas station brands. Speaking of strange, there's an absence of familiar cars. Instead of American muscle, Volkswagens, Corvettes, Porsches, and Datsuns, there are boxy sedans, scads of pick-up trucks, and a rare sports car sighting. And there's no sourdough bread in sight.

"Toto, we're not in Kansas anymore," I murmur under my breath as I slowly fill my cart with items emblazoned with more unrecognizable brand names.

Later, I walk a broader section of my surrounding neighborhood, getting the lay of the land. Businesses and most of the homes are red brick, with special details like bricked arches, herringbone walkways, and wrought iron fences and railings. It reeks of history and the past, while being quaint and sophisticated. Vastly different from the contemporary architecture in California, I soak it all in.

As I travel farther out, the shabbier abodes and patchy, unweeded lawns have me swiftly turning back, my internal warning lights flashing. I'm alone in the world now, my safety resting solely on my own shoulders. That harrowing night at the Self-Serve when I was robbed at gunpoint resurrected my sixth sense—the one propelling my feet faster now.

I breathe easier when storefronts come into view. I pop into a bookstore, instantly calmed by the familiar smell of books. Their diverse covers beckon to me from displays.

Browsing the titles—the worn wood floor creaking in spots, soft jazz playing from unseen speakers—my mood calms.

A few doors down, I treat myself to a double scoop of ice cream, licking the chocolate when it drips down my sugar cone, reveling in all the places to shop and eat as I make my way home.

I can't wait to explore the entire city and beyond.

~

I'm up ultra early Monday morning getting ready for my first day on the job. Professional outfit of black slacks and a white blouse? Check. Styled hair and light makeup? Check. Lunch made and breakfast scarfed? Check. Directions in hand? Check.

Mild jitters accompany me to work. I want to make a good impression, exceed expectations, make friends. Writing for publication is a competitive, cutthroat profession. Everyone's trying to make a name for themselves, get the top stories, and secure the byline. I don't kid myself that *Virginia Now* will be any different.

My lips purse before widening into a smile, thinking about Jay's parting advice: *Fuck you for leaving, kick ass don't kiss it, make it don't fake it, be your ridiculously gorgeous and fabulous self, good luck finding a better coworker than me, and for god's sake, get laid.*

After navigating through traffic, I make it to the building and park in the garage. An elevator whisks me to the nineteenth floor, and I push through the glass doors, greet the receptionist, and ask her where to go. She makes a call, and a woman named Valerie emerges. She seems close to my age but stands a head shorter with a thick mass of auburn curls reaching her shoulders. She chats me up while leading me through a maze of cubicles, finally stopping at one that's empty. With a wave of her hand, she proclaims it mine.

"Set your bag down, and I'll give you the nickel tour," she says warmly.

She guides me through various departments, past an expansive conference room where I glimpse a meeting in progress, smaller conference rooms, the employee lounge, and finally, the senior offices. Along the way, she makes quick introductions—most of the names forgotten by the time I'm back at my desk.

"Thank you, Valerie."

"Sure thing. And don't get comfortable...you've got an editorial meeting in ten minutes."

The meeting consists of writing staff for the Travel & Culture section only, immediately following an all-sections assembly every Monday. As a guppy in this pond, I'm happy to have a seat at the table at all.

Tyler strides in shortly after me, dressed straight out of *GQ* again with indigo designer jeans, a rich brown button-down, and a bolo instead of a tie.

"Has everyone met Jacqui?" he asks, not waiting for an answer as he scrawls something on an easel flipboard with a marker. "She's our newest staff writer. Be nice," he adds, glancing over his shoulder.

The six people present chuckle quietly, appraising me. Do they require a warning?

"You only need to watch out for Tanya," the male across from me says, his thick black glasses outlining a pronounced nose.

I scan for the woman in question, who promptly responds. "Greg's just jealous because I bag all the choice stories. You know what they say...talent talks, bullshit walks."

Well then. Greg's scoff rings out loud and clear. Tanya's smirk morphs into a smile my direction, though it smacks of disingenuous. She's young and attractive, although everything about her seems harsh: formidable dark brows, straight hair cut at a severe angle, military shoulder pads in her blazer, that tongue.

Tyler starts the meeting, reviewing assignments and deadlines, asking for new material, and following up on previously discussed story ideas. I listen, take notes, and do my best to get a bead on each team member, hopeful that some will become allies.

I score my first assignment: an article about a record store that once housed a speakeasy. I'll research its history, interview the owner and scan through the current offerings, hunt for old imagery, and schedule a photo shoot with one of our staff photographers. I'm also given assorted leads to dig into during my spare time, fleshing out any worth pursuing. I'm even encouraged to pitch my own ideas.

There's no missing Tanya's huff. *Did she want this story?*

The pressure to perform strangles me like a scarf tied too tight. *I can do this.* It's what I've worked for the past six years, damn it.

I SPEND HOURS GOING THROUGH ARCHIVED newspapers on microfiche at the library, pleased with the treasure trove of data it yields. Bleary-eyed after viewing all that magnified text on screen, I close my eyes and massage away the ache.

Once back at my desk, I review my scribbled notes and organize my thoughts.

"Knock knock."

I swivel in my chair, a hand flying to my chest.

An imposing, sandy-haired man in a navy suit stands before me, his arm thrown casually over my cubicle like he owns the joint.

He grins. "Didn't mean to startle you. I'm Don Jennings. Wanted to see how your first day was going."

Holy shit. I leap to my feet and extend my hand. He's the

publisher. He may not technically own the place, but he's still at the top of the heap with the biggest title.

"It's a pleasure to meet you, Mr. Jennings."

"Don," he corrects, a smile creasing his cheeks as hazel eyes pin me to the spot.

"Don," I repeat.

"The pleasure is all mine, Jacqueline Hall." He gives my hand a squeeze before releasing it. I'm surprised he knows my name. Isn't he too busy and important to remember the names of minions?

"Settling in alright?" His attentive gaze sends a weird shiver down my spine.

"Yes. All good."

"If you need anything, my door's always open." He winks.

"Um...thank you," I manage.

He saunters away, and I'm left flustered. A creepy twinge settles under my skin. Was he...? Nah. The boss man was just being friendly. I'm impressed he took the time to stop by and introduce himself. More so that he knew my name. Surely, I'm reading too much into it.

Thirty-One

I scrub a hand over my face, wishing the ache in my chest would just fucking leave. After four months in this new city, it's a constant one step forward, two steps back predicament.

Loneliness traps me in its familiar web as my foot taps against the cement floor, eyes hypnotized by my clothes tumbling in the dryer unit. I dislike this windowless room in the bowels of my apartment building. It always reeks of... something unidentifiable. Don't even get me started on the humidity. Virginia summers mean enduring thick, wet, suffocating heat. Temperatures fluctuate wildly and the oppressive mugginess permeates every nook and cranny that isn't air conditioned. Like this room.

Moving away from everything and everyone I know wasn't easy, even if I chose this adventure. It's the first time I've lived alone, and I miss the daily company roommates provided. My studio initially seemed cozy but sometimes closes in on me like a jail cell. I've pushed out of my comfort zone by exploring the region some...it just sucks to do activities solo, and my limited funds curtail me further.

There are ironic parallels to my location in Virginia to

California. The San Francisco Bay abuts the Pacific, while here, the Chesapeake Bay abuts the Atlantic. Like at home, within four hours I can be at the beach, mountains, countryside, or a major metropolis—not that I've gone that far yet. There's even reportedly a boardwalk in neighboring Maryland to rival Santa Cruz.

The landscape, architecture, cars, food, and vibes are different, and history is a persistent backdrop. I was barely aware of the Gold Rush while in my native state. Here, I'm steeped in the Civil War as if it occurred yesterday. Battlefields, landmarks, museums, and monuments abound—and Confederate battle flags fly everywhere, including the state capitol. Prior to this, I'd never even seen one—aside from the graphic emblazoned on the roof of the General Lee, the Dodge Charger in *The Dukes of Hazzard.*

Hallowed ground, where blood was shed, strategies planned, plantations burned, and lives lost, is profuse. I'm ashamed of how little I remember about this fraught conflict as taught in my history classes. I've got miles to learn and explore.

And I need to give Virginia a chance...even if I'm homesick.

My job remains the high point, and I've thrown myself into it. Under Tyler's mentorship, I'm improving, growing, and excelling as a writer. Every assignment challenges me, forcing me to do more, write better, find a unique angle or hook. Magazine life is fast paced, and we're always months ahead, juggling multiple balls to launch each edition. The *we're all in this crazy boat together* collaboration among our various departments helps. I've welcomed the late nights and weekends, voraciously learning aspects of production as I did at *San Francisco Life.*

Some of my newer daydreams include starting a magazine myself someday.

I've made a handful of friends at work, people to share a

drink with during Friday happy hours or to commiserate with over the occasional lunch, including Valerie. But they land firmly in the acquaintance category—not close friendships like the kind I forged back home. I celebrated my birthday alone earlier this week, which only left my thoughts marinating in the dangerous echoes of the past.

The bane of my existence is Tanya. As Greg predicted on day one, she's proven to be the wolf in sheep's clothing, her fake charm in place to mask the stench of her true nature. She undermines me constantly, vies for stories awarded to me, and seems intent on stepping on my face to climb over me.

Then, of course, there's Don, the publisher. He slithers by my office every other week under the guise of checking in, but I don't miss his obvious perusal of my tits and his not-so-subtle hints about how his door is *always open*. Or the gold band gleaming from his ring finger. Can't forget his insufferable dirty jokes, told with the ease of a practiced sleazeball.

My response sickens me more—defaulting to nervous laughter because I haven't a clue how to fight sexual harassment, especially from the person in charge. He holds the power to fire me, and not only do I want and need this job, but the thought of being unemployed on a foreign coast fills me with panic.

I live paycheck to paycheck with pathetically little in my savings account. It's debatable whether he's crossed any legal lines anyway. He's a pro scumbag, always skirting the edges, but it's still wrong. I've grown to fucking loathe the dude.

The dryer whines as it slows, shutting down my thoughts. I dump my warm clothes into my plastic laundry basket and haul it to my apartment to fold.

When I hang a blouse in my closet, I pause to study my dresses. I'm going on a date tonight and haven't decided what to wear. The whispers of resistance murmur. Honestly...I'd rather crawl into bed with a book than go out.

I'm such a bitch. Correction: *jaded* bitch.

I'm rarely attracted to anyone, not motivated to find a connection, still uncaring about this part of my life. Work is my boyfriend, sans orgasms.

My friends back home keep encouraging me to *"get back out there,"* so I'm remaining openminded. Or trying to. It's why I said yes to the guy who works in my office building. We continue crossing paths—in the elevator, at the newsstand out front, in line at the tiny cafe nearby—and after a few weeks of light flirting, Jeff made his move. He's an engineer, tall with a pleasant face, slim build, and great hair. While he seems perfectly nice, I haven't experienced spark one.

Maybe dates aren't about sparks.

Maybe staying walled off means the fireworks have zero chance to spark in the first place.

NOT WILLING TO GIVE A RELATIVE STRANGER MY address, I meet Jeff at the restaurant he selected in downtown Richmond.

Joe's Inn sits on a corner cloaked in brick with painted white ironwork and black awnings. Jeff idles on the sidewalk, flashing me a smile as I approach.

He holds open the door and as soon as I walk through, I'm instantly transported to Original Joe's in San Jose. The scent of Italian spices and sauces wafts around me, drenching me in nostalgia, a sharp pinch of longing on its heels.

Jeff speaks with the hostess, and we follow her to our reserved table. The narrow restaurant has a long wooden counter with stools along one side and matching booths on the other. More homey than fancy, it's another nod to my former employer.

We settle in across from each other, accepting menus.

"It smells delicious," I say.

His eyes bug out as he leans toward me. "This place is fantastic. Been around since the 1950s. I highly recommend... everything."

I study the menu, immediately spotting my heart's desire under the pasta selection.

He purses his lips and cocks a surprised brow. "You know already? Impressive."

I don't know if that's a genuine compliment or rag on women in general, but I'm giving him the benefit of the doubt.

A soft-spoken, middle-aged man with classic Roman features takes our order and leaves us with warm bread smeared with a garlic herb butter, returning shortly with glasses of Cabernet Sauvignon.

The conversation flows without much awkwardness. But then our salads arrive and my date inhales his, talking with his mouth full and reminding me of my father in the most unfortunate way. I steel myself when our entrees arrive, but there's no avoiding the front row seat to his egregious lack of table manners.

My delectable dinner makes up some of the loss. Brimming with sausage, meatballs, and melted cheese over a heaping mound of pasta, it will equate to three meals.

Jeff monopolizes the conversation, relaying stories from his fraternity days coupled with bad engineering jokes (*Any circuit design must contain at least one part which is obsolete, two parts which are unobtainable, and three parts which are still under development*), to which I feign polite laughter.

Just about the moment my eyes want to glaze back into my head, he seems to recognize the imbalance and coughs into his hand. "Oh boy...there I go again. I'm sorry, Jacqui. I talk a lot sometimes."

My eyebrows hike.

He holds his hands in surrender pose. "Tell me more about you. Are you from Virginia?"

"California. I moved here four months ago to work at the magazine."

"Wow, the Golden State, huh? Were you a beach bum?" He doesn't give me a second to answer. "Of course you were. Look at you."

I offer him a tentative smile, bracing for the stereotypical comments that people often blurt out. "I love the ocean. And I'm bummed the beach is so far. On the map, it seemed closer."

"You've got the massive Chesapeake Bay in the way. It's hours either direction to get past it to the big O."

I nearly choke on my wine, my brain going straight to orgasm, not ocean. "I haven't been yet. I'm dying to see how it differs from the Pacific coastline."

Jeff's expression turns optimistic. "I'm happy to take you. A buddy of mine has a house in Virginia Beach. We could hang for the weekend."

I smile noncommittally.

With concerted effort, I make it through dinner, dessert, and more of Jeff's long-winded monologues before begging off, citing work responsibilities in the morning.

"On a Sunday?" He's rightfully suspicious.

My shoulders shrug, head tilting. "Writer life."

"I'll stick with my nine to five," he answers, another indicator of how different we are. I'd spend every weekend working to become a great writer.

Once we're outside, he insists on walking me to my car. "Any chance you want to come back to my place?"

You've got to be kidding. "I really need to head home. Thank you for dinner—my kind of place."

"Cool. Let's do it again. I'll call you."

I don't answer, which he takes as a sign to lean in and kiss me. I break it quickly before he can insert his tongue.

"Thanks again," I murmur, yanking open the door and

climbing into my Toyota. I race off with a final wave, heaving out a long groan. What a letdown.

Zero sparks.

Zero attraction.

Zero interest in doing this again.

Thirty-Two

I'm awake early, depression coating me as I contemplate another failed date—and another empty day stretching before me. It's as if I'm barely tethered to the earth. Like an astronaut, floating without gravity, trapped in a little spaceship miles away from civilization. I wonder if "companionless" is my destiny. And if so, I need to figure out how to become better company. Learn how to fly solo *and* happy.

Throughout my life, I've looked to others to fill this gaping hole that lives and breathes inside of me. My parents. Friends. Boyfriends. Perhaps that's faulty thinking and *I'm* supposed to fill this goddamned cavern.

A memory flashes—the promise I made to myself as I drove across the country. About taking control of my next chapter, the one starring *me*. The one where I don't need anyone to fucking complete me or my story, damn it.

Flipping off the covers, I fetch my road atlas and lay it on the dining table. I'm going to the beach today, something I've failed to do so far. Despite longing for the soothing presence of surf and sand, it potentially invites an avalanche of hurt and pain that sticks to me like Super Glue. I don't know what

I'm in for because I don't know what's inseparable from Mick Callahan and all our memories surfside.

I don't care. I'm not letting that shit stand in my way. I'm at a crossroads, and nobody can press the gas but me.

Using the mile measurement bar on the map, it appears Virginia Beach is about 120 miles away, and that cheers me instantly. I write out the directions, eat a quick breakfast, throw on my bikini, and pack my tote.

Little traffic peppers the road on this quiet Sunday morning, making for pleasant, easy driving that allows me to absorb the landscape. I make mental reminders to plan outings to recognizable cities I pass: Williamsburg, Newport News, Norfolk.

Just over two hours later, I arrive. When I glimpse the ocean from my car, my heart fills with a familiar ache. A public lot comes into view, and I park and grab my things. Walking turns to jogging as anticipation courses through my veins.

And then I'm there.

I gaze at the deep blue before me, and my eyes prick with happy tears. Even though I'm staring at a different ocean, my soul understands where we are. The beach is my solace, my port in a storm, embedded in me at the atomic level. I physically experience my cells opening to this gift and reenergizing me. It's like surfacing after holding your breath underwater too long—and inhaling fresh air by the lungful.

I drop my bag, kick off my shoes and jeans, and wade into the Atlantic.

The early September sun kisses my skin, waves lap at my shins, and the sandy bottom shifts beneath my toes.

The whitecaps and breaks aren't as mighty as the Pacific, and jagged cliffs, evergreens, and familiar vegetation are conspicuously absent. *A goddamn blessing.*

Instead of pain, the crashing surf, salt air, stretch of sand,

and expanse of ocean from here to the horizon cradle me in comfort.

"Thank you. Thank you. Thank you," I murmur, swiping at the trickles down my cheeks, my heart filled to the brim.

This. This is what I needed.

THIRTY-THREE

I'm at the office early on Monday prepping for our weekly meeting and still riding yesterday's beach high. I'm crackling with vitality and eager for new assignments. I open my note pad, pen at the ready, and sip my fresh coffee.

Tyler breezes into the room last in his stylish clothes, hip loafers, and impeccably styled hair. "We've got a big agenda this morning, so I hope no one's hungover," he says with his signature snark. "Status updates. Starting with you, Greg."

We go around the table, each reporting on our current articles, with Tyler troubleshooting any issues.

"Next, we've got a special edition in the works for the new year. You've got exactly two weeks to pitch me your ideas. I'm looking for *fresh*, people, not the tired shit everyone prints. Do *not* come to me with resolutions, fad diets, or psychobabbly self-help BS, or it will be instant termination."

Is he joking? Sometimes it's hard to tell.

"We haven't settled on a theme either, so even though we're just one section of the magazine, think bigger...bolder... for the entire issue. Fourteen days. Got it?"

Heads bob, and I my brain takes off in a sprint.

"Now, onto new assignments," he announces, corralling my attention back to the meeting.

Tyler addresses me third—above Tanya—which is a first. He doles out the choice stories up front, so it means I've inched further up the list in a short time. There aren't a lot of *attagirls* given around here, so I'm glowing at his display of confidence.

"You're writing a feature on Hamilton Restorations. It's a car restoration business. Family owned, small town vibe, storied past, known clientele—celebrities, dignitaries, etcetera. It's a haul, down south, middle of nowhere. But I think you'll give this the right touch. You're into cars, if memory serves."

Pride surges again as I lap up his flattery. "Sure am. This is absolutely in my wheelhouse." My lips stretch into a smile as an old fire flickers. Cars? *Hell yeah*. I can't wait to dig in.

I don't miss Tanya's pen smacking her pad with force, but I can't bother with her passive-aggressive tantrums. I've got a great article—*a feature*—on the horizon, and a New Year edition to think about.

BACK AT MY DESK, I REVIEW THE ASSIGNMENT BRIEF, then phone my provided contact.

"Hamilton Restorations." The man's voice is sandpaper rough, which makes him sound old.

"This is Jacqui Hall from *Virginia Now*. May I speak with Gus Hamilton?"

"You got him."

"Hello, Mr. Hamilton. I'm—"

"Call me Gus," he clarifies, his definitive Southern accent emerging with every word.

"Thank you," I say, underling his first name in my notepad. "I'll be writing the article about your business for the magazine, and I'd like to schedule an interview at your earliest convenience. You can show me what you do and the kinds of vehicles you restore, and share your history, mission, and whatever else to tell the Hamilton Restorations story."

"Sounds agreeable."

"I understand your son works with you as well?"

"That's right. Between the two of us, we can cover everything you need." Despite his gruff tone, he seems more than amenable to meet. "I only have one condition. I want to see the article before it prints. I've been misquoted in the past by journalist types, but I've known Don for years and he assured me this wouldn't be a problem. He promised to send a crack reporter." The way his cadence emphasizes the word *crack* almost makes me jump.

Am I a crack reporter? If he knows Don, I hope Gus isn't in the womanizing douchebag camp with him. And why the hell wasn't I given a heads-up on this?

"I'll make certain you're satisfied with the outcome. We should plan on a few hours. I've got time available this week if that works."

There's a pause. "Friday. And if you show up before lunchtime, my wife will probably try to feed you."

A pleased chuckle leaves my lips. "She sounds like a lovely woman."

"The best."

His adoration for her touches a soft spot. We finalize the time, and I jot everything in my notepad then head to the library to do more research on the four stories I'm juggling.

It takes ninety minutes to drive to Hampton Springs, and once I hit state and county roads, it's downright scenic. I pass modest homes, acres of farmland, and vast woodlands, occasionally cruising through tiny towns with little else than weathered gas stations, walk-up custard stands, and small, independent grocery stores. It's a slice of Americana, one I've rarely glimpsed.

A sign comes into view, and I slow. Two chains hanging from a fancy wrought iron post hold a metal oval painted teal. The words "Hamilton Restorations" curve overtop a classic car with "Est. 1956" curving below in black. A white border brings it all together. Classy.

I turn into the driveway. A farmhouse gleams in the late summer sunshine with its white paint and black shutters, the front wrapped with a welcoming porch. A towering oak shades the house, and the abundant garden adds another dose of charm. I find the business farther down, housed in a vast, stately garage next to other outbuildings, the same oval sign—only bigger—mounted to the main building. A fenced parking area houses a smattering of vehicles in all stages of disrepair.

I park by the office next to a pristine Dodge Power Wagon, collect my satchel, and hop out. When I walk around the truck, my gaze catches and fixates on the first muscle car I've seen since leaving home. A Plymouth Barracuda, black as night, probably a late-60s model. Let the salivating begin.

The office door swings open, and an older gentleman greets me with a wave as a large, yellow Labrador squeezes by him and beelines for me, barking excitedly. The dog sidles up alongside and I offer my hand. Once I pass his sniff test, I venture a scratch on his head and am rewarded with tail wags and a lolling tongue.

"That's Hemi, and he's harmless," the man says. My lips lift at the name. "I'm Gus Hamilton," he adds, voice just as raspy as it sounded on the phone. "Also harmless."

I straighten and shake his proffered hand. He's noticeably tall, his brunette hair flecked with gray and his eyes a vivid cerulean blue.

"Jacqui Hall. It's a pleasure to meet you."

"Likewise."

"Quite a place you've got here."

He gazes in the distance, humming in agreement. "Eighty-three acres. Our family's lived here a century. And that old farmhouse has reared a lot of Hamiltons."

"It's very picturesque." The exterior is an open invitation —different from the hard, modern angles of California houses—and I long to see the inside. "I'm a big fan of this Barracuda. Yours?" *If so, you just raised your cool quotient by a thousand.*

"My son's," he admits. "But I've got a nice assortment of Mopars in my personal collection." His knowing smile says it all, and I nearly get a head rush thinking about what awaits in that garage.

"I'm looking forward to seeing everything today."

"Let me show you around and then we can sit and chat."

"Perfect."

Gus starts the tour outside, rattling off a brief history. His great grandfather owned the now-defunct Chrysler/Plymouth/Dodge dealership in town, which is why Hamilton Restorations specializes in Mopars, a word that's become synonymous with those manufacturers. Their downtown started crumbling after department stores moved to malls and larger entities eclipsed mom-and-pop establishments. I hear his despondency as he explains how the once-thriving Main Street now lies mostly vacant, housing a few attorneys, an insurance agent, two antique shops, and a pharmacy with an eat-in counter and soda fountain.

He points out some of the old vehicles. Even in their state of decay, I admire the exterior details: bulbous fenders, signature tail fins, chrome bumpers, hood ornaments, wing windows. These old gals exude real style, the kind long faded from today's automobile manufacturing.

"Gus, this is a little off topic, but I've noticed since moving here, and even on my drive across the country, the absence of makes and models I'm accustomed to seeing.

Where *are* all the cars? It's as if they don't exist outside of California."

"The car culture here is different. A big issue lies in our harsh winters. Cars rust. People also get rid of the old models in favor of new ones. Modern engineering means vehicles last longer with less maintenance, which is certainly attractive to many folks. There are enthusiasts and collectors here, and we take our cars to shows and meetups rather than use them for daily drivers. I've been fortunate to spend time out west, and you're right...it's not the same." He chuckles. "Bit of a culture shock both ways, I imagine."

Gus continues talking about the business while I jot notes. We enter the main garage, Hemi trailing behind us and then flopping down on the cement floor with a groan of contentment. I scan the beautiful cars in various stages of restoration. There are too many to see from one vantage point in the gargantuan facility and my gaze flits incessantly. I'm in car nirvana.

We round the bend into another section, and a steady clanging rings out. I surmise someone's working on a project —perhaps the son I've yet to meet or another employee. Gus keeps chatting as we walk toward the sound. A torso bent over the engine of an aqua vehicle that looks fresh off the set of *American Graffiti* comes into view. Long legs fill out a pair of jeans leading to black work boots. I swing my attention back to Gus.

"One of our repeat clients, an NFL player and car collector, brought us this 1959 Plymouth Savoy," he says. "It needs repair to the body, interior, and motor. My son is machining some of the parts by hand—he's our best fabricator. Let me introduce you."

The mystery man pops up from under the hood. Surprise crosses his face, followed by a grin that lights up bold emerald eyes.

"Sundance?"

THIRTY-FOUR

Shock reels through me as I gawk at Mr. Highly Memorable.

"Butch?" It comes out as a question but there's no question it's him.

"You all know each other?" Gus asks.

"We met once," Butch says, coming to the rescue. Not only have all words escaped me, but I'd rather not admit *how* we know each other...*one glorious, breathtaking afternoon of hedonistic sex.* And I'm damn glad neither of these men can see the images flipping through my head right now.

Mr. Afternoon Delight extends his hand, and I grasp it, the initial jolt almost making me flinch. I'm reminded how big he is—all of him—hands, height, dick... Heat engulfs me, and I step back as if burned. *Holy...* I clear my throat, choking on the awkwardness and hoping I'm not seven shades of red. Stealing another glance at Butch, my pulse races, recalling how his touch made me see stars. He scans me top to bottom and one side of his mouth lifts, like he's remembering too.

Goddamn, he's handsome—and filling out that black T-shirt nicely. My gaze shifts to the white letters rippling over his chest: *Mopar: You're with us or you're behind us.*

"Guess you got the job, huh?" His eyes narrow. "Magazine, right?"

"Good memory."

"Damn good." The satisfied smile on his face makes my entire body flush. Again.

Oh my god.

His expression morphs to one of understanding. "You're here to do the article?"

"Right again." I will my heartbeat to slow the fuck down.

"How about that," he muses. "What are the odds?"

About a million to one. I should make a trip to Atlantic City and bet my savings. "Yeah, yup, for sure." Great, now I sound like a blithering idiot. "Your dad was just giving me the official tour."

"Don't let me stop you. I look forward to catching up with you later," he says, a knowing grin on his face.

What does *that* mean? I absolutely cannot fixate on any of this now. Turning to Gus, I plaster a smile on my face, trying to exude the energy of *crack reporter*. "Please continue."

Gus navigates through the remainder of the tour, pointing out projects in progress and acknowledging the handful of workers he employs. When we land back in his office, I pull out my tape recorder and notepad and begin firing off questions.

The phone on his desk buzzes, and I pause the interview while he answers.

"We'll head over, my love," he says. Hanging up, he flashes a grin. "Lunch is ready. Let's grab Butch and you can meet my better half."

His obvious affection for his wife is just as endearing in person.

I brace myself for coming face to face with Mr. Lumberjack again—and the entire luncheon stretching before us. My nerves wrestle like a bucket of snakes.

"Butch, lunchtime," Gus barks.

Judging by the size of Butch's beaming smile, he's only too happy to join us.

"My son will fill you in on other projects this afternoon. He manages the day-to-day operations now. I mostly just get in his way."

"When *is* the last time you held a wrench, old man?" Butch teases, knocking his shoulder into his fathers'.

Gus gives him a sidelong glance. "Watch it. I can still tan your hide with one hand tied behind my back," he threatens good-naturedly.

Butch leans closer to my ear, speaking loud enough for his father to hear. "We'll let him believe all the lies he needs."

Gus guffaws. "You might be younger and stronger, Junior, but I'm smarter—and not afraid to fight dirty."

"Don't I know it." Butch grins down at me, all six foot four of him or whatever he is, as we reach the walkway to the farmhouse.

"Junior?" I inquire, directly to Mr. Hamilton. Butch groans.

"I'm Augustus James Hamilton Sr., and this chip off the ol' block is Jr. I'm more handsome, of course."

I can't stifle my delighted grin. Butch is *Augustus*. But now I'm confused. "So, why Butch?"

"It's a nickname," Mr. Tall, Dark, and Emerald-Eyed interjects. "Common 'round these parts when you share the same name." He leans closer to my ear, whispering, "And preferable when you don't want to be called Augustus."

"I doubt I can resist."

"Sure you can, Gold Rush."

I like the sound of that leaving his lips—in fact, all his nicknames for me—and for a second his lips are all I fantasize about as we stare at each other like two hungry wolves. My gaze darts forward, attempting to douse the rising inferno this man creates with one heated look.

The splendor of the family's well-tended garden

consumes my full attention, then the grand porch as we ascend its wide, painted stairway. Matching color bathes the floor while a light shade of blue dusts the beadboard ceiling. A swing for two hangs from one end, with ample inviting furniture arranged stylishly elsewhere. Potted plants add to the ambiance, and I surmise it's all the work of the woman I'm about to meet.

I'm meeting the parents of my one-night stand. Can this day get any more surreal?

Butch opens the door, holding it for me to walk through. I scarcely have time to take in the foyer when a woman bursts forth, wiping her fingers on a skirt apron, a welcoming smile on her face.

"I'm Jerri Hamilton," she says, extending her hand. It's clear where Butch inherited those beautiful green eyes. She's striking, and between her and Gus, their son got the best of both parents.

"Jacqui Hall. Thank you for inviting me to lunch."

She waves a hand. "It's my pleasure. You've come all this way to write about my two favorite men. And lord knows they will bore you to tears talking about cars. I'm sure you're ready for a reprieve."

I laugh. "Actually..."

She tilts her head. "You're a car gal?"

"Yes, ma'am," I admit a tad sheepishly. I sense Butch's eyes boring into me. "But I'd love to hear about your garden and this gorgeous home."

"How long you staying? I can talk about *that* for hours." She smiles, her southern lilt adding a layer of warmth.

Mrs. Hamilton steers us to the informal dining area off the kitchen, and Butch holds a chair for me, the same as his father does for his mother. Yep, surreal.

A sizable lunch spread fills the table on both sides of a lazy Susan holding condiments and an open jar of sweet pickles speared with a miniature serving fork.

"Butch and Jacqui already know each other," Gus says as he swipes two pieces of fried chicken from the oval platter.

"Really? How and when did y'all meet?" Jerri asks, offering me corn bread.

"Um...I was in town for a job interview, and he happened to be in Richmond at the same time." I take a warm square and pass the basket to Butch, who smiles like he has a million secrets.

"*Jacqui,*" he emphasizes, throwing back that he knows my real name, "and I met at a bar and wound up talking for hours. Once she stopped that incessant foot-tapping, if I recall."

I kick him under the table, attempting to wipe that *incessant* smirk off his face.

"Green beans?" A serving bowl balances on his huge hand, and I accept it with a saccharine smile.

"Isn't that something?" Jerri muses. "Small world."

"This is delicious," I say, steering us off the topic. "If it's not too personal a question, how did you and Gus meet? He said his family has lived here for generations."

"I love a how-you-met story," Butch interjects, resting his chin on his hand. "It's the kind of thing you can't wait to tell your kids someday."

While his parents stare adoringly at each other, I shoot him a death glare. He fights a laugh, toying with me and thoroughly enjoying it.

"It's actually a funny story," Gus says, only too happy to regale us with it. "Jerri worked at the local diner, and the first time I saw her, I became a smitten fool. When I asked her on a date, she turned me down flat."

Jerri's grin serves as corroboration.

"I went in there every day for a month. You know how much pie I ate? Gained five pounds trying to woo my future wife." He chuckles to himself. "I asked her out each time, and each time, I struck out. Can you believe that? A charmer like me?"

"Why did you say no?" I ask Jerri.

She wrinkles her nose. "He was a mechanic. I had lofty goals and assumed he wouldn't be a good provider."

"But then I found her stranded on the side of a country road, blown radiator still steaming, and suddenly, I looked like a knight in shining armor." Gus gets a devilish glint in his eye. "I told her I wouldn't help her unless she agreed to a date."

"Blackmail," Jerri confirms.

"Leverage," Gus corrects.

Jerri chuckles, eyes bright as she listens. In my periphery, Butch's fondness for both parents is obvious in his expression...and my chest twinges.

"The rest, as they say, is history," Gus concludes. "I'm more in love with this woman every minute, and I thank my lucky stars she agreed to be my wife."

AFTER LUNCH, BUTCH GUIDES ME BACK TO THE garage, chatting up the business along the way. The door snicks closed behind us, and I'm acutely aware we're alone. The air couldn't be more charged, and Mr. Lumberjack steals what's left of mine.

"Not to be unprofessional," he says, backing me against the wall, "but do you want to merge our lips together as much as I do?"

Yes. No. I shouldn't.

"No," I manage, unconvincingly.

"Really?" he purrs in my ear, and I gasp, my stomach somersaulting. "I'm getting mixed signals."

My heart rate ratchets up forty notches, my chest heaving at his deep, toe-curling timbre.

The scruff of his beard grazes my neck. How I remember that welcome burn. "You sure?"

No, I'm not fucking sure. I want to climb that redwood and frolic in his branches.

My resolve weakens and he knows it. His lips land decisively on mine, and we moan attempting to quench the thirst building over the last two hours. My satchel thuds to the floor as his hands find my hips and haul me closer. One of his arms wraps around my back, his massive hand pressing our bodies flush. His other hand snakes up the column of my throat. My arms slide under his and I clutch his broad back as our tongues tango, getting fully reacquainted. Fire licks through me, blazing like an inferno. And just like that, my panties incinerate.

My entire body lights up, floating and roaring at the same time. Our kiss blows through me like a tornado and then we're in the eye of the storm, as if nothing else exists.

Desire burns low in my belly as he engulfs me in all the best ways. Hands roving, frantic and wanting. Mouths angling, ravenous and tenacious.

Lord, have mercy.

"Wait," I pant, pulling back.

"Can't," he mumbles, his lips trailing to my neck.

"Oh god...that's..."

"Mm-hmm," he murmurs.

Stop! I scream in my head. "Butch. Wait." He continues kissing my exposed skin, cupping my breast through my shirt, pebbling my nipples. I'm momentarily lost.

"*BUTCH.*" I shove him gently and he meets my gaze with glassy eyes. "Not here. Not now. I'm *working*."

He sighs, adjusting himself in his jeans. "I'm sorry. You're right." He blows out a breath, raking those thick fingers through his brunette locks.

Look away from the fingers.

"That went from zero to sixty damn fast," I say, straightening my clothes.

He huffs out a laugh. "Could've won a land speed record at Bonneville."

"So, um, can we finish the interview? I still have some questions."

His emerald eyes cut to mine. "Yeah, Sundance. I'll give you whatever you need."

True to his word, Butch enthusiastically answers the remainder of my questions. Hamilton Restorations has all the makings of a fantastic feature: history, quality, values, known clientele, and heart.

We wrap it up and I stow the recording equipment. A significant pause hangs between us and the undercurrent of sexual tension I throttled during our discussion returns.

"How about a phone number, Sundance?" Butch pushes a notepad with the company logo printed at the top toward me. "I'd like to see you again. That is, if you're willing to rescind your 'one time offer' decree."

There's no hiding my wince...I did say that, didn't I? His stupidly dazzling eyes shine playfully. If I stare too long, I'll fall into an *Alice in Wonderland* rabbit hole. It happens anyway—no *drink me* potion required. "I'd like that too."

"Sure I can't convince you to stick around a while longer?" Those verdant emeralds sparkle with promise. So much promise.

"Tempting." *Garden of Eden level.* "But I need to get back to the office."

He doesn't push but continues studying me. "You are every bit as gorgeous as I remember."

My insides perform a big, swooning, swirling dip. "And you," I gesture with one hand, "are insanely good looking. And every bit as huge as I remember."

His eyes take on a dangerously sexy glint and combined with the pleased grin stretching across his face, he's glorious.

I blink, shaking myself from my daze. This charming, engaging man is quicksand. He could swallow me whole before I even realize I'm sinking. Something else skirts the edges of my awareness, something equally concerning. How easy all this seems—the kissing, groping, complimenting, talking.

Butch is both threatening and grounding. A warning and a comfort. A wild ride and a steady, quiet presence.

We exchange numbers, then stand. Butch's frame dominates the small office.

"I'll walk you out," he says, reaching for the door and holding it open for me.

I do like his manners. And his car. My head tilts toward the Barracuda. "Next time, I'd love to go for a ride in that. I'm kind of a freak for muscle cars."

"Yeah? What's your favorite?"

I don't hesitate. "A 1969 Camaro Z/28."

Butch groans, his head dropping in exaggerated agony.

Hand on my hip, I flash him attitude. "What?"

"I don't know if we can see each other again."

Is he joking? "Why not?"

"Because I'm a Mopar man, sweetheart. And we don't associate with Chevys, Fords, or any other makes." He sucks in a breath with a dramatic wince, letting it go with a loud whoosh. "It might be a dealbreaker."

Oh yeah? Walking away, I toss over my shoulder, "Your loss."

His chuckle follows me as I make my way to his parents, conversing in their front yard. I thank them for their generosity and say goodbye.

Upon my return, Butch opens my car door.

I cast him a flippant glance. "You still here?"

He smiles broadly as I settle into the driver's side. "I can't wait to experience more of that sass. *And incredible ass,*" he adds, leaning in lower and saying that last bit just loud enough for my ears.

Uhhhhhhh. I blink hard, my thoughts stalling.

"I'll call you," he promises. His green eyes fasten so intently on mine that my heart stutters.

He shuts my door and giddiness skids through me. Because goddamn, I really hope he does.

THIRTY-FIVE

I twine my fingers in the telephone cord as Butch explains his passion for Barracudas, making the case for why they're superior muscle cars. I'm stretched across my bed backwards with my hair splayed like a fan on the comforter and my legs crossed at the ankles up against the wall.

In this position, I feel like a teenager, more so because of the exuberant flutters dancing through my cells and the stupid smile on my face.

We've been on the phone thirty minutes. He called. *Like he said he would.* Didn't even wait twenty-four hours.

It doesn't seem like he wants the call to end, despite how much it's costing him in toll charges...and that fuels the flutters even more.

"I'm officially jealous." I sigh, defeated over never owning my dream car. "I drove a Beetle through college. My Dad thought it was economical. And he did pay for my gas. Still..."

"I'll deny it in a court of law if you repeat this, but VWs are great cars," he says.

"Hmm...not *dealbreakers*?"

He chuckles. "Still a dealbreaker."

"Wow, guess I'm zero for two. Why are you still talking to me?"

"I want to see you again, Sundance."

That sexy, smooth voice of his will be the death of me. And the sincere way he spoke those words has my stomach dipping. "I'd like that too."

"Tomorrow? I could take you for a ride."

I bark out a laugh.

He joins in. "I meant in my car."

"Digging a deeper hole..."

"You have a filthy mind."

Not usually, but you're crossing every barrier I've fought to erect. "I'd love to go for a ride in your car." And maybe take the other ride too. A full-body shiver courses through me, remembering Butch's king-size *everything*.

"Pick you up at eleven?" Mr. Deep Voice snaps me back to the present. "We can snag lunch somewhere out and about?"

"It's a date."

THE NEXT MORNING, MY INTERCOM BUZZES AT FIVE to eleven. His punctuality—eagerness?—pleases me.

"It's your handsome driver," Butch says, voice crackling through the system.

Cue idiotic smile. "Be down in a sec."

"Nuh-uh. I'm coming to get you."

"Even though we're going to turn around and go right back downstairs?"

"Don't question my chivalry, baby."

Baby? Instant access. And don't even get me started with the chivalry part.

At my door minutes later, the vision he presents damn near puts me on life support. Hair the color of aged bourbon framing his face. Get-lost-in-me eyes the shade of vibrant evergreens. The sheer *volume* of him packaged in jeans, a well-fitting Henley, and a broken-in, brown leather jacket. Lord, have mercy.

His eyes sweep me, and judging by his hungry gaze, my effort's paying off. My hair's styled, make-up natural, and I've paired a cat-black sweater with fitted Levi's and my favorite suede boots.

"You look gorgeous, Sundance."

"You too, Lumberjack."

"Come again?" he says, cracking a smile.

My hand swirls in the air, gesturing his way. "You know you're like a hot, foresty lumberjack, right?"

His head cocks, and one of his hands scrapes the scruff of his jaw. "Yeah...no." He looks almost embarrassed. "Ready to go?"

I nod and Butch takes my hand. My insides jolt at his touch, and that dormant heart of mine sparks to life.

We grin at each other in the elevator and out the lobby doors. Little palpitations skitter through me from our hands woven together, his nearness, his obvious desire. *He likes me.* Nothing is more ego-inflating than being wanted.

His Plymouth fastback comes into view, the chrome Barracuda emblem splashed along the rear. Once I'm secure in the passenger-side bucket seat, I scan the all-black interior, dashboard features, custom steering wheel, and Hurst shifter. The faint aroma of car cleaner mixes with Butch's woodsy scent with maple notes. *Eau de Lumberjack.*

My driver straps himself in and cranks the ignition, and the rumble sparks my other dormant body organ to life. God, I've missed that sound, that vibration, sitting front and center in one of these heavily horse-powered machines.

It's a little like taking a long, hot shower after a California drought, only tinged with a dash of bittersweet. Butch casts me another infectious grin, obliterating all thoughts.

He drives carefully through city streets, thrilling me when

he revs the engine or screeches off the line with just enough torque to lightly fishtail. Once we enter the highway, he opens her up. I *love* going fast, and when the familiar rush hurtles through my cells, I whoop loudly. A sidelong glance at the man expertly driving this machine shows a satisfied smile edging his lips.

I long to open the windows and let the wind kiss my face, but that's not happening on this September morning. It may be sunny, but it's cool outside with an even chillier breeze, and I'm grateful Butch turned on the heat.

After a stretch, he exits the highway, and I'm surprised how quickly we're passing undeveloped spaces with farms, fields, or towering trees only twenty minutes from a major metropolis.

"You like 'bacon roads,' Sundance?"

"What are those?"

"I'll show you, city girl," he says with another big grin.

He hauls ass along a winding country road, and as we hit a section of rolling hills, my stomach swoops on the down-strokes. Bracing myself, I squeal and laugh with each undulation like a lunatic.

"Get it now?' he shouts in between dips.

It's like driving on cooked bacon, the crisped fat creating those staggered peaks and valleys. My smile doesn't quit until we're through miles of hilly roads.

He reaches a T and pauses at the stop sign with the idle purring. Damn, he's a good driver.

"It's like a rollercoaster," I say, breathless.

He grins, eyes bright, and it's a heady combination. He turns left, flying through the gears as we reach speeds I'm afraid to monitor. He eventually slows through a small town, pulling into a spot at a diner.

It's the quintessential greasy spoon with a black-and-white checkered floor, red upholstered booths, and a counter lined with shiny metal stools. The type of place that serves breakfast all day and employs waitresses who call you "hon."

We snag an available booth, order, and get busy doctoring our coffees.

"I know almost zero about you," I say.

He cocks an eyebrow. "I'm not a serial killer."

"Whew, glad that's cleared up. But can I really take your word for it?"

"I mean...we've got to assume lying is a prerequisite for that kind of proclivity."

"At the very least."

He blows on his coffee, those tempting lips distracting me, and takes a sip. "Ask away."

My hands circle the mug as I wait for the liquid to cool. "Favorite color?"

"You're starting with the hard stuff?" he teases.

"Just answer the question, smartass."

He studies me, letting his eyes rove over my face. "Right now, it's yellow. You?"

"Currently, I rather favor..." I prop my elbow on the table, lean my chin on my hand and meet his gaze straight on. "Green." And I'm not lying. Butch's eyes are captivating.

That elicits another of his slow, gorgeous smiles.

"How old are you?" I'm dying to know.

"Thirty."

"Hmm...an older man." My brow arches. "I just turned twenty-four."

"I'm not exactly robbing the cradle." Butch shifts in his seat, hanging one arm over the back of the booth.

"When's your birthday?"

He casually lifts the cup to his lips, and I fixate on his throat working when he takes another sip. "January eighth."

I can't help my excited inhale. "That makes you a Capricorn. I'm a Virgo...our star signs are mega compatible."

He gives me a dubious look before his expression turns

amused. "Let me guess. You read the Bedside Astrologer every year."

My mouth drops. "You read *Cosmo*?"

He offers a half shrug. "A guy's got to learn about the G-spot somewhere."

Our food arrives, interrupting us. I've got to admit, he's a smart man; *Cosmo* is full of sex tips. That he cares enough to research shows me his ego is right-sized. And there's no question he knows his way around the female parts...hell, *I* don't even understand the elusive spot he just referenced.

We're quiet as we dig in: me to French toast and sausage links, and him to a cheeseburger and fries. I steal a few of his fries and he snags a sausage in unspoken agreement, as if we've been eating together for years.

Outside, after our meal, he presses me against the car. He cradles my neck and brings me closer, his lips claiming mine, revving my internal motor as he kisses me senseless. Heat shoots through me like a wildfire and a whimper slips out.

"I want to lick every drop of syrup from this mouth," he murmurs.

Yes, please.

Back on the road, Butch pushes in a tape and unfamiliar music filters through the speakers.

"Who is this?"

"The Marshall Tucker Band."

"Never heard of 'em."

"Have you been living in a cave?" he says, tone incredulous. "*Ohhh*...Californian. Maybe you ate too much tofu and alfalfa sprouts that it stunted your growth?"

"Maybe you ate so much fried okra and biscuits it affected your musical tastes?"

He chuckles and combs his fingers through his thick locks, leaving it tousled, and my gaze snags on it. "Marshall Tucker is the quintessential Southern rock band. Helped establish the entire genre. They're brilliant musicians."

I shrug. "Never heard of Southern rock either, but this doesn't sound very rock and roll."

"Do tell who you consider a proper rock band." He scrubs his jaw, a smile forming. "Let me hazard a guess. You're into the *hair bands*."

I smack him playfully on the arm. "I'm a huge Van Halen girl. Love U2, the Stones, AC/DC, Zeppelin, The Who, Pat Travers, Ozzy...a vast assortment." I don't mention Mötley Crüe in case he considers them hair metal.

He scoffs. "You have so much to learn, young'un."

I roll my eyes. "Suppose you'll have to teach me your ways, *oh wise one*." My words drip with sarcasm.

He chuckles. "Or just spank your pretty, bratty ass."

My breath catches at the instant visual. Me over his lap, behind bared, his big hand slapping my cheeks. It shouldn't sound so alluring...but does. "*Yes, please,*" I murmur.

Butch lets out a long, growly groan that shoots right to the spot already tingling from the image in my mind. "You're killing me, Sundance."

With a predatory gaze, he floors it. He's not the only one in a hurry to get back to my place.

THIRTY-SIX

Butch backs me into a corner as the elevator rises toward my floor. "I remember exactly what was on my mind our first time in an elevator," he murmurs. His tone heats my blood to a rolling boil.

"Which was?" I whisper.

"Exploring every inch of you." He presses closer, tilting my face up to meet his. "And that I was one lucky sonofabitch." Our mouths crash together, opening so our tongues can swirl and dance.

I'm weak-kneed and breathless when the elevator lurches to a halt and dings. He tugs my hand and leads me down the hall. Once inside, his imposing frame dwarfs my tiny studio.

Tossing my keys and purse onto the small dining table, I hurriedly shrug off my coat. "Want a drink or something?"

"Or something," he agrees, eyes fixated on me.

I gulp. My bed beckons, blatantly obvious in my one-room apartment. In seconds, he's got me flat against it, and we scramble to discard our clothing while only minimally breaking contact.

Our hands and lips and tongues rove everywhere, hard meeting soft, emerald and amber colliding, harsh breaths and low moans between us. Our bodies move in tandem, familiar yet strange, exploring, wanting, greedy, needy.

A sheen of sweat coats our skin as we come down from another ridiculously earth-shattering round. This shouldn't be so easy. So *right*. We hardly know each other.

Butch slowly withdraws, and our uncoupling leaves me bereft. His long arm snags the towel waiting on the bedside table, and he gingerly soaks up the residual evidence of our latest orgasms. Me first.

Engrossed in his task—one he's clearly enjoying—he murmurs, "I like how you trim this."

I shift onto my elbows. "What do you mean?"

His gaze remains focused. "Like a heart."

"Um, I don't do any . . . grooming . . . there."

"Huh. Your pubes are heart-shaped," he says, tracing the outline with reverence.

This is news to me and now I want to see for myself.

"It even swirls in the middle and leads right to this delicious entryway." His fingers follow, and command central perks up even though she's satiated. Or maybe she never will be with Mr. Sex God around.

"I don't have much experience with what other girls look like down there."

His head tilts. "Yours is . . . dainty. And fucking perfect."

Although he seems reluctant to leave my pubic region, he inches alongside me and props himself on one elbow. The fingers of his free hand thread through mine. Our gazes lock, and it's almost too intimate.

"I like you, Sundance." It sounds like a confession.

My lips lift. "I like you too, Butch."

"I haven't liked anyone in a long time," he admits.

"You've been burned." It's a statement. I recognize fellow burn victims well after the fire.

He nods, raking his top lip between his teeth. "It's hard for me to trust women."

Butch, we're parking our cars in the same garage. "It's hard for me to trust men."

"Guess we make a hell of a pair then." He smiles ruefully, squeezing my hand before exhaling a prolonged sigh. "Here's the deal. My life is complicated, my time scarce, and we're separated by enough distance to make this difficult. But I want to know you better."

I'm guarding my own castle and can't fault him for guarding his. I'm neither ready nor looking for a serious relationship, and yet our attraction is undeniable. "I'd like that too."

Butch pulls me in and wraps his arms around me. "So, we'll take it slow."

"Slow," I repeat.

"Even though we've already done dirty deeds."

I laugh. "Even though."

"To clarify, I'm not done with dirty deeds." He languidly strokes the planes of my back and over my ass.

"I hope not."

"This is new territory for me," he murmurs. "I want to let you into my life. There are things you need to know about me. Things that might make you run the other direction. I need to trust you first, and the only way to do that is time."

Can I ever tell him about Mick, Remy, and me? *Should I?* "And if I run away?"

Butch pulls back, his gaze pinning mine. "I'll chase you down and haul your pretty ass back into my bed anyway."

I bark out a laugh then ponder it. "That sounds kind of... hot." I doubt he's serious, but I like the idea of a man who would do anything to keep me. Or at least try. I don't want to think too hard about why.

"Yeah? I would live to fulfill your fantasies."

All body parts reawaken, standing at attention. "Really?"

His eyes gleam, expression rapt. "Mm-hmm. And judging by the flush of your pretty cheeks, something tells me you're into it."

Judging by his newly sprung boner, something tells me he's ready to start now. I'm a definite yes. Those Mick and Remy sandwiches were the stuff of fantasies, the kind I never knew I harbored, showing me an adventurousness that surprised me in the best way. Those two awakened my sexuality—then fed it—but I'm thirsty to explore it further. Something I'm just, this very minute, realizing.

I flash him a mischievous smile in answer.

He caresses my jawline, his thumb grazing my lips as he studies my face. "You're rocking my fucking world."

And you're rocking mine.

Thirty-Seven

Butch and I connect for late-night phone calls and the occasional conversation during working hours. It's probably a godsend that geography and life's priorities conspire to keep us apart; when we're in physical proximity, we wind up in bed.

I'm grateful for the forced "slow but steady" concept we agreed upon to see where our budding relationship—or possibility of one—goes.

We're getting to know one another.

After ripping each other's clothes off.

Backwards, and yet...forwards.

I don't want to lose myself again, and already, the telltale tug veers hard in his direction. He's likable. Fun. Principled. A gentleman. And yeah, fine...talented in the sack.

It's strangely intimate conversing into the night. We cover everything from the mundane to our upbringing to confessions. The absence of speaking in person provides a barrier, a false safety net to say...anything.

~

"Best subjects in school?" Butch asks.

"English, art, and gym. I was terrible at math and science. In eighth grade, we were forced to evacuate the class after I plunged my burning test tube into the wrong beaker and toxic gases filled the room."

He chuckles. "I can't write worth a damn, but math, science, and history all come easy. And I excelled in auto shop, of course."

Duh. "From here on out, I'll handle the writing, you handle the arithmetic."

"Deal."

"It's like together, we complete the Pi. Get it...Pi?"

"Are you attempting a math joke?" he says.

"*Attempting* may be the operative word."

"At least you know your jokes suck."

"At least you know my mouth can."

"That day we met? I thought—*KNEW*—you were the most gorgeous woman I've ever laid eyes on," Butch admits.

I smile, remembering the scene. "I've never done anything as impulsive as I did that day...asking a stranger to sleep with me." With whiplash force, the salacious threesome on *Seas the Day* blazes into my memory. Guess we can file that under impulsive too.

"A *handsome* stranger?" he teases.

"A deliciously tall, dark, mildly grumpy, and fine as hell lumberjack."

"Grumpy?"

"You were a little irritable," I amend.

"Any regrets?"

I swear, his voice is even lower on the phone, and it shoots straight between my legs. "Zero. If I think too long about it, I get turned on." My hand runs along the top of the comforter, smoothing the ripples. "And..." My throat tightens. Shit.

"And what?"

I pause.

"Sundance? You okay?"

I clear my throat, swallow the damn lump. "It gave me hope I could enjoy intimacy with someone again."

"You're giving me that hope too, baby."

THE FULL MOON GLOWS THROUGH THE WINDOW, casting its light across my comforter as I let another truth fly. Talking to Butch in the dark, right before I go to sleep, is fast becoming one of my favorite things. "I didn't go to my senior prom. My boyfriend and I broke up a few weeks beforehand. It still bugs me to this day—missing something I wanted to attend so badly."

"Your ex was obviously a schmuck," Butch says.

That elicits as smile. "It gets worse. He asked another girl to go the week before. So even though he pitched a bitch about going when it was on our docket, he was apparently not too depressed over our demise to ask some other chick in the eleventh hour."

"What a dick."

"Not even good dick."

"Ouch. If it makes you feel any better, I wore the ugliest tuxedo ever created to my prom. It was purple. *Purple*, Jacqui."

A chuckle bubbles out picturing 70s-style formalwear. "I'll bet you had the big, ruffled shirt to go with it too, huh?"

He groans. "Sure did...with purple accents. I looked like a jolly pirate."

"Doubtful, Lumberjack."

"I took solace in knowing I never had to step foot in one of those stupid dances again."

"I'm going to need photographic evidence of prom night. And I know just who I can ask..." I'm down for any family photo albums showing cute little Butch at all stages of life.

"You're never invited back. My mom already said she could tell you were bad news."

"Liar."

He chuckles. "You're my kind of bad news, Sundance."

"I NEVER EXPECTED TO STAY SO CLOSE TO HOME," Butch admits. "Sometimes I wonder how my life would be different if certain dominos hadn't fallen."

I pause. "Do you want to talk more about what dominos?"

"Not yet," he answers gently.

"I never planned to leave California, but now that I have, I realize how cool it is to live somewhere so vastly dissimilar and unfamiliar. Geographically, culturally, visually, all of it."

"Do you miss it?"

"Yes and no. It will always be home, I think. I miss my friends. And the cars. And sourdough bread. And what's a girl gotta do to get a turkey on whole wheat with avocado and sprouts around here?"

"I'll be honest. Never seen that on one menu. But you'll find creamed chipped beef on toast all day long. It's a southern staple."

Sounds disgusting. "I'm scared to ask."

There's a pause, almost as if we're both pondering where we hail from—two states, two coasts, three thousand miles apart.

"I've always wanted to visit the Sunshine State," Butch

says. His tone seems wistful, making me wonder about his secrets, those dominos.

"Yeah? I know a girl who could show you around..."

~

"TELL ME ONE OF YOUR FANTASIES," BUTCH COAXES.

I freeze.

"Sundance...you can tell me. Especially if you want it to come true."

"Uhhh..."

"Okay then, tell me something you like." His voice is warm, deep.

"Mint chocolate chip ice cream."

He growls. "Something sex related."

I stifle my laugh. "I think I may favor the taboo, kinky... uh, less traditional."

"Now we're talking. Like...?"

Way to put my foot so far into my mouth that I can't speak. I don't even know how to define *taboo*, aside from a threesome.

Except...maybe I do.

"Did you see the movie *9 ½ Weeks*? With Mickey Rourke and Kim Basinger?"

"I heard about it but haven't seen it."

"It was very...erotic. Bizarre. An interesting power dynamic."

"Rourke's got the power?"

"Basically. He made her crawl across the floor to him, and even though part of me was shocked by that, and more that she obeyed..."

"It made you wet?"

Then and now. "Yes," I admit, despite my discomfort.

"What else?" His tone is thicker, deeper.

"He blindfolded her and fed her different foods, but it

was sexy. And in another scene, she's so stirred up just thinking about him, she masturbates in her office chair." This scenes pops into my mind with regularity. "I've never seen anything like that on screen before...and oh my god, there's another scene where he takes her into a store and tests out a whip right in front of her, then buys it. She's alarmed, maybe aroused...I don't know, but it was all so provocative. Very master-slave stuff."

"And you'd like this, baby?" His low voice—and the desire oozing from it—steals my breath.

"I don't know, but the movie turned me on." At a time when almost nothing could.

"*You* turn me on."

I smile. "Back atcha, Lumberjack."

He snorts.

"What's your fantasy?"

"I'm dying to play with your ass."

As in...the inner sanctum? "Ummm."

"That a yes?"

I cough. "Could you be more specific?"

"I want to lick, finger, and fuck that beautiful hole. I dream about it."

Oh. A little spike of panic rushes through me. "No one's ever gone there, uh, before." My mind instantly calls up the line from *Star Trek's* opening credits: *To boldly go where no man has gone before.* Now I'm on the verge of cackling.

"Even better. It'll be all mine."

Something about that wiggles right between my thighs. Is it weird how much I like his possessiveness? And him saying *all mine*? I shake my head...I literally just told him my fantasy is to be his slave. "Does it hurt?"

"Not if you do it properly."

It bothers me that he's experienced at this, which is absurd. "So, you're an ass man?"

"It's one of my favorite things. But I'm an equal opportunity kind of guy...I will lavish attention on all your gorgeous parts."

～

"THIS IS GOING TO SOUND SO STUPID," I SAY. AND immature.

"Tell me," Butch urges.

"I resigned myself to becoming a spinster on the move to Virginia."

He barks out a laugh and I can't help laughing at myself. "Aren't you a little young for such a radical determination?"

"That, and decidedly melodramatic."

"How's spinsterhood going for you?"

"Not well. All I can think about is having sex with you again," I admit.

The words roll off his tongue slow and intentional. "I'm going to fuck any thoughts about spinsterhood right out of you."

Oh my.

～

"YOU SAID SOMETHING LAST NIGHT, AND IT MADE me think about my own situation."

Butch steals my full attention with that statement. I'm so eager for any tidbits about him. I make a little humming noise for him to continue.

"I haven't had a relationship with a woman for over six years."

He's only thirty, so this strikes me as odd. "Why?"

"I haven't wanted or needed to."

Cryptic. "But you've had sex?" I mean, obviously. I'm living proof.

He coughs. "Yes."

"I'll bet when I said no strings attached, you jumped for joy inside, didn't you?"

"Are you kidding? I felt like I'd hit the million-dollar jackpot."

I laugh, even though nothing could convince me I'm a million dollar lay. "Maybe you did. Our one-night stand was incredibly impulsive on my part."

"You aren't into casual sex?" Does he seem hopeful?

"Nope. I'm monogamous by nature." Unless, well...is being with two guys monogamous? Mono equals one. Technicalities be damned—we were committed to each other. *Until we weren't.* "I prefer commitment."

"I don't know if this makes me a caveman or male chauvinist or what, but I *really* fucking like hearing that for some reason."

I'm silent, working myself into a tizzy. What would Butch think of my threesome activities? Would he judge me? Reject me? Scorn me? Will my past forever haunt my future?

"You still with me, beautiful?" His voice forces my thoughts from their spiral.

"Mm-hmm."

"I know we're taking things slow, and haven't even broached this subject, but does that mean you want to be exclusive?"

A caught breath escapes. "Yes," I answer honestly. "Do you?"

"Fuck, Jacqui. I can't stand the thought of another man's hands on you...I absolutely want you all to myself."

My heart leaps even as my mind lobbies to stay grounded, reminding me not to get swept away or read too much into it. *Killjoy.* "Not into sharing then?"

"No fucking way," he practically growls, his timbre dipping lower, almost menacing. "And any man who'd agree to that is not only a fool but fails to understand your worth."

Well. His words swim in my brain, trapped in an eddy.

"I'm a possessive motherfucker. I protect what's mine—and will go any lengths to ensure you are safe, loved, and properly fucked."

My pulse hammers. I gulp down his intense promise like a shot of tequila. "I don't want to share, either," I say quietly.

"Good," he mutters.

There's a pause—as if we're both shell-shocked by our mutual revelations.

"What are you doing to me?" His agony is palpable.

"The same thing you're doing to me," I admit. The flutters amplify, taking flight once more. I'm falling for him, and it sure as hell sounds like he's getting feelings for me too. For two people determined to avoid a relationship, our trains are headed off the rails.

Maybe they've already derailed.

THIRTY-EIGHT

It's taken weeks to finalize the article about Hamilton Restorations, but I'm proud of the work. After a cursory review of the printout, I'm about to leave my cubicle to fax it to Gus when Don Jennings appears, blocking my exit. His brazen eyes linger on my body.

The nerve of this man. And I can't say a fucking thing. A flash of anger burns in my chest and frustration ripples through me like a set of ocean waves.

"That outfit is *very* becoming, Jacqueline."

My teeth grind together, and I forcibly relax my jaw. "Thank you. Can I help you with something?" *You lech.*

"Just checking on the status of the Hamilton feature."

Oh, right. "I finished the draft and was about to fax it. I believe it captures the essence of the business, their storied history, and state-of-the-art auto shop." My palms turn sweaty, and I slide one down my skirt. He tracks the movement over my hips, his hazel eyes practically bugging out. I stare at the floor. "I never thanked you for recommending me..." I shift my gaze back to his, trying to find my backbone.

"Don't mention it. I had a hunch Gus would like you." He winks.

This douchebag and his vulgar winks. With this one, I'm not sure what he implies; Gus was nothing but professional and clearly in love with his wife. I never got any weird vibes, unlike the inappropriate kind emanating from Don, as if he'd happily bang me in my cubicle this minute.

"Interviewing Mr. Hamilton was a pleasure. He was generous with his time and answered all my questions. Same with his son Butch." Who provided some extra...*details*.

"Is that it?" he asks, nodding at the papers clutched in my hand.

"Yes."

He gestures for it with his fingers. "I want to review this before you send it."

I hand it over, and my nerves take a fresh turn. The publisher is going to read my article, which is about one of his oldest friends. If I haven't done it justice...

"I'll give it a spin, and we can discuss it over lunch tomorrow."

Say what? "Oh, uh, okay."

"Don't be nervous. I'm sure coworkers have regaled you with stories about my vicious red pen, but my edits have helped every writer become better. That's the only goal."

I swallow the lump in my throat. A business lunch then. I can do this. What choice do I have? "Thank you. I appreciate your professional input."

He winks again and strolls out the door.

Fresh sweat trickles from my armpits and I hustle to the breakroom and buy a Coke from the vending machine. After chugging the cool drink, I dial Hamilton Restorations and ask for Butch. My pen taps against my notepad until his voice breaks the silence.

Instant comfort. "It's me."

"Sundance. What a pleasant surprise."

A smile edges my mouth. "The article is nearly finished.

Should be able to fax it over tomorrow. Just wanted to give you a heads up." *And hear your voice.*

"I'll let my dad know. If you're happy with it, Ms. Hall, he surely will be."

"Way to keep it professional, Mr. Hamilton."

"Hmm. I like the sound of that leaving your lips."

Now I'm sweating for an entirely new reason. "When *will* my lips see you again?" It's been a few weeks, and I'm jonesing to see Butch worse than I craved a cigarette after quitting.

"Not soon enough for me. I'm trying to arrange this weekend. Are you free?"

"Yes, absolutely," I exclaim, cringing at my obvious overeagerness. "I could head your direction if it's easier."

"No," he answers quickly—maybe too quickly. "This is your first fall in Virginia and Mother Nature puts on a hell of a display. I want to take you for a drive, show it to you. That cool?"

"I'd love that."

"Call you tonight?"

"It's my favorite part of the day."

"Mine too, baby."

～

Dread greets me shortly after I open my eyes; the expected lunch with my boss looms large. I dress conservatively in a black turtleneck and tan slacks. I sweep my hair into a basic ponytail. I'm fully aware of my efforts to downplay my assets, blend into the background, seem less attractive...and the lunacy of it. I shouldn't have to do anything different—*I'm* not the problem here.

As I cinch my hairband, the questions erupt. Did Don approve of my article? Did he slash it to smithereens? Does he doubt I'm talented enough to write for his magazine?

Despite my personal disgust for Don, I still value his

constructive criticism. He *is* the publisher, which means he's a seasoned pro—not just a seasoned scumball who hits on his employees.

Optimism prevails, and for good measure, I talk to my reflection in the mirror: "This is a working lunch. Nothing more."

As I drive to the office, Ozzy's "Crazy Train" plays on the heels of a Huey Lewis & The News song, and I blast the fuck out of it, attempting to quell my nerves. In addition to the anxiety of this impending work scenario, the memory of last night's phone call with Butch floods me with a weird combination of elated and skittish. Our dynamic constantly teeter-totters: mash the gas or slam the brakes.

It's hard not to push the pedal to the metal when he says things like *I protect what's mine—and will go any lengths to ensure you are safe, loved, and properly fucked.* But Butch has admitted trust issues. Secrets. And possibly legal troubles, which he alluded to the day we met. Whatever he's waiting to reveal until he's ready. If ever.

I can't exactly fault him when I'm trying (and failing) to hang onto my autonomy. Lord knows Butch makes it difficult; he's charming, complimentary, easygoing, and ridiculously attractive. The kind of handsome where I could forget my own name, let alone my mission in life. Yet in my deepest, messiest, broken parts, I'm wary of getting attached... or worse, falling in love. Especially with a man who can't trust.

I've traveled that path before, where I held up my heart on a platter, experienced a truthful, potent connection...and the loss of it fractured me, damaged me, obliterated me.

I'm not sure it's possible to experience a love like that again...if I can or should. Or how much of me is truly left to give.

Don summons me to the lobby at noon, and we make small talk on the elevator ride. He stands too close but keeps a reasonable distance as we walk the few blocks to the restaurant. I tug my coat closer from the nip in the air and ponder whether I have enough cold-weather clothes in my wardrobe. Having lived in California my entire life, I'm not used to temperatures below fifty degrees or sure what a Virginia winter promises.

We arrive and Don holds the door open, a blast of warmth hitting me when I step though. The place reeks of old money and business deals, with booths crafted of rich cherry and brass accents, Tiffany-style pendant lamps suspended overhead.

Our hostess seats us in a booth toward the back, and a waiter arrives for our drink orders.

"I'll take a martini, shaken, dry. Shall I make it two, Jacqueline?"

I hide my surprise. Is this a test? I've never had a martini, nor do I plan to start in the middle of a workday. "A Coke is fine, thank you."

Once he's out of earshot, Don asks, "Did you hear the one about a young guy who went to his doctor for a routine checkup?"

I brace myself for another crude joke and he plows ahead, not really waiting for an answer.

"When he came in for the results, the doctor said gravely, 'Jerry, I've got some good news and some bad news. You've got cancer. It's spreading at an unbelievably rapid rate, is totally inoperable, and you've got about three weeks to live.'"

Maybe this isn't another dirty joke.

"The guy says, 'Jesus. What's the good news?'

"'You know that cute receptionist out in the front office...the one with the big tits and the cute little ass?'" Don's hands lift to his chest, forming the universal sign for breasts, his gold wedding band gleaming in the lamplight. "'I'm fucking her!'"

Don cackles, and that goddamned traitorous nervous laugh of mine bubbles forth, even while a part of me withers.

Our drinks arrive, and we review the untouched menus. The faster we order, the faster this mandated appointment reaches its fucking conclusion.

After our waiter takes our selections, Don pulls out my article and slides it across the table. His scribbles pepper the margins, the volume of red slashes and circled and underlined words and sentences making it appear murdered.

"It's not as bad as it looks," he says, a smile lifting one side of his mouth. "You've got a natural talent for this work. It merely required a little polish. You captured Gus nicely." He grins, as if he shares an inside joke with his old pal.

I sift through his notes, finally glancing back at him. "Thank you for taking the time to review it. I appreciate your input."

"You know, I could be a tremendous help to you, Jacqueline. A mentor. Someone to guide you and ensure you're awarded assignments that tailor to your talents." His gaze drops to my chest.

My heart thuds so hard I want to press my hand against it.

"You're a beautiful young woman—and predators abound in our profession. That's another benefit to being under my wing."

Or under your sweaty body. I nod weakly, images of sordid casting couch stories projecting in my head, the kind where actresses are forced to their knees—or worse—to secure movie roles. I'm thoroughly grossed out, yet unsure how to respond. The threat of losing my job is glaringly front and center. This man holds all the cards. He's got a royal flush, and I've got jack shit.

I catch him staring hard at my mouth and realize I've

unconsciously sucked in my lower lip and am actively biting it. *Fuck.*

"Think about it," he says with a wink.

Our food arrives, and despite my roiling gut, I eat, desperate to end this lunch.

My boss prattles on about his golf game, and what a maddening sport it is—"his nemesis," he calls it.

And you're mine, buddy.

THIRTY-NINE

When Butch picks me up on Sunday morning, our mouths meet with such intensity—heady chemistry and longing churned together—that it's a struggle to get out the door.

"If we don't leave now, I'm going to keep you holed up in here all day." He grips the back of my neck. I arch into him.

"Mm-hmm," I mumble into his mouth. The straining erection behind his jeans fills me with need, and I grind forward.

He groans and forces us apart. "You win. A quickie."

"Yes!" I hiss with a fist pump.

He spins me around so I'm hugging the couch then yanks down my pants and underwear in haste, shoving them to my ankles. "Goddamn, you're a sight," he murmurs, buckle clinking as he flicks it undone. Anticipation floods my body, my ass bared to him in offering. His hand—that delicious working-man hand—cups my mound. A string of curses leaves his mouth when his thick fingers breach my opening and find me saturated.

Butch doesn't prepare me more than that; he thrusts his massive dick right into the promised land. Our moans ring out in the small space, and I nearly pass out from the pleasure, the crudeness, the rightness of it.

He fucks me like a man possessed, in hard strokes that ram me into the sofa enough that it skips forward. I want him to take it, take *me*. In this moment, there is nothing but this, us, his sheer power, and my desperation to receive it.

Yes. Yes. Yes.

He quickens, and I know he's close. It makes me whimper —his thrusts even deeper, unrestrained. I'm moaning loudly, desperate for everything he's doling out, spurred further by the masculine grunts giving him away. His orgasm erupts, and he grinds his hips as he spills into me with a husky groan. On its heels is angry pounding from the downstairs neighbors airing their grievance at the noise. *Oops.*

We both shake with quiet laughter as Butch collapses forward, pressing our bodies together. We're still clothed on our upper halves, but his arms around me feel like protection. Respect. More.

"Fuck, baby."

"I know..." I say, not even sure how to respond.

"I'm going to finish this when we get back."

I smile. He's worried about me getting mine. But he needn't be. I'm wholly satisfied...for now. "That was divine."

"You are the most extraordinary woman I've ever known."

Those words serve as their own caress, better than any climax.

It's cool and overcast, which turns out to be a vivid backdrop for viewing fall splendor. Butch takes his time as we travel the Blue Ridge Parkway, miles of scenic road that meander through nature's paradise, cutting through mountains, providing vistas that leave me speechless. The trees in their blazing golds, oranges, and reds are nothing short of dramatic against gray skies. It's as if God swooped down and painted the landscape, stealing my breath with its majestic glory.

I've never beheld anything so spectacular, even more poignant as I realize these leaves are singing their swan song. Once they fall from their branches, they'll wither, fray, and melt into the earth. I'm awed by its beauty, and that I'm glimpsing it right now, before it's gone.

"Mother Nature puts on one hell of a show, doesn't she?" Butch says.

I meet his exuberant gaze. "Magnificent."

We stop at overlooks. Steal kisses. Hold hands. Break for a late lunch. And then return to my place, where we spend a few hours in bed, exploring each other, talking and laughing, insatiable for all of it and more.

The witching hour arrives, signaling his imminent departure. Butch cups my face, staring down into my eyes for a moment before his lips find mine. We share a kiss that's gentle, sincere, and tinged with longing.

My heart tumbles in my chest, straining toward his like it's never been broken.

FORTY

"Best band you've seen live?" I ask Butch, my latest question fired through the contraption connecting us across the eighty-seven miles. The only rule is to keep our answers short. Tonight's been enlightening, funny, ridiculous.

"Bruce Springsteen and the E Street Band. They played *four hours*. Your turn."

"Queen...Freddie Mercury was *amazing*."

"Beach or mountains?"

"Beach!" I practically shriek.

"Very predictable, California. I'm going mountains."

"Very predictable, Lumberjack."

He snorts. "First kiss: good or bad?"

"Nerve-wracking and awkward. How about you?"

"I was scared shitless, had no idea what I was doing, but I liked it."

"You're acing it now," I say, remembering our smoldering first kiss.

He groans. "Do *not* get me started thinking about kissing you, Jacqui."

I snicker. "Moving on...celebrity fan moment?"

"I met Mario Andretti once at VIR and we talked racing for nearly an hour. Nice fucking guy. Didn't even act like he was anyone special."

"That's *mega cool*. Not sure if this counts, but I'm friends with a Major League Baseball player. Have you heard of Terry Walton? He plays for the Pittsburgh Pirates but we're all hoping he eventually gets traded to the Oakland A's."

"Don't know him, but that's a huge accomplishment."

"My friend Kendra wanted to marry him."

"Sounds like they're not together anymore."

"They're not. You ever had a tough breakup?"

"Yes," he says tersely.

"Me too," I whisper. "You were in love?"

He sighs. "Thought I was. She was my high school sweetheart."

"Even after the purple tux?" I joke.

Butch doesn't laugh. "I...I can't talk about this."

I've crossed a line, I think. "I'm sorry. I didn't mean to pry."

"It's not your fault. Sensitive subject."

There's a commotion in the background and he swears under his breath. "Hey, I've got to go. I'll call you tomorrow."

"Okay," I say, reluctant to end on this note. "Goodnight."

"'Night."

Did he get off the phone because of that noise, or did I upset him? I launch to my feet, unsettled, and yank open the fridge.

I'm overthinking this. It's nothing. He deserves his privacy.

I close the refrigerator, unable to concentrate and not the least bit hungry anyway. But my sixth sense hovers, casting doubt about Butch and his yet-to-be-revealed secrets.

What would make me "run the other direction"?

~

"WHAT ARE YOU AFRAID OF?" BUTCH ASKS.

I know exactly what he implies and it's not about phobias. I've thought about this a lot as my attraction to him grows. "Losing myself."

"How so?"

"I'm not sure how to protect my heart from breaking. When I care about someone, they get all of me. I lost myself once and it makes me reluctant to believe in anyone again."

Butch releases a long exhale. "You have no idea how much I relate to that. Are you scared of this...the potential of us?"

"*Yes*," I whisper. Am I seriously falling for another handsome, muscle-car-driving mechanic?

"Me too. It seems too good to be true, and that's my biggest fear."

"It does." My gaze latches on a water stain spreading across the ceiling.

"You aren't getting cold feet on me, are you?"

Isn't that a wedding-day jitters thing? *Do* not *weave marriage into this conversation.* "Not yet."

"But you've thought about it?"

"Truthfully? No. I really like you, Butch. And I mean everything about you. Do you have some ugly flaws you're hiding from me?"

He hums. "We already determined I might be a serial killer."

"I can put a hurtin' on some Cap'n Crunch myself."

After a pause, he barks out a laugh. Quieter, he says, "I more than like everything about you, Sundance."

But will you always? Will it be enough? My unspoken fears hang between us.

"I'm sorry you've lost faith in love," he adds. "Or at least in men. It takes a lot of resilience to push through heartbreak."

"Spoken like a true veteran."

"Yeah," he answers softly. "Which is why I'm fucked up about it too. I'd put the idea behind me."

His use of past tense doesn't escape me. Does that mean he thinks we have a shot? Why am I hopeful? Goddamn, stupid, motherfucking hope.

"And now?"

"Now I'm wondering if building a life with another person might be possible after all."

My breath catches. "Because of me?"

"Because we're good together. You feel it too, right?"

"Yes," I admit.

"What if two people who don't believe in love and never want to be hurt again took a risk?"

I tug at a loose thread on my comforter. "I don't know, and that's what worries me."

"What if it turned into something far beyond what they could have ever imagined? Became the greatest love known in the history of the universe? What would you say then?"

I'm stunned into silence, Butch's poetic words landing a direct hit. "I'd be inclined not to argue with the powers that be."

"My point is, baby...no risk, no reward. Let's stay open to whatever this is. Regardless of what happens, we both know we can get back on our feet again."

Before I can answer, his voice turns gruff. "The world ain't all sunshine and rainbows. It's a very mean and nasty place. I don't care how tough—"

"Are you quoting *Rocky*?"

"Just trying to lighten up a bit."

"If you were here, I'd kiss you. That's how much I love that you just quoted Rocky Balboa."

"I'll take a rain check on that kiss."

"Butch?"

"Yeah?"

"You make me want to take the risk. Just don't knock me out, okay?"

He hums. "You may not believe this, gorgeous girl, but you have the advantage in this matchup."

FORTY-ONE

Solitude can give my mind just enough rope to hang itself. Today's work commute topic: Thanksgiving—fast approaching. It's my first significant holiday in a strange place and Butch has yet to invite me to spend it with him. I assume his family gathers every year, but it's probably too soon for him to include me in that kind of thing. Or maybe he's reluctant tell his folks about us. I don't know what to think about that. By all accounts, we're progressing. Phone calls. A couple of dates. Sex. Slow-ish.

Will I be relegated to dining pathetically alone at some restaurant or forcing down a depressing turkey sub in my apartment? And is that better or worse than *years* of dismal Thanksgivings at my parents' house?

Why don't I come right out and ask Butch to spend it with me?

Answer: I'm a chickenshit.

By the time I arrive at the office, I've worked myself into a ridiculous, self-deprecating tizzy, caught between longing and reality.

That evening, Butch doesn't call until 9:30 p.m. He's distracted, not himself, and I'm still ruminating about Thanksgiving. I detest my insecurities about us—and it's making me reticent to talk about anything.

Then he drops the very words I didn't want to hear.

"I've got to cancel this weekend, Jacqui. I'm sorry. My parents are sick, and it...I can't—"

"It's alright. I understand," I cut in, my heart sinking. "You're a good son to take care of them." I wind the phone cord through my fingers, trying to strangle my anxiety and disappointment.

Butch sighs. "I wanted to see you."

"Same here."

"I'm burned out on my schedule, my responsibilities, all of it. It shouldn't be so difficult to balance everything."

"Yeah." It's all I can muster, wallowing in my own crap.

"Don't give up on me, okay?" His voice is dull and hoarse.

"I won't."

He pauses, clears his throat. "I'm still figuring things out."

What things? I want to scream. *What is there to figure out?*

"You still there?" he asks.

"Mm-hmm."

"You're quiet."

And you're unforthcoming. "Just not sure what to say, Butch."

"Tell me something you don't like talking about."

"What? Why?"

He sighs. "I don't know. Because I need to hear something real, anything to feel less fucked up in my head."

A part of me wants to tell him to go first. He's the one with all the secrets. But that would be a bitch move...he's despondent tonight. I pause, though it's not a challenge to call something up. "My mom's addicted to Valium and has been for years. She's so emaciated and fragile, I'm worried she's going to die."

"Damn, Jacqui. That's terrible."

Long breath. "I'm powerless to help her. I've tried."

He hums in agreement. "My uncle was an alcoholic. He killed himself driving drunk one night. Ran straight into a tree."

My eyes squeeze shut. "I'm sorry. That must have been devastating."

"It was my mother's brother, my favorite uncle until his drinking turned him into an asshole. He brought the chaos wherever he went."

"Is that why you limit yourself to two drinks?" I ask, remembering what he said in the bar the day we met.

"Yes."

"I had a sister who drowned when I was super young. It destroyed my parents. I don't think they ever recovered. Ergo, the happy pills." Except, they don't make her happy at all.

"Fuuuuuck," he breathes out on a long exhalation. We're both quiet for a minute. Then he clears his throat, his voice raspy when he speaks. "My mother had breast cancer and beat it, but it's the scariest thing our family has weathered. Thought we were going to lose her."

"Oh, Butch. That must have been awful...but also amazing to watch her overcome it."

"She's my hero, my inspiration when life seems too hard. I respect the hell out of her."

The burn hits me square in the chest. "I envy you. My parents are *not* my heroes." Bitterness coats my tone. "I think my mom drowned along with my sister. It's just taken longer for her to sink below the surface."

"I'm so sorry, baby."

"Thank you," I whisper.

"I wish we were having this conversation in person."

I exhale an audible breath, attempting to loosen the pressure in my chest. "Me too. I can tell you're struggling tonight."

"Talking to you makes it better."

That removes some of the sting from my disappointment. "Do you trust me yet?"

"Getting there. Faster than I imagined. What about you?"

"Getting there too," I echo. "I realized recently I need to trust *myself* more than anyone else."

"How so?"

"I tend to leap before looking, giving to others at my own expense. I'm still trying to figure out how to take care of Jacqui in that equation."

"I get it. Sometimes we're last on the list, and we give until it hurts."

I hum in agreement. "I'm not blind about the why. Not now, at least. Growing up with broken parents, forced to mature early, realizing I didn't have support...it turned me into a people pleaser." I found the term in a magazine article not long ago and knew immediately that it described me. "I've somehow believed if I give enough, I'll find what I'm looking for and fill that emptiness."

"But you're giving by nature too, aren't you?" he asks softly.

Bullseye. How do we stop an innate personality trait when it hurts us?

"Yeah, and it complicates matters, gets jumbled in my mind...like a drink in the blender."

Butch releases an understanding sigh. "What are you doing about it?"

"I'm learning, or trying, to be happy all by my lonesome instead of sitting around moping like a sadsack. I force myself to get out and see a movie, have a meal, visit a museum, whatever. It's not easy though, and borders on uncomfortable. I find loneliness suffocating."

"Are you lonely a lot?"

"*Yes*," I whisper. Admitting it sounds pathetic. "Lately I've wondered if I've expected others to solve that for me, while simultaneously realizing they can't."

"That's very insightful. Loneliness often has little to do with other people."

"Exactly. I've experienced it in rooms full of people, or out with friends, and certainly with my family, where I'm viscerally aware I'm not connected to anyone. Don't think I'm a loser, but... it's paralyzing, a hole I'm constantly trying to fill, only nothing plugs it up. It just gapes like an open wound." I squeeze my eyes shut, a small *ugh* escaping. "I can't believe I just admitted that out loud."

"You're not a loser, baby. But I don't think another person can fix it for you. It's your riddle to solve."

"Sometimes when I'm around other people, it's wonderful and nothing hurts." *Like with you.*

"Maybe you're with the right people in that moment, the kind who create those unseen connections, like when all the pistons fire to make your four-stroke run."

Mechanics. "You're wise beyond your years, Lumberjack."

He scoffs. "I don't know about that, but my parents infused a healthy dose of common sense into me. Or rather, it was beaten into me with a sledgehammer. I try and assess situations with logic. Except with you, Jacqui. You turn my world upside down."

"Ditto."

He's thrown me for a loop...or ten. When I'm with Butch, I'm not lonely. I don't understand if that's positive or not. Does he solve my problem...or camouflage it? I could lose myself in him so easily. Probably already have. And if I'm clear on one thing, it's that nothing lasts forever.

But what if we *are* pistons in the same engine that work together, like he said?

"I'm sorry again about this weekend. Are you going somewhere fun?" he asks.

No clue now. "I'll figure something out."

"I'll be exceptionally envious."

"Why?"

"One, because I'll wish I was with you, and two, you'll have time to yourself, something I rarely get anymore."

Hmm. "And I have more of that than I want. Isn't it strange how we each want the opposite?"

His rueful laugh travels across the miles. "It's completely fucked up. I can tell you this, Sundance. The more I get to know you, the more I want to be with you. I'll give you all my minutes, my hours, my years. You'll never be lonely again."

"That's downright romantic, Butch. But now I'm wondering if you're ready to offload a bunch of man crap—like your laundry—and I'm just the unsuspecting pack mule."

He chuckles. "Baby, you're a breath of fresh air. And right now, I want to gulp it down."

FORTY-TWO

Saturday, after some internal waffling, I force myself to go out and explore. It's another brisk day, clouds blocking the sun and dimming the light. I button my new black wool peacoat and draw the collar up as I walk several streets until I intersect Monument Avenue.

Beautiful homes line both sides of the street, and my gait slows to admire their trim details, masonry, and manicured gardens. There's no missing the gigantic monuments in the center strip, either. They seem a rather bizarre inclusion in a city neighborhood, but many of my coworkers said to check them out.

It's only a few blocks to the Virginia Museum of Fine Arts, where I spend a couple of immersive hours meandering the expansive halls of paintings, photography, sculptures, and featured exhibits. Art museums hold a special place in my heart, and this one is well worth the visit.

To cap off my day, I treat myself to an early dinner at a seafood restaurant, something I've missed since leaving my western shores. I order a bowl of clam chowder and a glass of white wine and nibble on warm French bread smeared with chilled butter in foil-wrapped rectangles.

I long for a book to keep me company and regret my decision to leave my current paperback at home. Solitary dining seems sad and pathetic—*look at the loser with no friends*—and I scan for anything to latch onto. When the body language of a nearby couple suggests trouble in paradise, I make up elaborate backstories for their argument.

My food arrives, and the combination of the creamy chowder, delicious bread, and dry wine eases my angst and is worth every penny.

I'd still be happier if Butch were sitting across from me, grinning at me like I'm the best entrée on the menu. Still, I can do this. Spend time with myself. Pamper myself. Take myself out on the town. And you know what? For Thanksgiving, I'll go to a double feature, stuff my face with candy and popcorn, and be thankful I'm alive. No more moping, no more hoping, no more hanging my happiness on what men deign to give me of themselves.

On the way home, my thoughts veer back to Mr. Tall, Dark, and Foresty. I do miss him, and he sounded like he needed a big hug. When I near the grocery store, I impulsively swing into the parking lot with the idea to make chicken noodle soup for Butch and his parents—a care package of sorts. He's inundated and they're sick. It's such an easy gesture. I'll drive it down tomorrow and surprise him with it.

As I push my cart through the aisles collecting ingredients, I admit it's not wholly altruistic. This provides an excuse to lay eyes and hands on my lumberjack. Will it seem pushy? Maybe. Or weird? I don't even know if Butch has told his parents we're dating. But he said he wanted to see me, so... green light.

Excitement rumbles through me as I pack up the chicken noodle soup, crackers, ginger ale, and chocolate chip walnut cookies I made last night. The essential healing meal. The anticipation of giving it to Mr. Foresty-eyed fills me with glee. That, and standing face to face after several long weeks apart.

I've got it bad.

Hey, I honored my commitment yesterday, standing on my own two feet like a big girl. What's wrong with liking Butch? Seeing where it goes, like he said?

My vagina sends up a high five...also stoked to see a particular man. But I steer my thoughts back on track. This isn't about sex.

I pack the car and head south. I'm in a bit of a predicament not knowing where the lumberjack lives. I didn't want to call and ask, effectively ruining the surprise, but he mentioned living near his folks, so I'll simply consult a phone book once I get to town and look him up. His address should be listed in the white pages. Easy peasy. Last resort: I stop by his parents' house. Would it be totally random and bizarre to show up unannounced? With a care package, no less? By the woman they only know as a writer doing a feature on Hamilton Restorations? Yes, yes it would. I cringe, wondering again if I'm making a mistake.

But then "In Your Eyes" comes on the radio, and I crank it up and belt out the words with Peter Gabriel. I don't need to second-guess an act of kindness.

As anticipated, the phone directory hanging in a gas station telephone booth gives me the goods. Consulting my map confirms he indeed lives close to his parents' house. My nerves amplify with each mile closer, pulse skyrocketing when the address affixed to his oversized country mailbox indicates I've arrived.

He might not even be here. Maybe he's at his folks' house attending to their needs, or at the store, or...calm your jets, girl. One step at a time.

The tree-lined gravel drive opens to a clearing. I spot his Barracuda first and let out a stuttered breath. My gaze swings to a charming, rustic log cabin, the logs separated by beige chinking, sheltered by towering trees. Firewood is stacked on one side and my lip curls in amusement. Because...lumberjack. Beyond that stands a huge garage. Of course, Butch would want one bigger than his house. I wonder what's in that massive structure.

I wonder more about how this man lives. Is he messy or fastidious? Typical bachelor or domesticated man? Does he cook elaborate meals or just grill everything? Sleep on luxurious or cheap sheets? Prefer books or TV? Does he chop all that wood shirtless? So many questions...reminding me how little I really know about this man.

Now that I'm here, I'm panicking again about surprising him. I'm both paralyzed and energized. There's still time to turn around...

Get out of the car.

With a heavy exhale, I collect my care packages and make my way to the door, manic dog barks coming from inside. I notice a small, pink bicycle on the other side of the Cuda, leaning on its kickstand. It's distinctly girlish with purple tassels dangling from the handlebars, and it looks wholly out of place. Whose is it? As I ascend the steps, I admire the wide plank boards on the porch, the swing for two, and the sculpted Labrador sitting by the door that sure resembles Hemi. But it's hard to concentrate with those sharp, incessant barks amping up my already unraveling nerves.

You've got this. Just fucking knock.

Shuffling my bags, I spy the door knocker—an actual gear shifter from a manual transmission (four on the floor to be exact) and can't help smiling at it. I clack it a few times and suck in another deep breath. There's a stampede of feet, more scrambling, continued howls. I plaster a smile on my face and wait, hoping that's Hemi and not an unfriendly dog planning to rip my face off.

When the door swings open, it's most assuredly Hemi, who bounds straight for me. And standing next to him, emerald-green eyes wide, mousy brown hair wild around her cherubic face, is a little girl.

FORTY-THREE

"Oh...hello." Words dissipate as I stare at the little girl...with eyes that match Butch's.

"Hi." She tilts her head, long hair falling to the side. "Who are you?"

"My name's Jacqui."

"I'm Emmy. My daddy wanted to name me Hemi, but my momma wouldn't let him."

The dog circles frenetically, trying to sniff my bags. Emmy lunges for his collar, holding him back. "Knock it off, you kook." Her bare feet poke out of *Cinderella* pajamas, and her free hand clutches a teddy bear. She fixes those vibrant green eyes back on me. "You're real pretty."

I smile. "So are you."

"Are you here to see my daddy?"

"Em, what the hell's going on down there? Why is Hemi barking?" Butch yells from within—and my pulse rapid fires again.

"Some lady named Jacqui wants to talk to you," she hollers.

"What?" his voice thunders.

Panic floods my bloodstream. "I shouldn't have come," I

murmur, dropping my bags by the door and backtracking, turning just in time to avoid plummeting down the steps.

Hurrying to my car, I reach the driver's side when Butch hurtles out the front, stumbling over the threshold. "Jacqui, wait!" His eyes blaze. Shock is splashed across his face. His hair is sopping wet and he's naked, save for a towel wrapped around his waist, the ends clutched in one hand.

My head shakes, my thoughts reeling and jumbling. Adrenaline roars through my system. I scramble into the seat. My hands tremble with such force the key won't insert, but I finally finagle it before Butch reaches my door, his pleas dulling in my ears. I back up enough to turn and floor it down the driveway, my vision tunneling. He has a daughter? Is he fucking *married*?

My stomach sours and bucks. I'm going to throw up or pass out. Maybe a combination. I would never, *never* be with a married man. Anger swirls with confusion, my guts roiling when I reach the end of the driveway and stop.

I need air. Now. With shaky fingers, I grip the handle and roll down the window. My car idles as I inhale deep breaths. Through the side mirror, I spot Butch hurrying barefoot and mostly naked down the gravel drive, still calling my name.

He reaches me, panting. His nipples are taut from the cold, green eyes wild, dark chest hair testifying he's every bit a man. His free hand braces the roof as he catches his breath.

I close my eyes tight.

"Jacqui—"

"Are you married?" I grit out, my hands balling into fists.

"No! Fuck. *No!*"

I face him now, meeting his penetrating gaze. "Is that your daughter?"

"Yes," he confesses. Fresh goosebumps flutter across his flesh. "Look, will you come back, come inside? Please? *Please, Jacqui.* Give me a chance to explain."

His clear angst gives me pause. My heartbeat slows

enough that I no longer want to hurl. And he is out here in only a towel, his feet likely torn to shreds, freezing his balls off.

I nod, not trusting myself to speak.

He lets out a long, relieved breath and taps his fingers on the roof of my Toyota. "Do me a solid and let me catch a ride. I feel a tad, uh, vulnerable."

My lips twitch, regardless of how fucking upset I am. "Fine," I spit out.

He makes zero haste hustling into the passenger side and we're both silent as I reverse back to his house. The only sound is his palms rubbing vigorously against each other. I lurch to a stop, yank up the hand brake more forcefully than is necessary, and climb out.

Emmy and the dog are nowhere to be seen, but my bags remain where I deposited them.

"What's this?" Butch asks.

"I made soup and cookies for you and your parents..." My voice trails off. I'm such an idiot. Me and my big ideas.

His gaze latches onto mine. It's brimming with warmth and maybe a tinge of awe. "Well, damn. You're just full of surprises."

"Oh...I don't know. Think you got me beat today, Butch."

He grimaces, then grabs one of the bags with his spare hand. I collect the other and follow him inside.

Emmy and the dog swivel their heads our direction from their post on the carpeted living room floor. They're prone in front of a television, watching cartoons. A big fireplace is flanked by bookshelves, and a matching brown leather couch and recliner fill out the space.

"Hi again!" she says with a wave.

My cheeks burn as I return it with forced enthusiasm. I've acted so foolish and immaturely, and yet, this little girl seems undaunted or unaffected by whatever vanishing act I tried to pull.

Butch leads me into the kitchen, and I set my bag next to his on the island counter. He stands close, his fingers grazing my arm, almost like he's afraid to touch me. And honestly... I'm not ready for that.

"I'll be right back. I need to get dressed. Make yourself at home, okay?"

Unable to meet his gaze, I manage a nod.

His footfalls recede, thumping upstairs, and I let another long breath loose, willing my nerves to stop behaving like live wires. *Give me grace.*

My thoughts attempt a hostile takeover, but that's about as useful as me learning chemistry. I'll stifle those urges—until I hear what Butch has to say.

Remembering the soup, I pull it from the bag and place it in the refrigerator. Colorful alphabet magnets clutter the door. The E, M, and Y peg a drawing at an angle—stick figures of a man, girl, and yellow dog with a bone.

The rest of the kitchen comes into focus, and it's striking. Masculine and efficient, and different than anything I've ever seen. The cabinets are painted black, with thick wood slabs for countertops. The stainless appliances remind me of the chrome on cars. A metal prep table with a shelf underneath serves as the island, and a round dining table with seating for six is tucked into the corner.

Butch hastens down the stairs. He exchanges words with Emmy in tones too low for me to hear then enters the kitchen, seemingly relieved to find me still here. He's wearing jeans and a navy henley with the sleeves pushed up his forearms and a pair of wooly socks.

His hand grazes my back. "Can I offer you a drink? Coffee or tea?"

"I'll take coffee, thanks."

He pours two cups and hands me one, then invites me to sit at the table. He brings milk and spoons, setting them down before settling into the chair next to mine. I hold the ribbed glass dispenser upside-down, fixating on the sugar granules drifting from the little metal flip top into my cup to avoid...whatever's coming.

"I married my childhood sweetheart," Butch says, getting right to it. "Met her at fifteen and put a ring on her finger once we graduated. We got hitched soon after. Emmy came along four years later and was...unplanned." He pauses, lowering his voice. "I used to say she was an accident, and now I realize what a shitty thing that was to say. Emmy is the light of my life. And sometimes life gives you the best surprises."

He's so earnest, and part of me wonders...hopes?...if he means *me* as well as his daughter.

"Before she turned one, her mother left us, saying she couldn't do 'this' anymore," he continues, air-quoting *"this."*

My chest squeezes at the image of a mother walking away from her child. It's so cold, so...cruel.

Butch inserts two fingers through the handle of his mug, the tips tapping lightly against the ceramic. "I never anticipated her leaving or ending our marriage. Never saw it coming. She seemed happy."

He scoffs. "Or perhaps that's my ego talking. Back then, I was still a kid myself. A little wild and self-centered, racing cars with my friends, getting in fights, acting like a total horn-dog. With her, I mean. My priorities were less clear then." He shrugs. "Maybe I was an asshole."

My heart flinches a little, that he justifies being discarded. They were young, in the years when most of us make poor decisions.

Butch's eyes stray to a spot on the wall. "She had dreams of moving to a big city," he admits. "She hated small town life, and what she called 'small town ways.' She found it suffo-cating. I figured she'd grow out of it, realize the opposite is true. But then..." He hesitates.

"What?" I prompt.

"Then I started working for my dad, and she wasn't happy about it." He strokes his jaw with his thumb and forefinger as his eyes connect with mine. "It was a way to make money, but also, I *wanted* to. I love cars, and I was eager to learn all I could about them plus participate in the family business. The gearhead gene runs strong in our family."

I raise my eyebrows. "I've noticed."

"I'd wager, after that, she believed we'd never leave. And honestly? I'm not sure we would have, or if I could have, which is a pretty fucked-up situation."

I nod and sip my coffee.

"But how could she walk away from her own daughter? As a parent, I've thought about it a lot, and there's nothing— *nothing*—that could pry me away from my little girl. Not only because I'm responsible for her, but because...she's my world. The air that I breathe. The reason I get up in the morning."

That knot in my throat enlarges and I swallow hard. "She's never come back or contacted you or Emmy?"

Buch lets loose a long breath. "Actually, she did for the first time about six months ago. Remember the day we met?"

I instantly make the connection. "Your legal troubles?"

"Yeah. Darlene appeared out of nowhere and wanted to see Emmy. I refused, for obvious reasons. Then she blindsided me with a custody lawsuit."

Yikes. "Does she have legal grounds?"

"The lawyers are figuring that out, but it's not been the slam dunk I assumed it would be. A hearing is being scheduled, and it's all taken a lot longer than I anticipated. It's very fucking unsettling. I just want it to be over."

"I'm sorry."

He runs his fingers though his thick brown hair, scratching the back of his neck once he reaches it.

"When did you divorce?" I realize I'm clutching my mug and loosen my grip.

"She served me with papers shortly after leaving."

"And you've raised Emmy by yourself this whole time?"

"I've had help, thank God. My parents and sister are saints. They love that little girl, and she loves them. But I try not to take it for granted because Emmy is my responsibility. It's fine for her to sleep over at Mimi and PopPop's house sometimes, and they enjoy having her...as long as it's within reason and I'm not taking advantage of their goodwill."

I'm floored. Butch gets thrown a curveball and he hits it out of the damn park. My parents get a curveball and forfeit the game.

"She's the center of my world, but I'm also hers. I'm who she relies on. I'm where the buck stops. And she's a handful. A spunky, precocious, tiny female who scares me to death."

A small smile inches across my lips.

"And I have no earthly idea what I'm doing, but I try my best. She does well in school, takes dance, works on cars with me, parades everywhere in dresses and crowns, and I attempt to keep her in line while not giving in to her every whim. She probably knows I'm wrapped around her little finger."

Butch is laying his heart out to me. He's obviously smitten, caring, and...sheltering...and it's all so beautiful.

"Does she ask about her mom? Miss her?"

Butch grimaces. "She doesn't remember her mother, and I've watched her like a hawk for years looking for trauma or emotional damage, wondering whether she needs outside help or to talk about it. So far, I don't see anything. But here's the other thing. I'm very protective of Emmy. I don't want..." He clears his throat. "I haven't introduced her to anyone that might leave her. Hurt her. Put her in the position to love someone who doesn't love her back."

My chest seizes again. *"Of course,"* I whisper. "That's why you didn't tell me about her. You're rightfully cautious."

"In all honesty, I was going to tell you soon. I know that sounds like bullshit, but I promise it's not. And this is not how I wanted you to find out about my daughter. I'm damn sorry about that."

"I get it." I do. I don't like it much, but it's understandable.

"Emmy hasn't gotten close to women aside from my mother, sister, and grandmothers, and a part of me knows that's not...maybe that's not what's best for her? I'm a man. I know man stuff. She's a girl. She needs to know girl stuff. And while some of that can probably wait, I'm thinking it's important for her to have that soon."

Yeah. Before her period comes. Sooner, really—the school years can be brutal. I don't say anything, though; I just nod.

"I like you, Jacqui. A lot. I want to let you into my life, to pursue whatever's happening here. I haven't experienced this," he gestures between us, "in years, which tells me it's something special. I trust you." His hand skates toward mine then stalls. "I want you."

"Daddy?" Emmy interrupts, peering around the doorway.

"What do you need, sweetheart?"

She shuffles over, still dragging that teddy bear in one hand. "Can I have a snack?"

"Sure, baby. How about an apple?"

She nods, her curious gaze fastening on me. "Want some apple too?"

I smile at her. "No thanks, but that's nice of you to offer. I bet you got those good manners from your daddy."

She shakes her head, a big grin crossing her face. "My PopPop."

"Hey!" Butch chides, grabbing her like a rag doll, hefting her into his arms, and tickling her.

Emmy squeals with pure delight, her giggles echoing in the kitchen. She's breathless when he relents.

"Pay the toll, kid."

She dutifully plants a kiss on his cheek.

He sets her down and she runs off gripping a ruby apple her father rinsed under the tap.

Butch's smile fades, as if he's remembering our sobering conversation. He pours us more coffee and sits back down. "You're awfully quiet, Sundance. I've laid a ton on you here, but can you throw me a bone?"

My thoughts remain scattered. "I'm not sure what to say. It's...a lot to absorb."

He hums.

"Emmy is adorable. The two of you together..." I grasp for words. "It's heartwarming. Admirable. I respect the hell out of you for how you've stepped up as a father."

"But?" he prods.

But I know nothing about being a mother. My mom wasn't a great role model. I can barely take care of myself. This is way out of my league. I could fuck it all up...this *one thing* that's more important to Butch than anything else. Plus, he's embroiled in a legal battle with an ex-wife that sounds messy and equally beyond my purview. My mind races with intrusive thoughts, but I voice none of them.

"I just need some time to digest this."

His shoulders sag. He's not convinced.

He's laid himself bare, and I'm backtracking like a spooked animal.

I'm proving him right about women. About trusting others.

I'm also, unwittingly, sealing my own destiny.

FORTY-FOUR

Butch clears our cups, and we stand. I'm hoping the long drive back to the city will give me the space and time to sift through my emotions.

"Will you stay a while?" he asks. "We don't have to talk about anything heavy. Just...stay. Hang out with Emmy and me. Please."

I'm torn...wanting to, not wanting to. "Alright," I answer.

He's standing close, and our eyes connect. Cautiously, he pulls me against him. When I don't resist, he tightens his grip. Tears threaten the minute I inhale his scent, the inexplicable safety and surety of him, the longing and ache that follows.

He presses a kiss to my forehead, and the warmth leaves its imprint even after his lips are gone.

Butch gives me the nickel tour of his home. There's a spot probably meant for dining that serves as a playroom for Emmy. It's brimming with toys and games, a desk, and a crafts table piled with various supplies and some project in progress. A powder room and laundry facilities fill out the first floor.

Upstairs are three bedrooms. Emmy's is adorable with a sparkly pink bedspread, bright pillows, and a purple plush chair tucked into a reading nook crammed with books and more toys.

A Jack-and-Jill bathroom adjoins with a spare bedroom that only contains a bed and nightstand, but a copse of lush evergreens fills the rear window. Butch's suite is the largest and has a private bathroom with a huge tub, separate shower, and double-sink vanity. It's impossible to avoid staring at the king-size, four-poster bed made from rough-hewn logs. A black comforter is draped on top of gray sheets and pillows. A stuffed leather chair, end table, and a sizable dresser give it a masculine vibe. His room also benefits from those glorious trees out his windows.

"It's so...homey," I say.

Butch raises an eyebrow. "That's why they call it a home?"

I elbow him. "It's just interesting to finally see where you live. You're neater than I thought."

He hums. "I try."

My gaze lands back on his bed.

"I've thought of what I would do to you here," he whispers, brushing a lock of hair behind my shoulder. I shiver and he notices. "I hope you'll give me the chance."

We head downstairs, and Woody Woodpecker's signature laugh punctuates the air as we near the living room.

Emmy's head rests on Hemi's torso. The pair seem as thick as thieves.

"A certain someone mentioned you wanted to name her Hemi."

He grins. "I did. It was vetoed." *By her mother.*

"For a girl, Butch? Really?"

"What's wrong with that? The Hemi engine is superior, powerful, badass. Sounds perfect for a female. That's a don't fu...mess with me kind of name."

"You have a point," I concede.

"That's now moot."

I shrug. "Suits the dog perfectly." As if Hemi hears, his tail swooshes back and forth across the rug.

Butch smiles at the canine wistfully. "I got him for Emmy's first birthday and named him Hemi so fast it would make your head spin."

I do the math. They probably both needed this furry companion in those brutal early days when they became a father-daughter duo.

Emmy unglues her eyes from the TV. "Do you have a pet?" she asks.

I shake my head. "Unfortunately, they aren't allowed where I live."

She shrugs. "I could loan you one of my stuffed animals. They're literally like pets, and real good company." She squeezes her teddy bear for emphasis.

I hold back a chuckle at her use of the word *literally*. It sounds so grown up, and her misuse of it is even more endearing. "Might take you up on that."

Turning to Butch, I ask, "Do you want to take the stuff I brought to your parents?"

"I'll drop it off once you leave. They're both down with the flu and are probably sleeping." His fingers graze my arm in a gentle gesture. "Thank you again for doing that; it was thoughtful of you."

I spend a few more hours with Butch and Emmy, finally relaxing enough to absorb their dynamic and the fact that Butch is a father. *A father*. It turns me inside out...and fills me with awe. Daddy Lumberjack loves with undiluted purity and a sure hand. It's jarring—in a good way—and potent to witness.

I'm still on shaky ground when he kisses me goodbye, a kiss full of yearning and questions and possibility.

When we part, the angst in his expression adds to my own turmoil. Although uncertainty percolates beneath the surface, I squeeze his hand reassuringly...because I'm hopeful. Even though hope is foolish. And dangerous.

I also can't process this fully until I'm alone. And I must, for clear and obvious reasons.

The avalanche hovering silently in the recesses of my mind descends before I'm even out of Hampton Springs. It's unavoidable, smothering me with its blanket of icy reality as I'm bombarded with thought after thought.

A part of me absolutely wants to run from Butch and his daughter.

I know nothing about parenting. And I lack a roadmap. Plus, if my DNA is responsible, I've got no business dipping my toe into that pond.

I will not do to another what's been done to me.

I. Will. Not.

But God help me, nothing in my heart wishes to turn away from that man.

We've developed intense feelings in a short time. I blame those late-night phone calls. We talk nearly every night, and it's helped us know each other intimately—without convoluting it with sex...much. We've shared everything from the mundane to the serious to the sacred. And the laughs...Butch is funny. Insightful. Teasing. Kind. Sexy. Dirty. We're friends, not just lovers.

And when we *are* together in the flesh, that's damn fine, too. Off-the-charts delicious. It's chemistry. Working in my favor for once. *Or is it?*

Can two people simply possess the molecular structure that scientifically latches onto one another...emitting those pheromones and leading nature by the nose?

Because despite my best efforts to buck a relationship, to avoid falling for another guy with devastatingly beautiful eyes, to keep the sex casual...here I am.

My gaze slides to the passenger seat, where a three-foot

stuffed lion sits. Emmy solemnly placed it into my hands before I left, saying she picked this "pet" because he matched my hair. She made not-so-idle threats about my caring for "Lucky" and reiterated he was a loaner, nothing permanent. A smile edges my lips at that precocious seven-year-old.

I've never spent time around kids. I'm too young for any of my friends to have children, and I basically grew up an only child. Which makes the prospect more frightening than it already is, like charging into the ocean before you know how to swim.

Is she going to be upset her daddy wants to spend time with me, taking time away from her? Will she become resentful if she thinks I'm trying to be a mother figure? A threat? What if she doesn't like me? What if it disrupts the life they've carefully created?

I vaguely remember being young. Some father-daughter outings like miniature golf, A's games, camping a few times. My mother was slowly receding by that point. And eventually, I fended for myself, preparing my own breakfasts and lunches and sometimes dinners, tidying the house, inventing imaginary friends, and attempting to fly above the gloom permeating our unhappy household.

Watching Butch and Emmy together blew my mind. Understanding dawns, and I inhale sharply as if I've poked a deep bruise. *That's what it's supposed to be like.* My tears trickle as I lament how more than anything, I wish my dad loved me the way Butch loves Emmy. Unconditionally and with enough affection to power the entire damn planet. She trusts him completely, respects him, throws herself into his arms without thought. They revolve around each other...a gravitational tether made of pure love.

I swipe at my wet cheeks, well aware I didn't get that type of paternal love and never will. There's no changing the fact, and no point succumbing to self-pity, even if justified.

I'm happy Emmy's living a life where she's cherished.

And I like her already. She was friendly, welcoming, brave. I mean, she sent *me*—a strange woman—home with one of her beloved stuffed toys just to keep me "company." Butch *loved* that. It guaranteed my return, and he likely perceived (correctly) that Emmy melted a chunk of my frozen heart. How could she not? She's like a little ray of sunshine.

But the cold, hard truth remains. *I can't give away something I never received.* It wouldn't be fair to anyone. Butch and Emmy deserve a female presence that complements the love they already share...someone who embodies motherly instincts and intuitive behaviors, not some broken shell who probably needs therapy.

FORTY-FIVE

Butch sends me two dozen roses at work Monday. They're a bright, rich yellow (still his favorite color), long-stemmed, and positively stunning. The card brings a sappy smile to my face and tugs on emotions I'm struggling to deny.

> There's a reason Butch & Sundance are so good together. Give us a chance.
>
> Butch
>
> P.S. Do you know how to swim?

"Oh shiiiiiiiiiiiiiiiiit," I murmur under my breath, channeling Robert Redford from the movie. But seriously, *oh shit*. This scene *does* kind of mirror my current reality. Do I need to jump off a cliff to save myself, even if I don't know how to swim?

Butch must intuit I'm waffling on how to proceed, but he doesn't know why. Not really. My head tells me I have no business screwing up their family dynamic with my ineptitude, inexperience, and lack of maternal DNA. My heart... well, that organ's always beat whatever direction it wants without a shred of sense, and it thumps to life whenever Butch materializes in any form: on the telephone, in bed, or via lovely flowers I can't stop admiring.

On impulse, I make the call. It's only a short wait before Butch's voice reaches through the line, his familiar, deep tonality like a caress.

"It's me."

"Hey, you."

"Thank you for the roses, Butch. They're gorgeous."

"*You're* gorgeous. Did you see the note?"

"Mm-hmm."

"You know how to swim, baby?"

"*I do,*" I whisper.

"Are we going to sink or swim together? Because I'm ready to jump off that cliff with you, Sundance."

He's so fucking sure. It makes all this worse. "I...like hearing that." And I had the same thought less than three minutes ago.

"I'm sensing a 'but'..."

"I have zero privacy here at work. Can we continue this tonight?"

"Yeah."

"Thanks for making my day," I murmur.

"You make mine every day."

"You're going to make this tough, aren't you?"

"Impossible."

We hang up, and my eyes flick from the phone to the roses. *He's fighting for me. For us.*

BUTCH CALLS AFTER PUTTING EMMY TO BED, AND IT dawns on me that's why we always talk after 9 p.m. I'm perched on the couch with a hot cup of tea. There's a knot behind my sternum—and no question I'm dreading this conversation. The likelihood we can swim vs. sink seems unimaginable.

"Do you have a bedtime routine?" I ask. Delay. Delay. Delay.

"I read her a book or two, tuck her in, kiss her goodnight. And I keep her door cracked...we joke it's to let the monsters roam freely instead of camping out under her bed."

A choked chuckle escapes. "My dad read to me when I was little. Unforgettable stories like *Treasure Island*, *Wind in the Willows*, *The Many Adventures of Winnie the Pooh*, and *Charlotte's Web*. It's probably why I'm a reader to this day."

"My mom did too...in our early years, and I remember it fondly. It's damn cool to be the guy reading to my daughter now, a tradition getting passed down the generations, you know?"

The knot tightens, turns heavy, like a boulder pinning my chest. I manage a humming noise.

A thick pause hangs between us. "You liked the roses?"

My gaze fastens to where they sit on the coffee table. "I love them. Staring at them right now."

He makes a satisfied grunt. Then pauses, as if gearing up to ask The Tough Questions. "Put me out of my misery, Jacqui. Tell me what's on your mind. I'm going fucking crazy since you left."

"That's fair." My knuckles rub circles on my upper chest. "Yesterday was...shocking, realizing you had a daughter. It blindsided me. And I admit my initial reaction was terrible. I jumped to conclusions, couldn't handle all the emotions, went into freakout mode. But when you asked me to stay, and explained...shared everything, it helped. I'm sure reliving that was difficult."

Butch acknowledges this with a throaty sound.

"Watching you with Emmy, being there with you both, was good for me."

"Okay," he says, exhaling a sharp breath. "I sense that almighty 'but.'"

My lips don't want to move. "*But*... I don't see how this can work," I admit. "Knowing you're a father and that your life revolves around raising and protecting Emmy, I don't think my presence is in her best interest."

"Why?"

"Because I lacked a mother most of my life. Mine is a drug-addled, absentee figurehead. My father is only slightly better. He provided the essentials but failed at any emotional connection. Jesus, you showed in me in one afternoon how a father should treat his daughter—more in one day than I've experienced in a lifetime. So, it's doubtful I possess any attributes along these lines aside from knowing what *not* to do, which means I have no business being around any kid, especially one who is your whole world. Regardless of how much *we* want to be together, this obviously changes things."

Butch heaves out a breath. "I'm trying to understand your thought process but I'm not buying it. You think any of us have a clue what we're doing before we become parents? There's no manual—it's on-the-job training. And yeah, some are better at it than others. I go day to day just attempting—hoping—not to fuck it up, knowing all the while *I probably am*. And I'm clueless about where nurturing comes from, if it's DNA, innate to your personality, or what you learn watching your own mom and dad. Likely a combination. There's no way of predicting the type of parent you'll be, and you're selling yourself short by speculating and assuming. You could be the best mother on the planet."

"Or the worst."

He scoffs. "You're kind, empathetic, and not afraid to dish things straight. You're way ahead with those skills. But I get it if this is too much for you. You're twenty-four years old and maybe don't want anything to do with a kid at this stage of your life. You're not looking for a package deal. And I'm absolutely a package deal. I have responsibilities, and a young girl to rear by myself."

"That part doesn't scare me." A surprising realization. "Just all the rest. What if Emmy doesn't like me? Resents me? Or gets mad at you for bringing me into your lives? What if I screw it up? What if she thinks I'm a poor substitute for a mother?"

"Pump the brakes for a minute. I'm not asking you to be her mother or parent. Right now, you're just Jacqui, my girlfriend."

My girlfriend. Damn my fool heart for skipping.

"Think of this as an opportunity to get to know each other. If we decide to go the distance, let me assure you that you're going to fuck some part of this up...we all do. Because *we're* screwed up, imperfect humans with shortcomings. At some point, your crap will impact your kid and there's nothing you can do except fail better. It's committing to doing the best you can, like any relationship."

"It still sounds like an experiment...and you know how bad I was at science."

Butch huffs out a laugh. "It *is*, Sundance—one I'm willing to collaborate on with you. All I'm asking for is a chance. Let this ride, see where it takes us. We'll still go slow, but also forward. I understand it's overwhelming, so...baby steps."

"Baby steps," I repeat.

"Is that a yes?"

It can't hurt to try, right? We can break up at any time if it's not working. Except, that's a whole other problem. "I don't want to hurt you or Emmy." Or myself. "And you said yourself that's why you've avoided relationships."

"That's true. But what's happening between us is worth the risk. *You're worth it*, Jacqui. Is it scary? Hell yeah. But I've never felt as fucking alive as I do when I'm with you... so say yes, goddamn it."

This man. My heart thumps wildly as I search one last time for a reason to say no. He's making this easy...and difficult.

"Good," he says, even though I haven't uttered a word.

My husky chuckle causes him to expel what sounds like a relieved breath.

"I'll need guidance. Maybe a little hand holding." My voice is quiet, hesitant.

"It will be my pleasure to hold your hand, and every other part of you, gorgeous."

My chest loosens. I'm still overwhelmed, but there's a lot to be said for Butch's enthusiasm, support, and how much he wants me, us, this.

"Hey," he adds softly. "I didn't ask you about Thanksgiving for obvious reasons and I've felt like a complete asshole about it. Here you are, separated from family and everyone you know, and if it's not too late, I'd love for you to join us. So would my folks."

I'm taken aback. "Your parents know about us?"

"Mm-hmm. They're quite taken with you. My mother hasn't shut up since you were here for lunch. And then you really blew things up by making homemade soup and cookies, which we all loved, by the way. My parents genuinely appreciated the gesture. It ratcheted you up to all-star status."

I let out a surprised snort. "Wait. Back up a minute. Explain that first part about your mom."

"She sensed there's something between us—or could be —and she's been bugging the fuck out of me about it."

My unfiltered laugh rings out. "Wow, seriously?"

He pauses again. "It's been a long time since she's seen me...interested in a woman." He groans like it's painful, but I'm coated in warmth.

"Your situation was probably hard on your mom. She only wishes for your happiness and would have wanted your marriage to be lasting and fulfilling with your family intact. It must have been agonizing for her to see you hurting."

He hums, almost smug. "Damn, Sundance. Sounds a lot like something a mother would say."

I'm dead silent, mulling over my last words.

Because he's right.

Forty-Six

Thanksgiving brings a cavalcade of thoughts and emotions. Normally I'm focused on surviving another *Hall-iday,* but this screams high stakes. Or maybe I'm being overly dramatic.

Wanting to make a good impression—the entire Hamilton family will be there today—I don a shirred ruffle, rust-orange dress that hits mid-calf, and my favorite suede boots. I leave my golden hair long, my makeup tasteful, and damn if I don't look like a walking advertisement for autumn. I gather my purse, coat, and the sweet potato pie I made from scratch. My coworker Val assured me this was an appropriate southern dessert for the occasion.

My mind chants *we're doing this...we can do this* all the way to the car.

As my Toyota warms up, I sift through my tape collection, searching for anything to ease the trepidation shadowing my every move. Oh yes...Van Halen's *1984* will do nicely. The synthesizer intro plays, bringing a pang of melancholy. It's their last album before David Lee Roth quit the band. Granted, he was a total prima donna but replacing him with Sammy Hagar—as much as I love me some Hagar—

ruins a good thing. Another reminder that *nothing stays the same*.

I make my way to the interstate, volume cranked. Roth sings, "Go ahead and jump" and I wonder if Van Halen is imparting wisdom specifically for me. A grin erupts before I belt out the lyrics.

Singing, headbanging, and tapping out guitar riffs on the steering wheel keeps my nerves from taking over for most of the ride. Good call.

After I exit the main highway, the landscape illustrates just how fast indeed everything changes. The grass leans toward gray. Trees are barren, their once vivid leaves browning and seeping into the earth. As sad as this transition to the next season looks, I'm excited for my first winter on the east coast, stoked at the prospect of snow. The only time this California girl previously experienced that phenomenon was if I drove four hours to frolic in it—a rare event.

Entering Hampton Springs proper, I slow my speed and reduce the volume on John Mellencamp's "Scarecrow," but my heart pounds harder and faster with every mile closer to the Hamilton household.

Butch. Emmy. The parents. Other family members. Overwhelm creeps up, but then again, there's safety in numbers. Maybe it will be easier, put me less on the hot seat? *Right*. My hunch is this brood protects their own, which means I'll be scrutinized and interrogated...and I might not measure up.

I steer down the drive, exhale a long breath.

Might as well jump.

Butch jogs out of the house and down the porch steps before I've shut my car door.

He doesn't say a word, just pulls me into his arms and kisses me. My heart lurches at the intensity in it. His lips find my ear, his words raw, honest. "I'm so fucking happy you're here. That you're giving us a chance. Thank you."

I stroke his cheek, grazing the coarse hair from the beard

he's growing, and he sinks into my caress. "Thank you for believing in me."

He closes his eyes a moment, as if savoring my touch.

We part and his brow lifts. "You ready for the circus?"

"As long as there are no clowns. I just can't add the stress of that into my day."

Butch chuckles. "We're all clowns, baby."

I collect the rest of my things, and he offers to carry my pie. He escorts me to the door and as we step inside, I'm assaulted in the best way by Thanksgiving aromas: roasting turkey, cranberry, citrus, cinnamon, and nutmeg. Music plays underneath a chorus of voices coming from different directions.

Thundering footfalls round the corner. Emmy tears through the foyer wearing a cape, as are the little boy and girl on her heels. "Hi, Jacqui!" she squeals as she runs past.

"Hi, Emmy!" I call out.

Butch takes my coat, letting out a slow whistle when he sees my dress. "Hot damn," he murmurs.

He leads me into the kitchen, where his mom envelops me in a hug like we're already the best of friends.

"So pleased you could join us."

"Thank you for having me." I collect my dessert from Butch and hand it to her. "It's sweet potato pie. I, uh, made it." *And hope I didn't butcher it.*

Mrs. Hamilton lets out a happy gasp. "It's official. We're keeping you. That's my *favorite*!" She's effortlessly warm and welcoming, setting me more at ease.

"I hope I did it justice. I'm a little nervous about it."

"I'm sure it's fabulous. We're all pie fiends, but I'm not sharing this with anyone. Except you." She raises her eyebrows and flashes another smile.

An older couple waits expectantly, and Butch guides me there next. "These are my grandparents on my mother's side, Henry and Mabel." They both have those signature green eyes, only paler—clearly a defining feature of this clan.

We shake hands and exchange pleasantries.

Butch leads me into the living room to continue introductions. A fire blazes in a massive brick fireplace under an elaborate wood mantle. Hemi stretches five feet long on the rug before it, barely sparing me a sleepy glance. I greet Gus and meet his mother Dot, then Butch's sister Liz and her husband Dan. The next time their kids run through (the pair chasing after Emmy), Liz threatens them with no dessert if they don't stop "the ruckus." Her tone brooks no argument, stopping them in their tracks.

A breathless Emmy swivels toward me and scans me from top to bottom. "Your dress is pretty. I want one."

"Emmaline Rose Hamilton, you *hate* dresses," Butch says.

"Nuh uh. Not if they look like that."

A furrow forms between Butch's eyebrows as he scrutinizes his daughter. After she runs off, his perplexed gaze finds mine. "I think you have a fan."

A smile inches up my lips. I know what I'm buying one little girl for Christmas.

Liz snags my hand. "I'm stealing her. Don't try and stop me," she tells her brother as she tugs me down the hall.

"She just got here!" I'm nearly out of the room when he yells, "You don't have to answer any of her nosy questions!"

Liz shuts the door on a study lined with brimming bookshelves, abundant light casting a glow upon the titles. A cushioned reading nook nestles in a bay window—a refuge if I need it. I can't help scanning the spines...until Liz pulls me from my happy gaping.

"Not to freak you out, but I wanted some girl time," she says with a sly smile. "Big brother *never* brings anyone home, which means you're special."

"Oh...I don't know about that."

"I do." Her grin grows wider. Liz isn't lumberjack sized like Butch but stands about my height. Her long brunette hair blazes with auburn hues, and her blue eyes sparkle gleefully. "Tell me about you."

Where to start? "I'm from California. I moved here in April to work for a magazine in Richmond. You probably heard I wrote the article about your family's business?"

She dips her chin. "Pop was happy. That's saying something. You live in the city then?"

"Crammed into a studio apartment that's all mine. It's convenient for work but also cool being near all the metro stuff." I leave off *and lonely*.

She makes a face. "Oof. That's a drag of a drive for you and Butch to spend time together."

"A bit," I agree. "But it's forced us to take things slow, which we both need."

"Mm-hmm. Guess if there's a silver lining, it gives you the chance to get to know one another. Become friends?"

"Exactly."

"But y'all like each other, don't you? I mean, *a lot*."

My expression, even without verbal corroboration, clearly pleases her. "Are you here to warn me off or threaten me if I hurt him?"

She barks a laugh. "Butchie can take care of himself. Although..." She turns thoughtful. "He's been hurt, and by hurt, I'm talking almost mortally wounded, by what happened with Emmy's..." She falters. "I can't even say the word. Let's just call her the...incubator. I would do anything and everything in my power to stop that from happening again."

I nod, my affection for her growing. It also makes me wonder how the family's coping with Butch's ex-wife trying to insert herself back into Emmy's life. "You're a good sister."

"And you're making my brother happy for the first time in years."

Our eyes meet, hers reflecting nothing but sincerity.

"He's doing the same for me."

AS THE DAY UNFOLDS, THE HAMILTON FAMILY dynamic sets me further at ease. They get along, tease each other, help when needed. Butch wrestles with the kids, throwing them around like they're weightless. The younger generation frolics...like they should. No one drinks too much or zones out in a haze of narcotics. No one yells. No one gets angry or upset. No one's ignored.

Delicious food flows, from the appetizers to the big meal to the array of desserts, giving me my fill and then some. I've never eaten homemade stuffing the likes of Jerri's and the cranberry sauce isn't from a can but made with tart berries sweetened by sugar. Every dish—the mashed potatoes, sides, salads, and pies—were crafted from scratch. The time and energy infused into making this beautiful spread fills me with a foreign emotion. It's so personal, generous, meaningful...as if love is the main ingredient in feeding us all.

Butch is attentive, but not overly demonstrative. When his hand finds mine under the table, he lightly strokes my skin, and even that simple touch electrifies.

As we're nearing the end of a collective cleanup effort, Butch's lips graze my ear. "Want to go for a walk?"

My body protests from overeating. "Mm-hmm, but you might have to roll me."

He snickers, and I return the dish towel to its hook.

"We're sneaking out of here. *I want you all to myself*," he whispers.

Liz gives us a covert thumbs-up. I glance at Butch, who mouths "thank you," to her. *Ah.*

We steal to the foyer, and he helps me into my coat, buttoning it up as his gaze burns into mine. Just like that, I'm floating, my stomach flipping, heart pattering. He throws on his own jacket, and we quietly escape out the front door.

Butch leads me to a well-worn path, and we're soon enveloped in nature. Tall pines stretch to the sky, and the undergrowth is a combination of dropped cones and needles along with patches of luminous moss. Our breath plumes in the brisk air as waning sunlight filters through the trees.

"It's so beautiful here." I stoop to admire a cluster of tiny, star-shaped ferns.

"It's a kid's paradise—and not too shabby for the grown-ups, either."

Indeed. But I wonder... "Have you ever wanted to leave?"

"Once upon a time," he admits, as we continue walking. "But life took such a U-turn with Emmy, and having the family's support helped. I'm sure I could've managed without it, but it would have been a bitch. Now I don't want to take her away from the people she loves and who love her."

"Your parents would take it hard." I've witnessed how they've doted on her today.

"You ain't kidding."

We round a bend, and I gasp in delight as we come to a short, arched bridge over a stream. I hurry toward it, stopping dead center on the wood-slatted span, taking in the tall trees and babbling brook, captivated by this wondrous place.

Butch cages me against the railing and holds my gaze. "I stopped thinking about myself, my wants and needs...until you."

I stare into those serious, beautiful green eyes. *The forest's got nothing on them.*

His lips caress mine softly, gently, and I close my eyes, sinking into his touch and savoring it. His grip tightens as he deepens the kiss, staking his claim and making me forget my own name.

"I want you," he breathes.

I whimper. "I want you."

"C'mon," he says, taking my hand and urging me down the path. Our pace turns brisk. Soon we arrive at Butch's cabin, cheeks flushed from the cool air.

He locks the door once we're inside and wastes no time pushing me against it. His kiss is searing. Our tongues twine, hungry and desperate. Heat shoots through me like lightning, dampening my panties in seconds. We strip off our coats, and I moan when we finally grind together and his erection presses into me. It's been weeks since we had sex, and we're ravenous. Our hands roam as greedily as our tongues tangle, and every inch of me trembles with yearning.

He drops to his knees. "This dress," he says, clutching the hem. "I've been waiting all day to get my head underneath it and taste you."

I'm panting as I watch his eyes darken...and his head disappears beneath the fabric. Butch whips my panties to the side and slides in his tongue without pretense, dragging it through my center. His groan rumbles through me as my own rips from my throat.

He laps up the proof of my desire, spearing me, suckling me. His obscene noises of gratification reach my ears. He pins my dress and me in place with a sure grip, his other hand holding my useless underwear out of his way. My shoulders anchor against the door, my legs widening of their own volition as I take the pleasure he doles out. He's relentless, and my repeated whimpers confirm I'm a willing victim.

I rub an aching breast with one hand and sink the other into Butch's thick hair, using it for leverage as my pelvis thrusts toward his talented mouth.

He pauses, handing me the hem of my dress. Repositioning his hands, he spreads me wider where he feasts. His beard abrades my inner thighs, scraping my skin then obliterating the discomfort with his lavish attention on my pulsing clitoris.

It's...*ohhhhhhhh.*

My core begins a familiar dance. Coiling, tightening, tensing.

Shockingly, I'm about to orgasm. Standing up...fully clothed...at his mercy.

My breath halts, and a minute later, I combust, the edges of my vision tunneling, darkening, stars exploding behind my eyelids. My unbridled wail echoes in the space against Butch's long guttural groan. I can't think or speak or apparently, hold myself upright because when my legs buckle, Butch pins me in place and continues consuming what's his.

Only when my shudders abate does he stand. "Bed. Now," he commands.

With an unfocused gaze, I attempt to walk, quickly forced to stop and get my bearings.

He assesses me and without a word, dips and throws me over his shoulder in a fireman's carry. Then my giant lumberjack takes the stairs by twos.

Butch sets me down, and my eyes snap to the raging hard-on straining through his jeans. My energy jolts back to life. I long for him—*need him*—in my mouth.

"Clothes off, Sundance, before I fuck you with them on. I'd hate to ruin this pretty dress."

I'm quick to obey, and we grin at each other while disrobing with impressive speed.

I sit on the bed, eying the swollen erection grazing his abdomen. "I want to blow you." I barely recognize my own voice, or the desperation in it.

"Jacqui..."

"*Please.*"

He doesn't hesitate again, giving me what I want. My lips wrap around his length with gusto and we both groan as I take him deeper. I love his size, his masculinity, his taste. I've never wanted anything so much. My enthusiasm, the sounds I'm making...they're almost embarrassing.

Too soon, he separates us, muttering about his lack of

control and *that fucking mouth*. I swipe the saliva from my face and let him push me flat against the mattress.

His eyes are pure green fire as he sinks into me, feeding me his cock inch by gigantic inch.

"Butch, Butch, Butch..." I pant. Then he fills me completely and all words evaporate.

His eyes close and his neck muscles pulse as he collects himself. Except there's no such thing as restraint in this universe where we're coupled together.

"Holy fuck," he murmurs.

Our eyes meet, his burning into mine. I wrap my legs around him, stroking the curves of his honed build as our eyes stay locked.

He pulls out. Thrusts deeply. Then he stills once more. "I'm never surviving this," he mutters, and a soft chuckle leaves my throat.

He thrusts again and all laughter leaves.

He thrusts again and my brain silences.

He drives all the way in, and then it's just us, joined at our centers, our gazes, our hearts.

Butch moves with raw, magnetizing strength, his muscles flexing, undulating under my fingers. With each piston of his hips, he steals my breath.

My legs widen, beckoning him closer.

Fill me, obliterate me, own me.

Our bodies create new music, writing a melody never heard before and finding a rhythm that eclipses everything... my pain, my heart, maybe my soul.

Something shifts.

It's then I realize: We're not fucking.

We're making love.

FORTY-SEVEN

Butch and I revel in the aftermath. The air is heavy with unsaid words.

"Sundance?" he whispers.

"Hmm?"

"Say you're mine."

A languid smile unfurls. "I'm yours."

"Glad that's settled."

I chuckle and grip him tighter.

He groans near my ear. "I don't want to leave...but we should probably get back."

"M'kay."

He pushes up with those strong arms, and our sweaty bodies stick to each other like they aren't ready to part either. The affection in his eyes strikes my chest like a meteor, setting off a blinding happiness that threatens to crater my soul and light the world.

His lips find mine, ardent but controlled, before he slowly pulls out of me. As he fetches a towel from the bathroom, I admire his glorious backside—everything from his broad back to how it tapers into a toned ass, leading to those burly legs.

We clean up and get dressed, camouflaging our clandestine tryst, then walk the path, hands clasped, back to his parents' house.

THE SKIES DARKEN, SIGNALING I SHOULD HEAD back to Richmond. I have to work tomorrow and still need to call my parents. Although Jerri offered to let me use her phone, I declined. It's long-distance, plus I didn't want to risk upsetting myself. Talking to my mom and dad is always a crap shoot.

Butch's grandparents have already departed, and Liz and Dan are corralling their kids to leave too. I'm standing with Butch and his parents in the kitchen, and Jerri's attempting to send me home with leftovers.

"That's nice of you to offer, but—"

"Better just do what she wants," Butch interrupts. "Don't want to get on her bad side."

His mother shoots me a pointed look, her brows raised in challenge, as if her son knows what he's talking about.

I accept her offering with a grateful smile. "Today has been wonderful. Thank you, really, for the best Thanksgiving I've ever had."

Surprise crosses Jerri's face. "It was our pleasure, Jacqui. And if you're free next Saturday, we'd love you to join us for cookie day. We get all the ladies together and bake and decorate an unholy amount of Christmas cookies. Some we give to the shut-ins nearby, folks who are elderly or sick and can't get out much. It's a Hamilton tradition."

I don't sense this is lip service from his mother. She wants me around. And something about this annual cookie-a-thon also hits me hard—but what, I'm not sure. "That sounds wonderful."

Emmy careens into the kitchen, her socks sliding on the hardwoods. "Are you leaving?" she asks, a touch breathless.

"Yeah, honey," Butch answers. "Jacqui has a long drive."

Emmy's brow furrows. "Why don't you just spend the night? We can have a slumber party!"

Butch chokes and I smile gently, squatting down to her level. "Wish I could. Rain check?"

She tilts her head. "It's not raining."

The adults chuckle and I grin. "It's just an expression. It means can we do it another time?"

She smiles, nodding enthusiastically.

"Looks like I'm coming back for cookie day," I add.

"Good. We can have our slumber party then. Don't forget Lucky," she says.

Oh boy. Did I just stick my foot into a puddle of rubber cement? Butch might have to smooth this over. "Will do. See you later, Emmy."

"Bye!" She runs off again.

"Can I bring anything Saturday?" I ask Jerri.

"Not unless you have a recipe you enjoy making this time of year. Otherwise, we've got everything covered."

Before I can say another word, she offers up a warm hug, followed by Gus. I'm so unaccustomed to free-flowing familial affection, it startles and soothes me simultaneously.

Butch holds my care package in one hand, and his other finds the small of my back. "I'll walk you out."

We intersect his sister and her family on the way and say our goodbyes.

"Heard you're joining us for cookie day and *having a sleepover*," Liz says, eyebrows raised and expression full of mischief.

News travels fast. "I am. See you then?"

"I'll be here, sis."

I laugh. "Troublemaker."

She winks and I experience a tug of longing to become friends.

Butch escorts me to my car, waiting while I stow the leftovers I'm seriously stoked to have. "Are you good with all that? Coming back for cookies and...a slumber party?" The look on his face is so genuinely hopeful, it pulls at my heart like he's lassoed it.

"I am if you are. What about Emmy? I know you're easing her into us."

"She seems immune to my easing. She's taken to bulldozing. As long as she's comfortable—and clearly that little firecracker is taking the lead—I'm fine. But make no mistake," he says, pressing me against the car. "You're sleeping in my bed."

"Is that a threat, Mr. Domineering?"

"It's a promise, sweetheart." He lets one of his charming, wicked smiles loose and my insides liquify.

"Savage," I tease.

"You have no idea. You've awakened a monster."

"Mmm," I muse. "Yes, please."

He chuckles low. "Look at you, baiting the monster."

"I know what he likes to eat," I taunt, recalling just how voraciously he ate a few hours ago...right up against his front door. *Whew.*

"Baby, my appetite for you only grows."

My breath hitches. "Same here. Now stop looking at me like that or I'll never leave."

A lascivious smile draws my attention to his lips. "Tempting."

We eye each other a moment longer, staring like a couple of lovesick idiots. He grasps the back of my head and guides me to his waiting mouth. He kisses me earnestly, melting me from head to toe.

"Call me when you get home so I know you're safe." More pitter patters.

"I will. And Butch?" The emotions of the day almost overpower me as I collect my thoughts. "Thank you for inviting me today. It meant a lot to be here. I'm sorry I fought you on it."

He shakes his head decisively. "No apologies, Sundance."

He pulls me back into his grasp. "You came, and I couldn't have asked for a more perfect day. All my favorite people in one place. It was my best Thanksgiving too."

My eyes glisten and I nestle into his chest a little deeper. Hearing his heartbeat thud so reassuringly under his clothes, it's as if it's talking to mine. Two hearts, reaching toward the other, finally free to seek love again.

No lasso necessary.

FORTY-EIGHT

I return to the Hamilton household on the morning of cookie day. It's strange coming straight to his parents' house, but I'll see Butch later, after he returns from a client meeting with his father.

All females from Thanksgiving are present, plus two cousins close to Liz's age—Shelly and Barbara.

Jerri wasn't kidding about the production aspect. Long folding tables are set up for decorating, one holding tubs layered with the hundreds of sugar cookies and gingerbread men baked yesterday. Jerri names the new varieties underway: cherry pecan balls, thumbprint cookies, molasses crinkles, peanut butter kisses, and Grandma Gray's melt-in-your-mouths.

Christmas music from the radio plays softly in the background as we chat, bake, snack, and decorate.

Once I've helped Jerri make several batches, I'm steered to a table brimming with royal icing colors, assorted sprinkles, edible silver balls, and small candies. The two grandmothers, Dot and Mabel, are old pros and deftly school me on technique.

I've never decorated a cookie in my life, but I get the hang of it quickly and enjoy the deliberation and experimentation. After the first half-dozen, mine even start to look pretty.

Funny stories are swapped, good-natured teasing abounds, and more cookies get produced than in a commercial bakery. I'm not sure what to label the sensation blanketing me...it's like being transported into a heartwarming holiday movie.

Emmy races in—this girl favors running as her main mode of transportation—plops into the chair next to me and is about to grab a blank when Liz reminds her to wash her hands. Emmy drags her feet to the sink, but she cleans up without complaint.

"Need any help?" I ask when she returns. As if. Jerri said this was tradition; the kid's probably been at it for years.

She shakes her head. "I'm literally going to make a whole gingerbread family."

I give her an encouraging smile, inwardly cracking up over her constant use of *literally*. "That sounds fun."

Emmy lines up two large gingerbread bodies next to a couple of smaller ones. Wasting no time, she dives in with different colors, obliterating each with candy. It's an utter mess when she finishes—a big, beautiful mess. Her expression lights up as she shows everyone her masterpieces.

Later that afternoon, Butch strides in and the sight of him makes my stomach dip. The energy between us crackles... everything supercharged since Thanksgiving. He's greeted warmly by the crew, and when Jerri slips her arm around his waist, he stares down at her affectionately and squeezes her closer.

"Smells terrific in here. I think I just gained five pounds. And by the amount of frosting on Emmy's face, she ate more than she decorated."

I'm midway through adorning another sugar cookie when he heads my way.

"Hey, gorgeous." He gives me a tender kiss on the top of my head before he slides into the chair his daughter recently vacated. His smile reaches those pretty eyes, and all I can think is, *mine.*

"Hey, Lumberjack."

"*What* did she call you?" Liz asks. Butch ignores her, casting me a withering stare.

"Lumberjack," I supply, unable to suppress my grin.

Liz guffaws. "*Priceless.*"

Butch glares at her. "You will refrain from ever repeating it, dear sister."

"Good luck with that, Paul Bunyan!" she teases.

"I'd like to find me a big, strong lumberjack," Shelly says.

"Me too, sweetie," Grandma Mabel adds.

"Jesus Christ," Butch mutters. "I've got to get out this sorority. When are you coming over?"

I stop icing and bite back a laugh. "We're wrapping up, so soon."

He presses a kiss to my lips...in front of everyone. And believe me, this crowd's watching—albeit discreetly. "Hurry," he whispers.

"'Bye lumberjack,' on three," Liz rallies. "One, two, three."

Butch bolts for the foyer.

"BYE, LUMBERJACK!" we chant in chorus, chasing him out the door before we burst into fits of laughter.

AFTER TUCKING EMMY IN FOR THE NIGHT, BUTCH joins me downstairs. She let go of the "It's a slumber party, so Jacqui needs to sleep with me" pleas once her father explained that grown-ups stay up longer and will be sharing a bed when it's our bedtime. She clutched Lucky as a consolation as I read her a story (another plea). I wasn't denying her that too—but was I ever unprepared for how such a small act would choke me up. Maybe it's the memories of my own dad reading to me, or how important books and writing are to me now, or simply that it's the first time I've read a storybook to a child.

Butch stokes the fire to roaring and joins me on the sofa. I place my mug of hot tea on the coffee table and curl up next to him.

"I could get used to this," he says quietly. He presses a kiss to my temple, and I sigh into it.

"You have no idea how easily *I* could get used to this." With each hour logged with Butch, Emmy, and his family, I swear my heart recalibrates—almost tangibly—as if it's patching up all the holes. It's wonderful...and terrifying.

I tilt my head to look at him, and he tucks me closer into his side, cupping my jaw. When our mouths merge, it's soft with an undercurrent of heat.

We part, and his expression turns roguish. "Ready to watch the movie?"

My eyes narrow, mining for clues. "Which one?"

"Something tells me you're going like what I rented." He picks up the remote, clicks a button, and the VHS plays.

The 20th Century Fox logo appears with its signature searchlights and drumbeats. It fades to black before an old timey movie screen pops up. As the sepia film rolls, so do spots, scratches, and flecks as if it's aged celluloid. I squeal as soon as I see "The Hole in the Wall Gang," then clamp my palms over my mouth, remembering that Emmy's sleeping.

It's *Butch Cassidy and the Sundance Kid*.

Some couples have songs, but us? We have a movie. *This one.* Butch's answering grin only makes me happier. Pulling his face toward mine, I press my lips against his cheek. "You're the best."

The title sequence begins, and I settle in next to my man to rewatch this gem. Across the two hours, we hold hands, steal kisses, and laugh. Once it ends, we creep up to his bedroom, settling into his huge bed like we've done it a thousand times. We're both zonked, content in each other's arms.

"G'night, Sundance."

"G'night, Butch."

We share one last kiss in the dark, and my eyes close.

I could get used to this, I think again, drifting into sleep.

FORTY-NINE

Butch calls me at work the first Wednesday of December, and his strained greeting sets off my internal alarms. Before I can ask what's wrong, he blurts it out.

"The custody hearing's been scheduled. The fifth of January at 10 a.m."

He hasn't spoken much about this looming court battle, and I've been reticent to bring it up. From the tidbits he's shared, it sounds as if he's done all he can and given his attorney everything she asked for, including details, dates, and names for affidavits. As a man of action, he's not treating it lightly, but he also doesn't dwell on it.

I grapple with what to say. "Finally."

"Yeah. I'm ready to put this behind me," he says tersely. "It's dragged on long enough."

"Do you want me to come with you? Or if you need me to watch Emmy, I can do that too." It's a leap, but I'll support him anyway I can.

"Let's talk about that later, once we figure it all out, okay?"

"Of course. Is there anything I can do for you right now?"

My heart aches, knowing how scary this is for Butch and what it means for not only him, but his entire family.

"Just...don't bail on me. I'm worried this will scare you away," he admits, his vulnerability laid bare.

"Baby...no. It won't." What kind of callous human would I be to leave him high and dry? Especially when more and more, I believe we have the potential to go the distance.

"It's a lot."

"I'm here for you." *I think I'm in love with you.*

He lets loose an audible breath. "Okay."

"Can I..." *Just say it.* "Ask you more about this tonight, when we both have privacy?"

"Sure." He sounds so stressed, I second guess myself.

BUTCH CALLS AFTER EMMY'S ASLEEP. "HEY, BABY."

"Hi." I sit up straighter on the couch and mute the television. "How are you holding up?"

"I'm a fucking wreck."

The center of my chest twinges and tightens. "I know this is awful."

"It's all the unknowns." He exhales a strong breath. "Will the judge think it's in Emmy's best interest for her to stay in only my care? If he awards joint custody, what will that do to Emmy? How can I protect her? How can I trust Darlene ever again?"

"What does Emmy know about her mom?"

"She thinks her mother left because of what I described as 'the troubles in her mind.' I've made sure to emphasize it wasn't Emmy's fault."

"You thought Darlene was mentally ill?"

"I don't know if, technically, that was accurate, but it's my perception and perspective. I mean, it's not natural to up and leave your child. Maybe she does, or did, have mental health problems."

"Was she depressed?"

"Not that I was aware of, but she struggled after Emmy was born. Never really regained her typical disposition."

I sink further into the sofa cushions, trying to make sense of it. "Do you think she had postpartum depression? I don't know much about that other than it's real for some mothers and sounds scary. I've heard stories where their anxiety or despair makes them a danger to their child."

"Thankfully, it was nothing like that. Darlene just wanted to get out of our small town and live a different life. At least, that's what she told me." A weariness coats his words.

It's hard to fathom. "Do you think Emmy would want to know her mom?"

"It's not her mother," he snaps. "*Shit*. I'm sorry."

I pause, giving him space to explain.

"That's the rub, isn't it? I have no idea. Maybe it would be good for my daughter to know her... Darlene. A bond could probably still form. But goddamn it, how do I trust her ever again? What if she hurts Em?"

It's agonizing, all of it. "I don't know," I whisper, hoping the justice system makes the right choice.

FIFTY

Christmas nears, and with the office closing for two days, I'm scoring a four-day weekend. I'm not crazy (or rich) enough to fly home, and I've already told my parents I'm staying put. They understood, and as expected, didn't fight me on it or offer to buy my plane ticket. *Shocker.*

It seems a bit much to believe the Hamiltons will adopt me for such a significant holiday. Although they've been nothing short of welcoming, I'd never presume an invitation, nor does the idea make me super comfortable. It's their family time.

As if he knows, Butch broaches the subject on the phone.

"You could drive down Christmas Eve and stay through the whole weekend." When I pause, he barrels forward. "If you want. Because I want it. Emmy will too. In fact, pretty sure everyone here is a big fucking yes."

God, this man. No hesitation at all. Just open arms. He was the one who said we'd take it slow, yet he's done nothing but mash the gas and redline the RPMs. He makes it easy to take the ride even though a part of me wonders if we'll crash.

Emmy's voice chirps in the background, and Butch tells her he's speaking with me. After a bit of scuffling, she commandeers the phone.

"Hi, Jacqui."

"Hi, Emmy."

"Are you coming for Christmas?"

Oh lord. "I'm thinking about it. Your daddy just invited me."

"I think you better. He gets darn tootin' grumpy when you're not around."

"Emmy!" Butch scolds.

I can't help but laugh. "Is that right? Are you sure I'm the reason?"

"Uh huh. He's been mister cranky pants ever since you left."

This girl and her vocabulary. "I'll bet you're excited for Christmas. What do you want Santa to bring you this year?"

"Presents. Lots and lots of presents."

"You want to be surprised then? I like it."

"Give me the phone, you spoiled brat," Butch says in the background, doing something that makes her shriek then giggle. After a beat, he's back.

"Your daughter's a trip."

He sighs long and hard. "Affirmative. And I have not been grumpy. Much."

I chuckle. "I miss you already too."

"Good. That means you'll come back. Now, don't you want to know what *I* want for Christmas?"

"I'm pretty sure I've got Daddy Lumberjack's wish list covered."

He barks out a laugh. "Here I thought lumberjack was bad. You're absolutely not allowed to say that in front of Liz —or anyone. Even my grams made a lewd comment."

"Are you forbidding me...*daddy*?"

He groans. "Christ, woman. You're killing me."

My grin widens, then fades. I've been on the fence about asking Butch to accompany me to our office party, only because I don't want to go...which is one hundred percent due to my skeevy boss. Mr. Possessive Gorgeous Hulk by my side would equal a giant, intimidating, human security blanket.

"I know it's super late notice, but the magazine's throwing a holiday staff party next Friday. Any chance you could be my date?"

He pauses, then hisses under his breath. "Shoot. Wish I could, but Emmy's got a dance recital that evening. We meant to invite you, but it obviously slipped through the cracks."

Damn. "I'd much rather join you than attend this company affair, but it seems like bad form to skip it."

"I'm sorry, baby. Really. How about I try coming up that weekend? We can walk downtown and check out the department store windows, see the lights, have dinner."

"I'd like that."

"And you'll think about Christmas? I'm dead serious about you staying all four days."

His words burrow into the intended spot. "Mm-hmm." It sounds perfect, honestly. Not like I want to sit home alone, crying into my pillow. "Thank you. It means a lot, Butch."

He makes a little scoff. "Baby, you're all I need for Christmas."

Swoon. "Feet-sweeper-offer."

"Who's your daddy?" he says, lowering his already sexy timbre, and we both burst out laughing.

∼

THE OFFICE CLOSES PROMPTLY AT FIVE ON FRIDAY, with the holiday party immediately following at a restaurant two blocks away. Most people dressed up for work, but some scramble to change before heading over. I'm still wearing my day-to-night outfit: a scoop-neck crimson sweater with a black skirt and matching heels. Val and I touch up our hair and makeup in the restroom, then walk over together, keeping a brisk pace despite our coats barricading us against the frigid air.

Welcome heat blasts us upon entering the establishment. We navigate through the crowded bar to the reserved back room, where *Virginia Now* employees mingle. An open bar beckons, alongside tables brimming with appetizers and desserts.

"Alcohol first," Val says.

"Definitely," I agree.

We wait in a short line, then score our drinks. The first sip of my gin and tonic slides down easily, hitting the spot and serving as a primer to get through this party.

Val and I join a group of coworkers, where a discussion about a new Oliver Stone movie is underway. I half-listen. A Vietnam War setting. *Platoon*. Starring Charlie Sheen, the memorable degenerate in *Ferris Bueller's Day Off*. Based on Stone's personal experiences. Academy Award buzz. Maybe Butch and I will see it at the theater.

The room grows louder as staff filters in. A band threatens to douse conversation with its cringey covers. Currently: *Beat It*. I give them twenty minutes until they trot out *Y.M.C.A.*

I slip away to fill a small plate with nibbles, then stand in line for another drink. After a wait lengthy enough to polish off my food, I get my second cocktail in hand. As I crane my neck searching for Val or anyone recognizable, Don sidles up alongside me.

My whole body stiffens. I'm trapped.

He leans in close. "You look ravishing, Jacqueline."

Gross. It takes effort to force my lips into a weak smile.

"Hav…a…time?" he asks.

I don't catch what he said over the music, and he repeats it next to my ear.

I flinch, my body jolting away from his hot breath. I school my features, lift my drink, and lie. *Yes, having a great time, boss.*

He grins, those hazel eyes twinkling, then leans in again. "I thought … see … before…" I'm only catching about half of what he says.

Pulling back, I shrug, pantomiming that it's impossible to hear him above the noise. The band launches into *Macho Man*. Still the Village People, and ten bucks says *Y.M.C.A.* is on the finale playlist when people are drunk enough for dance moves.

Don presses in so close to my ear that he touches the shell. This time, his voice rings loudly. *"Follow me."*

Fuck. Fuck. Fuck.

My blood chills in this now-humid room crammed with bodies as we navigate through the throng. The lyrics to the song they're butchering only makes it worse.

Body…wanna touch my body

My boss gazes back, ensuring I'm following along like a dutiful puppy. Everything in my head screams *RUN*, but at what cost? How should I handle this? What are his intentions?

Every man wants to be a macho man

He exits the banquet room into the expansive bar, leading me to the darkest corner.

"This is better," he says with a smile, then holds out his glass. "Cheers."

"Cheers," I reply, politely tapping my drink with his as he clearly expects.

His eyes pin mine, his expression turning wolfish. "I thought I'd hear from you by now."

I raise my brows.

"About the mentorship offer." He winks.

Those fucking winks.

He moves closer, and one of his arms snakes around my waist to pull my head near his mouth. "I'm a powerful ally, Jacqueline. And powerful...in other ways as well. I believe you'd find it a very satisfying experience."

My heart races, fear and disgust rioting behind my sternum. I balk, but his vise grip holds me hostage.

"You scratch my back, and I'll scratch yours, if you catch my drift." His breath reeks of alcohol. "For now, how about a friendly holiday kiss?"

I recoil as his lips graze my cheek.

He chuckles, releasing me. "Playing hard to get? You have no idea how much I love that game. And how patient a man I am."

He eyes me hungrily, and it reminds me of a hyena circling a fresh kill on one of those old episodes of *Mutual of Omaha's Wild Kingdom*. I shrink, wondering how I can continue working at *Virginia Now* if this is my future. If there's going to come a day when he takes instead of asks. Or fires me without cause other than his warped expectations that I acquiesce to his request—demand—for sexual favors.

His raises his glass. "Relax. It's just a bit of fun." His lascivious grin creases the corner of his mouth.

For whom? My stomach roils.

"Now, if you'll excuse me, I need to get back to the party, make the rounds. Merry Christmas." He winks, his palm grazing my ass with the barest of touches through my skirt.

He doesn't wait for a response before striding off, leaving me with my pulse pounding in my ears. I slam my drink on the table with such force the liquid sloshes out, splashing my hand. Without a word to anyone, I bolt outside and back to my car.

My thoughts spin. What are my rights? How has Don

incriminated himself? Should I be logging all of his comments somewhere? Can I report him? How...when he's the publisher where the buck fucking stops? Or damn close. There is a parent company but would they even believe me if it's my word against his? *Fuck.* How can I deal with this? Protect myself? Will I have to quit my job?

By the time I make it to my Toyota, my breathing's so ragged, I strain for air. My keys clang to the pavement. My heart races as I scan the area, my nerves threatening to snap out of my skin.

Get in the car. Get in the car. Get in the car.

I finally slide into the driver's seat, lock the door, and speed off. I clutch the steering wheel so hard my knuckles whiten. Adrenaline tears through my body, undiluted rage throbbing within. I can't afford *not* to figure this out. Don made it perfectly clear he's looking forward to the chase and has every intention of reigning victorious. He's sat on his throne, unchecked, for a decade. How many victims have bowed to his harassment? How many were unceremoniously canned for resisting? How many have cried themselves to sleep feeling cornered, helpless, and alone?

I make it to my building's garage. Pulling my purse to my chest, I make a mad dash for the elevator, relieved when it's empty and hauling me to my floor. With trembling hands, I open my apartment door and quickly lock it behind me. My forehead slumps against it as I steady my breathing.

There's only one person I long for right now. *Butch.* I desperately want to tell him about my slimy boss, ask his advice, see if I'm crazy...

But I can't. His father has a longstanding relationship with Don, and Butch would probably want to kill the motherfucker for doing this to me. No matter how I dissect it, there are consequences at stake, so I can't—won't—involve the Hamiltons.

Not telling Butch seems wrong—like a lie—but I don't see an alternative. I sink into my couch, cloaked in the familiar loneliness I've fought against my entire life. Regardless of how hard I fight, it finds me again and again, returning like a boomerang.

I'm in this by myself. I have no one else to turn to.

FIFTY-ONE

The office closes early Christmas Eve, which allows me to drive to Butch's in daylight. My car's packed with presents and enough clothing to hang out until Sunday—if I choose. An undercurrent of excitement hums under my skin. It's my first Christmas truly on my own, and I have zero desire to reminisce or dwell on the past. Instead, I'm warmed by the idea of spending it here in Virginia with this close-knit family who've already endeared themselves to me.

I'm not even parked when Mr. Hot Lumberjack emerges from the cabin with a huge grin lighting up his rugged good looks.

He pulls me into his arms and off the driveway, searing me with a kiss before uttering one word.

Butch draws back. "Hi."

Falling into his emerald gaze, I flash him a smile. "Hi."

"You're a sight for sore eyes," he says, easing me to the ground.

"You too."

"Merry Christmas Eve, gorgeous."

I'm about to answer when Emmy and Hemi scramble out

the front door. Emmy throws her arms around my legs in greeting. It's the first time she's done this, and the affection thaws any reservations I have about being here.

I give her a squeeze, and when the dog nudges me on the other side, my fingers slide into Hemi's golden fur then rumple his ears.

"It's Christmas! It's Christmas!" Emmy squeals. Grabbing my hand, she tugs me impatiently toward the house. "Come see our tree!"

Her enthusiasm is infectious. I shoot Butch a backward glance, all smiles, and he's already beaming.

Emmy tows me up the steps and into the house, making me jog to keep up. But *oh my*. The evergreen standing in the living room brims with ornaments and big colored lights and nearly touches the ceiling.

"It's beautiful, Em."

She keeps tugging until we're inches from the tree, then highlights some of the decorations. "I made this one. And this one. And this one..." Several branches display her crafty, glittery, bedazzled handiwork.

"You're very creative," I say.

She smiles proudly, then points to one that looks decidedly...awkward. "Daddy did this one. He's not artistic."

I chuckle.

"I heard that," Butch says, playfully indignant.

"We saved some for you to hang," Emmy continues, lacing her tiny fingers with mine again as she leads me to a stash on the bookshelves. My nose stings from this unexpected gesture. When I steal a glance at Butch, his eyes shine with tenderness.

"That is so thoughtful." I crouch lower. "Can I give you a thank-you hug?"

She nods, and I squeeze her, blinking away happy tears.

"Wanna put 'em on?"

"Emmy, let her get settled. She just got here," Butch says.

I respectfully shake him off. "It's okay, I'd love to."

They saved me a popsicle-stick reindeer, a fancy crimson ball with white painted swirls, a glass pinecone dusted with snow, and a wooden sleigh glued with sequins and my name spelled in purple glitter. The "u" and "i" are squished on one end, where she started to run out of room, but it only makes it more endearing. I whisper to Emmy how special it is, trying not to lose my cool.

Carefully hanging each, I realize I've found a spot of my own, one where I might just belong.

WE SPEND THE EVENING AT BUTCH'S PARENTS' along with Liz and her family. Once again, the kids race tirelessly through the house, Hemi flops before the fire blazing in the hearth, conversation and teasing among the adults abounds, and there's food, drink, and love aplenty.

During dinner, I learn about their Christmas Eve traditions. The children receive holiday-themed pajamas and will leave out milk and cookies for Santa, time-honored books are read aloud, and one lucky individual will get the privilege of putting baby Jesus into the Nativity manger. It's obvious the latter is an area of contention, with everyone vying to be picked.

"Me, me, me!" Kayla demands. "I want the baby Jesus!"

Liz and Dan lock eyes, sharing an exhausted-parent moment.

"You literally did it last year," Emmy says. "I haven't had a turn in forever."

Butch scoffs. "You? You twerps have taken over. It's like Liz and I no longer exist."

Liz mock-glares at her mother. "For once, I agree with you, big brother."

"That's ridiculous." Jerri scoots her chair from the table and stands. "I don't play favorites. I love you all equally."

Gus snags her hand in his. "But me the most. Right, honey?"

She lowers her face to his and kisses him gently. "Maybe."

Everyone guffaws.

"What about you, Dan?" I ask.

"I got it one year, but it's so cutthroat, I was constantly watching my back, you know? Frankly, I don't need the stress." He cracks his knuckles. "Now I just try flying under the radar and doing what I'm told."

More cackling, except from his wife. "Really? Strange. I still don't have the flower beds I asked you to make *three years ago*."

He sighs loudly and narrows his eyes at me. "Thanks for helping me stay out of the spotlight, *Jacqui*."

"My pleasure," I answer with a toothy grin.

"I don't know why we bother trying to sway Mom." Butch squeezes my thigh affectionately. "Jacqui's a shoo-in this year."

"Yup," his sister agrees. "She's a first timer. Although I could argue I'm more deserving as a beleaguered parent of two hellions."

"So am I," Gus says, causing more laughter.

"The decision's already been made," Jerri quips, returning to the table. "You'll just have to wait to find out who it is. Now quit your bellyaching and help clean up."

We all pitch in before reconvening in the living room. Butch and I claim one end of a sofa, and his arm wraps around my shoulders. The children tear excitedly into their tissue-wrapped gifts then scamper off to don their pjs. Jerri distributes the reading material. Many are Little Golden Books, and I'm offered one to read. I select *The Littlest Angel*, which I've never seen.

Butch taps the vintage cover. "That's one of my favorites."

The kids thunder back into the room and flop down in

various places, and the readings begin. *How the Grinch Stole Christmas. The Biggest, Most Beautiful Christmas Tree.* A new addition called *The Polar Express.*

When it's my turn, Emmy crawls between her father and me, making a shared lap so she can see the illustrations.

The Littlest Angel turns out to be a surprisingly meaningful story about angels and earth, not fitting in but eventually finding your heaven, and the night Jesus was born. Parts of it are so touching that I'm forced to pause when my voice wavers.

As the family patriarch, Gus reads the grand finale, *The Night Before Christmas.* Even my father read this to me, without fail, every Christmas Eve of my formative years.

We all applaud when he finishes.

The room falls silent as Jerri unearths the baby Jesus, holding him reverently in the air for all to see. "The honor this year goes to..." She pauses, clearly for dramatic effect. "Jacqui."

Oh...wow.

"Called it," Butch says.

Liz rolls her eyes. "So predictable."

"Not fair!" Kayla pouts.

"Don't be a brat," her brother Trevor scolds, even though he's only seven.

I stand and meet Jerri's warm gaze as she places the tiny ceramic figure into my hand. *"Thank you,"* I say, wondering if I should give it to Kayla.

She smiles sweetly and guides me to the Nativity scene, pressing close to whisper, "Don't even *think* of giving the babe to anyone else or allowing them to guilt you into it. This is tradition, and they've all had plenty of turns."

The rustic stable is nearly as big as those popular microwave ovens, with painted figurines and animals huddled around a little wooden manger, empty save for a small scrap of material mimicking a blanket.

The kids gather round as I place the baby Jesus into his cradle, all gripes tempered for now, and the group sighs a collective breath. There's something both funny and poignant about the moment, and I'm flattered to be the chosen one.

Jerri corrals the grandkids to set out Santa's treats, and I rejoin Butch on the sofa.

"You're one of us now," he murmurs.

That might be the best Christmas gift I could receive.

FIFTY-TWO

Emmy paces outside Butch's bedroom door, and the dog's nails scrape the hardwoods as he scrambles along with her increasingly agitated steps.

"Daddy?" she ventures.

Butch groans and props on one elbow to read the alarm clock. "It's 5:54 a.m., for fuck's sake," he mutters.

I don't bother fighting a smile. It's Christmas morning... *of course* she's raring to go. A part of me is too, the giddy anticipation of giving and receiving already surfing through my system.

"Are you awake?" Emmy asks.

My sleep-rumpled, vaguely annoyed man glances at me. "What are you smiling at?"

"You, Lumberjack. Merry Christmas."

He sweeps the hair off my face, caressing my cheek. "Merry Christmas."

"Daddy! I hear you in there."

Butch flops back against the pillows, all but admitting defeat. "Come on in, kid."

Emmy plows through the door with Hemi at her heels

and climbs onto her father's chest. "Time to get up! It's Christmas!"

We both recoil at her shrieking.

"Sweet daughter of mine," he says, cupping her face in his giant hands. "It's still dark. We can't go to Mimi and PopPop's for a couple of hours. Go back to your room and play with your toys or watch TV."

"Gah! This is literally torture," she huffs, a scowl forming on her pretty face.

My giggle bubbles out. "Merry Christmas, Emmy."

"It *will* be if we ever get going."

Butch kisses her forehead. "Now scoot. And shut the door on your way out, please. I'm trying to sleep."

"How can you sleep at a time like this?" She huffs again and heads for the door.

"Easy." He pretends to snore—loudly.

"C'mon, Hemi." The dog pads after her, the door snicks closed, and their footfalls disappear down the stairs.

"The joys of parenting," he mutters.

He extends his arm, and I roll into his side, hiking my leg over his. "I think it's sweet. She's excited."

"I know. But more shuteye sounds wonderful."

My fingers lightly trace his pecs. "Mm-hmm...or would you like an *early* present?"

He groans softly as my hand skates lower. "Sundance..."

I push down the covers, free his growing erection, and wrap my hand around his length. Using a feather light touch, I stroke him from top to bottom, trailing my pinky below to gently graze the boys downstairs. He's smooth as silk but a rod of steel, and the sight and sensation whets my own appetite.

"Goddamn, that feels good," he rasps.

I tongue his nearest nipple, flicking it lightly, rewarded when it stiffens from my wet strokes. He releases a constrained moan and his hand grips me where it lands on my back.

"Fuuuuuuuuuck," he whispers.

It's not long before Butch's body tightens in multiple places at once: his chest where I suckle, his taut scrotum—a dead giveaway he's about to blow—and his hand fastening me in place.

Give it to me.

I shift, positioning my mouth over his tip and catching his release as he bucks. Our eyes meet and I'm fixated on how his lips part in a silenced cry as he finishes. What a glorious sight. He regains his breath, slowly coming down as we watch each other.

"You give the best fucking hand jobs I've ever had," he murmurs.

I resituate to nestle into him. "Happy to be of service."

"I don't know how you do that without any lube. It's so… smooth."

"Magic hands?"

"You have a magic everything, baby." He kisses the top of my head. "Now I wonder," he adds, his fingers coasting along the outer lace of my panties, "how wet are *you*?"

I arch into his hand with a whispered admission. "Not going to lie. That was a massive turn-on."

A satisfied hum leaves his lips. "I like how you use the term *massive* when talking about my dick."

I stifle a laugh.

"Can you be quiet?" He plants kisses along the column of my neck while he teases me below.

"Mm-hmm."

"Then spread those pretty legs."

He doesn't have to ask me twice.

"Good girl," he says as his fingers wiggle under the fabric and begin their own masterful strokes. He growls quietly as he explores, probes, and coaxes me to orgasm. It takes every ounce of control to smother my moan when I explode. I ride his hand through waves of contractions, gasping for air, my entire body soaring from the high.

He wraps me in his arms afterward, where we lay satisfied and content—until we worry Emmy will light the house on fire if we don't get moving.

Christmas Day is a bounty of stockings and presents, food and drink, teasing and laughter, ease and comfort, and most of all, unity. The more I'm with the Hamiltons, the more I realize how authentic they are. No one pretends. No one acts ambivalent. No one ruins the day.

They love each other, even when they occasionally snipe. As a unit, they're strong and unshakable. I never knew family could be like this. I mean, hypothetically, sure. But in reality? I've never witnessed it. They're all living the fairy tale.

And even though Butch's marriage ended coldly, leaving Emmy motherless and him to raise her alone, his family's response gives credence to their solidarity. They stepped in—unwaveringly—and helped rear her together. There's proof in the power of that, and her name is Emmy. Her self-esteem appears fully intact, and she overflows with joy, spunk, wit, and affection. The result of watering her daily with the same substances.

The easy way the Hamilton family welcomed me into the fold astounds me, fills me, and heals a part of me that remains so shattered I'm not sure it's completely fixable.

In the afternoon, Butch and I take a breather, inhaling the fresh air with Hemi at our side as we meander the rear acreage. We walk hand in hand, and my eyes tear from the cold. I finger the fourteen-carat-gold necklace he gave me with the initials B&S hanging from the front, smiling. It reminds me of a similar one I wore in junior high spelling out

"Jacqui." I didn't expect such an extravagant, personal gift—and I adore it.

"How's it going, baby?" he asks. "Missing your parents... or home today?"

I scoff. "Hardly. This is the most beautiful, heartwarming Christmas I've ever experienced."

He pauses, finding my gaze. "That makes me really fucking sad—and happy at the same time."

"Me too," I admit quietly.

"I hope..."

"What?"

He smooths a lock of my hair from my face. "I hope it will be the first of many."

"Nothing would please me more," I say, placing a hand on his jaw and coaxing his lips to mine.

Hemi drops a stick at our feet and Butch hurls it into the field. The dog runs after it as if it's a side of beef. "My family loves you, you know."

I immediately call up how they unexpectedly showered me with presents earlier. "I feel the same toward them. They're incredibly easy to be around. You're lucky to have them. You all blow my mind."

"What do you mean?" Hemi returns and Butch throws the stick in a different direction.

"The way you get along, respect each other, want to hang out together. I've never really witnessed that kind of dynamic," I say, burrowing my hands into my coat pockets.

Butch cocks his head, a crease forming between his brows. "It seems normal to me, and I'm sorry it wasn't like that for you."

"I could get used to it."

"I could get used to you getting used to it."

We share a knowing smile just as something wet and flaky tickles my nose. I look up and gasp. *It's snowing.*

"Oh my god!" I squeal, entranced by the delicate snowflakes dropping from the sky.

"Well, would you look at that," he says, squinting up at the heavens. "It hardly snows here, and rarely in December."

My smile broadens as I twirl in circles, my arms spread wide as snow dances across my cheeks and hair. "I've never seen snow falling before. It's magical...and beautiful."

Butch moves close, studying my upturned face. "I've never seen anything more beautiful."

The way he stares at me melts the ice. "Will we get a lot?"

He shrugs. "It wasn't in the forecast. Maybe this is Mother Nature's gift to you."

"This day just gets better and better." More of my happy squeals erupt as I catch Butch grinning. He's unfazed by the snow...but not, apparently, by me.

When we return, Emmy's running around in the new dress I gave her and dinner preparation is underway, so I hunt down his mother and ask if she wants help.

"Have you talked to your folks today, honey?" Jerri asks.

"Not yet."

She levels me with an undecipherable look, then herds me down the hall to their home office and insists I call. "Take your time." After she squeezes my arm reassuringly, Jerri leaves me in privacy.

I dial the number and my father answers.

"Merry Christmas, Dad."

"Jacqui! Merry Christmas. It's good to hear your voice."

He sounds cheerful and isn't slurring. "Yours too."

"How's your day going? You're with your boyfriend's family, correct?"

"Yes, the Hamiltons. It's going well. There's quite a crowd here, and everyone's been so nice."

"Did you get our gift?"

"I did. Thank you for the money. It was generous, and I

can always use it," I say with a self-deprecating laugh. "Did you get mine?"

"Sure did. Your mother's wearing the sweater you sent, and I look forward to reading the Chuck Yeager autobiography. He's had a hell of a life. Respectable."

"I knew you'd like it. Mom put on the sweater already?" Seems out of character.

"She misses you. We both do. It's strange not having you home for the holiday." He sighs. "I guess our little girl has grown up."

My eyes prick suddenly. "Mm-hmm."

"Let me grab your mother." He puts the receiver down and hollers for her. It takes over a minute until she's on the phone, and I stem the guilt over talking long distance on someone else's dime.

"Jacqui," she says, her voice wan and hoarse, as if speaking is an effort.

"Hi, Mom. Merry Christmas."

"Same to you, honey. How's everything?"

"Great, honestly. I love my job, and my boyfriend's wonderful..." Despite knowing the answer, I ask anyway. "How are you?"

"You know...the usual. Nothing new." She pauses. "Alright then, I'll let you go. I know it's costing a small fortune to say hello, but I'm glad you did. Be good."

"Okay." I falter. "I love you, Mom—"

The receiver clicks in my ear. My chest heaves and I tamp it down. Before the undertow sweeps me away, I speed-walk out of that room and back to the kitchen.

I force my best fake smile at Jerri, who hands me an apron. She puts me to work peeling russet potatoes, and it's another sign I've been accepted into the Hamilton family fold. Liz and Grandma Mabel stroll in, receiving tasks for table setting and unearthing fancy serving pieces. Jerri chatters with me as she bustles around wrangling more dishes and ingredients, effectively keeping my attention in the present. At one point, she checks on the biggest roast beef I've ever seen. The wafting aroma makes my mouth water.

She tells me a cute story about younger Emmy, and it's then I remember.

"Hey, Jerri?"

"Hmm?"

"I would love to see any old photos of Butch, especially as a kid. Do you have albums?"

She crows. *Do I have albums?* Does a one-legged duck swim in a circle?"

When I stop cackling, I add, "Don't tell Butchie," stealing Liz's pet name.

She winks. "Wouldn't dream of it. We'll figure out a time for a *secret* viewing while you're here this weekend."

We share a knowing smile—the partners-in-crime kind.

That evening, stuffed to the gills and overstimulated from nonstop activity, Butch and I say our goodbyes, sharing hugs with everyone. A passed-out Emmy doesn't wake when her father lifts her into his arms, lays her in the back of the car, drives us to his log cabin, and plants Miss Literally Crashed in her own bed.

Butch and I don't last much longer, opting to crawl under the covers and talk quietly before passing out ourselves. His large body spoons mine, wrapping me in comfort, safety, surety...and something I think might be the essence of home.

FIFTY-THREE

We sleep in until Hemi whines to go out. "If it's not kids, it's dogs," Butch mutters, swinging his legs off the edge of the bed. Seconds later, he's rubbing Hemi's head, intoning: "Whosagoodboy, whosagoodboy, whosagoodboy."

I lean on my elbow, watching. "You like to put on a grumpy front, but inside, you're nothing but mashed potatoes."

He harrumphs, then pulls on yesterday's jeans and leaves his chest bare.

"Mmm...that may be the best lumberjack look yet."

He gives me an inscrutable look.

"Let me know if you plan on chopping any wood like that. I'll bring my camera."

He stops at the door, casting a baffled stare. "You're ridiculous. You realize that's not even remotely practical...or safe."

I shrug. "Sex appeal is dangerous, Butch. That's just a fact you'll have to accept."

He shakes his head, but I see him fighting a smile as he disappears. And it pleases me immensely.

Although I hate leaving this comfortable, ginormous mattress, I'm on a mission to make breakfast. I throw on some sweats and a T-shirt, brush my teeth, and pull my hair into a ponytail.

When I enter the kitchen, Butch looks up from making coffee. "Hey, I was coming back to bed."

I slide my hands around his waist and trail kisses down his back, pressing one into the hollow between his shoulder blades. "I was worried you'd start breakfast, and I want to make it this morning."

He shifts to face me, tugging me closer. "You do, huh?" His eyes are the same shade as the tiny ferns along the path. "Did I mention how much I love waking up with you today?"

"Not yet," I answer with a smile.

"I *love* waking up with you, baby."

I shrug. "I could get used to it."

He grins at what is fast becoming our saying. His lips press against mine and we share a languid kiss.

Emmy startles us when she enters making kissing noises. She promptly launches into the song immortalized in elementary school. "Daddy and Jacqui, sitting in a tree, K-I-S-S-I-N-G. First comes love, then—"

Butch lunges at her, and she flees, shrieking. The chase is on, but he catches her handily and hauls her back to the kitchen. Nosing her pjs off her belly, he blows a loud raspberry on her ivory skin. Her giggles fill the air, and it's the most glorious sound.

He releases her, bending on one knee to meet her at eye level. "Em, does it bother you if I kiss Jacqui?"

Her eyes flicker between her father and me. "I mean, it's literally gross, but it's your mouth."

Butch and I both fight a laugh as he nods thoughtfully. "You know if something upsets you that you can tell me anytime, right?"

"Sure."

"Good. I love you, kid."

"I love you too, Daddy."

DURING OUR BREAKFAST OF PANCAKES AND BACON, Emmy announces it's Game Day. Essentially, the day you sift through your Christmas presents and play with any toys and games, read your new books, or mess around with whatever you want. It's another Hamilton tradition—and a lovely idea.

After we finish our meal, Butch starts a fire in the hearth and goes upstairs to shower. Emmy asks if I'll help set up her Lite-Brite, and I jump at the chance. I haven't played with one since my own childhood, and it was always a favorite toy of mine.

I open it up and pull out the familiar light box with its black screened front. Next are all the colored pegs that fit into the holes. Several picture templates with pre-printed outlines are included (that's new) plus the standard paper blanks.

"Want to freeform your own design or try one of these?" I ask.

"Let's create one from scratch," she says.

"I like your style, Emmy."

She beams her cute smile, and I plug the unit into a nearby outlet and slide in a blank. I grab a bowl from the kitchen and dump in the pegs from the plastic bag. Emmy and I lie on our stomachs on the living room rug, and I wait for her instruction.

"Let's make a butterfly!"

"I love that idea. Big enough to cover the whole screen?"

"Uh huh."

"You push in the first peg. Do you see how it fits?" I ask, demonstrating without pushing one in all the way.

She picks up a purple peg and punches it through the paper. Her face lights up after seeing it illuminate. "Oooh. That's pretty."

"Isn't it? What colors are we making our butterfly?"

"All of them!"

We alternate punching in the various pegs, consulting occasionally on placement to keep our insect shape. When I glance at Emmy midway through, her face is the portrait of concentration, the tip of her pink tongue poking through her lips. Once the outline of the butterfly emerges, her smile radiates.

"This is so neat," she gushes. "Let's make the inside thingies now."

We begin adding smaller shapes within the wings. Playing with a Lite-Brite after all these years does my heart good, especially collaborating with Emmy.

In that moment, I'm struck by how easy she is to be around. That if I simply be myself, follow her lead, and let things flow naturally, this "parenting" stuff isn't so daunting after all. She's merely a tiny human. The only difference between us is I'm bigger, older, and hopefully wiser.

I was relieved by her response to her father kissing me. We've mostly stowed our PDA, giving Emmy time to adjust and get to know me, and to not pressure or overwhelm her. But she seems to take us in stride, accepting me like her dad brings women home regularly.

Shit. Has he? Butch already said he's cautious about who he introduces to his daughter.

"Emmy, may I ask you a question?"

"Uh huh."

"Do you like me being here?" I fight a wince at how insecure that sounds. Do kids pick up on that kind of thing?

"Mm-hmm. And my daddy likes it too."

"That makes three of us then. You don't mind him having a girlfriend?"

She shrugs. "He's never had one. But he seems happier now."

I study her face, which stays focused on our butterfly in

progress, now lighting up most of the screen. "Was he... unhappy before?"

"He was just Daddy. I think he was lonely. Daddies are literally supposed to have mommies."

I bite back a chuckle. "You mean a wife?"

"Uh huh."

"It's nice when people fall in love and get married." Ideally.

Emmy looks at me now, nodding. "Like Cinderella, when she finds her Prince Charming!"

I flash her a smile. "Exactly. Who doesn't want to find their prince?"

I may have found mine...in lumberjack form. Because I am definitely, irrevocably in love with Butch Hamilton.

THAT NIGHT AFTER EMMY'S ASLEEP, BUTCH TAKES Hemi out for a quick walk, and I tiptoe into the bedroom. Wanting to sleep in one of my boyfriend's shirts, I open one of his larger dresser drawers and find a stack, rooting around for a soft one. I tug one out, shaking my head when I read what's on it: *Mopar or No Car*. I've never seen such brand loyalty before. I strip off my clothes and pull on the shirt, which is comforting two ways: it smells like Butch and the well-worn cotton lays softly against my skin.

Now I'm cold. I open one of the smaller drawers in the middle looking for socks, but it's more of a catch-all receptacle for his stray items. I barely notice what because my eyes fixate on the photo laying on top...of us. Someone must have taken it at Thanksgiving without me noticing. It's a beautiful shot of Butch and me standing in the living room. He's talking and I'm laughing, our expressions bright and happy. I pick it up and take a closer look. We really are a stunning couple.

And how sneaky of Butch. Why didn't he didn't share this with me? I've half a mind to steal it.

I momentarily startle when my memory flashes on a picture of Mick, Remy, and me from our Christmas in Half Moon Bay. We took it before things got X-rated. It's the only photo I have of the three of us. Taken with my Polaroid, Remy held the camera aloft, we all squeezed together on the sofa, and he pushed the button. It came out perfect.

That picture is hidden away with other treasures from my days with Mick and Remy...my "Mick's tape," a journal, the story I wrote.

I'm about to replace the photo when a piece of paper flutters to the floor. Maybe it was stuck to the back? I bend and retrieve it, unable to miss what's so plainly scrawled in a woman's handwriting.

I don't love you anymore, and I don't want this life.
I'm sorry.

I nearly choke on a shocked inhalation as I bolt upright. My eyes widen as footfalls draw closer, but I'm rooted to the spot. Hemi shuffles into the bedroom followed by Butch. He shuts the door and turns to me, assessing my panicked expression.

I'm still frozen in place, the picture in one hand, note in the other, the dresser drawer ajar.

I see the second he pieces it together. The recognition. The flicker of pain. Brows drawing tighter, shoulders sagging.

"I'm so sorry...I didn't mean to pry," I murmur. "I went to borrow a shirt and then some socks and it just...fell out." Is he angry? Upset?

He moves closer, takes the note from my hand, then pulls me against his chest. "It's alright, Sundance. Ancient history."

I hold him, offering whatever modicum of comfort I can.

In the past or not, what's written on that piece of paper is wounding, horrible... heartless.

"I'm not sure why I kept it all these years. A fucked-up reminder, maybe. It's a good thing I did though. I dug it up and showed it to my lawyer and she added it to the evidence. I didn't know what to do with it afterward, so I chucked in here."

"*Butch,*" I whisper. "I'm so sorry." It's an awful note, and I've clearly dredged up a tough subject, one that he's mired in dealing with *again*, this time through the legal system.

"Forget it, okay? Let's go to bed."

He undresses and we crawl under the covers and hold each other. I trail my fingers through his hair, along his arm, across his back. Over and over.

"You look good in my shirt," he mumbles, half asleep.

I smile in the dark as I continue stroking him. Finally, he succumbs, his breathing evening out with Hemi's soft snores.

It's a long while before sleep finds me.

FIFTY-FOUR

Butch takes Emmy to her dance class on Saturday morning. He asked me to join him when we were having dinner at his folks' house last night, but Gus intervened, saying he wanted to pick my brain about an idea he had. Without realizing it, his father unwittingly provided the perfect opportunity to view those family photo albums on the sly if our conversation doesn't take too long.

I'm waiting for Gus in the living room, those painful words replaying in my mind for the nth time no matter how hard I try to shut them out.

I don't love you anymore, and I don't want this life.

Butch and I haven't spoken of the note again, and I'm wondering if we'll ever go there. It sure helps me understand some of his pain. Childhood sweetheart. Married young. Unplanned pregnancy. Then poof, everything you thought was forever...gone.

I thought Mick was going to be my forever. Would have met him at the altar in half a heartbeat. Then poof, everything was gone. I realize that doesn't hurt like it once did. It's more of a bee sting than a gut shot.

I take a sip of coffee as Gus enters and sits in his favorite plaid wingback chair. I'm not sure what I was expecting, but it wasn't his next words.

"I want to start a magazine about car restorations. A quality publication, something upscale, different."

"Well, *that's* exciting."

"You helped spark the idea, actually."

"Me? How?"

"Back when you mentioned the lack of car culture on this coast. It got me thinking about a way to share about the classics, resto jobs, show vehicles, barn finds...all of it."

"It's a cool idea." *Very cool.* "There's nothing on the market like that now?"

"There are plenty of car magazines, but nothing like what I'm envisioning. I'm talking about every issue being a collector item with professional photography, longer layouts, and articles that carefully detail the restoration process and showcase the result. Maybe it's a quarterly, so it can be done right, and thick enough that it's printed on better paper, perhaps bound instead of stapled like the flimsy magazines on the rack."

"It sounds worth pursuing." Not that I'm any expert.

"Since you're in the business, I thought you could advise on what I should do next."

"Not sure I'm qualified to answer," I say, clearing my throat. But actually, I do have some suggestions. "I'd start with market research, so you can identify what's out there now. Then I'd sketch out a few editions to crystalize some ideas for content and how you'd plan to write the articles and handle the photography. It'll require an advertising staff, which you may be able to hire on a freelance or contract basis. You also have production concerns, such as who will print the magazine, how you'll distribute it, and what entities could handle subscriptions and newsstand sales. You eventually need to figure out if it's a venture worth taking on in terms of costs, time, projections, and viability."

Gus grins. "Sounds like you're perfectly qualified to answer."

I smile shyly. "I'm happy to help any way I can."

"I'll give Don a call this week. Pick his brain. He'll probably try to talk me out of my harebrained scheme."

My heart drops into my stomach, and it's all I can do to nod my encouragement and keep my qualms about my boss internalized. "That's smart. He obviously knows much more about the magazine industry."

"You've given me plenty to think about. Right now, it's just a notion, but maybe one day it will materialize into the real thing."

A sheen of sweat coats my skin and when I register the tremor in my hands, I surreptitiously press my palms against my thighs and force myself back to the present. "You're in a unique position with your restoration business to offer something of value. You have the perspective, clientele, connections, and history. Car enthusiasts would respect that."

Jerri strides into the living room balancing photo albums, effectively halting all conversation. I'm relieved. I don't want to think about Don or the wedge he could drive between me and this family I'm starting to belong to.

She drops the stack onto the coffee table. "There are more, but we can get started with these." She glances at her husband. "You all finished in here?"

Gus stands. "Yes, my love. And knowing you as I do, you're going to do what the heck you want anyway."

"You know me well," she answers.

He winks. "That I do."

Jerri joins me on the sofa and hefts the first thick volume into her lap. Our eyes meet and hers turn scrutinizing. "You look a little pale. You alright, sugar?"

I'm not. I'm in a nightmare that hasn't played out yet,

one I don't know how to stop from unfolding, but which probably won't end well. "I'm fine," I say, rallying my most reassuring smile.

She opens the album, balancing it between us, allowing me to fall into their family archives. There's cooing, squealing, and laughing as I soak up the precious, awkward, hilarious images of Butch through various stages of youth.

A half hour later, Butch groans when he busts us. "Mom! What the...? That is so..." He grapples for words. "*Wrong*."

Jerri frowns. "What? You're adorable."

"Spoken like a true mother," he mutters.

"You were *hot* in that purple tux," I say. "And that long hair? *Mmm*."

"Stop. No. We're not doing this." He's truly annoyed, stepping closer and looming over us.

He lunges for the album, but I clutch it to my chest. "You're such a spoilsport."

"Am not."

"Are you five?" I tease.

"Give it. Or else show me all *your* awkward pictures."

I shrug, giggling. "They're in California."

"Convenient." He rubs the scruff of his jaw.

I hand the object of his ire to Jerri and rise from the sofa, placing my hands on Butch's forearms. "You were a handsome devil at every iteration." He glares. "Naked in the bathtub with your sister." He groans. "On your bike with the banana seat and sissy bar." He narrows his gaze. "At the science fair, proud of your potato-powered lightbulb." I push up on my toes and kiss his lips, which stubbornly don't respond.

"Really?" he mumbles into my mouth.

"Really," I say, not taking my lips off his.

He relents, his arms opening as he tugs me closer and kisses me back.

"That's my cue to leave," Jerri says.

Laughter bubbles out of us both, forcing our mouths apart.

"Where's Emmy?" I ask.

"Dad intercepted her outside. She's probably shredding her tutu running on all cylinders. Did you have a nice time here?"

"Are you kidding? *Purple. Tuxedo.*"

He rolls his eyes.

"To answer your question, I did. Your parents are awesome."

"Yup. Case in point, Emmy's staying over tonight so we can go on a date."

Alone time. As much as I've enjoyed all the family togetherness, Butch and I are rarely on our own here, and I crave it.

Butch enters the cabin near sunset, swinging some keys around his finger. "Ready for an old-school date, gorgeous?"

More than. He's been secretive all afternoon about the details, but when we go outside, I audibly gasp. I'm staring at one of the most stunning classic cars I've ever seen. "*Wow.*"

"It's a 1958 Plymouth Fury."

My eyes dart to his. "The *Christine* car?"

"One and the same."

It even looks like the Fury from the movie with its cherry red paint, sleek lines, and cool fins. "I stayed up until three in the morning reading that damn Stephen King book and then I was too scared to fall asleep. For some moronic reason, I doubled down when the movie came out and saw it too. Color me terrified." Moving slowly toward the vehicle, I outright ogle it.

Butch chuckles. "Maybe I should have gone with the Special Deluxe instead."

"Are you kidding? This is perfect." I continue soaking in the car's beauty. The white top. The grille that looks beautiful *and* frightening. The long swath of chrome across the sides into the fins.

Once I finish my circuit of the entire vehicle, Butch opens the passenger door like the gentleman he is, and I slide onto the bench seat. The interior is matching red, but the steering wheel is two-toned in cherry and white. Totally bitchin'. Scooting over, I check out the driver's-side dash. The classic dashboards are jaw-droppingly cool, and this one doesn't disappoint.

I'm ogling Butch now, at ease behind the wheel of this big sexy car, one that seems to comfortably fit his big sexy self.

The engine rumbles to life, a steady cranking in the idle. Butch takes off, and she rides so smoothly, it's as if we're gliding. The seat has a noticeable bounce to it, and I can't help whooping.

My handsome driver flashes me a pleased smile. Then he rattles off some interesting history about the Fury. It's a rare, low-production car. The nickname for the 350-cubic-inch high-performance engine is Golden Commando. The custom paint is a nod to *Christine*, as the originals were white and gold or beige. He relays some insider restoration gossip on how hard it was for director John Carpenter to wrangle enough Furys to make the movie, most of which were destroyed during filming.

Well, yeah...they were crashed, set on fire, crushed. *Christine* was a murderess.

An old-style, drive-in burger joint comes into view and when Butch pulls in, I bounce in my seat. Maybe *I'm* five. I've only seen these in movies, and I'm marveling that one exists, let alone that I'm here.

"Is someone going to roller-skate over and take our order?" I ask.

Butch chuckles. "No on the skates, yes on the order. The menu is printed right here." He points to his left.

I slide closer and peer out his window, checking out the limited offering: burgers and dogs, fries and onion rings, sodas, shakes, and malts.

"We can't spill anything, or my father will have both our hides."

"Hell, I'm nervous about eating in ol' Christy. Maybe she'll eject or kill us before we leave the parking lot."

Butch's mouth lifts in one of his amused smiles.

A peppy teen with blond braids approaches. She's wearing a checkered uniform shirt with the Flip's Drive-In logo emblazoned on the front. After we order, my considerate date thanks her and rolls the window back up to keep in the heat.

The waning sun casts a nuanced light into the car. For a minute, it's quiet except for the radio turned down low.

Butch lifts his brows. "Wanna make out?"

I snort but...*yeah*.

We chuckle as our lips meet before he cranks up the volume and leaves me breathless.

After polishing off our meal (no spills) we arrive at the local theater (alive) to see *Brighton Beach Memoirs*. It's a grand but intimate space that was formerly an opera house, popular in these old small towns. Along with the usual staggered seating, there's a charming loveseat-for-two option and Butch guides me right to it. He wraps his arm around me, holding me close, and his woodsy scent with the maple notes invades my senses. There's no place else I'd rather be.

Afterward, Butch takes us home. I don't know why I'm suddenly nervous, my insides fluttering. Maybe because of the palpable shift in my awareness that what we share is special, and the unspoken vibration pulsing between us.

He holds my hand and leads me upstairs to the bedroom. We both want one thing: to get our bodies naked and closer. We shed our shoes and meet at the foot of the bed.

His emerald eyes latch onto mine, and he cups my face. "I'm so fucking in love with you."

He says it so earnestly, my heart takes flight, the flutters amplifying. "I am totally, madly, wildly in love with you." It's sheer relief to utter that truth.

"Thank fuck." He clutches me against his chest. "I've tried waiting, but I can't any longer. *I love you*, Jacqui."

Our mouths connect. It's impassioned, touching, claiming, and I melt into him, my heart opening, recalibrating again.

He undresses me slowly, kissing my skin as it's revealed. Goosebumps skate across the surface. His warm breath teases me as he licks and strokes and kisses me, leaving nothing unattended.

When I'm fully naked, his gaze sweeps me top to bottom. "You are so beautiful."

Smiling at this glorious man, I let myself hear and believe his words.

I make a move to undress him, and he seems like he's about to brush me off, then doesn't. I want to return the worshipping he just lavished on me. There's pure pleasure in peeling off his shirt, belt, jeans, socks, briefs. My hands coast across his skin, caressing his sinewy planes and valleys. My lips graze along the way, and his flesh ripples in their wake.

Butch responds to being touched differently than any man I've been with. It's like oxygen to him, or proof of life. He is loved, but he's also been deeply wounded—starved of this kind of human interaction, the type of intimacy only shared by people in love.

We're both so vulnerable in this moment. It's not only our bodies that stand naked...but our hearts.

Making our way to the bed, we converge, hands roving, legs and arms wrapping, mouths desperate and seeking.

My insides are on fire, my heart full to bursting. He swallows my whimper and holds me so tightly, there's no space left between us. Our tongues dance as if we'll never get enough.

Butch shifts, rolling me to lie flat. "I'm going to make love to every inch of your body."

His breath hits my ear. He licks the shell and ventures inside, and I shudder. His kisses trail down my neck and along my chest, his lips landing on my nipple. He palms one into his mouth while fondling the other and I writhe under the attention, arching toward him. I'm a mass of need, clamoring for more, but Butch takes his time, going at an agonizingly slow pace that's both reverent and greedy.

His tongue laves its way down my torso, across my belly, and skirts my soaked center. His fingertips trace my legs all the way to my ankles, then reverse up along the inside. I part my legs, and by the time he's made it to the apex of my thighs, my essence provides visible proof of my pleasure.

"Absolutely gorgeous," he murmurs. When his breath breaches where I'm exposed, my skin ripples, an inferno blazing through me.

"Butch," I beg.

He answers with his mouth, his fingers spreading me wider as he claims me fully. I let out a strangled cry of relief, desire...longing.

He's probing, licking, sucking, fingering...and my body contorts of its own volition, desperate to be closer. It's a dance of sensations. His appraising groans fuel the flames. His rough razor stubble abrades my inner thighs. I'm drenched with his distinctive scent, melded into the sheets.

A storm brews at my core. Gathering. Quickening.

My breath stills. My mind blanks.

POW. I blow with dynamite force, my orgasm jerking in spasm after delirious spasm, my thoughts so obliterated I scarcely register him milking me for every drop. I'm only vaguely aware I'm wailing.

Butch shifts to hover over my face, as if memorizing my details. "Beautiful," he repeats.

I'm punch-drunk from an explosive orgasm, viewing him through a heavy-lidded gaze.

He positions himself between my legs, which widen in welcome expectation, eager for our bodies to merge. As he pushes inside slowly, our eyes lock, both of us breathing through the glory of it. The profoundness.

He stills. "Goddamn. Each time with you feels like the first."

"So good." My breath catches as tears prickle against the back of my lids.

"I love you."

"I love you." My words are a hoarse whisper.

We move in exquisite tandem. There's a rightness, a completeness, to the way he fills me, and the way I receive him. Those green irises darkened by his dilated pupils fasten on me. His thrusts are sublime, decadent, intense.

A declaration.

Mine.

Yours.

A tear escapes, almost as if my body's unable to hold so much sensation.

"You okay?" he whispers.

I can't speak or I'll lose it, but I manage a nod.

Our lips meld, another *I love you*. The space connecting us thickens with emotion. My legs shift higher and wider, wanting to be closer everywhere we're joined. We moan at the adjustment, our pleasure transcendent, authentic, sincere. Our heavy breaths and sighs float between us, and more of my tears leak as the potency of our lovemaking breaks through any remaining barriers.

Butch's pace quickens from slow and languid to hard and fierce. Claiming. Asserting. Demanding.

You're mine. I'm yours.

Maybe forever.

He roars through his release, meeting my cry. His hips buck as he spills into me, grinding like he never wants to stop. We cling to each other, breathing heavy, bodies merged, hearts undeniably fused.

FIFTY-FIVE

I awaken in Butch's arms, my back glued to his front. His erection, stirring before he does, lodges against my ass. A smile creeps up. My man is nothing short of virile...we spent hours pleasuring one another last night. Even though I'm big dick sore, the memory causes stirrings of my own, and my hips grind into him purposefully.

"Mmm," he groans, pulling me tighter.

"Mm-hmm," I answer.

"I could get used to this." His voice is even deeper still laced with sleep, and hearing it this close to my ear ignites my blood.

We take a quick break for human necessities, then reunite for another rousing session of sex...the loud and unrestrained kind, since little ears aren't around.

Lying on his chest after, listening to his steady heartbeat, a comforting happiness fills me.

Butch breaks the silence. "I probably shouldn't say this... it's too soon."

Now I'm curious. I lift my head to meet his gaze, resting my chin on my hand. "Say what?"

He heaves out a breath. "Don't bolt on me?"

I level him with a stare. "I just admitted I love you. I'm not going anywhere. And I seem to recall you saying if I did run, you'd just haul me back to your bed anyway."

"Right. Still stands."

"So?"

He strokes my hair, moving a section away from my eyes. "I don't know about you, Sundance, but this sure as hell feels a lot like forever."

I nod because it does, although voicing that sentiment aloud gives it a credence that scares me. Like it's too good to be true? And it's *way* too soon to be making even stronger pronouncements than we have already. A laugh huffs out. "Guess we really didn't heed 'going slow', huh?"

"You know, maybe if Emmy had paused, even just for a second. But she didn't. She sees exactly what I do...a bright, sparkling light. You're so easy to like. And the window dressing ain't bad, either." He graces me with one of his most charming grins.

I sink into those compliments.

"Window dressing isn't enough to sustain a relationship though," he adds. "I mean, don't get me wrong...it's a mighty appealing package—"

"Speak for yourself, Lumberjack. Your looks are pretty much responsible for keeping me around."

Butch flips me onto my back and tickles me mercilessly.

"I give, *I give*!" I shout through giggles.

His gaze turns serious, and my laughter dissipates. "Let me finish. Where your beauty really shines is in your nature. You're giving, loving, empathetic, funny, and damn good company. It's why you fit in so well with everybody here, like you were meant to be a Hamilton all along."

He's knocking my socks off. That's what he sees? That's who I am?

I bury my forehead into his neck. "You're embarrassing me but also winning me over." I lift my head and our smiles collide. "Who you are takes my breath away. When I saw into your heart, the kind of father you are, son, brother, man…it was everything. You're a protector. A champion for others. Reliable, loyal, faithful, giving, so much more." I place my palm on his chest. "It's the most beautiful thing I've ever seen in a human being before, and I've never felt so at home with someone in my entire life. In fact, I've truly never *felt* at home." My voice cracks. "Until now."

"Did I mention how in love with you I am today?"

"*Not yet,*" I whisper.

"I love you, Jacqui," he says, his emerald eyes earnest.

Those three words are like CPR to a drowning victim. They revive me, make me want to live. "I love you too."

We kiss, the soulful kind. The kind with unspoken promises.

Butch shifts his body alongside mine, resting his head on his crooked arm. "How are you doing with the whole…Emmy thing?"

"It's been surprising," I say. "Natural-ish? Easy? I'm going with the flow."

"You've been great with her. She adores you, and I can't even begin to tell you what seeing the two of you together does to the ol' ticker. You two gals are shredding it."

"It's still early, but honestly, it's not as difficult as I imagined. She's a tiny human, nothing to be afraid of."

He barks out a laugh. "Oh, she's plenty scary. Like all you women."

"I beg your pardon."

"You're part of the club, sweetheart, the giant sorority. None of you have a clue how much power you wield over us."

I stare incredulously. "You must be high, Mr. Hamilton. Do you not understand how men *shatter* us?"

"Psh. It's all posturing and ego and bullshit. You have what we want. *Desperately want.*"

I roll my eyes. "Pussy?"

"Well, that, sure. But way more. Women are far more interesting and complex."

"On that, we can agree."

His lips quirk before he turns contemplative. "You provide depth...add meaning to everyday life. A woman's love is rare, precious, and powerful."

Whoa. "That's actually kind of deep, Lumberjack. And beautifully expressed."

"But don't get me wrong, the pussy's a major draw."

I smack him playfully and he laughs, then gets up to run us a bath.

Bathing with Butch is fast becoming one of my favorite activities. The lumberjack has an oversized tub that fits both of us perfectly. It's not only romantic, but seeing this tall drink of water with his arm hanging over the side, eyes fastened on me as I climb in, is sexy as hell. The way he looks at me as if I'm the only person on earth who matters. Like he wants to devour or spoil me with every second of his day. Come to think of it, he looks at me this way all the time.

I nestle against him, immersed under the bubbles floating on the surface like fluffy clouds.

Mr. Slippery and All Mine kisses the crown of my head. "I've been wondering...what if we're like old cars that just needed the right person to come along and restore us? You know, fix the engine, replace the upholstery, fabricate damaged sections, give us a fresh spin in life. An opportunity to shine, press the gas, and go for a hell of a ride."

"I'm thinking *you* should be the writer."

His gently pinches my waist under the water. "Nah, that's your area of expertise."

"It's a poignant analogy, Butch," I say softly. "Perfect, really."

"Maybe we just needed someone to show us a little love after we sat rusting and neglected."

Now I'm getting teary. "Don't you make me get all weepy, Butch Hamilton."

The arm he's casually slung across my chest tightens. "I'm your mechanic, baby, and you're mine. And I'm damn glad we're putting in the effort. It would be easier to ignore the rot, shy away from the work required, and let the paint peel. But what a waste, you know?"

He's so damn poetic. I manage a nod. "We've still got miles to go, and plenty of gas. I'm thankful for you, for us."

He squeezes me and plants another reassuring kiss to my temple. "You sure you have to leave today?"

"Unfortunately."

"Now that we're letting all the truths fly, I'm going to float something else out there. We've been doing the distance waltz for months. At some point, we need to talk about getting in the same zip code."

He's right. The miles separating us make everything difficult. "I don't disagree. But I also have no idea what to do about that."

"Me neither. Let's stay open to talking more when we're ready."

"Okay," I whisper.

As I drive back to my empty apartment, the ache deepens with every mile logged between Butch and me. Once inside my studio, surrounded by dead silence, I'm struck by the difference in what I left vs. what I have. And the quiet is louder than it was prior to Christmas...because I just experienced an earthquake-leveling dose of home, family, and love.

FIFTY-SIX

The day of the custody hearing arrives, and I drive to the Richmond courthouse. Adrenaline spikes as I walk toward the imposing structure that looks a century old. Pushing myself through the doors is akin to steering your ship into a hurricane, knowing you can't avoid it, so you put your head down and blindly hope everyone comes out unscathed.

I go where directed and spot Butch first, huddled with his parents and sister in the corridor outside one of the smaller rooms designated for family court. Tension radiates from the group, even from a distance. As I hug each of them tightly, I try infusing positive energy from my body to theirs.

There's scant conversation as we wait, and really, what is there to say? By the way Butch yanks at the knot in his tie, I can tell he'd like to rip it off—and probably the whole suit. He's too antsy to even hold my hand.

His attorney arrives, briefcase in hand, and pulls Butch aside for a private discussion.

It's obvious when Darlene shows up because Liz mutters "bitch" under her breath. Never seeing her before, I'm riveted, sizing her up while she speaks to the man at her side. Her face is plain but pretty with round features, her mousy brown hair badly permed into too-tight coils. She's average height and wears a navy V-neck dress with shoulder pads and two rows of white buttons down the front. Scuffed vinyl pumps complete the ensemble.

She's accompanied by a short man whose belly threatens to pop through his starched shirt underneath a brown suit that screams polyester. An oily sheen coats his face, obvious even from twelve feet away. There is nothing attractive about him.

He waddles over to Butch's attorney, and I'm dismayed when the pair shake hands even though they're about to do battle. The man extends his hand to Butch next and is met with a stony stare. Yeah, buddy…that's not happening.

Butch strides back to our group, not even sparing Darlene a glance, but I don't miss how she glares at him. He takes my hand, and I return a firm, reassuring squeeze.

Sweat trickles from my armpits as we wait. It's incredibly awkward hanging out in the hallway with his ex-wife. There is zero acknowledgement of Darlene by any of the Hamiltons, and it's no surprise. Her abandoning both Butch and Emmy is unfathomable. I wonder if Darlene truly understands what she lost, how deeply she hurt them, and how much strife her current actions are causing.

My criticism of her is harsh. Even as a relative newcomer, I've come to adore this family and all they stand for. I can't imagine blowing it all up like she did. Nor can I fathom ever abandoning my own child, but clearly my judgments are born from my own unfortunate personal experience.

The bailiff opens the door and calls our names, and we file into the small courtroom. Two tables are placed in front of the elevated bench for the plaintiff and the defendant. A half-dozen rows of seating are set up on either side of the aisle.

It's seems ludicrous that Butch is the defendant in this case—defending his position when *Darlene* is the one who did something indefensible, but she's the one who filed the petition for custodial rights.

Butch, Darlene, and their respective attorneys take their seats. The Hamilton posse and I sit directly behind Butch.

Please let this man keep custody of his daughter.

My mind skirts to Emmy at school, none the wiser that an event of tragic magnitude—affecting her fate and those in this room—is about to go down. Maybe she's at recess, swinging from the monkey bars, or playing hopscotch with a rock to mark her place. Maybe she's working out a simple arithmetic problem, face scrunched in concentration. Her grandmother will be waiting when she gets off the bus if this runs longer than predicted.

An officer calls the court into session, and we all rise as the judge enters the courtroom. He addresses us all, introducing himself and the official case. Tension remains thick.

I listen with growing indignation and outright fury as Darlene's attorney lays out their case, making her sound like a model fucking citizen who realizes—*now*—how much she has to offer her child and why, as her biological mother, she's owed it...especially with the father labeled "uncooperative."

I force my breath to slow. In and out. In and out. In and out.

Then it's Butch's lawyer's turn, and she makes an excellent argument why that's not in the child's best interest, providing the details of Darlene's abandonment and the ideal life Emmy leads now in the care of not only Butch, but his extended family.

The judge checks his watch three times, giving me the vibe he's more concerned about his lunch break than the heart-wrenching case before him. It's a big fucking responsibility and it hits me how ludicrous this whole thing is. What a farce. How can a stranger decide something so pivotal, affecting precious lives for years to come, based on thirty minutes of attorney jockeying?

With each minute that passes, I become more appalled, more worried, more livid.

The arguments end, scads of important information left unsaid. The judge looks at his watch *again*, then steeples his hands.

I hold my breath as I'm sure every Hamilton does.

The judge prefaces his decision with a long string of court-speak, Virginia Code citations, and how he's prioritizing the best interests of the child. Finally, he says the magic words.

"The father has taken sole responsibility for the upbringing and care of the child and there is no indication that Emmaline's mother has contributed in any form since voluntarily abandoning the child. As she is essentially a stranger to the child, the court believes awarding any custodial rights would only be confusing and potentially damaging to the child. The court finds in favor of the defendant, who will continue to have sole custody."

Our collective cries of relief rise on our side of the courtroom. Butch turns in his chair and our eyes lock. We share a quick smile before his gaze lands on his parents and sister. His attorney leans in to talk with him, and I glance at Darlene, who's slumped forward with her head in her hands, shoulders shaking as she succumbs to tears. I'm happy about the judge's decision but still have a smidgeon of empathy for her. Regret is a powerful emotion.

We surround Butch, sharing fierce hugs and congratulations. He throws an arm around me and our posse heads for the exit.

"Butch, wait!" Darlene calls out.

He swings her direction.

"Please let me see her. Get to know her. Please."

A look of incredulity crosses his face. He shakes his head, not bothering to answer, and we keep walking.

"The Butch I knew would *never* do this!" she shrieks.

He stiffens beside me but pushes through the door.

FIFTY-SEVEN

Mid-January, I'm in an irritated rush, arms full, racing to the corporate copier on the opposite side of our floor because the one I normally use has jammed and this project is expected in ten minutes.

I freeze when Tanya exits Don's office...looking freshly fucked. Hair slightly disheveled, lipstick smudged, blouse partially untucked.

Her gaze narrows. "What's your problem?" she snaps.

"Um...are you okay?"

"Never better." She casts me a smug look and strides past.

I swallow hard. Did she? Did he?

Forced to stow my concern for now, I hustle to the copy room and get on task.

At the next staff meeting, Tyler awards Tanya the top story. The following week, she gets another plum feature. The third week, I'm almost to the bottom of the feeder pool, and I'm sick to my stomach. Not only am I questioning my own abilities, but if my assumptions hold any veracity, it's fucking terrifying.

I'm a day away from approaching Tyler when he summons me to his office. The verifiable shit-ton of debating I've done in the past few weeks has made me question my sanity. Maybe I'm about to get answers.

"Hey, Jacqui. Shut the door and take a seat." I may be imagining it, but he sounds beleaguered.

I've got a million and one questions but I bite my tongue.

He folds his hands, his collective fist tapping against his desk as if he's deciding what to say.

The printing press that now resides in my gut starts up, churning out fresh newsprint.

He clears his throat. "I'm sure you've noticed that you're getting fewer features lately, and I wanted to explain what's happening."

"I appreciate that."

"There's been a complaint."

My stomach lurches. "About me?"

"Partially, yes."

My eyes widen. "By who...whom?"

"I'm not at liberty to say, but this person alleged you were receiving special treatment regarding story assignments. The complainant suggested your longevity in the industry and skill level weren't in alignment with theirs."

Of course it's Tanya. No one else stands to gain as she has *already*. "That's why I've been underutilized these past weeks?"

Tyler acknowledges with a quick dip of his head. "I've been mandated to give appropriate assignments to senior staffers. It's not a reflection of you as much as a necessary part of the process."

This isn't totally true, and we both know it. Other staff members are still scoring primo stories instead of being reduced to the slush-pile dregs I'm getting.

"Do you believe the allegations are credible?" I notice my knee bouncing and still it with my hand.

"I'm not at liberty to say." Again.

Right.

"I'm sorry, Jacqui. For what it's worth, I value your place on the team. You're a good writer, professional, meet your deadlines, go the extra mile. I have no complaints with your job performance whatsoever. Quite the opposite."

That's effectively my answer. His hands are tied. He's probably galled by it too. How I long to unload about Don and seek Tyler's advice...but that's far too risky. And likely useless.

I rub my brow, choking back the injustice. "Am I going to be fired?"

"No," he assures me.

But I don't believe it. This is Don's way of showing me who's boss—and what happens if I don't play ball.

Fifty-Eight

Emmy turns eight in February, and I'm at Butch's house for a weekend-long celebration. Today is the skating party. A dozen of her friends will gather at the roller rink, then her two closest girlfriends will sleep over. Liz and her kids are coming, and Jerri dropped off a homemade sheet cake for the party because she's amazing like that. The family shindig will happen tomorrow, and I'm pretty sure Jerri's making *another* cake for the occasion.

Butch borrows his dad's Power Wagon, and we pile in and head for the rink a half-hour away.

Ten minutes in, he slides his hand across the bench seat and threads his fingers through mine. "You're vibrating. One might think it's your birthday."

"It's *my* birthday," Emmy chimes in from the back.

"Yes, it is," I say. She looks adorable in pink jeans and a white top with sequins that will glow under the rink's strobe lights. Turning back to Butch, I continue. "For the record, I'm *stoked*. I love roller skating and haven't been in years. I'm going to rex my heart out."

His brow furrows. "No idea what that means."

"It's like a shuffle step where your skates kind of cross in front..." I try—and fail—to pantomime with my hands.

Now he's squinting. "California thing?"

"Not even." Except, maybe it is?

"I've got a few moves."

"Really?" I smile broadly, trying to picture this massive man on skates. "You'd better ask me to couples skate."

"You know it." He winks.

Turns out, the lumberjack can skate. And with most of the parents hanging around to watch their own kids, Mr. He Can Do Everything and I get plenty of glide time on the floor together. Including the romantic couples skate in the near-dark to Earth, Wind & Fire's "Reasons," their best song ever.

Holding hands, skating to popular music, and seeing Emmy's face lit up with joy and laughter is marvelous. Until Emmy takes a fall, skinning her elbow. Tears waterfall down her face, and to my surprise, she comes crying to *me*. Without any thought, I pull her onto my lap, rubbing her back in soothing circles while Butch checks her wound.

"We should clean this up," he says. "It's bleeding a little."

"I'll take her to the ladies' room."

A small smile edges his lips as I smooth Emmy's hair and tell her we'll have her back out on the floor in no time. Her head rests against my chest as her tears dry. Minutes later, with her hand in mine, we head to the bathroom. Butch stares at us with love in his eyes, and possibly a little wonder.

That night, we supervise three shrieking girls hopped up on junk food. By the time we get them settled for bedtime—after several attempts—Emmy's room has finally fallen blessedly silent.

Butch and I quietly shut down the house, get ready for bed, and crawl under the covers in near collapse. He spoons my body, tucking me as close to him as possible and letting out an appreciative groan of approval. It's heaven how our bodies fit together. It reminds me of two spaceships docking. A slow, sure, steady dance until *click*.

THE NEXT DAY, EMMY TEARS INTO HER BIRTHDAY presents, the portrait of glee. The whole gang is here at Butch's parents'—the central hub for Hamiltonian events— to celebrate. She's the belle of the ball, princess for a day, and lapping up the attention like a thirsty dog. She's unwrapped half of a large pile of gifts, and sits surrounded by the colorful paper and ribbon remnants strewn across the living room floor.

Emmy squeals, bringing me back to the present. She's holding a pair of red boxing gloves. She takes the five steps to reach her father, dangling the gloves by their strings. "Put 'em on me, Daddy!"

Butch fits them to her little hands. "You ready for your big-girl lessons?"

"You know it. You literally made me wait until I was eight."

I'm dumbfounded. *She wants to learn boxing?*

He finishes lacing her up and Emmy throws her arms around her father's neck. "Thank you, favorite person."

"Love you, kid."

"Love you, too." She turns and jabs a few punches, then exits the room, fists blazing.

Something grips my chest...something foreign and fighting for space, a realization clawing for air. "She wanted this?" I ask Butch, my voice low.

His eyes follow her movements, full of pride, and he nods. "She's watched me for years. I've got a bag out in the garage."

No wonder Butch's muscles are so defined.

"It's important she learns how to defend herself," he adds. "Boxing not only gives you usable skills should you ever need them, but it's a confidence booster, makes you stronger, and requires discipline. I want Emmy to have all those tools."

The thing in my chest sharpens.

"There are lots of creeps out there. Predators. And I'm not just talking about the weird guys, but the boys she'll see every day going to school. The assholes who take without asking, or pressure girls into doing shit they don't want. I want to give her a voice she can use and back up with her fists."

I'm overwhelmed by how incredible Daddy Lumberjack is for teaching this to his daughter so she'll be prepared. Because he's right—the world is full of dicks, literally and figuratively. It's a monumental, responsible parenting display.

And I'm flooded with the bone-deep knowledge of how much *I* need it. *Now*. Yesterday. Most of my life.

"Will you teach me too?" I ask.

Butch's head swings my way. "Yeah?"

I meet his gaze, trying not to sound desperate. "Yes. Please?"

"I'd be happy to, Sundance. I'll pick you up a set of gloves and we'll start the next time you come down."

I squeeze his forearm. "Thank you."

FIFTY-NINE

Boxing turns out to be the most empowering activity I've ever experienced. In a month's time, I've learned the basics. The correct stance, how to stay on the balls of my feet, turn my hips. Essential punches like the jab, cross, and hook—plus combining them. The importance of breath work, exhaling on every strike. And how to hit a heavy punching bag.

Today Butch watches me practice straight punches on the bag, just jabs and crosses. I've done them slowly so far, focusing on my footwork and relaxing my fist until I land each punch. I pick up the pace incrementally, ready to speed it up.

"That's it, Sundance," Butch praises from where he sits on a workbench. "Your form's looking good."

My lips tug up slightly. *Bap bap, bapbap, bapbap.* I love hitting this dense, stuffed cylinder. The sweat coating my skin is proof of my effort and exertion—and this demonstration of power makes my cells crackle with energy and blood hum.

I don't kid myself about my boxing skills. It's only been weeks, so they're fledgling at best, but the entire act fuels me.

Strength over weakness. Confidence over fear. Badass over coward.

Another month of shit assignments. *Bapbapbap.*

Leering and winks from Don. *Bap bap bapbapbapbap.*

Bitchy, smug looks from Tanya. *Bapbapbapbapbapbap.*

Being trapped, stuck, scared. *Bap bap bapbapbap.*

I drop my hands, leaving the bag swaying from where its bolted to the rafter. Strands of hair loosened from my ponytail cling to my face. I grin at Mr. Handsome Trainer, whose eyes scan me top to bottom with a satisfied smile on his lips.

He crooks his finger and coaxes me to stand between his legs, which dangle from the sturdy wooden table he's sitting on.

Butch grips my waist. "You look so goddamn sexy right now. If I wasn't worried about snooping young eyes, I'd bend you over this workbench."

His words hit the intended spot and a little bomb of pleasure spreads through my system as a whimper leaves my mouth. Boxing may empower me, but I'm putty in Butch's hands. There's something extra filthy about the idea of getting it on in here with grease, dirt, cars, and tools. Perhaps on the hood of a car...

Our mouths collide hungrily, and I don't even care about the sweat. Just this. Just now.

We part, sharing a moment of mutual understanding. My heart leans fully toward his now with zero reservations. Maybe it's caution-to-the-wind stupidity, or blind faith, but it seems bigger than that.

I used to think we were like two halves of a broken glass. Once glued together, we formed a whole, but the cracks were still visible. Now I see our broken shards were melded in hot fire and blown together to create something original, strong, and colorful.

Butch unlaces my gloves. "You're improving with every session. I'm proud of the work you're putting in."

"I didn't expect to like it so much."

"Yeah? Why'd you want to learn so badly?"

"Everything you said about why you were teaching Emmy? That all applies to me. I wish I'd had a father who understood what kind of protection women need in the world."

He assesses me as he pulls off the second glove. "Have you dealt with some assholes?"

I nod. "I've fought off several." *Still am.*

He grimaces. "Fuckers."

"And when I worked at a gas station one summer, some jerk robbed me at gunpoint."

"Jesus." His stare turns steely. "Did he hurt you?"

"He tied me up and shoved his nasty tongue into my mouth before leaving. But that was the scariest night of my life...and I've never felt more powerless." Butch strokes the top of my hand with his thumb as I fight the unease ramping up in my chest.

"I'm sorry that happened to you. I can only imagine how terrifying it was."

"I don't want to be helpless, and living in the city multiplies my risks exponentially. But this," my head dips toward the leather gloves, "is helping."

His gaze turns calculating. "We should work on how to defend yourself barehanded."

Those words only fuel the emerging strength I desperately seek...and am beginning to experience. "That would be amazing."

He wraps me in a tight hug. "I will do whatever it takes to help you stay safe, Jacqui."

As I lean into the surety of this man, not one shred of doubt exists. His formidable size isn't even the main reason. It's his lionheart, the protective instinct that's bred into his blood, and his innate moral compass pointing him the only logical direction.

"Or you could just move in with me, and I'll beat the crap out of any fucker who tries messing with you."

I pull back, eyes flitting to his. Is he joking?

He laughs—nervously? "I'm showing you *all* my cards."

"Are you serious?"

The phone trills and Butch's head swings toward it, debating before he ignores it. "I'm dead serious about fucking up anyone who touches one hair on your head. And you know I want us living in the same zip code...but you probably want an apartment nearby as a next step."

"I know the distance is a drag, but is it a becoming a deal-breaker?"

He holds my face in his hands. "Baby, there are no deal-breakers with you. I'm in love with you."

Emmy runs into the garage, breathless. "Can I go to Mimi's and help bake brownies?"

"That's who called?"

She nods, frenetically.

"Sure. Have fun." Emmy starts to scurry off. "Call when you get there!" he hollers after her.

She waves in acknowledgment.

My mind hits overdrive. *Game on.*

Five minutes later, Butch hangs up the phone with confirmation Emmy made it to his parents' house.

I lick my upper lip, then playfully bite the lower one.

Butch's eyes track it. "That mouth," he mutters.

My hand travels up my torso and coasts across one breast. Again, his eyes stay glued.

"Are you baiting me?"

I offer a slow, alluring shrug, like I don't know what he's talking about. But my gaze stays boldly fixed on his, silently begging him to take charge, possess me, make each nerve ending crackle.

"You're being a very...bad...girl." Every word is measured, a menacing caress as he stalks closer.

I turn around and walk a few steps, pausing to leisurely bend at the waist and massage my ankle, teasing him with a view of the ass I know he craves.

His growl hits me right between the thighs. "Very bad." His footsteps draw nearer. "And bad girls get what's coming to them."

Victory.

Butch hauls me upright and propels me toward a 1969 Dodge Charger he's restoring in one of the bays. When my knees bump the metal grill, he yanks my ponytail. "Give me that fucking mouth," he says, kissing me hard.

The fire sears from my lips to my groin. The slight pinch from where he grabs my hair to the invasion of his tongue, slicking with mine, floods my center. He's possessed—and so am I.

He forces me flat against the sanded hood, ass up, my pussy tingling with anticipation. "Teasing me with those big, luscious tits of yours, your nipples poking through your fucking top." He spreads my arms like eagle wings as my cheek flattens upon the smooth surface.

He yanks down my shorts and underwear in one go, exposing me to him. "Shaking this perfect peach ass every-where you go."

I want him to spank me and silently plead for it.

"Now it's mine to do with as I fucking want."

"Yes, *please.*"

He lets out a satisfied groan...then his hand slaps my right ass cheek. The sting lifts me onto my toes—and unleashes a small flood from between my thighs.

I moan my approval. *Yesssss.*

"This ass," he says, spanking me on the other side, harder this time, testing to see what I can take.

My garbled ahhs meet his triumphant grunt.

"This pussy." *Smack.* "These tits." *Smack.* "And that fucking mouth." *Smack.* "Are mine."

I'm arching, writhing, bucking—and I'm embarrassingly drenched in that sacred space I hope he plows very soon. This is other-fucking-worldly. I'm acutely present, fully in my body. Aware of everything...from the contour of the hood beneath me to the bite of his palm against my skin to the ache Butch creates that only he can fill. He takes me places I've never imagined, and I trust him more than I've ever trusted another human being...especially when I'm this vulnerable, this defenseless.

"Say it," he demands.

"All yours," I rasp.

"What am I going to find if I reach between your legs, huh, Sundance? You getting off on this, my naughty, dirty girl?"

I whimper, desperate to widen my stance, but they're trapped by my shorts. And god, those words. I've never wanted anything more than to be his plaything.

"You are a stone fox," he murmurs. One hand skates up my thigh and explores my throbbing vagina, discovering it's flooded. He plunges two thick fingers inside me, groaning out a long "Fuuuuuuuuck" as I wail from the delicious intrusion. His erection is a steel rod, pressing against my tingling ass with a promise for what's to come. He pumps his fingers deep and stars fleck my vision. I'm so wet, the squelch fills the air. It's raunchy, depraved, obscene.

Butch stops, and my breath hitches. *Nooooooo. Don't stop.*

"Grind that pussy and fuck my fingers."

Ahhhh. My body obliges, overriding any hesitant inner voice as I do exactly as I'm told.

"That's it, baby. God, you're a horny fucking broad. Keep moving that beautiful ass."

Between the way I'm driving my hips, forcing his fingers deeper, and how those key nerve endings press against the car, I'm gone in sixty seconds. My orgasm rips out of left field, without the usual buildup, and my scream echoes in the space.

Butch keeps penetrating me as shudders of release rock through me. "Such a good, bad girl...my hot, slutty girl." His praise in that resonant low tone sends fresh chill bumps rippling across my skin.

My vision turns black, and my brain is thoroughly blown as I come down. Butch's hand disappears, and my lips open in protest. Before I utter one syllable, his cock thrusts into my pulsating center and more waves of pleasure erupt.

"Clean up your gorgeous mess," he commands, stuffing his wet fingers into my mouth.

I groan around him, sucking my essence eagerly off his hand as he invades me in two places.

"Good fucking girl," he says in reward.

He unmercifully takes what's his, driving into me possessively and holding me hostage with my shorts tethering me in place. Each thrust claims and dominates, and when he removes his hand, I nearly cry from how much I need this, want this.

Not this...*him.*

"You drive me fucking insane," he grits out. "I want you every second of every day. Your body. Your mind. Your heart." He grips both of my hips as his impaling strokes pound into me.

I'm too full of sensations to respond, my breaths coming hard and fast. All I can do is take it, give in to it, and enjoy the ride.

My release, still undulating through me in slow waves, starts shifting into something...different. In this position, my man's big dick spins new magic in combination with my pussy rubbing against the angled hood. My cries grow louder and faster.

Butch knows. "That's it, baby. Give it to me. Give it all to me."

A second orgasm rips through me as Butch growls his approval. I'm delirious as he continues his assault, hands digging into my hips. He holds me in place and drives into me with delicious force—my center spasming around him where we're joined.

"I love how...we fit...baby." His words come out strained. "How...perfect you...are. I will...never get enough...of you...of this."

All I can do is whimper, his words swimming in my soul. We are perfection.

Butch quickens, roaring out his own release as he spills into me. We both gasp for air, our chests heaving as his body cocoons around mine.

It's minutes before we speak.

"You okay, baby?" he murmurs.

"I loved every second."

"You're turning me into an animal."

"I don't even recognize myself, in a good way. And...I trust you." Something I wasn't sure I could do again.

His lips brush my shoulder. "You'll always be safe with me, Jacqui."

THE FOLLOWING WEEK WHEN TANYA AND I CROSS paths in the ladies' room, her appearance is again slightly disheveled. A hundred barbs linger on my tongue about how she's screwed her way to the top and effectively fucked me too, but I'm not a shrew.

She senses my heavy stare and glares at me in the mirror. "What?" she snaps.

"You don't have to..." I pause, lathering my hands. How do I word this?

"Spit it out, Barbie." She's two sinks down, pumping soap into her palm.

God, she's a bitch. "You don't have to do what you're doing."

"What am I *doing*?"

She knows exactly what I mean. "With Don."

"Mind your own damn business." She shuts off the water, leans toward the towel dispenser, and yanks a few out.

"It *is* my business when your actions affect me. Assignments are being distributed based on something other than merit. You think I don't know it was you who complained?"

"I deserve everything I get."

On that we can agree. "Do you know Don has tried getting in *my* pants? And likely many others before us?" I dry my hands more roughly than needed.

She shrugs, applying a new coat of lipstick. "Guess you were too stupid to see a good thing when you had the chance."

A dumbfounded scoff leaves my lips. "Yeah...no thanks."

"Grow up, Jacqui. This is how the world works." Her tone drips condescension. "And keep your fucking mouth shut if you know what's good for you." She exits the restroom, her threat still hanging in the air.

If this is how the world works, I quit. I'm not rising to the top on my back or my knees. I'm getting there on ability and performance. And Tanya may be keeping Don occupied, but I know it's only a matter of time before he corners me again.

SIXTY

In April, Butch whisks me up to Washington, D.C. for the National Cherry Blossom Festival. Thousands of trees bursting with pink and white blooms line the Tidal Basin reservoir and surrounding National Mall area. I couldn't have asked for a more glorious welcome to the nation's capital.

The walk among the flowering trees dazzles but visiting each iconic monument fills me with awe. The Lincoln Memorial, with an enormous carving of Abe sitting in a chair overlooks the famous reflecting pool, the Washington Monument visually arresting at the opposite end. The Jefferson Memorial is an open-air rotunda featuring a bronze statue of Thomas Jefferson standing atop a pedestal, surrounded by quotes carved in marble. Our time at the Vietnam Veterans Memorial is silent and solemn as we walk the entirety of "The Wall." It's etched with rows upon rows of names honoring the fallen soldiers forever lost in that controversial war. Countless flowers and trinkets are placed in front of panels as remembrances.

Through it all are the trees in bloom and miles of lawn

greening up now that spring has arrived. Spending time in the heart of our nation, one that carries the weight of our history, blankets me in humility.

We venture to the White House, passing poignant quotes carved into sidewalks along the way, then head to our hotel.

When we arrive at the Willard InterContinental, it's so fancy, I worry what it's costing my lumberjack. The palatial lobby is the epitome of elegance with huge marble pillars, inlaid ceilings, golden details, oversized ferns, and polished floors that makes the kid in me want to see how far I could skid in socks.

In the elevator, I joke, "Do you think we might be able to order canapés?"

Butch grins down at me, leaning close to my ear. "The only thing I want on the menu is holding my hand." His eyes caress mine, looking at me like I'm priceless.

He opens the door to our room and *wow*. "Oh, Butch," I murmur.

I take it all in. Spacious, stylish, and stunning. An accent wall outlines the plush king bed with a very presidential-esque headboard. An upholstered bench sits before it. I peer out the window, glimpsing the Washington Monument jutting to the sky. And the bathroom holds its own glamour with a variety of soaps and lotions I'll peruse later—plus a ginormous tub that easily fits two.

I throw myself into Butch's arms, tackling him against the mattress.

He grunts, then laughs. "You like it, baby?"

Exuberance dances through me. "I love it. You're spoiling me." I gaze into those emerald eyes I also love.

"It's my pleasure, believe me."

"Are you secretly wealthy? I mean, this place must cost a fortune..."

He chuckles. "I'm not a closet billionaire or anything."

I pretend to be crestfallen. "What a shame. That's kind of a dealbreaker."

"Because you could get used to this?"

Laughter bubbles out of me. "Exactly that."

Butch pulls me down to his lips and we share a languid kiss.

He lands a sharp smack on my ass, and I yelp. "Let's clean up and eat dinner so I can have my way with you back in this bed."

"Sounds like a plan, handsome, non-billionaire, lumberjack man," I say before hoisting myself off him.

We take a cab to Georgetown and walk along M Street, home to a smorgasbord of restaurants and bars. A fair number of preppy college students mill the sidewalks. When we pass the Third Edition, I do a double take.

"What?" Butch asks.

"This looks familiar," I say, staring at the facade. "Isn't that the bar from *St. Elmo's Fire*?"

"Didn't see it."

I nudge him with my elbow. "Not a Brat Pack guy?"

"More of a *Rambo, Red Dawn, Dirty Harry* kind of guy."

"Blood, war, destruction then? No comedies? Dramas?"

"I liked *Beverly Hills Cop, Cannonball Run,* and that one with Kurt Russell?" He pauses, then snaps his fingers. "*Big Trouble in Little China.*"

"So...*action comedies*? Way to branch out."

He gives me a sidelong glance as we reach the restaurant. "Let me guess...you only like romances?"

My brows furrow before I give him a flat look. "Wrong-o-rama. I'm game for almost anything."

"Good. Because I'm putting that to the test later."

It's a promise, one far more delicious than what we're about to eat.

I emerge from the hotel bathroom in my emerald lace teddy. It's not only a nod to Butch's arresting irises, but it pairs nicely with my honey-blond hair. A deep V splits the material to my navel, and the high cut over each hip dissolves to a G-string in the rear. This audacious getup emboldens me.

Butch has stripped down to his jeans and stands by the window, low lamplight casting a sexy glow across his muscular frame. He's already turned down the bed, and the crisp white sheets beckon in open invitation.

I strike a pose, watching him for a minute. Because the view is spectacular—and I'm not talking about the city. "Hey, Lumberjack," I coo.

His head swivels, body following as he drinks me in. He takes his time, eyes growing hungrier by the second.

The ache thrashing within me intensifies. I'm a woman starved. For him.

"Come here, gorgeous," he murmurs, holding out a hand.
Gentlemen, start your engines...

I join him at the window. A furtive glance convinces me we're high enough that no one can see us.

Butch places my palms against the glass and nudges his knee between my legs, forcing them wider. His lips graze my cheek. "Mine," he says, that bass tone a lightning strike to my groin.

"*Yours,*" I breathe, already so aroused my nipples ache.

He nuzzles my throat, trailing his tongue over to the sensitive area by my ear. His hands stroke the length of my arms, across my breasts, along my hips, and tease the apex of my thighs. He growls appreciatively and my flesh ripples in response.

"You look like such a sexy, naughty girl...so beautiful, baby." His kisses trail down my back as every one of my cells responds to his words.

I'm panting. *Yes, yes, yessssssss.*

"Are you my pretty whore tonight? My toy? Mine to do with as I please?" His fingers tease my entrance and the other hand travels across my front to pinch my nipple through the lace. It's scratchy against my tender skin, but I like it.

"Yes," I croak.

He hums deep. His erection strains behind his jeans, pressing into me so hard that whimpers leave my throat. His assault continues and I'm so taut I may spontaneously combust.

"Butch," I plead.

He spins me around. "On your knees, baby. Open that fuckable mouth."

Oh, hell yeah. I sink to the carpet, salivating for him. He's already unbuttoned his jeans and pulled his zipper partially undone. The teasing glimpse of his bulging cock floods my center anew.

He caresses my hair, stroking down my face, and lifts my chin. Our eyes fuse, and his burn with raw hunger. "Do you know what the sight of you like this does to me?" He doesn't wait for an answer. "Now pull out my cock and suck it like it's all you'll ever need."

My eager hands obey, sighing with choked desperation when my fingers wrap around his girth. I draw him hungrily into my mouth. He's so hard, I marvel at all that strength. His dirty talk has me spun up and I've never wanted anything more than to be used and defiled by this man for hours. Butch's king-size dick is difficult to manage in its entirety, but I'm on fire. He leaves one hand fisted in my hair, feeding me every inch. My throat opens to take him deeper and deeper with each pull of my hollowed cheeks.

"You can take it, Sundance, *all of it*," he murmurs.

I work harder, and a low "*fuuuuuuuck*" rolls from his lips.

Moaning around his girth, I revel in his rigidity, stark

masculinity, at how he's using me while revering me. It spurs me on, all my nerve endings tingling.

A quick glance shows his eyes blazing, focused on me inhaling him, pleasuring him. Barely distinguishable words tumble from his lips…"heaven" and "death of me" and "mine."

My jaw labors at being stretched for so long, but then his strokes come faster, his hand steadfastly keeping me at his mercy as he fucks my mouth with abandon.

"I'm…coming…baby. Swallow every…drop."

I moan just before his hips thrust and grind, bottoming out in my throat as I breathe quickly through my nose. Warmth spurts with his final thrusts, and his hand nearly rips my hair. Tears from the intensity leak from my eyes as his gaze latches on mine.

He pulls out, still partially hard, and I gulp down the essence pooling in my mouth. Inhaling some deep breaths, I tilt my freed head up at my towering lumberjack. He stares down at me, green eyes blacker and hazy with lust. He lifts me from the floor, kissing me with renewed energy. His tongue sweeps mine, surprising me a little, considering. But he's resolute, claiming my mouth with intensity.

"I love that fucking mouth," he says, palming the side of my face.

I smile up at him, gratified at pleasing him…not to mention myself.

"Get on the bed on all fours." His deep, captivating voice brooks no argument.

I'm feral for dominant Butch, willing to do whatever he demands. I want it, all of it, whatever *it* is. I crawl onto the ready sheets as instructed, my vulnerable assets on display.

"Stunning," Butch murmurs, his breath warming my ass before he kisses me there. He unsnaps the teddy and the material springs away from my crotch. His fingers coast along my pussy and slip inside.

I moan, my entire body trembling from his touch, the anticipation, the desire surging unchecked through my veins.

He hums. "Baby, you're dripping. Did you like sucking my cock? Did it make you want to come?"

"Yessssss."

"Such a good slutty girl."

His thick fingers venture in further—*god, I love his fingers*—two, then three. I'm gasping when he licks up the underside of my ass cheek and lands on my...my...um, *other* hole. I'm ripped from my delirium as his wet tongue probes. When I stiffen, he stops.

"Relax, baby. I promise this will feel good if you get out of your head."

For real?

"I've wanted this since the day we met. You have no idea how sexy you are, or what this means...you giving this to me. I want all of you, Sundance. *All* of you."

I whoosh out a breath. "Okay."

"Trust me?"

"Yes."

"Mine?"

"*Yours,*" I breathe.

"Relax. Get ready to come like you never have before."

That's one hell of a promise, and I force myself to chill. Butch resumes exploring the playground. His fingers and tongue create a symphony of sensations, pushing through my remaining resistance with surprising ease.

Oh...*my*. What he's doing back there, everywhere, it's an advanced level of dirty sex with a hint of taboo. We're crossing new barriers tonight.

His tongue seeks, soft but persistent, as he groans against my flesh. Then a finger replaces his mouth, gently swirling and probing. He pushes in the very tip, allowing me time to adjust. My breath comes in pants, my center wiggling and pulsing and then pumping toward him, begging for more.

And he gives me more.

The pressure...fullness...of this foreign pleasure steals the air from my lungs. With his other hand strumming my pussy into a frenzy, I have zero notice before I combust with such force, my eyes squeeze shut and I wail through a powerful, raging orgasm. Tremors wrack my body, my limbs shaking uncontrollably.

"*Ohhhhhh*, baby...*that's* my good girl," Butch croons, voice husky with wondrous praise.

My eyes tear from the sheer intensity. He pulls me gently onto the bed and into his arms, kissing my hair and whispering *I love you* and *baby, baby, baby*. I'm shook...speechless...spent, my mind and body blown.

Butch rolls over top of me and kisses my forehead, eyelids, cheeks. He's reverent and tender, tugging my heart nearly out of my chest. My legs part, wrapping around his waist as he eases his hard length into me, his massive size stalling my breath until he's all the way home. His strokes start slow and decadent but soon lead to hard, possessive drives, the kind that hammer *mine mine mine* with each thrust. If I wasn't his before, I am now. Fully. Unequivocally.

The revelation knots my throat as I stare up at my beautiful man and find his eyes fastened on mine in an unspoken love letter. A man who pulled me from the trenches of despair and healed some of my brokenness. Patched the worst holes in my heart. Restored my faith in men, in desire, in two hearts beating in harmony.

I'm yours.

After, he wraps me in his arms, murmuring more praise, adulation, appreciation.

When we've sufficiently recovered, Butch draws us a bath and pops the champagne. With a lazy smile, he holds out his hand to help me into the tub. My back slides against his front as I sink into the soothing bubbles.

He lets out a contented sigh. "I could get used to this."

Without even looking, I know he's smiling. My toes peek out of the froth before submerging again. "Better get busy making those billions."

The arm he has wrapped around my chest squeezes as he kisses the top of my head. "I'm already the richest man alive."

SIXTY-ONE

I decide to look for another job. It's April and I'm still getting crappy assignments with the occasional feature, just enough to keep me dangling on the proverbial hook like a sucker fish. When I ask Tyler for an update on the bogus "complaint," he says there's no new information, meaning this is now the status quo.

Don appears to be waiting me out—or maybe he no longer cares, now that Tanya's fulfilling his needs. Insufferable, predatory, chauvinist pig.

I'm casting my net wider in hopes I can move closer to Butch. Moving would be difficult for him, between Emmy and his role in the family business, but there's nothing shackling me to Richmond aside from more opportunities.

Unfortunately, the early prospects prove dim. The only publication in Hampton Springs is *The Gazette*, a weekly newspaper, and they're not hiring. No magazines operate in the small towns and the next one worth applying for is based in Virginia Beach—just as far from the lumberjack as I am now. I'm trapped until further notice.

I relay all this to Butch on Friday night when I'm back at his place.

"Something will open up," he says with confidence.

"You're refreshingly optimistic."

He shrugs. "*You* happened. I never predicted that, so now I think anything's possible."

I move in closer and circle my hands around his waist, tilting my head up at him. "You sure know how to sweep a woman off her feet."

In answer, he corrals my legs from under me and hefts me into his arms, bride-style, causing me to squeal.

Emmy barrels into the kitchen with the dog scrambling behind her.

"Dogpile!" she chants, jumping into the fracas.

Hemi follows, and Butch exaggeratedly falls to the floor without letting me go. Our peals of laughter fill the air as our limbs tangle and Hemi gives our faces big sloppy licks.

AFTER EMMY'S DANCE CLASS, WE STOP BY HIS parents' house so I can say hello.

"Come here, cutie pie," Gus hollers at his granddaughter. "Give your PopPop a squeeze."

"I'm not pie!" she answers with a touch of irritation, as if she's explained all this to her grandfather before.

"You know I think you're sweet enough to eat." He bends down and Emmy wraps her arms around his neck and kisses his cheek.

I'm awarded hugs by Gus and Jerri too, par for the course these days.

"I just made coffee cake," Jerri says. "You all come in and have a slice."

My stomach rumbles in agreement. "Sounds delicious."

"I'm glad you're here, Jacqui," Gus adds. "I've got a proposition for you."

Now I'm intrigued.

We settle around the informal table with slices of the

crumb-topped cake and coffees before us. I groan at the airy first bite bursting with brown sugar and cinnamon. Jerri returns my satisfied smile with her own.

"You are the best cook," I say.

Gus clears his throat, and my gaze swings his way. "I want to pursue the magazine, and if you're willing, I'd sure appreciate your help."

Butch's head jerks in my periphery as my eyes stay fastened on his father. "How exciting. You figured out the logistics, printing, and all the nitty-gritty details?"

He shakes his head, looking a little sheepish. "That's where you come in."

"I'm listening."

"I'd like to hire you to nail down the specifics, outline the first year of issues, determine its overall viability. Since you already have a job, I figure we can iron out a consultant fee. A lot of this you can do on your own time, of course, and then we'll get together in person as schedules allow."

Butch scrubs his jaw. "Are you sure you want to take this on, Dad? It's going to be time consuming. I know you're less hands-on with the restorations now, but I don't want you stretching yourself too thin. We're swamped with business."

"That's why Jacqui's helping to sketch out the details. I won't make any final decisions until I see the numbers, time investment, and fine print, so to speak. Right now, it's just a possibility, but a damn attractive one. And there's clearly a hole in the market, that much I know. This will put Hamilton Restorations on the map."

"We already are," Butch answers, an edge to his voice.

Gus raps his knuckles on the table. "Let your old man tinker around with this idea. It's something I dreamed of years ago, a dream that's never faded. I only have more of a contribution to make in our industry by creating this magazine."

I gently squeeze Butch's forearm. "It would be a niche publication, and those can do very well because they're so specialized."

"Whose side are on you on, Sundance?"

"Team Hamilton all the way," I answer with a grin.

Butch rolls his eyes, muttering under his breath.

"Gus, I'd be happy to consult on this, but you don't need to pay me or anything."

He snorts. "I'm paying for your expertise, and I won't hear another word otherwise."

We don't hang around long once the conversation ends. Emmy opts to run home through the wooded path and Butch and I drive the car back. He's turned broody and quiet; the energy between us tense.

"I can tell you're unhappy about this," I say, reaching behind his head and stroking down his neck. "Why though?"

He grunts. His jaw muscle pulses.

I knead this taut skin and watch his lids droop as he sinks into it. Butch loves being touched...even if he's mad.

"Baby..." I prod.

His eyes flash my way, then back on the road. My hand falls to my lap.

"First, I meant what I said," he explains. "We're stretched thin at the business, and him gallivanting around with a time-consuming new venture is going to make everything harder. That negatively impacts you and me, and I think we can both agree the last thing we need is less time with one another, correct?"

"True."

"Second, you getting involved in your spare time? Same impact. *What fucking spare time?* You think I want this taking away from the paltry minutes we patch together? He had no right to ask that of you without talking to me."

"Whoa, now. You're not my keeper."

He rakes a hand violently through his hair. "That's not what I meant."

"What *do* you mean?" I cross my arms.

"He's told me very little about all this when it directly impacts my life, my livelihood, my time, and now my girlfriend."

I soften at his words but remain stern. "You don't want me to help your dad then?"

"I don't fucking know." He steers the Barracuda down his driveway and pauses halfway with his foot on the brake, spearing me with a gaze blazing with intensity. "What I want is more of you, as much of you as I can get, every goddamn fucking day."

My heart melts. Butch's love is ferocious, and he's not afraid to own it or display it. I unbuckle my seatbelt and finagle my way onto his lap—not the easiest feat since the man is massive and the car...not.

"What are you—"

My lips collide with his, my tongue running along the seam and demanding entry. The kiss says everything: *I love you, I want you, I need you, I'm yours.*

He responds, gripping the sides of my face. His tongue ravages mine, taking what I'm offering.

We part, our foreheads touching as our collective breath mingles.

"I love you, Butch."

"I love you more."

"We'll work all this out, I promise."

His head dips wearily. I climb back into my seat, and he drives to the house. Emmy's waiting on the porch then breaks into a run toward her father, worry creasing her features. He hurries out of the car, and I fly out my own side in time to witness her clutch his body.

"Hey, you okay?" he says. "What's wrong?"

Emmy nods, solemn. "I needed to love you."

Butch chuckles and hefts her into his arms. "I thought something terrible had happened."

"Love withdrawal *is* terrible."

Be still my heart. And damn if these two haven't stolen mine.

Sixty-Two

"Will you go to prom with me?"

I pull the phone away from my ear and briefly inspect it. I must have misheard because it sounded a hell of a lot like a...*prom invite*. Only we're grown-ass adults, long out of high school, so that's impossible.

"Come again?"

"I said, Jacqueline Hall, will you go to prom with me?"

A chuckle bubbles forth. "I don't understand."

"You need me to explain prom?" Butch says.

"Okay smartass, yes, I do, since I graduated from high school in 1981 and it's now 1988. Unless this is a *Back to the Future* kind of situation. Do you have a DeLorean time machine with a flux capacitor?"

"Better."

"Really?"

"I've got a badass car, a hot fucking date that I'm betting is a sure thing—"

A loud laugh erupts from my mouth. "And let me guess, a purple tuxedo?"

"And *no* purple tuxedo."

"And this prom is where and when?"

"Next month. It's an annual event for adults about an hour south of here, and I know you didn't go to yours, so I thought maybe I could take you to this one."

Oh shit. Oh shit. Oh shit. Insta-tears.

"Jacqui? You there?"

"Mm-hmm," I manage. *Get a hold of yourself.*

"Is that a yes?"

I'm at a loss for words. I swallow and take a deep breath. "You took me off guard there, Lumberjack...in the best boyfriendy way. It's a *hell yes.*"

"Had me worried there for a minute."

"It's really a prom?" I breathe.

"I've never been, but it's supposedly the real deal. Cheese-ball decorations, a professional portrait photographer, disco ball and DJ, formalwear, the works."

"Oh my god. That's epic." So cool. "I'm touched you remembered."

"I remember everything you've said, Sundance."

I'm goo. Scrape me off the floor. "And no way I can get you into a purple tux?"

"If that's a requirement, I must rescind my invitation, beautiful."

"I'm kidding. But you are expecting to get laid, if I heard your earlier reference correctly?"

"I don't mean to presume, but it's customary for the girl to put out on prom night."

We share a laugh. Of course I'm putting out. No prom required. "But it's formal?"

"Formal-ish. Men don't need to wear black tie, for instance. A suit will suffice."

"Mmm...I'm kind of drooling about Daddy Lumberjack in a suit."

"I will do anything to get you drooling, baby. Especially if it involves my dick."

I chuckle. "Is it going to be, like, old folks?"

"Maybe? I'm not sure. But ask me if I care."

"I'm betting not."

"All I care about is taking my hot girlfriend to prom, because every woman should experience that in her lifetime if it's what she wishes."

"Have I told you how much I love you today, Butch?"

"Nope."

"You are the most wonderful man—and you've straight-up ruined me for anyone else."

"That was my evil plan. And baby...there's no one for me but you."

A FEW WEEKS LATER, THE BIG NIGHT ARRIVES. Butch insists on picking me up for our date, as he would if it were our high school prom, so I stay at his house to get gussied up and he changes at his parents' house. He tried taking Emmy with him, since his parents are babysitting her overnight anyway, but she wanted to hang out with me while I got ready.

She's been attached to my side through makeup, hair styling, and donning my dress and jewelry, peppering me with questions.

How do you keep the mascara from getting in your eyes? Carefully.

What does the blow dryer feel like? I point it at her head, the blast billowing her long strands as her giggles erupt.

When will I wear a bra? When your breasts start to grow —and show.

Will mine look like yours? There's no way to know until they mature, but whatever size they become will be perfect.

Do you love my daddy? So very much.

Do you think you'll marry him? I don't know how to

answer so I lob back my own question: *Would you like that?* And she nods.

You're so pretty. Am I pretty? Yes, you are beautiful. And you're beautiful inside, where it matters most.

Then she says, "I love you, Jacqui." It's the first time.

Hugging her tiny body, I whisper, "I love you too, Emmy." Double goo.

Butch knocks on the front door of the cabin right on time, and Emmy answers, allowing me a grand entrance moment down the stairs. I hold onto the railing, steadying myself as I descend in strappy, elegant heels, careful not to trip over my floor-length, flowing black gown.

My date comes into view. Our eyes connect briefly before mine travel down his masculine frame. He's wrapped in a black suit with a crisp white dress shirt, opened a few buttons at the top with no tie. He's clean shaven and my insides flutter as if it really is prom night.

His gaze rakes over me. He's taking in the halter top, attached to two panels covering my breasts but providing a peek between, how the material hugs my curves and flares at the bottom, and the enticing slit up the left leg. My hair is styled in an updo with loose tendrils framing my face.

He holds out his hand and I take it.

"You are breathtaking, Sundance. A vision beyond my wildest expectations." He spins me to see the open back, then hums his approval.

"Stunning," he murmurs.

"Likewise, handsome. I mean, *whew*. I could get used to that."

He grins. "Maybe don't get *used* to it. But tonight? It's all for you."

I appraise him another minute then narrow my eyes.

"What?"

I shrug. "I'm a little disappointed."

His expression falls. "Why? What did I do?"

"Jeez, Butch...I really thought you were going to give me the purple tux."

"Trust me on this." He flashes a smile I can't quite interpret.

The two of us stand there openly admiring each other until Emmy says, "Sheesh...why don't you marry her already."

Oh my god. I must be fifty shades of scarlet and Butch nearly chokes.

"On that note, missy, get your butt over to Mimi and PopPop's. I'm not leaving until you call and let me know you got there."

"Where else would I go? It's literally next door."

Butch cocks his head, a warning, then leans down to her level. "Pay the toll, kid."

She kisses his cheek. "You look real nice, too, Daddy."

"Thanks, sweetheart. I love you."

"Love you too."

She leaves with Hemi, and we stand in the foyer grinning at each other.

"Is that for me?" I ask, spying something clutched in his hand.

He looks down as if he forgot he was holding it. "What a dumbass. Yes, this is for you." He hands me the box, and I open it, finding a corsage.

It's not one of those tacky, over-the-top varieties that dwarfs your forearm, but a tasteful, demure bracelet made of white mini roses. Butch removes it and slips it over my wrist.

"It's lovely." And unexpected.

"You look so beautiful, Jacqui," he says, taking my hand. "I'm a lucky son of a bitch."

I trail my fingers down his suit lapels, coasting over the smooth material and loving the way it hangs on his large frame. My shoes close our height gap by four inches, putting me closer to that kissable mouth, and I plant one lightly on his lips. "You look good enough to eat."

"Uh...sold."

We share a smile, interrupted when the phone rings and Butch gets the confirmation he needs from Emmy. It really is convenient that he lives next door to his parents, and in this safe, small-town enclave where his daughter can run between houses.

Butch tucks me into the Barracuda, which he's washed, waxed, buffed, and cleaned. It's *very* prom night all around. We get on the road, all smiles, just as the sun begins to set, coloring the sky in vivid hues. He's even got Van Halen in the tape deck.

We arrive at the restaurant on time for our reservation. Rich aromas waft through the air and my stomach rumbles in response. We crack jokes and steal kisses, then settle in for a delicious meal.

Adult prom is everything Butch promised and more. The decorations with an "Under the Sea" theme. The mostly older couples. The cheesy photos, for which we absolutely pose. And all the glorious dancing. My suitor isn't afraid to bust out some moves, and the slow songs, when my head rests on his shoulder, make me sigh like a lovesick girl. Because I *am* a lovesick girl, one hundred percent gone for this man who gave me a prom do-over on a silver platter. What kind of man does this?

The one I have the privilege of loving.

He is the consummate date: attentive, selfless, focused purely on me having a wonderful time. I inhale it all, from his mesmerizing scent to the soft twinkling lights to the music flowing across us when he holds me in his arms. Classics like "At Last" by Etta James, "Let's Stay Together," by Al Green, and "Unchained Melody" by the Righteous Brothers.

Once we get home, I happily put out—the perfect ending

to this wondrous night. And my date doesn't disappoint either.

He's wearing briefs in a shocking shade of purple.

SIXTY-THREE

The shit hits the fan two weeks later when Don calls me into his office. He positions me in a chair in front of his imposing desk, assessing me with his pale eyes.

"Are you happy here, Jacqueline?"

"At the magazine?"

"Precisely." His eyes remain fixed on me, reminding me of a lizard that never blinks.

Why not say it out loud, call him out on his bullshit? "I'm unhappy with the prejudicial way assignments are distributed among our section."

He doesn't react. "Be more specific."

Like you don't know. "Ever since a complaint was filed—full of *false* allegations—I've received significantly fewer features and top-tier stories."

"Why do you assume the allegations are untrue?"

"Because I've done nothing to compromise my ethics, and previous assignments were awarded on merit."

He clasps his hands. "Perhaps the quality of your writing deteriorated."

Or maybe I just refused to fuck the boss. "That's not the

case, and Tyler can verify. Even these past months where I've been unjustly underutilized, I've given a hundred percent, like always."

He straightens his fingers, leaving them threaded, and points them my direction. "How do you propose resolving it?"

"Let Tyler decide who deserves assignments based on merit."

Don stands, walks to my side of the desk and sits against it, arms crossed. "You know you have a get-out-of-jail-free card."

His proximity sends a jolt of adrenaline through my bloodstream. The door's closed, louver blinds drawn, and he's standing close. *Too* fucking close, lording over me in a power play.

"Sure do. It's called work ethic." *Or we could just go with ethics, something you're severely lacking.*

"About that." He cocks his head, tapping a finger against his lips. "I heard something interesting about you through the grapevine."

The way he hovers, casting me a glib smile, gives me a vivid flashback to the children's tale about the spider with the fly. Tornado-alert panic rushes through my system.

"I hear you're looking for another job."

"Excuse me?" *How could he know that?*

He arches an eyebrow, and maybe I'm reading into it, but his expression turns victorious. "I see my comment hit the mark. You *are* searching for employment elsewhere?"

I swallow hard, unsure how to respond.

"Additionally, you're *consulting* on a magazine for the president of a company you met working for us. There's nothing ethical about that, sweetheart."

My heart falls. Did Gus tell him this? Why? I grasp for something, anything to say. "You spoke with Mr. Hamilton?" Shit, now I've confirmed his suspicions.

"It matters not where this knowledge was derived. What matters is, one," he extends his index finger, "you go behind my back to work with contacts you made through *Virginia Now*—at the very least, ignoring professional courtesy. And two," he uncurls another finger, "sneaking around to secure employment elsewhere is just ungrateful. You've only worked here a year, and we've invested in you. Now you're complaining about assignments you deem insufficient instead of buckling down and being a team player."

My breathing labors, heart jackhammering against my ribcage as I stare at the ground. I'm about to get fired.

I'm barely cognizant of Don standing until he moves closer, his voice next to my ear. "But you and I both know how easy it would be for me to forgive these transgressions." His hand grazes my breast through my blouse, and my body jerks so violently, I lift from the chair.

Was that an accident? It happened so fast. Yes? No? He's still uncomfortably close but not touching me as I perch on the chair's edge, ready to bolt.

"You can open your mouth, or you can collect your things."

My gut roils. Is he saying what I think—? My lips part, my response stalling as I grapple for words.

"Good choice," he says, unzipping his slacks in front of my face.

"N-no, no!" I push off the chair and his hand whips out, digging sharply into my shoulder and forcing me back down.

He looms over me, confidence written all over his face. When I thrash, he smiles, using both hands to restrain me. "I knew you'd be a tiger."

Revulsion shudders through my body, my limbs trembling uncontrollably. I summon my voice. "I said *no*," I croak. Goddamn it!

"Be a good girl and stop fighting. This was inevitable," he grits out.

He grips my throat, pressing against my windpipe, and fresh panic rises. With the other hand, he releases his engorged, veiny penis, cloaked in an angry purple hue.

My eyes widen as adrenaline and fear pump through my blood. Bile bucks from my stomach, and I dry heave, choking and sputtering.

His hand relaxes. "Don't gag yet. You haven't even had a taste." He lets out a low chuckle, lines up in front of my face, and yanks my neck toward that disgusting violet monstrosity.

I reel back, my neck springing loose from his grasp and nearly hyperextending. He scrambles to straddle me, trying to bridge the gap. I rally every ounce of courage and strength to launch one leg skyward, kneeing him in the groin. The squish of his genitals is unmistakable. He falls back against the desk with a strangled groan.

"You bitch!" he hisses.

I clamber to my feet, dodging his flailing arm. Don staggers in my direction. Clenching my fist like Butch taught me, I assume the stance I've practiced for months and punch his jaw as hard as fucking possible.

Don reels, eyes flying wide, and drops to his knees.

My hand stings like hell and I debate whether to throw another. "Fuck you, you predatory asshole." I turn on my heel and reach for the door.

"You're fired," he rasps. "And you're *through* in this industry. Should've played ball, you stupid cunt."

"You're pathetic." With a final backward glance, I rip open the door with enough force it nearly flies off the hinges.

Adrenaline rampages through me as I stalk past the empty desk where Don's secretary greeted me fifteen minutes ago. My eyes dart like a wild animal as I continue down the hall and into the sea of cubicles, the roaring in my ears eclipsing thought. Focus. I need to focus.

Clean out your office.

I chuck essentials from my desk and shelves into a canvas

bag. Souvenirs from companies I've profiled. A paperweight Emmy made me. My movements are jerky, my thoughts careening all over the place.

Leave the building.

I stride to the elevators, avoiding curious stares, desperate to flee. I have no idea what Don's capable of anymore. Will he sic security on me after spewing lies? There were no witnesses. The only potential for that would be his secretary—and she was conveniently, conspicuously absent. The elevator arrives, and I scurry inside, depressing the button for the garage a dozen times until the doors close, fervently hoping no one else gets on.

Get to your car.

Full-body trembling hits once I'm in my Toyota, but I manage to start the ignition, reverse out of my parking spot, and screech out of the garage...for the last time. I've been *fired*. The absolute nerve of that fucking asshole. Fresh anger blazes a path from head to toe. I floor the gas, racing recklessly through the streets.

Butch.

He's the only person in the world I want. *Need*. I veer away from my apartment and head south.

"FUUUUUCK!" I scream, pummeling the padded seat next to me. My hand vibrates, stinging from that punch. I'll take pain in exchange for the satisfaction of hitting Don—and hurting him—any day of the year. I hope I bruised his dick.

What a motherfucker. Loser. Douchefuckhole.

And he's going to get away with it. How many times has he already? *How is this right?*

It's egregious. Unfair. It must be illegal. But what recourse do I have...really? It's my word against his *again*. If anything, *he* might press charges. For assault? Or is it battery? Both? Technically that may be accurate, but what of *his* despicable actions? Attempted forced oral, strangulation, coercion, manipulation. What's considered rape?

A wave of revulsion ripples through me, what could have happened...what nearly transgressed. Watch me go to jail and Don live to fuck another employee. I bark out a sarcastic laugh. What a fucking joke.

It's not like I want my job back. I can't—*won't*—work there ever again. And how did he know—

It doesn't fucking matter. Can he blackball me industry wide...is that even possible? Is he going to ruin my life?

With a sinking realization, I start to understand I blew it. I should have screamed at the top of my lungs, not slunk away out of fear just because Don ordered me to leave. Now he can spin this story any way he wants. He's just the type to lie his ass off...say I'm crazy, or a nightmare to work with, or that *I* came onto *him* and then went ballistic when he refused my advances.

"Fuck. Fuck. Fuuuuuuuck!"

As the hopelessness of my situation invades, my fury and ire recede liked scared rodents. A sob catches in my throat... followed by a deluge of tears. The desperate, alien sound of my keening fills the car and my chest heaves as hyperventilation nears. I steer through the blur coating my eyes and soul, unsure how to deal with it all.

Butch.

I cling to that name, and the waterfall emanating from my eyes slows. *Pull yourself together.* He will help me sort this out. He loves me...and he's there for me.

But I haven't said one word about my problems with Don, and I have no idea if Butch will understand my reasons why.

SIXTY-FOUR

As much as I don't want to be seen by anyone other than Butch, he's somewhere inside Hamilton Restorations. I inhale a deep breath and with tremulous fingers, push through the main door.

One of the shop hands sits at the desk on the phone with a sandwich and a Dr. Pepper before him. I offer the briefest of waves and keep moving. My neck cranes past classic cars in various stages of repair, jolting when I hear a drill whir and tools clank over the loud music. It's some of that old rock Butch loves, something I'd tease him about if I weren't nose-diving off an emotional cliff.

I round the corner and spot two figures in the distance bent under an open hood. One man relocates to the driver's seat; the other is clearly Butch. He spots me from twelve yards away and does a double take. His smile falters from whatever visual cues I'm presenting. My heart thuds hard with a mixture of churning lava-level anxiety and relief I'm here.

My face falls, tears spilling down my cheeks as I throw myself into Butch's sturdy frame and cry my thousandth tear.

"Jacqui, what's wrong?" He wraps his arms loosely around me, chin resting on my head.

I mumble incoherently.

"Jeff, go ahead and take lunch. We'll finish this up later," he tells his coworker. The car door squeaks open and shuts soundly. Heavy boots recede. Butch raises his hands. "I don't want to get grease on you."

"Don't care," I blubber. "Just hold me. Please."

He squeezes tighter and doesn't pressure me, giving me precious minutes to cloak myself in his comfort.

"Baby, you're scaring me. Tell me what's going on."

I nod into his chest, inhale a breath. "Somewhere private."

"My place?"

My head bobs again, and he lifts my chin to meet his warm, searching gaze. He gives me a reassuring kiss and keeps an arm around me until I'm in his car.

Butch casts concerned glances my way as fresh adrenaline sprouts in my system. By the time we make it inside the cabin, a new layer of sweat coats my skin. He guides me to the couch, and even though I'm jumpy as fuck, I force myself to sit down.

Then I start my story...from the beginning.

Butch's expression and posture morphs multiple times during my monologue—mostly pissed, judging by his ticking jaw and clenched fists. I finish, and he breathes heavily, pushing his fingers against his temples.

"Right now, all I want to do is drive to Richmond and rip that prick's throat out. And much, much worse." His voice is lethal, a tone I've never heard from him before. He cracks his knuckles, pins me with those enraged green eyes. "Is this the reason you wanted the boxing lessons?"

I bite my lower lip and nod.

He stands, paces, stops by the mantle. "I'm proud of you for kneeing that fucking scumbag in the balls and throwing a punch. You took care of business today, stood up for yourself, and that's exactly what you were supposed to do."

I'm proud of me too. For that part.

"But goddamn it, Jacqui, why didn't you tell me about this fucker and what was happening?" His eyes blaze. "We agreed not to lie to each other or keep secrets. Help me understand why you kept this from me."

My shoulders sag. "Your father is friends with him. I assumed there'd be fallout and I just...I didn't want to cause problems for your family."

Butch vehemently shakes his head. "We're going over to my parents' house right now—"

"What? No!"

"And you're going to relay this entire goddamn travesty to them. My dad is honorable, and he will not stand for this, any more than I will. Mark my words, it will make him sick to his stomach."

I rake my fingers through my hair. "Oh, god. What will they think of me?"

He looks incredulous. "Of you? *Of you*? Jesus, Jacqui, you're not the asshole in this equation."

Butch pulls me to standing and wraps me in his arms. "I'm so fucking relieved you're alright, and here with me now. You did the right thing."

My breath catches, thwarting another sob.

"We're going to figure it all out—together. It's going to be okay, baby. You can stay here as long as you need."

"But I was fired. And—"

"Hey," he says, cupping my face. "I've got your back, your six, your everything. The rest we'll work out. Now, let's go—I want my dad's input, and my mom's."

I nod, blindly trusting his advice.

Turns out, it's marginally easier regurgitating the whole sordid affair again despite my embarrassment, angst, and reticence. His parents are aghast and disgusted by what I relay, their expressions shifting with every lecherous, degrading detail. In addition to Don's transgressions toward me, Gus fumes over my boss using him as leverage. He intends to call his personal attorney to find out what legal action is possible, including contacting the publishing group to get Don terminated. Jerri declares Don always gave her the creeps.

I'm awed by their genuine concern, steadfast belief, and instant defense of me. It's bolstering and helps me stop questioning whether I did something wrong. Gus isn't worried one iota about his friendship with Don—that's now over. He's only pained that it caused me to stay silent.

Jerri wraps me a fierce hug, whispering about men acting like animals, reassuring me, comforting me. She clutches Butch's hand, praising him for teaching me to protect myself.

We all know, without saying it aloud, that the outcome could have been much worse.

"The prick won't get away with this," Butch reiterates. "I don't care what it takes."

Gus flashes a warning look. *"Son."*

Butch's jaw is clenched in such a hard line it might break. What does Gus think he's going to do?

"Son," Gus repeats, placing a firm hand on his shoulder. "I'll handle it. Do we understand each other?"

Butch grumbles in reluctant agreement.

I stay with Jerri while Butch heads to the garage to dole out responsibilities. He's quitting early, despite my protests. I'm no longer a total disaster, but I'm not fine either and he knows it. My entire life was just tumble-dried, and I'm screwed in more ways than one.

Jerri brews tea and suggests we sip it on the front porch, a place I've come to love. On another day, I'd think it was a pleasant afternoon. The spring flowers are fully in bloom and the temperature moderate, reminding me of Bay Area weather. It's normally a comforting setting, but I'm the opposite of calm.

"I'm sorry I turned your world upside-down today," I say sullenly.

"Jacqui," she chides. "Don't be ridiculous. We're family. That's who you turn to in times of trouble."

My nose stings and I fight against more tears as that statement hits me squarely in the chest.

Jerri notices my struggle. "What is it, sugar?"

"It's just...I've never had a healthy family. Mine is super messed up." My stupid eyes leak, even though it seems biologically impossible for my tear ducts to be operational at this point.

"Oh, honey." She pauses, her gaze sympathetic. "Not everyone gets lucky where relations are concerned. Thank goodness we get to choose our family later in life, whether through marriage or friends. You're not alone."

"You say the most reassuring things," I rasp out, wiping my damp cheeks.

"I say what I mean."

"And you consider me family...even though Butch and I are just dating?"

She flashes a knowing smile. "You two are more than *just dating*. You're in love with each other, as plain as that azalea bush is bursting with blooms. Butch has been through a lot, and I wasn't sure he would find his way to loving again. But he has, and I couldn't be happier about the recipient."

My spirits lift. "I'm head over heels for that man...and I adore your whole family."

"I'm glad to hear it because I couldn't bear to watch him get hurt again. Butch has always been a little tender-hearted. When he loves, he gives the full hundred percent."

Don't I know it. "I'm amazed by it actually...that he has a hundred percent to give after all that."

Jerri's eyes fasten on me, assessing. "Your heart's still a little broken, isn't it?"

I nod, gnawing on my lower lip. "I'm realizing my parents

broke it first. Then...others. But Butch has patched me back together in a way I never expected."

As if he's heard us, Butch walks out of the shop and his gaze swings our way, zeroing in on me.

Jerri leans back in her rocker. "He's gifted that way, has always known how to step up for people." Her eyes flit to mine. "He's a good one to have in your corner."

I'm so lucky. "I'm grateful...for all of you. Thank you for being so welcoming. And kind. It's a privilege to be included."

She squeezes my forearm across the small table between us. "We're glad you're here."

I steal another glance at my boyfriend. "Can I ask why Gus seemed worried about Butch earlier?"

Jerri drops her head, as if collecting her thoughts. "I'd wager my son would like nothing more than to drive to Rich-mond and beat that man to a pulp. The Butch of yesterday would be gone already. His fists have gotten him in trouble before."

My eyebrows hike.

"He's...protective. But not a bad guy, if you know what I mean. More like the hero seeking justice."

I stare into the distance, mulling that over. I totally see that in him. *Still...*

"What kind of trouble?"

"He's familiar with the county jail," she says ruefully. "Bar fights—often from defending women. Admittedly, he was a little hot-headed in his youth. I'm sure my husband saw the murder in his eyes today. It doesn't sit well with Butch to let a man like Don go unpunished, especially when the person he wronged is someone he cares deeply about. It's probably eating him alive."

Oh.

"He can't afford to be on the wrong end of the law, even if he's in the right. Gus will help him temper that inclination."

The school bus tires squeak to a halt, and we swivel toward the sound. Emmy barrels down the driveway. Butch crouches to meet her at eye level and she falls into his waiting arms. The joy on his face is undiluted as he converses with her, too far away for me to hear. Then he nods at the porch, and her eyes follow. She squeals and runs full tilt in our direction with her pink backpack bobbing behind her. She races up the stairs, dumps her bag, and beelines straight for me.

Emmy launches herself at me. "You're here! On a school day!"

I squeeze her back, getting a whiff of her apple shampoo, startled by the comfort she brings. I hide my angst and respond with as much cheer as I can muster. "I am. Surprise!"

"Guess I'm chopped liver," Jerri mutters good-naturedly.

"Hi, Mimi," she says, still breathless, letting me go and hugging her grandmother.

"How's my pumpkin?"

"Hungry." She turns the linings of her shorts pockets inside out. "My snack holes are empty."

Jerri and I chuckle.

Butch stomps up the steps and his eyes latch on mine. "Do you want to go home...or stick around here?"

He said home. Not his house. *Home.*

These Hamiltons are efficient little knitters, working to stitch my heart back together. My answer comes easily. I'm exhausted, emotionally drained, and I long for a hot shower to wash away the memory of Don's intrusive hands.

"Home."

I SCRUB OFF THE DAY'S ATROCITIES AND SINK INTO bed, crashing in Butch's arms with him stroking my back. When I wake, it takes me a befuddled minute to realize where I am and why. The day's events replay, paralyzing me like there's a knife to my throat. Tears spring to my eyes, and I heave in a big breath. A glance at the alarm clock shows it's near suppertime. When I hear muffled voices downstairs, I stagger into the bathroom and splash water on my face.

It's going to be okay. It's going to be okay. It's going to be okay.

Father and daughter are parked on the sofa watching a movie. Emmy appears to be engrossed, but Butch's unfocused gaze tells another story. My footsteps bring him back to the present and his green eyes slam into mine. There's a multitude of emotions pooling in his. Part of me inwardly flinches.

He stands and tilts his head toward the porch. I follow him out the front door and we sit on the stairs with the last rays of sunshine kissing our faces.

"How're you doing, baby?"

"I'm a train wreck."

He nods thoughtfully. "I get that. Probably going to take a while to regain your bearings." He pauses, one hand scrubbing his jaw. "I'm struggling too."

My fingers rest against his thigh, and my gut twists uncomfortably.

"I'm not trying to overburden you, but if I don't say this, I'm going to detonate, and it won't be pretty."

I swallow, waiting. He puts a hand over mine.

"I've given myself over to this relationship—and I'm fully committed. It's a small miracle you showed up in my life and that I recognized what you were, *are*, which is a second chance. An opportunity to open my heart, share something meaningful with another person, and expand the possibilities for a future I'd abandoned."

My breath suspends as I freeze.

"A huge part of us—this—working...is about trust. Very early on, I brought this up to you as my biggest problem. After what happened with my ex, I lost faith. A piece of me died, and I let it stay buried. I've intentionally kept interactions with women impersonal and short-lived...until you. Because it's not just my heart on the chopping block but Emmy's. The stakes are enormous."

I manage a nod, fear lodging in my throat as I sense where he's going. He's upset with me. Is he ending it?

"You slammed into my life like a fucking hurricane. Even that first night, in your hotel room. We just...hit it off. It was easy, comfortable. And the sex? Unbelievable. You rocked my whole world in a few hours. Part of me hated leaving you without a name, a phone number, a chance to explore what it could be." He huffs an incredulous laugh. "And then you show up on my damned doorstep, gift wrapped. I knew within *minutes* I was screwed."

"Me too," I murmur.

"Despite my good intentions to go slow, we've sped right along. Let me be clear, I have no regrets. I love you, and I know you love me."

"But..." It comes out as a whisper, barely a breath.

"But goddamn it, you blindsided the fuck out of me. I had *no* idea you've been dealing with your scum boss harassing you. What happened at your office party *months ago* and then *today*? And everything in between? You kept this to yourself, as if you don't...trust me. That hurts." His voice turns hoarse, his pain broadcasting straight into my chest. "It's making me question what we're doing here."

I clutch his hands with mine, willing him to look at me. "No!" I choke out. "Please... I was scared. Confused. And wrong. I desperately wanted your advice. You're the one person I *can* turn to, but the whole thing with your dad...I didn't know what else to do. I didn't want to cause problems for your family."

His head hangs, shakes as if he doesn't think that's a good reason, and our hands separate.

I try to form the right words. "I'm not used to people being in my corner. Everyone leaves."

His face turns toward me, eyes softening.

"I've been so lost..." Tears trickle down my cheeks. "But you make me feel like I *matter*. I've never had anyone show up for me like you have. I'm starting to believe you have my back in a way no one ever ha...has." My voice breaks and I swallow. "Not even my own parents." The truth of it cuts deep.

Butch's hand covers mine. "You do matter, Jacqui."

"And your family...they've all opened their arms. Act like I belong here. Your mother told me..." The tears fall harder now and my breaths stutter. Butch strokes the back of my hand with his thumb and I cling to the sight of it. "She told me that I was part of the family today—and I almost went to pieces."

"Everyone here has fallen for you, Sundance. Not just me."

I meet his gaze through watery eyes. "With you, I see nothing but possibility. I see an incredible man who values and treasures the people closest to him. A man who is selfless, giving, and loving."

"And a total stud in the bedroom?" His eyes shine, lighter now.

A wet laugh escapes, and it brings some relief. "Beyond. Way, *way* beyond."

He fingers shift errant strands of hair away from my eyes and across my shoulder as he stares at me intently. "You know why, right?"

"Because we love each other?"

"This is bigger than love. I got a taste of it even that first day. I couldn't explain it, tried ignoring it, but there's no denying it any longer. It's like an exploration every fucking time. You mean more to me every minute."

My tears slow, and he thumbs them away. "I'm sorry," I whisper. "Please don't give up on me, on *us*. I trust you with all of me. And you did protect me today by teaching me how to be on the offense, not just defense. It's the first time I didn't feel powerless." I shove away the visual of Don's penis in my face. "I will never lie to you again."

Butch's eyes turn glassy. I crawl into his lap, and we embrace tightly, his heartbeats thumping against my own.

"I love you so fucking much," he rasps.

"I love you more. You mean everything to me."

Our mouths meet in a desperate, healing kiss swirling with hope for all that we are—and can be.

Sixty-Five

Following the advice of counsel—the attorney Gus paid for on my behalf—I meet with police and file a formal report. A visit to the emergency room documents the damning thumb-shaped mark Don left on my neck.

In preparation for the attorneys filing a written complaint, I meticulously log a record outlining the harassment and provide a list of employees who might corroborate some of my claims.

The formal complaint asks for damages, financial compensation, a letter of recommendation, and the immediate dismissal of Don fucking Jennings. I'm hopeful. I may have lost my job, but he will not ruin me.

Butch convinces me to move out of Richmond and in with him. He's worried about Don confronting me, or worse.

Do I mind living with the lumberjack, being under his protection (and under him, period)? No, I do not. Was I bolstered by Emmy's enthusiastic response? *"We'd be together every single day?"* *"Daddy will never be grumpy pants again!"* Yes, I was.

As if all that weren't amazing enough, Gus insists I start consulting on his magazine right away. He puts me on his payroll, saying it's "easier this way," but it seems like too much —he's already footing the attorney bill. So, I work hard, digging in to comprehensively research his venture.

I'm energized by the excitement of creating something from scratch. Butch offers his spare bedroom for a makeshift office, and we add a desk, worktable, and large cork board, where my notes and plans begin taking shape.

Everything's put in motion shockingly fast. I'm relieved to be out of the city. I'm more comfortable with the charming, engaging Hamilton family by the minute, and their enclave is a sanctuary with its towering oaks, babbling brook, and soothing landscape.

I'm wanted. Embraced. Safe. And my future holds real promise.

~

A month later, Don's been fired, I have glowing letters of recommendation from senior management, my wrongful termination is termed a layoff, and I'm awarded some financial compensation in the form of back pay.

What sticks in my craw? There's zero admission of wrongdoing or apology, and I *wasn't* "laid off."

It's the best deal the attorneys could negotiate, so I take it. They said these types of cases often drag on for months or years, but the police and hospital report scared them enough to ante up hush money.

Truthfully, my sanity demands putting it behind me. I don't want to think about it anymore even if it's not exactly what I wanted. I'm David and they're Goliath, only I don't topple them at all. I'm no more than a ripple in their ocean.

Butch finds me on the porch, leaning against the railing as

Emmy chases after lightning bugs. Their brief flares of light pop in the twilight hour and I find them simply magical, never having seen them before moving here. He slides his arms around my waist and presses a kiss to my temple. I sink into his touch, my arms crossing over his.

"You doing alright?" he asks.

"Mm-hmm. Just glad it's over."

"I'd still like to kick his ass. That would give me the peace of mind I crave."

I blow out a laugh. "Tempting, but no." I don't need Butch going to jail.

Emmy lets out a celebratory shriek as she catches two bugs in a canning jar. Butch poked air holes in the top so they can survive, but he'll make her let them go in a while.

"I will never get over these wonders of nature," I say. It does put life in perspective. No amount of Dons in the world can diminish the awe and magnitude of Mother Nature's gifts.

"You've got to admit, it's a clever mating system."

"The good old, 'I'll show you mine if you show me yours'?"

Butch chuckles, squeezing me tighter. "You can show me yours anytime. You know I'm happy to show you mine."

I try to elbow him but he's holding me too close.

"I've got a really cool thing we can go do right now if you're up for it."

Turning in his arms, I find his handsome face. "I'm up for it."

"Em!" he calls. "C'mere. We're all going on a little excursion." He takes my hand and steers me toward the car.

"Is ice cream involved?" she asks.

"Something even better," Butch answers.

"Nothing is better than ice cream," she mutters. "Can I bring my bugs?"

"Sure. Get your little butt in the car," he commands.

We pile into the Barracuda and drive about fifteen minutes to a park. Butch grabs a flashlight from the glove compartment and leads the way down a nearby path.

"What are we doing?" I whisper.

"Can you keep a secret?" he asks.

"Of course."

"So can I," he answers.

"You are a maddening man."

His white teeth shine in the dark. "I'm not ruining a good surprise, Sundance. If you don't agree, I'll make it up to you later."

I smile to myself as we continue walking the dirt path, an occasional lightning bug blinking in search of a mate. Night is closing in quickly as we arrive at a long wooden bridge, suspended above a pond surrounded by an expansive lawn and trees. Butch stops when we reach the center, shuts off the light, and we fall silent.

Like magic, they appear. Fireflies. Hundreds and hundreds of them, as far as the eye can see, emitting their luminescent green glow across this woodland paradise. My breath catches as I absorb this phenomenon of the beetle world. Even Emmy's speechless.

Butch's hand finds mine and squeezes.

"It's amazing," I whisper, almost unable to grasp what I'm witnessing, it's so extraordinary.

"They're like little fairies," Emmy adds in a hushed tone.

We watch in silence for a long while, gradually crossing the bridge to view from different vantage points.

Emmy opens her jar and releases her fireflies, whispering to them, "Go be with your kind."

When we've had our fill, Butch stoops to let Emmy ride him piggyback and I shine the light as we make our way back to the parking lot.

Emmy chatters animatedly but my thoughts veer to how lucky I am. To observe the miracle of life in so many forms, to experience true love even when I thought it was lost, to realize I'm but a speck in the cosmos, here to make the most of my own blink of time.

Sixty-Six

I'm on the porch steps watching Butch split wood. *Finally*. I've fantasized about the lumberjack doing this task for months, and he's not disappointing me. It's a beautiful Saturday in late September, with a breeze rustling the trees against azure skies dotted with billowy clouds. Hemi's stretched long beside me, snoring softly, no movement aside from the occasional twitch. Butch wears faded jeans and a T-shirt. Sweat coats his skin, and those muscular biceps and forearms are on display as they flex and exert with each strike.

"Don't you want to take your shirt off?" I call out.

He rolls his eyes, flips his ballcap backward, and resumes.

Yum. "This is like my birthday and Christmas all rolled into one. Definite video material." His parents purchased one of those VHS camcorders recently and we've all had fun with it. It would be the perfect medium for lumberjack porn, if it exists. And if it doesn't, it should. I've got the model right here in all his six-foot-four glory.

He ignores me and continues chopping, a quirk of his lips betraying his amusement.

I rest my chin in my palm and ogle.

Butch lodges the ax in a fresh log and walks those long legs over to me. He lifts the hem of his shirt and uses it to wipe his brow, giving me a direct view of his torso.

Double yum. "Goddamn, Lumberjack. I'm about to slide off the steps."

He smirks and hikes an eyebrow. "Sounds like a problem."

"One you could solve," I offer with a wink.

He braces his arms on either side of me and leans in close. "What, exactly, is your fantasy here?"

"You're already knocking it out of the park, Mr. Glistening Axe Man. But if I was going to expand on it..." I turn around and check that Emmy's still inside, then change to a whisper. "I might just want you to force me to my knees right there in the dirt...or have you tie me to a tree and fuck me senseless."

"Shit. Now I'm getting a boner."

"Me too. Or, you know, the female equivalent."

His lips land on mine in a blistering kiss, and tingles erupt down my spine.

"You are pure trouble, Sundance. Now do me a favor and bring me a glass of water."

"Because you're hot?" I run the pad of my finger across my lower lip.

He cocks his head. "Um...yeah?"

"No, I want to hear you say, 'I'm hot.' Because you. Are. Hot." I rub my palms together for emphasis.

"You're ridiculous."

"Good thing you love me."

He grunts an acknowledgment and adjusts his package. My gaze snaps to his crotch. "We'll continue this conversation about your lumberjack fantasy later." It's a promise.

I shake my ass at him as I walk up the steps.

"Tease away—I'm coming for that."

"Promises, promises." I smack my right cheek for good measure before slipping through the front door.

When I rejoin Butch and hand over his water, Hemi is steadily barking at a car crunching down the gravel drive. "Who is it?"

"Goddamn it. I think it's Darlene." He slugs down the entire contents of the glass and hands it back to me. "Baby, go inside. Keep Emmy occupied, okay?"

"Alright." I head in and check on Emmy, who's still playing with her Barbie Styling Salon, pretending to give the redheaded doll in one of the chairs a haircut. She chatters away, nailing the stylist role to the max.

I quietly walk back to the window overlooking the front. Darlene stands by her faded yellow Valiant. Butch's defensive posture says it all: arms crossed, stance wide. Hemi growls, hackles raised, and Butch hushes him.

Darlene approaches, her pink-and-white striped short-sleeved blouse tucked into high-waisted pale denim. Her perm has relaxed, those tight curls now loose waves. Within a few minutes, she's gesticulating wildly with her hands as she glowers at Butch.

He grows increasingly agitated, his own hand jerking into the air for emphasis before he casts a nervous glance toward the house.

The two verbally spar several more minutes while Emmy continues prattling on to her hair customers without a clue about what's transpiring in the front yard.

Butch frowns, his hands balling into fists at his sides. More words are batted between them. Then he gives Darlene a final, vehement head shake and she stalks to her car. Her head whips, eyes flaring at Butch as she yells one last thing. He doesn't answer, but I can tell he's pissed, his jaw visibly pulsing from here.

When the car's out of sight, he picks up a nearby rock and

hurls it down the driveway. Then he turns abruptly and strides in the opposite direction with Hemi hot on his heels.

I launch out the door and jog to catch up. "What did she want?"

His irate eyes meet mine. "She's not letting this go. Despite what the courts decided. She wants to see Emmy."

"Oh no."

"Obviously, I told her no fucking way," he spits out. "But now I'm wondering if she's just going to keep showing up."

"Yeah...that's not cool."

He rakes his fingers roughly through his hair. "And one of these days, Emmy's going to be outside when it happens. And then what? What will she think? What will she want? Am I doing what's best? Should I talk to Emmy about it?"

"I don't know, but you said when the time was right, you'd tell Emmy about her mom and then she can decide. It's alright to not have it all figured out this second."

He looks toward the house, then squeezes his eyes shut. "I just don't want Em to get hurt. And I sure as shit don't know how I'd ever trust Darlene to be in our daughter's life again. I thought all this fucking bullshit was over. Maybe I need to get a restraining order."

Helpless to do much else, I wrap my arms around him. "Just keep being her dad, Butch. You're doing a wonderful job with her, and until your gut tells you something different, just stay the course. Trust your instincts."

Butch's instincts propel him to act in the week ahead. He speaks to Emmy's elementary school principal to explain his concerns. He holds a family meeting. He reiterates to his daughter how careful she needs to be at her age, reminding her to be suspicious of strangers. And he doesn't leave Emmy unattended.

They're all precautions, but hopefully, Darlene will abandon this mission and disappear, just like she did when Emmy was young.

SIXTY-SEVEN

Emmy and I play in the colorful autumn leaves, raking them into a big pile before running and jumping in, both of us shrieking with laughter. Leaf confetti sticks to our hair and clothes—and in Emmy's case, sometimes catches in the sparkling tiara secured to her crown with combs.

Emmy considers herself a princess—with vast costumes, tiaras, wands, and attitude to back it up. You won't find me arguing. Right now, she's the princess of the forest, framed by the glorious ruby, auburn, and golden hues of nature's palette as she lies flat on her back.

Hemi circles us, barking animatedly. He wants to be part of the fun but refuses to step one paw in the pile. Butch tried taking him over to the restoration shop, where he's attempting to catch up on the backlog of work, but Hemi seemed hell-bent on staying with us.

Emmy's shushing the dog when my stomach roils with a sudden, sharp distress. I blow out a harsh breath.

"I need to use the bathroom," I say.

"And I'm thirsty," Emmy adds.

I stand, offer my hand, and hoist her up. She runs toward

the house as I wade out of the pile. "Brush off before you go in," I yell just as another twinge hits my gut.

When I get to the door, I hastily add my detritus to hers, another cramp hammering my insides as I hurry to the restroom. What the hell?

Awarded a moment of reprieve—even though my guts are tight as a drum—I flip through the magazines stuffed in a basket: *Reader's Digest, Car Collector, Muscle Car Review,* and *Cosmo.*

Emmy's footsteps thunder down the hall and stop by the door. "I'm going to see Daddy. M'kay? Bye!"

"Wait!" Sudden pain doubles me over, and I break out in a cold sweat. "Em?" I croak, trying to breathe through it. "Emmy!"

She doesn't answer, already gone.

Damn it.

The next assault strikes, this one bringing a wave of nausea. What is happening to me? I need to catch Emmy. But my body has other plans, hitting me with spasm after spasm.

Hemi barks outside and my head jerks toward the sound. His barks turn insistent. Unrelenting. Alarm shrieks in my head, but I can't hear anything but the dog. What's going on?

A fresh cramp hits. Goosebumps skitter across my flesh. My vision darkens at the corners, head woozy, and I slump forward. Bile edges up my throat, and I pant through the attack.

Hemi howls.

Oh god, I'm going to hurl. I scramble to my knees and retch into the toilet, trapped in my own personal hell. My stomach empties, and I'm at the mercy of biology, just here for the revolting ride.

It takes several offensive minutes and when I think—hope—it's over, I rest my forehead against the cool porcelain of the upended seat and get my bearings.

The dog has fallen silent.

I pray Emmy's alright. And that I am too.

I'm weak but need to pull myself together and find her. I splash cold water on my face then hasten on unsteady legs to the front door. Flinging it open, I lurch onto the porch, sweating head to toe.

Hemi stares down the driveway, growling menacingly at a faint cloud of dust hanging in the air. That's when my eyes catch on something sparkling near his feet.

Emmy's tiara.

"Emmy!" I scream, eyeballing the empty drive. There's no answer.

I glance down the path, debating whether to take it, but stagger inside to the phone instead and call the shop. "Pick up. Pick up. Pick up."

I slam the receiver down. What should I do? Nausea rears again and I pant through it, then try calling again. "Pick up. Pick up. Pick up."

"Hamiltons." It's Butch.

Thank God. "It's me. Is Emmy there?"

"No. Why?"

"We were playing, then she told me she was going to see you—"

"When," he snaps.

My pulse throbs, my nerve endings crackling like popcorn kernels in hot oil. "Maybe ten minutes ago. I was stuck in the bathroom—"

"And she just left?"

"Yes, before I could stop her. Hemi started barking like crazy, and when I finally got outside, he was howling at the driveway and there was dust like a car was here, and..." I sob, "I found her tiara on the ground."

"Stay there. I'll see if she's here somewhere. If not, I'm coming to you." He hangs up without another word.

"Please, please, please be alright," I chant.

I will never forgive myself if something happens to her.

My head swims with doomsday visions, and I gulp deep breaths. Losing my cool won't help anything. Maybe she's just at her grandparents'. Maybe she's on the path collecting rocks. Maybe she climbed into one of the vehicles to play race car driver.

Or maybe something terrible has happened.

Bile rises and I run to the bathroom—and retch again.

"Jacqui!" Butch yells as he bursts through the front door, boots thudding against the hardwood floors.

"In here," I say weakly. I'm slumped on the floor, scared to stray too far from the commode.

He looms in the open doorway, his gaze flitting over me, frantically taking in the scene. "Is Emmy back?" He's breathing hard.

"No. Oh my god. You didn't find her?"

"No! Tell me everything that happened. And what's...are you ill?"

I nod. "I think it's food poisoning."

He squeezes his eyes shut and presses his fingers into his temples. "Fuck! What the hell happened over here?"

My eyes well. "We...we were playing in the leaves. I felt sick to my stomach, so I came inside to use the bathroom, and Emmy came with me to get a glass of water."

"So how the fuck did she disappear?" he yells, and I flinch.

Everything is loud and bright and horrible. Tears slip down my cheeks. "When I was in here, she told me she was going to see you—"

"And you didn't think to stop her? To tell her to wait for you?" he demands.

"I tried. Butch, I tried, but she left. She didn't wait for an answer. She just—"

His arms cross, eyes steely and forbidding. "Disappeared,

Jacqui. That's what she did. She walked outside, and now she's gone."

My sobs intensify. "I'm so sorry. I didn't..." My words trail off. They're meaningless.

I see a flash of anger, pity, sorrow. Maybe regret. "I'm calling the police," he says as he strides away.

My head falls into my hands, muffling my heaving sobs. Panic and remorse twist my guts anew. A cavern of despair forms, one that seems black, cold, and bottomless.

POLICE ARRIVE TO INVESTIGATE, TAKE STATEMENTS, and determine the next course of action. It's been one hour since Emmy disappeared. One hour for Butch and his parents to conduct a cursory, property-wide search. One hour to for me to become wracked with fear, grief, and self-loathing.

I can't stand to witness Butch's stark anguish.

I can't stop blaming myself.

I can't help but think of my sister, drowned before we could even develop a friendship. Drowning my entire family in the process.

Now I'm drowning too.

The obvious suspect is Darlene. A stranger could also have forced Emmy into a car and driven away, the irony being that Emmy's biological mother *is* a stranger to her. At minimum, Darlene remains a person of interest and police issue an all-points bulletin for her 1970 pale yellow Plymouth Valiant, which Butch describes in detail. He doesn't remember the full license plate number but provides a partial, and the state: Illinois.

Butch excels under pressure: giving officers a recent school picture of Emmy, answering every question from her age, eye color, and height to the birthmark above her right elbow. We describe what clothes she wore, the brand of sneakers.

I provide a comprehensive statement, explaining how a

violent gastrointestinal attack prevented me from going after Emmy or witnessing what caused her disappearance. The officer seemed concerned, said I looked white as a sheet. I'm still shaky and weak and can barely keep water down but I'm not thinking about me. Only Emmy—and Butch.

A search ensues. The sergeant, a personal family friend, explains most missing kids are off playing somewhere or they've wandered over to a friend's or neighbor's house. But we know, the way you sometimes do at the bone-deep level, that Emmy is not playing, hiding or lost.

She was taken.

Family, friends, and neighbors arrive to look for her across the massive acreage where the Hamiltons live and canvass the entire neighborhood. The community grapevine works its magic, spreading the word and putting everyone on alert. The Hamiltons are well known and respected in these parts, and one of their own has gone missing. The whole town rallies, doing whatever they can to aid in the search.

Even mired in numbing heartache, I'm awed.

But as the sun sets on this horrific day, Emmy remains missing.

Neighbors drop off food and flashlights.

No one can bring themselves to stop searching. To admit defeat. To do...nothing.

The search is more for us now.

Even weak and nauseous, I continue walking, looking, hoping. The image of her tiara sticks like a thorn in my mind. Emmy would never leave that behind. Was there a struggle? Did Darlene harm her? Is she hurting her now?

Eventually, with heavy limbs and even heavier hearts, we trudge home. People are exhausted—mentally and physically. It's in the hands of law enforcement now. Between the new computer technology at their disposal and the APB they issued, we pray the police locate Emmy quickly.

Butch and I haven't spoken in hours. There isn't anything

to say. I'm devoid of comforting words. None can or will fix this anyway.

I'm waiting for him to break things off for good, to demand I leave. At the very least, to blame my incompetence, rail about my inability to do the most important task at hand —safeguard his child.

A real mother would do that.

Sixty-Eight

Butch's sobs awaken me. We're on the couch; neither of us could stomach getting into bed or even think of sleeping. My eyes snap open and swing to him. He's slumped over his knees, his broad shoulders heaving.

My heart breaks anew.

Something in my chest squeezes at seeing a big, strong man like Butch so shredded, powerless...vulnerable.

Crawling behind him, I wrap my body around his and hold him close. His massive frame shakes as he weeps, wracked with that bottomless, consuming grief and pain.

He doesn't push me away, an encouraging sign. I remain, anchoring him, reminding him *I'm here. I love you. I'm sorry.*

Fresh tears spring from my own eyes, rolling down my cheeks and splashing onto his shirt. I tenderly kiss his back.

His anguished cries hang in the air, each another blow to my bruised heart. Hemi lumbers to all fours and rests his head on his Butch's thigh.

I rub Butch's back in slow, smooth strokes, over and over.

I'm here. I love you. I'm sorry.

Slowly, his sobs cease, his breaths shuddering as they normalize.

It's dark outside, impossible to guess the time, but not yet near dawn. My brain screams questions for which there are no answers. Have the police found Emmy? Has anyone spotted her from the photos we provided? From the community search team? From the flyers getting made and distributed? Where was she taken? Is she hurt? Hungry? Scared? Is she with Darlene? What if they can't find her?

What more can we do?

Butch stands. "I'm going to get some water," he says hoarsely. "Want some?"

"I'll get it for you," I offer.

He waves me off and walks toward the kitchen. I hear him open a drawer, shake what sounds like pain relievers from a bottle, and use the sink. He returns with two glasses, setting them down on the coffee table.

I take a few token sips.

He reclines on the sofa, silently beckoning to me to join him. He cradles me against him, and I sag as his arm closes around my chest. We remain wordless, but his breath floating past my ear provides the proof of life I need—and a smidgeon of hope.

Then again, hope is dangerous.

∼

We don't leave the cabin—hoping, praying, waiting for the phone to ring with news that Emmy's been found. The absence of her little footsteps, giggles, and tea parties attended by stuffed animals surround us like ghosts.

Gus, Jerri, and Liz cycle through at intervals, bringing food we barely touch, offering hugs, and fighting tears. No one knows what to say in these circumstances. No words exist in the English language to provide solace for this atrocity.

We turn on the television...but find it depressing, not

distracting. The silence without it deafens. How can quiet be so loud?

Butch relieves some of his stress by pummeling the punching bag in the garage. Splitting more wood and stacking it high for wintertime. Throwing a tennis ball for Hemi to chase. During those times, I stand vigil by the phone.

There is nothing more agonizing than sitting around, idle and helpless, knowing Emmy is out there...scared, in trouble, worse. And yet we are relegated to it, chained here, impotent.

SIXTY-NINE

Seventy-four hours after Emmy disappears, the phone rings—a shrill, jarring sound in a household turned mute. Butch pounces on it and I bound to his side.

Will this be the call to tell us she's alive and well...or that the unthinkable has happened?

He lets out a loud whoosh, eyes tearing, and gives me only a few head nods until the call ends. *She's alive.*

His beautiful eyes finally meet mine. "Emmy's been found. Unharmed. In South Dakota."

My hands fly to my face. "Thank God," I rasp.

His chest heaves as he processes. "Darlene took her," he confirms, "and she's now in custody. Taking her across state lines made it a felony, and she could serve a lot of time for that."

We hold each other tightly as relief streams down my face in the form of tears. *Thank you, thank you, thank you.*

"When will she be home?"

"She's on her way. They're flying her."

"Oh, Butch..."

"I know, baby. I know."

My voice catches. There's relief, but also...remorse. "I'm so sorry."

He pulls back, shaking his head. "Jacqui, none of this is your fault. *I'm* sorry I made you think that for one second. I was a jerk for lashing out at you. It was wrong and misguided, and I hope you'll forgive me."

The pressure weighing on me lifts—just enough to breathe. Maybe it's not ending between us? "But..."

"You're not the delusional person who abandoned your own daughter for almost eight years before kidnapping her. Emmy's safe and coming home. That's all that matters."

He's right. I need to set aside my faulty internal monologue and see the reality. I couldn't help the circumstances surrounding this egregious event. The blame is fully on this woman's warped actions.

~

Butch and I stand in the driveway as the cruiser pulls to a stop. Emmy's out of the car in a flash, leaping into her father's arms. His smile is wider than I've ever witnessed. The love, joy, and relief are so achingly palpable between them, it almost hurts to watch. An impatient Hemi jumps on his hind legs to cover Emmy's face in slobbery kisses, and she grabs onto his fur as he licks at her tears.

And then she reaches for me. Clutching her solid little body reminds me how precious and tenuous life can be, and I'm flooded with gratitude. She's here. She's alive. *Thank you. Thank you. Thank you.*

"I'm so happy you're home," I murmur. "I love you so much."

She grips me tightly, her voice barely above a whisper. "I love you too."

Butch closes his long arms around us, and we stay in our cuddle huddle for several minutes.

The officer waits patiently, and finally Butch releases us to shake his hand. "Thank you for everything you all did for us. I'm forever grateful."

The tall, lanky man gives a curt nod. "Just glad we found her and brought her back unharmed. We still need to tie up some loose ends. We'd like you to bring Emmy in tomorrow so she can meet with our children's advocate. She understands how to talk to children who've been traumatized. She'll ask your daughter about her experience, assess her mental health, make sure she's alright. She may even find additional evidence to assist our case."

Butch listens, a hand shoved in his pocket. "I understand. And I'm worried about what Emmy's been through so this... advocate...could help with that?"

The officer nods. "After the interview, she'll speak with you about whether she thinks Emmy would benefit from additional counseling."

Butch's expression calms. "I want to be with her for this. No offense, but I'm not leaving her side."

"You can stay with her the entire time. We just need to do it quickly, while details are still fresh."

"Of course. Tomorrow's fine."

The officer holds out a hand. "I'll give you a call in the morning with a time."

Butch and the officer shake. "Thank you, and please extend our gratitude to everyone at the station."

The officer leaves and Butch sweeps Emmy back into his arms. "I know a whole bunch of people who'd really like to see your pretty face. You up for it?"

On his call with Butch earlier, the police chief suggested we not pump Emmy for information right away, but rather shower her with love, security, and family time. Tomorrow's interview might be the safest way for Emmy to share about her experience, especially with her father by her side.

Emmy nods solemnly. "I want to see Mimi and PopPop."

Butch plants a kiss on cheek. "I'm never letting you out of my sight again."

He sets her down and we each take one of her hands and walk the path to his parents' house.

Our little family is whole again.

SEVENTY

Emmy bounces back with surprising aplomb. The children's advocate was kind, gentle, and thorough. While the ordeal scared Emmy, she proved resilient both during and after the three-day kidnapping.

Despite her mother being a stranger, Emmy initially trusted Darlene, who deftly pulled, then played, the mother card. She confessed to being Emmy's mom, explaining how much she loved and missed her, apologizing for ever leaving. She asked if she could treat her to a sundae at the pharmacy downtown, promising that Butch approved and she'd have her back within the hour. Darlene shed a few tears and Emmy felt sorry for her, plus her own curiosity took over. She *wanted* to spend time with her mother and learn why she had left, where she had been, and if she was staying now.

Darlene steered Emmy to the passenger seat, but Hemi attempted to physically come between her and Emmy. When Emmy leaned over and gave the dog a big hug, calming him down, she thinks her tiara probably fell off because she didn't notice its absence until Darlene sped off.

There was no stop for ice cream. There was no stopping at all.

And as Emmy watched the woman nervously driving her away from her hometown, she began to realize something was very wrong.

Emmy cried to go home, and Darlene said she'd like to provide her with a new home. Give them a chance to get to know each other. Give her a chance to do things right. When Emmy asked where they were going, Darlene remained vague. When Emmy asked to call her daddy, Darlene answered, "in a while." But a while never came.

Emmy cried more, scared she might never see her daddy, dog, family, or me again.

Her mother's volatile emotions scared her too. Darlene was smiling and laughing one moment, fearful and anxious the next. She wept. Pleaded. Railed about Butch and how he'd prevented any interaction she tried to have. She deftly pulled on Emmy's heartstrings by telling her about the night she was born and other memories of her first year.

Darlene stopped only when necessary and was careful when she did, keeping Emmy in line using promises to take her home or let her call Butch only if she obeyed. She made Emmy stand quietly by her side during gasoline or food stops. They slept in the car only in remote places, just a few hours at a time, limiting her chances to escape. But Emmy was also wary and unsure what Darlene would do if she ran or screamed.

Emmy intuitively understood if she complied, she'd eventually get to a telephone or find help. So smart, that girl. She also figured those boxing skills in her back pocket might prove useful if the opportunity arose.

When the Valiant was spotted at a Shell station matching the APB in Lymon, South Dakota, Darlene was apprehended quickly.

Since Emmy's return, we've watched her like a hawk, looking for signs of distress. She's had a few nightmares, but even then, this brave girl understands how to take care of herself—she simply crawls into bed with us and falls asleep with the assurance we're there. Emmy's therapist said her resilience is likely due to how she's been raised, with love and security surrounding her. She has strong self-esteem, a level head, and wisdom beyond her years.

Butch hasn't bounced back quite as gracefully. He compulsively checks on Emmy—when she's sleeping, doing crafts, watching a movie. He won't let her run the path to her grandparents' house alone. He doesn't want her outside without an adult. He's needy and worried and riddled with guilt.

When I gently suggested he try a few therapy sessions himself, he scoffed me. So I've taken to soothing him my way, through touch. Stroking his hair, his arms, and his body anywhere and anytime—on the sofa, as he drifts to sleep, in the car. He says it grounds him, so that's what I offer. My words attempt to assuage his conscience, reminding him what a good, loving father he is, imparting strong values, common sense, and useful skills.

I understand what happened to Emmy presses all his buttons, not to mention his pride. He identifies as the protector—the one who keeps us safe. Between what transpired with me and my boss and now this, it shakes the foundation of who he thinks he is. But he's not responsible for what others do. And I don't think he understands the foundation he lays for all of us, which is not only mighty, but allows us to rise beyond life's uglier moments.

Family boxing resumes with gusto, along with "what you should do if this happens" scenarios—Butch's bid to help the women in his life anticipate the evil in the world.

I think he also grapples with what happened to Darlene. Emmy experienced uncertainty and fear while with her mother but still came home worried for the woman's fate— and still curious.

Darlene told the authorities she didn't set out to kidnap

Emmy. She showed up that day to confront Butch again and reason with him. But when the opportune moment arose, she spontaneously snatched Emmy up, thinking it might be the only way she'd ever see her daughter.

Butch is compassionate enough to wonder if Darlene *should* have a role in Emmy's life. Despite what she's done—an act of desperation he believes he's guilty of contributing to—he doesn't know what's in his daughter's best interest. And it's all complicated further by Darlene going to prison. We talk some about how and when to broach that, aware it's a choice his daughter can make when she's older.

Sometimes relationships are tangled, confusing, and complex. I know that the hard way.

~

OUR LIVES RETURN TO A NEW NORMAL. I'VE FOUND A groove living with Butch, putting the unpleasantness from *Virginia Now* behind me, and outlining the parameters for Gus's dream.

Gus not only greenlights the magazine but offers me the job of managing editor. *Editor.* After intensive research, pulling together costs and vendors and distribution companies, plus sketching out the first four issues, I'm thrilled to take on that role. Granted, it's a big title for a ton of work. Maybe it's false confidence, but I believe in myself.

I credit two of the most important men in my life for getting me here: Mick, for always encouraging me to pursue my dreams, and Butch, who lavishes me with praise, support, and unflappable faith. He is unwavering in his love for me... and it makes me sturdier on my feet.

I'm not discounting what I've brought to the party either. I've stood on shaky ground, navigated uncertainties, and sometimes worry I'll never fill the holes received from heartbreaks and heartaches. But through it all, I've endured. I've overcome. I've risen.

I once believed my destiny was to live solitary, alone, relegated to self-reliance. It's understandable why. But loving again is a choice—a risk, yes, but a choice. An opportunity to blossom, to share companionship, to experience a profound connection. It's a gift to myself, honestly. Believing I'm worthy, embracing it, letting it flow through me, and returning these same things to the spectacular human being who adores me.

I'm a better person because of Butch. Perhaps the best version of myself to date.

I hope he's a better person because of me.

And when you allow someone you love, respect, and trust into your life, you reap all the dividends around them. For me, that's priceless.

Emmy has shown me what motherhood means. It's not about biology. It's about who shows up for you every day. Who nurtures you. Who loves you without condition.

Gus and Jerri have shown me what it means to have parents. People who are in your corner, heading up your posse as a guiding, loving force that values inclusion at its core.

Liz has shown me another sister exists in my world, and she is alive, funny, and a special brand of cheerleader.

And family...a word I thought meant only one thing. Family is not always the people who gave you life, with whom you resided in your formative years, or blood relations. No, the definition is so much more prolific and profound.

And thank God for that.

I've always craved love. Connection. Belonging.

And now I have it.

SEVENTY-ONE

Butch and I escape the first weekend of December for some alone time. He takes me to Cape Charles, a quaint historic town on the Eastern Shore.

Although some residents live here year-round, it's clearly a place that bustles with tourism in the warmer months, with gorgeous bay views, beaches, a long pier, and a downtown full of shops and restaurants.

We spend Saturday exploring, stealing kisses, and winding down over a decadent dinner and a shared bottle of wine. Our inn—an old spiffed-up Victorian—has beautiful floors, intricate crown molding, and high-ceilinged rooms. Our bedroom features a four-poster bed with spires that shoot close to chandelier height. The floral wallpaper, antique furniture, and gas fireplace add to its charm.

When we return from dinner, wrapped chocolates lay on our pillows and the fireplace warms the room. I shrug off my coat and walk over to the hearth to help take off the chill.

Butch joins me, his arms wrapping loosely around my waist. "I want to watch the sunrise with you tomorrow."

I squint one eye. "And that means waking up at what time?"

He grins. "Not that early, sleeping beauty. If we leave here by 7:30, we'll be fine. The beach is only a few blocks away."

I place my hand on his chest, meeting his gaze. "As you wish, Lumberjack."

"My wish is in my arms, baby."

"Mine too," I whisper.

We share a lingering kiss.

"Today was wonderful, Butch. The drive here, the walk through town and along the beach, this beautiful inn, being alone together..."

His eyebrows lift. "You don't miss Emmy bothering us every five minutes?"

I chuckle. "I love her, you know that, but having you to myself comes with special fringe benefits."

"Really? Do detail these benefits."

I smack him playfully on the arm. "You know very well what I mean."

His mouth hovers over my ear, his warm breath sending a jolt straight between my legs. "Like fucking you senseless for hours?"

Whimper.

"Making you come so hard you see stars?"

Whimper.

"Licking that perfect pussy?"

Moan.

"Having your mouth around my cock?"

"Yesssssss," I beg.

"As you wish."

THE NEXT MORNING, BUTCH GENTLY WAKES ME. WE brush our teeth and quickly dress, bundling up for our short walk to the beach. We snag a couple of to-go coffees downstairs, and he retrieves two blankets and a flashlight from the car.

We stretch one blanket across the sand, then he sits and motions me between his legs and wraps the other around us. The sky is washed in a purplish pre-dawn luster, the stars still visible. We're quiet, watching and waiting. Butch presses a kiss to my temple, and I nuzzle in tighter.

The light shifts, a deep orange bursting against the dark depths of the water. Slowly, the sun breaks the horizon, lifting the color higher, painting the heavens with its brilliant hues. We're mesmerized by this simple, beatific act of illumination, one of nature's daily miracles.

The rays breathe a murmur of warmth onto my face.

"You see that?" Butch asks, his timbre sending a shiver through me.

"Mm-hmm."

"You're like the sunrise, emerging from the unknown, gaining strength as you rise, bathing me in your warmth, your abundant light, your rare beauty, all with the promise of a new day."

My heart stutters.

"You brighten my entire world, Sundance. And I want to wake up every single day for the rest of my life with your sunrise."

Before I can say one word, a jewelry box appears in his hand.

Oh my god.

"I want you to be mine forever."

My eyes prick, my throat constricting as I open the black velvet box with trembling fingers. My breath catches. A sizeable pear-shaped yellow diamond surrounded by a double halo of smaller yellow and white diamonds sits in the center of a platinum band. I've never seen anything similar or so stunning.

I can't believe this is happening.

"Marry me, Jacqueline Hall."

I twist enough to press my palm against his rugged, spectacular face. My gaze fastens on his emerald eyes, so full of love and hope and promise. "Augustus James Hamilton, Jr., it would be my honor to marry you."

Our mouths join for a deep, intimate kiss, sealing our sentiments.

"May I?" he asks, holding out his palm.

I surrender the box and seconds later, Butch places the ring in its rightful place on my left hand.

"Thank fuck it fits. I had to measure your finger while you were asleep."

My laugh rings out as I return my gaze to that gorgeous symbol of our love, and of light—the light between us. "It's so beautiful, Butch."

"Like you."

"You're an incredible man. What you said...bringing me here this morning. I'm...you're full of surprises." I'm so over-come, I'm practically inarticulate.

"I'm full of love. For *you*, wife-to-be."

"And Emmy's okay with this?"

He stifles a laugh. "After we've lived in sin for months?"

I mock glare.

"After my parents lectured me to make an honest woman out of you?"

"So...you're proposing under duress?" I tease.

"This proposal is all mine, Sundance. From me to you, because of what *I* want. You're mine. And I'm yours. But making it official matters to me. Living with each other has only proven to me what I already knew. We're good together. Was everyone else on board? Hell yeah."

He fishes out a note and hands it wordlessly to me.

Please marry my daddy. Then we can be a family forever and he'll never be a grumpy monster again.

Your favorite 8 ¾ year old,
Emmy

My teary laugh bubbles out. "God, I love this girl."

"She loves you too, baby, and that's another big reason this works."

We kiss again, tenderly.

"There's only one last bit I need to say." His eyes trace the horizon before locking with mine. "Regardless of what difficulties we face in the future, promise me we'll always work it out. Let's agree right here and now that leaving each other is not an option. Even if the going gets tough, no matter what, we figure things out. That's my commitment to you, and I couldn't bear it if—"

I won't make him say it, let alone think it. "I agree a hundred percent. I commit myself to you and to us. I'm not going anywhere, Butch."

His expression relaxes.

I lean back into him, and our mouths connect, binding our promise of a forever together.

SEVENTY-TWO

Butch heads to his parents' house so we can pick up Emmy en route to heading home. Maybe for the first time, I truly, bone-deep, believe it's also my home. Where I belong. With my family. That's about to be legal since he's making an "honest woman" out of me. I smile broadly at that.

The tires crunch down the familiar drive, and I'm reminded of my first glimpse of this haven over a year ago. Looks like Liz and her brood are here, plus Jerri's parents, which means we can tell them the good news. I glance at Butch wondering if this was his plan all along and discover he's wearing a shameless grin.

Before he's opened my car door, family members stream onto the porch with Emmy running full tilt down the stairs and straight for us.

She barrels into me, throwing her arms around my legs, her head angling toward mine. "Did you say yes? Did you say yes?"

"I absolutely said yes!"

She screams, hugging me tighter, and my heart flips. *She really does want this.*

One by one, we're congratulated, embraced, and kissed. My entire being beams with unbridled, unfiltered happiness —like a sunray.

When we get home, I have a few calls to make, the first to my parents, who both get on the call. They aren't surprised...because unbeknownst to me, Butch called and asked my father for his blessing after sneaking the number out of my address book. Of course he did. He's a gentleman with values and this aligns with everything I know about this man. Correction: *my fiancé*.

"You're happy for me then?" I ask.

"We haven't met Butch," my father answers, "but if you think he's the right man for you, you have our blessing."

A twinge of irritation snaps thinking back to how that was *not* his take on Mick. My father thought less of Mick because he was a blue-collar mechanic, assumed he didn't have a *life plan*, accused him of taking advantage of me, of not being good enough for me. All shortsighted, judgmental bullshit.

"Thank you. He's most assuredly the one for me."

"We're thrilled for you, honey," my mother adds, a slight tremor in her voice. "Have you set a date or location?"

"He just proposed this morning, so no, but I'm sure we'll discuss details soon."

"Perhaps you can plan a trip home, and we can go dress shopping?" My mother sounds jarringly optimistic, yet I can't imagine she's got the energy for wedding undertakings.

Honestly, I just hope she can survive the big day without a handful of Valium and gallon of Chardonnay. Can I even expect her to travel here, when it's so far? Until this minute, I assumed we'd marry in Virginia. But maybe it should be in California...except that would require all of Butch's family to travel. My head swims.

"Jacqui?"

"Sorry, Mom. Spaced for a second. I'm thinking about the details."

She laughs softly. "It's an exciting time in every woman's life. Just let us know."

"I will. Thank you."

"And send us a picture of your ring!"

"We'll be happy to help pay for the wedding," my father inserts. "Within reason."

Right. "That's much appreciated."

"Alright then, I'm sure you have other calls to make."

"I do."

"Give Butch our congratulations," he adds.

They both say goodbye at the same time, and we hang up. I phone the only other people who matter, getting a hold of Kendra and Jas (unfortunately, Kit's not there). It's wonderful to catch up and hear their genuine excitement about my engagement. I tell them about the proposal, and they squeal and sigh at all the right moments. A pang of homesickness surfaces, and I wonder if a trip to California to see everyone and shop for my wedding dress makes sense.

"Everything good?" Butch asks.

"Mm-hmm," I say, pushing all intrusive thoughts away and returning to riding the high of *freshly engaged*. My head tilts and my lips purse. "But *someone* didn't tell me he asked my father for permission."

A sly smile spreads across Butch's face. "You think I'd half-ass something as important as this? You should know by now I have a code, do things properly."

My eyes spark. "No argument here, Lumberjack. Although..."

"What?"

"You didn't get on one knee."

Butch's eyes flare in a familiar way. "You want me on my knees, baby? You know how much I like that." His salacious grin speaks volumes, giving me a twinge in my lady parts.

I shake my head, stifling a laugh.

He pulls me into his arms and kisses me, grabbing a big handful of my ass in the process. "Hello there, sexy fiancée."

I return a languid smile. "God, I like the sound of that."

"I like the sound of *my wife* even better."

"Mmm...*possessive*."

"You have no idea," he murmurs. "You're mine. Forever trapped in my net now, gorgeous girl." He traces my lips with his finger. "Mine." Grabs my ass again. "Mine." Rubs between my legs. "Mine." Caresses my breasts. "Mine." Lands on my heart. "All fucking mine."

SEVENTY-THREE

"So...are you guys having an engagement party or what?" Liz asks, tapping a Christmas-red manicured fingernail against her coffee mug as we chat in her kitchen.

My mouth drops. "Seriously? I feel ambushed."

It's the day after the annual cookie-a-thon, where I was bombarded with wedding questions I couldn't answer before Liz rescued me, telling everyone to back off and let me breathe.

She cackles like the devil herself. When her daughter and Emmy shout from the den, Liz cocks an ear, waiting to see if it warrants investigation. Their resounding giggles confirm they're fine, and she refocuses on me. "Clearly, you need guidance. Which brings us back to your engagement party."

"We haven't talked about it. But Butch isn't, you know, formal like that?"

Her face lights up and her fingers snap crisply in the air. "We could make it lumberjack themed!"

I snort in the most unladylike way. "Sold!"

Her eyes gleam as if her brain is working a mile a minute. "Wait, are you serious?"

She pins me with a stare. "As a heart attack. I'm dying to plan a soiree, and this is the perfect opportunity. Did you already exchange gifts?"

"Gifts?"

"Oh my god. You don't know about the presents?"

My eyes flit from her to my coffee. "No," I answer, a tad defensively.

"It's customary for you to get each other engagement gifts. And later, wedding gifts."

I'm utterly baffled—and it's obvious.

"Didn't you spend most of your tender youth planning your wedding?"

My face scrunches up. "I never gave it a thought, actually."

Liz's mouth drops. "You're a mutant."

I pin her with a stare. "Look, I'm not the fussy type. More of a no-frills, low-maintenance kind of girl. I didn't have grandiose ideas about flowing gowns or tiered cakes or fancy receptions. I never thought about marriage, aside from assuming I'd do it one day."

After watching my parents, did I even believe getting married was all that enticing?

"Consider me your guide to help you plan the wedding of *my* dreams since you don't have any." She lists items on her fingers. "Engagement party. Wedding location. Dress. Hair. Bridal party. Readings." She sighs breathily. "We have so much to discuss."

And she thinks *I'm* the mutant? I freeze like a mouse under the hungry gaze of a hawk—just like yesterday.

"Trust me."

"Famous last words." Another sip of coffee fortifies me. I'm going to need gallons. And note to self: *brandy.*

Liz cocks her head, assessing me. "Don't you *want* some help? You seem overwhelmed. Stop staring at me as if I'm the firing squad."

She's right. Wedding prep should be joyous, not akin to death. "Fine," I squeak. "I could use your help. I'm clearly out of my depth."

She beams, her blue eyes practically glittering. "It's settled then. I'm so excited about this. And honestly, I'm just thrilled my brother met you and wasn't too stupid to recognize a good thing when he saw it." She winks. "Plus, we need to beef up the sorority around here."

I chuckle. As if. Turning serious, I place my hand on hers. "Thanks, Liz. I couldn't ask for a better sister-in-law."

"Let's hope you still think so after the wedding."

"You're going to push me way out of my comfort zone, aren't you?"

Liz just smiles knowingly.

LATER AT HOME, I FIND BUTCH IN THE UPSTAIRS bathroom fixing a leaky pipe. He's on his back, head in the vanity cabinet under the sink, long legs begging me to climb on top. Unable to stop myself, I straddle him.

He grunts, a lazy smile crossing his lips when his gaze tilts to study me. "Have a good time?"

I nod, smiling. "You?"

"Buckets of fun. I've gotten greasy, wet, and had to run out for parts even though I have an entire shed full of hardware except, of course, the one part I needed."

"Maybe I can improve your day."

His eyes shift, considering my offer. "Where's Em?"

"Downstairs."

He sighs. "I'll take you up on that later." He motions me off and slides out from under the cabinet.

"Did you know it's customary for us to exchange an engagement gift?" I ask, following him out.

Butch rightfully seems perplexed. He did, after all,

purchase the extremely expensive-looking ring on my finger. I've fallen deeply attached to it already. "Nope."

I glance at said ring. "This is more than enough for me. I love it so much."

"And you're more than enough for me," he says, carefully planting a kiss on my lips without touching me with his dirty mitts.

"You didn't properly warn me about your sister," I say, trailing him down the stairs and into the kitchen.

"Meaning?"

"She's hell-bent on being our wedding planner."

"Christ." He squirts some Gojo on his hands and works in the degreaser. "Good luck calling off that dog."

"Not even going to try."

"Look at you, beautiful *and* brains."

"As if you didn't already know that."

He grins. "Like I said, lucky SOB."

Emmy runs into the kitchen. "I literally have the best idea. Wanna hear it?"

"Can't wait," Butch answers.

"Ice cream. We should all go out for ice cream."

Butch crouches down to meet her face to face. "And what have you done to deserve such a treat?"

She scoffs. "Exist."

It's right then, staring at these two individuals who've claimed my heart, that I know what to give Butch.

THE NEXT DAY, I POP INTO THE CORNER PHARMACY and read through dozens of greeting cards pertaining to love. Realizing the important part is my personal sentiment, I purchase a blank card with a deep scarlet front and silver embossed heart. Once home, I carefully print my message—

ten little words that speak volumes—sign my name, then tuck it inside the envelope and place it on Butch's pillow.

When we climb into bed later, he picks up the envelope. "What's this?"

"Something for you," I say, my pulse instantly racing.

He reads it. Reads it again. And again. He glances up, eyes watering. Swallows hard, his Adam's apple undulating with the effort.

"Now you can throw the other one away," I whisper.

We fall into each other's arms as he crushes me to him, gripping me so tightly I almost can't breathe. We share a meaningful kiss. He lies back, bringing me with him, and I snuggle into the crook of his arm. He holds the card aloft, reading it again, as do I, even though I know exactly what it says.

I love you and I want this life.

Forever yours,
Jacqui

SEVENTY-FOUR

As we flip the calendar to 1989, the future's so bright, I've gotta wear shades, just like the song. Butch and I are getting married in October. The magazine I've worked so diligently on will launch its first three volumes, if all goes as planned. Emmy's unfettered disposition continues, and Butch's overprotectiveness relaxes more each month since her disappearance. Making a trip home to California stays on my mind, but with everything going on, I worry about taking a week off and it lands on the back burner.

Before I know it, it's Major League Baseball's Opening Day, and I'm glued to the television for Terry's debut as an Oakland Athletic. They're playing the Seattle Mariners in our hometown. Kendra told me he was traded over the winter, and I'm not missing this for anything.

Emmy pokes her head in the living room. "Whatcha watching?"

I pat the couch cushion, inviting her to join me, and she clambers alongside. "See number forty-three?" I ask, pointing at the screen.

She nods.

"That's my friend Terry. He's a professional baseball player. Isn't that cool?"

She shrugs, watches all of sixty seconds, and runs off. Apparently not that cool.

Even Butch doesn't totally get it. He grew up in Virginia, where there are no professional baseball, football, or basketball teams. In fact, many other states on the east coast don't have teams. I realize how fortunate I was to grow up with several in the Bay Area.

Sports united our city, which splintered into factions over crime, class, racial divides, culture, and more. And on a personal level, they bonded my father and me during those early, difficult years.

Needless to say, I'm vibrating with excitement. *Terry made it home.*

I'd give anything to be at the Oakland Coliseum watching him live, and I wonder which of our friends are at the game. Mick and Remy? Kendra? Vinny? Jeremy? I hope they're all there cheering him on. A flash of grief washes over me, and I pull the bowl of popcorn onto my lap and shove a handful in my mouth. No crying over the past. The players finish warming up and I only recognize some on the roster: Rickey Henderson, Jose Canseco, Mark McGwire, Dennis Eckersley.

It's an exciting few hours of shrieks, pride, and glee— enough to make Hemi abandon me eventually too. Oakland jumps into the lead in the first three innings, and Seattle answers in the middle innings, but the A's prevail 3-2. Terry gets one hit and scores, thanks to an RBI by McGwire. I leap into the air once it's over—I'm so proud of him, elated he's back in our hometown, and riding the high of a real success story. The guy couldn't deserve it more.

Two days later, Terry is dead.

SEVENTY-FIVE

Terry's death by cocaine overdose dominates the news. Sportscasters discuss rampant cocaine abuse among MLB players. Calls for drug testing resume. Various general managers and players weigh in on how player drug use has affected performance and cost them games and pennants.

I'm utterly drained, a gaping maw of grief left in the wake of my sobs. Leaning against the kitchen counter, I massage my forehead as a headache threatens.

Butch's hand strokes my back, and I meet his tender gaze. "I'm going home for the funeral."

He wraps his arms around me for the hundredth time this week. "Want me to come with you? I will in a heartbeat."

My whispered "no" is muffled by his soft cotton T-shirt, and I sink into the familiar scent and reassurance of his stable presence.

"You sure?"

I angle my face toward his. "Yeah. I just need—*want*—to be there, and I'm overdue for a visit with my parents anyway."

"I understand, although..."

"What?"

"It sounds trivial in light of everything, but it would be nice to meet your parents before our wedding day."

He's not wrong. It's weird that he hasn't...but this isn't the right time. I can't face the collision course of Terry's funeral, my past, and parental interaction with the stress of introducing my fiancé around too.

If I'm honest, Butch seeing behind the curtain of my fucked-up home life holds zero appeal. It's safer if he meets them out in the wild—for our wedding in Virginia—instead of in their natural habitat where alcohol and Valium and infidelity and bitter unhappiness prevail.

I book a flight, rental car, and hotel for the following day. It might be shitty, but I don't let my parents know. I don't want to field questions or deal with my folks until after the funeral. Next I call Kendra, and we decide where to meet the morning of the service. I graciously accept her invitation to stay with her afterward for as long as needed.

As I pack, a growing current thrums through my veins, gaining volume and speed. A lingering question. A small sliver of light that will not be snuffed. A tiny, reawakened voice.

Mick and Remy.

I know they'll be at the funeral. They're among Terry's closest friends.

And I'm not sure how I feel about seeing them.

But by the electricity sparking my cells, it's got unfinished business written all over it. And the guilt hits me like a hammer. I'm engaged. Why do I have questions? What does this mean? What's going to happen when I see my dynamic duo? It escalates my heart rate enough that I sit on the bed and put my head between my knees.

Butch jogs up the stairs and finds me in this position. "Are you okay?"

Fuck.

My pulse pounds in my ears. I need to get a hold of

myself. "Yeah," I whisper. "Just..." *Just what? Thinking about my ex-boyfriends? Ex-lovers?*

The mattress dips as my husband-to-be sits beside me, one of his huge hands rubbing up and down my spine in a soothing gesture. "What's wrong?"

This is the moment of truth, isn't it? The moment I tell him about my past, and he either shuns me or continues loving me.

I have to tell him, don't I? Otherwise, it's like lying...or at least, keeping something important from him. I promised never to do that again.

The pounding of my heart amps up again as I sit upright and rub my knuckles over my chest, avoiding his gaze. "Can I talk to you about something you might find difficult?"

"You know you can tell me anything, Jacqui."

I reach for his hand, and he squeezes it against mine. It's comforting, and I'm in blind faith mode. "There will be old friends...and ex-boyfriends," I say slowly, "at the funeral."

He makes a humming noise.

"I'm a little stressed about it, I think because one particular relationship was...non-traditional...and ended badly."

"Non-traditional?" he questions.

My heartbeat escalates to battering ram status and I force out a breath. "I loved two guys, who were best friends, and they loved me too."

He freezes, eyes darting away as he takes a minute that I desperately try not to fill with nervous chatter. "Sounds messy. And like a recipe for disaster."

"It had some messy moments," I admit. "Until we..." I can't say it.

Butch squeezes my hand reassuringly, urging me on, reminding me that he's my rock. God, I love him. It's this thought I cling to as more words spill. "Please keep an open mind when I say this."

He nods.

"We all decided to share each other and our love." I venture a glance at my fiancé and his eyebrows raise, but there's no condemnation. Yet.

His expression turns puzzled as he probably tries not to think about the physical equation. "I'd ask how that all worked out except you're here, engaged to me, and not there, so..."

A humorless laugh escapes. "Pretty much. It went surprisingly alright at first. Then it blew up spectacularly."

"Do you still have feelings for these guys? Are you having second thoughts about us?" There's tension in his voice.

"No!" I turn to Butch, cup his jaw and press my lips to his. "No," I reiterate.

He pulls back, green eyes blazing with intensity. "Then you changed your mind and want my domineering presence by your side as I stare those motherfuckers down?"

My loud laughter erupts. "Not necessary, Mr. Possessive and All Mine. There's a little unfinished business, and I'm just...I haven't thought about any of this in years." The result of so many blessings, chiefly the man sitting next to me. "Happily so," I add.

Butch sighs, sounding frustrated. "What kind of unfinished business?"

Remy. A pang pulses through me. "The kind where there was no goodbye of any sort with one of them, during which he met and married someone. I was hurt and angry for a long time about how he treated me. I'm wondering if seeing him will lead to a confrontation."

"I don't like it."

I stroke Butch's hair where it curls at the nape then let my fingers travel down his thick muscular neck. "It might not happen. I'm there to pay respects to Terry and his family. I'm not trying to worry you."

"What about the other idiot?"

Mick. Another pang. "He gave me a proper break-up, if there is such a thing." Boy, did he. A part of that still zings.

His gaze fastens on me. "I guess it's safe to assume these guys are morons for letting you go."

"True statement." I smile at him, forcing all my love and adoration into my expression.

"You're going to keep that rock on your left hand the whole time, right?"

I nod, grinning now.

"Tell the world you're engaged to the *best* man you've ever known?"

More nodding.

He cups my face. "Say you're mine, Sundance. Only mine."

"I'm all yours, Lumberjack. Only yours. There's no question about it."

"I still don't like it, but I trust you...and I trust us."

As he kisses me, I fully absorb these words I needed to hear and tuck them inside my heart for safekeeping.

Butch takes me to the airport. After opening my door at the curb in the departures drop-off area, he sets my suitcase beside me on the sidewalk. His hand threads through mine. "I hate that you're going alone."

"I'm fine...I promise. I love you."

He cradles my face and my hair whips in the wind. "I love you, baby. Call me so I know you arrived safely."

We share a fierce kiss, our bodies pressing against each other, then I take my bag and disappear through the automatic glass doors.

Ninety minutes later, I'm in the air, my thoughts swirling.

It's been five years since I've seen Mick or Remy. My best

friends. My lovers. The men who left a gaping hole—one that's been hard to repair—in my heart.

I'm not naïve enough to believe that what we shared could last forever, especially with the complications of our...*unusual* relationship.

But god, I miss them.

Shifting in my airline seat to gaze out the tiny oval window, patches of landscape blink through the clouds as this titanium contraption hurtles across the earth, California drawing me to my native shores.

Even though I've moved on, the nagging feeling something tangible is missing lingers, like the soldier who experiences a phantom limb after an amputation.

Maybe a part of my heart will always be missing because it will always be theirs. Or perhaps seeing them will heal this fissure and make it whole again.

Inhaling a fortifying breath, I settle against the headrest.

Endeavoring to open the box we shut all those years ago may very well be a fool's errand, but with my wedding on the horizon...I need to close that box once and for all.

My gorgeous engagement ring snags my attention, and I press it to my lips, reminding myself of Butch's essence. His strength is my strength, and even through this symbol, it infiltrates me, soothes me, grounds me.

I read, doze, and allow thoughts to come and go like summer insects.

When the aircraft touches down in San Francisco, I deboard and make my way to the rental car company. A short while later, I'm driving toward the Pacific, needing to see, smell, and inhale the coastline I've missed so terribly.

I'm out of the vehicle at the first opportunity, and every cell in my body jerks awake and alert, gulping the ocean air and reminding me viscerally of where I am.

California.

Home.

A huff of surprise leaves my lips. I stand before the majestic sea as realization dawns. No matter where I go, where I rest my head at night, California is in my bones, my blood, my DNA. It will always be home along with whatever state I currently reside.

"DID YOU GET IN OKAY?"

Butch's deep voice is a salve after a long day of travel. I cradle the hotel phone, curled on my side in the middle of a massive king-size bed. "I did, baby."

"I've got a surprise for you when you get home."

My heart performs a little flip. "Really? What is it?"

He chuckles. "Yeah, like that's going to happen."

I know. He's like a fucking vault when it comes to secrets. Something I love about him. "A girl can try."

"Don't bother to guess."

My mind whirs, then slows. I'm exhausted—and if I'm honest, anxious. There's no energy to mentally sift through a list of presents I could want. "I miss you."

"I miss you more."

"I'm too tired to argue." I stretch my legs, joints cracking in my ankles.

"Just how I like my women...pliant."

I bark out a laugh. "*Pliant* my ass."

"I like a pliant ass too."

"Well, that's true. You *are* an ass man." A loud yawn escapes.

"Get some sleep, Sundance. I'm sure tomorrow will be tough. What time is the funeral?"

"Midmorning."

He pauses. "I should be with you."

God no. Potent images of Mick and Remy flash unbidden in my mind. "That would be like coming to my high school reunion, a total drag. No one cares about the plus-one. You're just the guy everyone is morbidly curious about because they're nosy and want to know if I wound up with a hot guy or some balding loser." *And I need to do this alone.*

"Which one am I?"

"If you have to ask..." My lips curve into a smile.

"Ouch."

"I'll call you later tonight, hot guy."

"And then you better get your pliant ass back home."

"Soon, baby. Soon."

SEVENTY-SIX

Even though I arrive early at the Chapel of the Chimes, the only Oakland facility large enough to accommodate the mourners streaming into Terry's funeral, it's already packed. I wonder how many people here actually *knew* him and aren't just fans. I walk toward the imposing structure and find the fountain in the front, spotting Kendra. Like me, she's wearing a black, knee-length dress. Her hair is longer and in a new style.

Our eyes meet, and mine instantly well. We fall into each other's embrace, clutching tightly. I've missed her and never expected to reunite over something tragic. It's bittersweet. We pull apart, our hands connecting.

"Despite this fucked-up situation, you look amazing," I say.

"And you're still a fine-ass white girl," she answers, and we share wan smiles. "Let me see that ring."

I lift my hand.

"You better hang onto that man. That's exquisite, Jacqui, and so perfect for you."

"I know," I murmur, but it's hard to be excited about this with grief hanging so heavy between us. I sniff, reaching for the travel pack of tissues in my pocket. "You ready for this?"

Kendra tries to speak and chokes on a sob. "Nope. But we've got no choice."

"Let's get in there and find a seat before we're stuck in standing room only." I silently hand her a tissue.

We infiltrate the throng, scanning for open seats in the towering chapel. A dominating stained-glass scene looms behind the pulpit. We make it midway and push into a pew, then clasp hands tightly.

My gaze flits, panning the crowd, trying to study the pews around us. It's impossible with the constant motion of people standing, sitting, or squeezing into seats.

I know what I'm doing, who I'm looking for, but I can't make myself stop.

And then a flash of copper halts my breath.

The light hits Remy's hair as people shift enough for me to catch it. The sight of him barrels into me.

In a blink, he turns.

His eyes land on me.

We share a moment frozen in time, and I feel it...the caress of his gaze, warm and something else. *Damn, he looks good.*

He offers a subtle smile, but I don't return it. Despite the electricity flowing between us, I'm still hurt and fucking angry. His lips fall, and my eyes naturally gravitate to the seats beside him. His wife Sherry sits to his left. The crowd moves again and another head swivels my way with purpose.

Mick.

Our eyes collide and stick. My heart thunders and my chest floods as we stare for a full minute.

Surprise. Marvel. Regret. Reality.

His head tilts, providing a better view. His hair is short. He's freshly shaved. Suit lapels visible. The whole getup is likely giving him hives. His cryptic smile morphs into a warm one and I freely give one back.

The organ music begins, and Mick's eyes leave mine to face the front. I've got a firm grip on Kendra's hand, and she's more than happy to be my anchor in this storm.

The service starts, full of biblical excerpts, hymns, religious platitudes about death and resurrection, and somber remembrances by family, friends, players, and coaches. It's followed by Terry's burial in the adjacent Mountain View Cemetery, which most attend, and where I catch a heart-fueling glimpse of Jeremy and Vinny, other members of our ragtag friend group.

But the finality of Terry's shiny black casket, next to the freshly dug hole where he'll remain, snaps the last tether of my control, and I'm wracked with sobs.

As we make our way to the reception, my pulse rapid fires, roaring in ears as my nerve endings crackle with trepidation. This is where I'll come face to face with Mick and Remy— possibly for the final time in my life. Then again, I never expected to see them again, and here we are. The universe has a cruel sense of humor at times.

Am I tempting fate?

Kendra and I detour to the ladies' room to spruce up, our waterproof mascara unable to do the kind of heavy lifting required today.

And do I care what I look like? Undeniably so.

Look what you passed up, boys. Look and weep.

God, I'm pathetic.

MOURNERS PACK THE RECEPTION HALL, WITH people vying to fill their plates at the extensive buffet or already sitting and talking. Their mingled murmurs sound like a roar in my ears.

"I'm going to get in line," Kendra says, motioning to the buffet.

Sweat trickles down my back. "I need some air. I'll come find you."

I'm not four feet into the hallway when a hand touches my forearm.

"Jacqui, wait."

I whirl, coming face to face with blue eyes under cropped copper hair, and my body goes rigid.

"How are you?" Remy asks.

I have fifty retorts but can't summon one.

"Are you...are you upset with me?"

My scoff is harsh. "Remy, you cut me off without a word. One minute, we loved each other, the next, it was as if I didn't exist. And now you just want to, I don't know...shoot the shit, make small talk, swap pleasantries?"

His face contorts.

"You treated me like trash. Literal trash..." My eyes water. "After everything we shared? After what we..." I swallow. "Why?"

His gaze shifts to the floor before meeting mine. "I was really fucked up back then. For a long time." He runs a hand through his hair. "I treated everyone who mattered like shit. You never deserved that."

Fire blazes through me. "You hurt me. And you *destroyed* Mick and me."

He winces. "I know," he admits. "If I could go back in time and change it, I would. I'm so fucking sorry, Jacqui."

I shrug and look away. Sorry just doesn't cut it.

"I don't blame you if you don't want to talk to me. But I hope you can forgive me one day. I'm trying to be a better man. It's part of my recovery."

I soften a tad, and my gaze swings back to his. "Are you clean?"

His sapphire eyes radiate sincerity. "Coming up on two years."

"Good. If today was any reminder, it's that any of us—especially you—could be in that casket."

Remy squeezes his eyes tight.

"And you're happy? Happily married?" I can't disguise my interest.

A slow grin crosses his face. "Yeah." He shakes his head like he can't believe it either. "I wound up marrying my best friend."

That stings more than I expect. "Then I guess it was all for the good."

"And you?" He glances at my left hand. "You find a decent one?"

My own smile unfurls. "The best."

Remy holds out his hand. "So...friends? Or at least off the shit list?"

Fuck. Maybe it's the severity of the day, his stupid apology, or the part of me that's genuinely relieved he's clean, but I take his hand. "Not enemies," I offer. Because friendship is a stretch.

"I'll take it."

He squeezes my hand and returns to the reception. A minute later, I straighten my shoulders and follow.

A few steps in, I bump into someone and spin to find Remy's wife. Her light brown hair is styled into a flattering blunt cut with bangs.

"Oof, I'm sorry," she says, extending a hand. "I'm Sherry, Remy's wife. You're the famous Jacqui, right?"

"Um...yes?" I answer, shaking it. Her big hazel eyes are assessing, but not cold, and damn if she isn't pretty in a wholesome, girl-next-door way.

"Remy and Mick have talked about you for *years*."

They have? The warmth spreading through me like honey is undeniable. It's quickly doused by a flash of resentment. "We were really close." *And because of you, we aren't.*

Wrong, I internally scold. *Remy is the only one to blame here.*

"It's nice to finally put a face with the name," she says.

Sherry clearly doesn't know the extent of my relationship with Mick and Remy, or I doubt she'd say that. Why does she have to be so sweet? The petty brat in me wants to dislike her but the truth is, under different circumstances, we might even be friends. Remy doesn't deserve her.

"It's great meeting you too," I say.

"Well, nature calls." She chuckles, then places a hand over her belly, which reveals its slight protrusion. "We're expecting our first child, and I swear I'm peeing every five minutes."

"*Oh*. Co...congratulations," I sputter.

"We've got a table in the back. Come sit with us." We share a smile as she hurries off.

I find myself behind Leland in the buffet line and give him a long hug. He's known Terry since they were kids, and grief is etched indelibly in his tear-stained eyes.

After I fill a plate, Kendra waves me over as a few recognizable men bellow my name. It's the old gang and they're all smiles as I head toward them.

One by one, I'm hugged and welcomed.

"Bella!" Vinny greets me, swallowing me in an embrace. "Don't mind the fluffification," he jokes, patting his expanded middle as we part. "My wife likes it."

"I do?" the very pregnant woman at his left says before Vinny introduces us. We share a knowing smile.

Jeremy's next, lifting me off my feet.

"You a congressman yet?" I ask. His once perfectly feathered hair is now gelled and styled in line with his political aspirations, and an impeccable navy suit hugs his frame.

"State senator, baby. I see the years have done nothing but make you more gorgeous." He sets me down.

My smile stretches wide. "Still single and devastating all the ladies?"

"Unless you want to finally give me some of that." He blatantly checks me out top to bottom, always the flirt.

I slap him on the chest and roll my eyes, but underneath, I'm vibrating from Mick's nearness, aware he's biding his time, watching and waiting.

His chair drags along the floor as he stands, and our eyes clash. His absorbing gray irises send ripples through me. His gaze rakes down my body and lands on my left hand. Sorrow or pain tinged with grief swim in those memorable eyes before he schools his features.

We embrace, and his ocean scent wafts around me like nothing has changed. Only everything has.

"Hey Jax," he murmurs.

Thump thump. It's been years since anyone called me that, and truthfully, that name belongs to him. *"Mick,"* I breathe.

We part, I think both torn between wanting and hating to let go.

"You look well," he says, then blows out a laugh. "Fucking great, actually."

"Thank you. You—"

...also look amazing, like the motherfucker you've always been.

Do not get Micknotized. Do not get Micknotized. Do not get Micknotized.

"...too," I add lamely.

He dips his chin toward my hand. "Engaged?"

I nod, my emotions rioting.

"I'm not surprised." He opens his mouth as if to say more, then stops himself.

My eyes scan his hand and come up empty. "No one's stolen your heart yet?"

He stares at me for one molten moment. "I think we both know one woman did."

Thump. Thump thump. Thump thump thump. "You were stupid to let her get away."

He nods slowly, thoughtfully. "Agreed."

I'm relieved our friends aren't listening to us. Mick and I have gotten shockingly intimate—and honest—in just a few sentences. My heart thumps erratically, traitorously.

Mick breaks the spell, motioning to two chairs. "Tell me about the great things you're doing in the world. I want to hear it all."

"I think we all do," Remy echoes.

I start my recap, glancing at each person around the table. Remy and Sherry, Vinny and Stephanie, Jeremy, Mick, and Kendra. It evolves into each of us providing updates on our lives, reminiscing, and sharing Terry stories. There's laughter, good-natured ribbing, the poignant, familiar reminder these individuals are my first true family—the ones who made me whole, gave me life, and bestowed gifts too numerous to count.

The crowd thins as the reception comes to a close. We stand after two hours of reuniting. It's natural, intimate, soul-fueling. Terry would approve, despite the circumstances. I gaze fondly upon these four men who grew up playing Young America baseball with their pal, Terry, friends until the end.

Remy grips Mick and Jeremy each on the shoulder. "Let's go say goodbye to Terry's parents."

The guys nod in unspoken agreement, and the two wives squeeze their husbands' hands and walk toward the exit, leaving the remaining six of us to say our goodbyes.

We start the rounds, and it's surprisingly difficult.

When it's Remy turn, he hugs me tight, and I don't miss Mick's gaze fastened on us. I get a hit of nicotine and it damn near transports me to 1982.

"It's done my heart good to see you, Jacqui," Remy murmurs. "That you're flourishing, doing this writing stuff you always wanted, and living a good life. It's..." He releases me, tapping a hand against his chest. "It's awesome."

Seeing you healed something inside me too. I blink the emotion away.

"I'm grateful I didn't drag you down with all my bullshit," he adds, his head cocking in his signature way. "I'm clearly a selfish prick consumed with my own shit. But I really am sorry."

"I appreciate that," I manage. "I've hated hating you all these years. You were one of my favorite people...and one of the most important in my life."

Remy's throat works.

"I'm relieved you're doing well too. And about to be a damn father." I shake my head. Watch out, world.

"Weird, right?"

"Rem?"

"Yeah?"

"Don't fuck it up, okay?"

He snorts, salutes.

And that leaves Mick.

Saying goodbye to him is the hardest of all.

His gray pools find my amber, holding them captive like they always have. He's still so fucking handsome, still has some claim on this stupid contraption beating in my chest.

"I'm so proud of you, Jax. For pursuing your dream and embracing a new life far from here. I've only ever wanted you to thrive and seeing you the way you are now brings me a sense of...peace."

"I feel it too, about you—and Remy. It's given me closure, healing, whatever's been missing." I'm grappling for the right words. "I gave you my heart and it's been hard to repair it. Really hard. I wasn't even sure at times that I could."

He looks anguished. I'm guessing it was similar for him.

"All I want is for you to find your happiness. You deserve it, and you need to stop fighting it. Let yourself have a good life full of love, Mick."

He pauses. "I won't make you any promises, but I'll try.

Seeing you gives me hope that maybe that *is* in the cards after all."

"You're too good of a human being not to share your heart with someone."

He drops his head for a few seconds, then nods. He won't allow it to become morose or debate the merits of what he deserves...I know where he stands. Instead, he shoots me classic Mick.

"Live large. Kick ass. Keep shining, beautiful."

We hold each other close, and all the little fissures in my heart knit together. I breathe in his touch, scent, and body I've gotten lost in, allowing myself to experience it one more time...and let it go.

Today bestowed unexpected dividends: healing, a full-circle revolution, and a potent reminder of those who loved me when I didn't know how to love myself.

There's only one place now I want to be.

SEVENTY-SEVEN

I tap my foot as the Boeing 747 taxis. I'm ready to bolt, my belongings already in my arms, yet forced to wait until half the plane empties.

Interminable minutes later, I'm finally on the gangway to the terminal, stuck behind the same lollygagging passengers.

I scan the area as soon as my feet touch the solid airport floor, spotting him in seconds—my tall lumberjack, standing head and shoulders above these mere mortals.

Our gazes intersect and those arresting green eyes stroke mine as we hurry toward each other, smiles erupting. And then I'm in his arms, sharing a voracious kiss as everyone surrounding us at Gate 21 fades away.

"Missed you, Sundance," he murmurs, not letting me go. He looks exceptionally striking with his latest mustache and neatly trimmed beard.

"I missed you so much."

His body heat, woodsy scent, and firm grip ground me. He's forever my port in the storm.

"You good baby?"

I nod into his chest. "Especially now that I'm here with you...where I belong."

He kisses me again, and in that moment, we're the only two people on earth.

We part and head to baggage claim, hands linked, as he shares tidbits about Emmy's antics while I was away. I won't see her until tomorrow; Butch made it clear he's keeping me to himself for twenty-four hours. No argument here.

As we pass subsequent gates, I witness people reuniting, a young couple fighting, a toddler whining, a teenage boy scoping out a girl...a microcosm of life happening with our departures and arrivals. It perfectly summarizes my state of being—I've departed and arrived. I know who I am...my wants, my needs, my worth.

I know it without any doubt: this man holding my hand offers an enduring love, one full of mutual respect, kindness, exploration, and togetherness.

On the long ride home, I fill Butch in on my visit with my parents. My mother's improved health and demeanor, her excitement about the wedding, how she engaged with me... truly *with* me...unlike most of our interactions the past decade. She's finally trying instead of succumbing. If my heart hadn't already lifted from time spent with friends and mending the Three Musketeers, giving me closure and peace of mind, this put it over the top.

Even my father shared enthusiasm over our upcoming nuptials and meeting the Hamiltons. He offered praise for how I've handled difficult situations and the professional strides I've made. Regardless of my complicated emotions about Fred Hall, his pride in me holds weight.

The entire visit with my parents landed squarely in surreal, but I left more hopeful about salvaging our relationship than ever before, and I tell Butch that too.

He squeezes my hand, pleased. Butch understands the value of family and these revelations lift his heart. Because this man only wants what's best for me. I almost laugh, realizing these are the same words Mick, Remy, and I shared when we said our goodbyes. But isn't that the essence of "real" love? Wanting the people who matter to us to live their optimal lives, be happy and cherished?

SEVENTY-EIGHT

Butch wakes me with his tongue between my legs. I'm still sore from last night after we went several rounds, acting like we spent months apart instead of five days. If it's possible, something has shifted again with us...moved us another layer closer and deeper. And sex with this man rocks my world, pushing boundaries, ripping orgasms from my depths, and forging trust at the soul level.

I widen my thighs further. "God, I love your mouth." *And your mustache rides.*

His muffled answer sounds more like a groan.

Thick fingers. Hot breath. Slick tongue.

The tension mounts, and he senses it, pulling out all the stops as he strums me to pleasure oblivion, his lips suctioned to command central, a finger filling the other orifice he's claimed.

Ka-POW.

I grip his hair, my convulsing, quivering pussy arching into his mouth as he pushes my thighs impossibly wider, intently watching the show. Even when I try clamping shut, he holds me agape and bare, mesmerized.

"Butch," I plead.

"What do you need, baby?"

"You know what I need. *Please*."

"Tell me. You know it turns me on when you say what you want."

"Please push your big, beautiful dick inside me right fucking now."

He growls in approval. "You want me to fuck you, gorgeous girl?"

"Yessssssssss."

"Hard or slow?"

"Both. Hurry, Butch. *Please*."

"I will never get tired of hearing that," he murmurs, positioning himself. He thrusts all the way in, stealing my breath. Our eyes connect and fuse. His lips graze mine, providing a small taste of my own essence. "And I will never stop craving you."

My eyes roll back in my head as his hips move with purpose. The pleasure is intense. Our collective moans and ragged breaths fall between us as my hands grip his broad back. My legs spread wider to bring us even closer where we're intimately coupled, his hips fitting fully into the cradle of mine.

It's sublime. Consuming. Charged.

Our eyes meet as he drives harder, giving and taking. Claiming and surrendering.

He quickens and explodes, a sight to behold in both beauty and strength.

Our foreheads touch, our breaths heavy and hearts intertwined.

"I love you."

"I love you, wife-to-be."

Butch lifts his head, a sliver of emerald present around his dilated pupils as a devilish grin overtakes his handsome face. Before I can ask what he's smiling about, I'm hoisted into his arms and clutch his neck to hang on. He kicks open the bathroom door, deposits me on the mat, and starts the shower. It's giant sized, like him, with two heads—one positioned higher to accommodate his height, the other lower, perfect for mine.

What's going on? "Where's the fire, Lumberjack?"

"Patience," he says, that secretive smile back in place.

My brain stops guessing what he's up to as the hot water slides down my body. I sigh from the heaven of it, tilting my head back and closing my eyes.

Butch's finger traces my breast, pulling me from la-la land. "In exactly thirty minutes, I want you to come outside. Do not go downstairs before then. Do not peek out any windows. Get ready to go but stay in the bedroom until it's time."

My eyes narrow. "Is this the surprise you were talking about?"

He doesn't answer, just flashes a satisfied smile.

"You are a terrible tease and—"

He presses me against the tile and lays another dizzying kiss on me, effectively shutting me up.

I'M GYRATING, *DYING* TO KNOW WHAT HE'S HIDING from me. Three more minutes. I finish tying my shoes since he said we're going...somewhere. I'm in the dark on how to dress, so I donned my standard Levi's, T-shirt, and sneakers.

Time.

I bolt downstairs and out the front door, and my mouth drops open. I'm stunned into silence, frozen in place.

The lumberjack stands *in front of a Camaro,* one of his hands resting lightly on the roof. It's painted Rally Green with fat white stripes on the hood and rear. My breaths escalate. It's not just *any* Chevy Camaro... it's the kind I've always wanted.

A 1969 Z/28.

I stop gawking and finally descend the porch steps, eyes locked on the vehicle. "It's gorgeous. Beautiful. Sexy."

Butch's eyes meet mine. "I couldn't agree more."

"But you're a Mopar man. What is this?"

"Baby, this is a true testament of my love for you. It's an early wedding present."

My heart skips, tumbles, crashes. I stare disbelievingly.

He holds out the keys. "I restored it for you. As much as it pained me, it's your dream car, and you're *my* dream, so it's yours, Sundance."

My eyes tear and I throw my entire body at him, leaping into his arms and almost knocking him to the ground. I pepper his face with kisses—over his eyes, cheeks, nose, lips. I whoop loud enough that Butch winces, but I'm grinning and he's grinning as I overflow with sensations.

I jump down, grab the keys, and make a full revolution of the...*my*... Camaro.

Cowl induction hood. Pristine paint. Mag wheels.

Butch holds the driver's-side door open, and I slide into the seat with my heart thudding wildly against my ribcage. My hand grazes the shifter—four on the floor—then over the immaculate black dash, white upholstery, and steering wheel.

Butch climbs into the passenger side and I squeal, the natural high soaring through my veins.

"Start her up," he says.

The smile on my face can't stretch any wider, even when the motor cranks out that growling, sputtering, rough idle. I rev the gas just to hear it roar.

"It's got a 302 cubic engine and 450 horsepower."

She's gonna go fast.

"And—"

It dawns on me then. "*You* painted it green?"

He grins with a sheepish shrug. "Your favorite color."

"God, I love you," I say, planting another kiss on those generous lips.

He traces my jaw. "Clearly, I love you. Now show me whatcha got."

I depress the clutch, shift into first, and gun it down the driveway, spraying a little gravel, then slow...I don't want to scuff the paint. Once I get on pavement, all bets are off. The car roars and my gleeful laugh nearly eclipses it as I let it fly. My movements are fluid as I navigate through all four gears on these country roads, amazed at how this emerald machine handles, accelerates, and sounds. It's possibly the most elating thirty minutes of my life—and that's saying something.

Even though I could happily drive all the way to the Florida Keys in this all-mine muscle car, I reluctantly return home. When I shut off the ignition, my brain whirls, overwhelmed at the magnitude of this gift. It's of mind-boggling proportions, and I'm caught somewhere between jubilant and bawling.

"You okay over there?" Butch ventures.

I shake my head, biting my lip.

"Come here, baby."

I maneuver myself onto his lap in the most awkward, ungraceful, crawl-plop move ever.

"What's wrong?"

"It's just...so...awesome. Such an enormous present," I croak, stupid eyes welling *again*. And now I hear it...the voice that's accompanied me too long. The one always whispering that I'm not worth a damn.

But I *am* worthy. Worthy of Butch, the pursuit of happiness, abundance and gifts, and anything else. I have self-worth.

Butch tilts my face toward his. "I think you underestimate the depth of my affection for you, Sundance." He pauses. "What we've got is the real deal. My love for you grows every day, and it's the kind of perfection you don't question or try to explain. You hold onto it, nurture it, treasure it...and mash the fucking gas."

A tear slips from my eyes, absorbing his reassuring and beautiful words.

"In my mind, I've seen our life unfold all the way to the finish line—and it's blinding in its brilliance but also comforting and steady. You and me? We're meant to be. I thought I knew what love was before, and I was wrong. This, baby, *this* is it. I'd give you a hundred Camaros if it made you happy." He squints as if the idea pains him, and I chuckle.

Our lips meet, tasting of worship and longing, tenderness and passion.

"You are the most wonderful man. I don't know what I did to deserve you, but I'm going to love you with every ounce of my being for the rest of my life."

"That's all I want. You by my side."

"Like the real Butch and Sundance?"

He mulls that over. "Our rendition...partners *and* lovers."

I lift an eyebrow. "You want to christen this car, Lumberjack?" I whisper.

He answers with roving hands, his lips searing me with a kiss.

"I love that you're mine," he says. "And I'm yours."

My palms frame his face, his warmth seeping through my fingers. "Thank you for all that you are, have been, and will be. I can't wait to love you forever."

"I could get used to that." His pointed gaze—a bright, happy green—caresses me even more effectively than his hands, and I'm lost in his forest once again.

Up Next

California Dreaming Book Three
This emotional, delicious perspective from Mick's point of view spans not only his feelings about Jax but digs into his formative years. Treat yourself to the first two chapters. *(Download or see Bonus on my website)*

California Dreaming Book Four
This epic love saga concludes with a redemption story for Mick (because he asked...okay, begged) that takes place in another decade.

California Dreaming Book Five
This standalone spinoff features Kit and Jas with Kit's super cool age-gap love story. And of course, a few cameos by our favorite characters in the series.

Bonus
If you never read the highly satisfying bonus epilogue from *When There Was Us*, I highly advise you do! It's both heart-warming and gives you another potent hit of the Three Musketeers. *(Download or see Bonus on my website)*

Never miss an announcement or release
Subscribe to my newsletter *(or sign-up through my website)*.

Afterword

I chose to include workplace sexual harassment in this story because of the prolific amount I experienced for decades. This type of behavior was rampant in these years, and while it surely still exists, there are more policies and laws in place now to thwart, prevent, or punish it.

Regarding my personal experience, the first violation occurred in 1980, the first night of my very first job at age sixteen. I was hired to work at a movie theatre selling concessions and the assistant manager cornered me in a dark hallway near the storage room and forcibly kissed and groped me before I finally pushed him off and ran back to the lobby. I never returned after that night—but I also was too scared to tell the owner what happened, even when he gently prodded.

My next job (still sixteen) was at a cafe selling the newfangled product of frozen yogurt. The owner asked me to drop acid naked with him in a dark flotation tank.

My college internship was at an advertising agency with some prestigious clients despite it being a one-man show. Before my internship finished, my boss tried kissing me too, effectively cutting this credited requirement short.

Directly after college, I worked for a big, well-known

corporation. One of the vice presidents groped my breasts at a bar right out in the open; he didn't even bother to hide it.

When I moved to Virginia, I began working for a sizable company swanky enough to garner me a window office. My boss, the co-owner, was the biggest harassment offender of them all. He regularly leered at me, complimented my outfits as he openly gawked, told me dirty jokes, tried kissing me at an office party, and then fired me without just cause. While working at the same firm, a male client told me, "I want to fuck your brains out" (direct quote). You can probably surmise how my lech of a boss responded when I reported it: "Ignore him—he's harmless."

I've lost track of all the men who've made me uncomfortable with off-color jokes, sleazy compliments, and overt and inappropriate gestures in the workplace, but they occurred at nearly every job I held until I started my own company in 2000 (which, coincidentally, is when policy development, awareness, and court cases about this topic increased).

All this barely scratches the surface of the sexual violence, harassment, and unwanted attention I've experienced outside of the workplace.

It was impossible to report these issues when the problem took place at the top. But even when I did file a complaint, the owners/CEOs (always male) consistently counseled me to ignore the transgressions, saying these men/comments were "harmless."

It debilitated and frustrated me to feel so powerless, which is why I wanted to put Jacqui in the same position, only give her an empowering moment. I also loved spotlighting how parents can help their children understand the reality of the world that awaits and tangibly aid them to be better prepared for whatever comes their way by using Butch as an example.

I'm not alone in experiencing harassment, so I hope its inclusion was helpful or validating to readers.

PLAYLIST
IN ORDER OF APPEARANCE

- "Waitin' for the Bus" by ZZ Top
- "Oh Sherrie" by Steve Perry
- "Willie The Wimp" by Stevie Ray Vaughan and Double Trouble
- "Let's Go Crazy" by Prince and The Revolution (*Purple Rain* soundtrack)
- "Don't Look Back" by Boston
- "Valley Girl" by Frank Zappa
- "Suicide Is Painless" (theme from *M*A*S*H*) by Johnny Mandel
- "Nobody's Fault but Mine" by Led Zeppelin
- "Afternoon Delight" by Starland Vocal Band
- "I'll Be Loving You" by The Marshall Tucker Band
- "Crazy Train" by Ozzy Osbourne
- "Thunder Road" by Bruce Springsteen
- "Somebody to Love" by Queen
- "In Your Eyes" by Peter Gabriel
- "Jump" by Van Halen
- "Small Town" by John Mellencamp

- "Raindrops Keep Fallin' On My Head" by B.J. Thomas (*Butch Cassidy and the Sundance Kid* soundtrack)
- "Macho Man" by The Village People
- "We Belong Together" by Robert & Johnny (*Christine* soundtrack)
- "Reasons" by Earth, Wind & Fire
- "Dance the Night Away" by Van Halen
- "At Last" by Etta James
- "Let's Stay Together" by Al Green
- "The Future's So Bright, I Gotta Wear Shades" by Timbuk 3
- Bonus track (for my anti-hair band lumberjack Butch—complete with rockin' chainsaw solo): "The Lumberjack" by Jackyl

ACKNOWLEDGMENTS

My dear husband, love of my life, the man who's always had my back, my "touch her and die" IRL* protector, and a guy who really did read Cosmo in his younger years for additional "tips" on how to please women, you've ruined for me for anyone else with your big, unconditional love. I know you were skeptical about *my* love when I allowed Fords and Chevrolets and other makes into *When There Was Us*, but I told you redemption was coming, and didn't it? The Hamilton family and their restoration business is Mopar all the way. I even gave Butch a Barracuda—this is how much I love you. You are my redwood and have steadied my path since our chance meeting almost 40 years ago. Thank you for your incredible support of my writing, even when it puts me "in the bubble" for days on end. *Note: IRL stands for in real life. "Touch her and die" is a vibe some of us romance readers like in fictional men. I'm explaining these pop culture references since you pretend to live in the 1950s.*

Thank you, Mom, for reading every book I've ever written... and wanting to. Even though it freaks me out to know you're reading some of my explicit scenes, I absolutely adore how much you support me in chasing this long-held dream. I also get teary each time I think about how you said Emmy was unwittingly just like me at her age...outspoken, speedy, and light on her feet.

Massive thanks to my editor, Josie Juniper, who is thorough, questioning, snarky, smart, and so freaking deft. Your suggestions always push me to make the implausible plausible, the character arcs aim higher, and the open loops close. I will always laugh at your comments (along with curse and cry). P.S. I'm sorry you had to endure an FMC who was lacking at math and science—I know it presses your STEM-girl buttons. Also, romance fans: go read Josie's romances... they're wonderful!

A special thank you to author friends who listen, encourage, and laugh with me on this artistic, emotional journey. I'm grateful for your presence, especially Cynthia Brubaker, Nicole Devonne, and Claire Stibbe. A massive grateful shoutout to the authors in our Indies Do It Better (Tits out, girls!) group for their support, rapport, and generosity. Love you gals.

Much appreciation to the K.C. Lake Street Team...I thank you one and all for trying to elevate the California Dreaming series so more readers can fall into this world. This includes Crystal Marie DiBlasio, Rebecca Ferrel, Chloe Graham, Jenn Lynette, Beth Franchina-Melito, Hope Myers, Jennifer Naval Peak, Julie Peden, and Leialohaioi Tassillio.

A huge shoutout to my beta readers Crystal Marie DiBlasio, Beth Franchina-Melito, and Amber Tischio. I appreciate you, your excitement, and your love of these characters so much! Thank you for coming for the ride. Thanks also to my ARC readers. You help propel this bus forward, and your willingness, kindness, and enthusiasm are greatly appreciated.

Thank you to Marisa Gelfand, licensed professional counselor, for her consult on responses children and adults would have from trauma that occurs in the book. In addition to her practice, Marisa is also the creator of The Character's Toolkit, which explores coping skills and mental health concepts through characters in popular novels. Listen to the podcast!

To my wonderful cousin and attorney Linda Redlisky, thank you for your guidance on plausible legalities in my fictional world. You are one of my favorite people and the way you've supported me in my author career makes me feel blessed.

Thanks to Tom Fitzgerald, former Virginia law enforcement, for his consult on police procedures.

And from my whole heart...THANK YOU to everyone who read, posted, reviewed, and loved *When There Was Us*, then became feral for book two. I appreciate every one of you for taking the ride and experiencing it the way I'd hoped. These two books are literally (*ha*) my heart, infused with huge, unearthed emotion from my younger years and bruised heart. It's a love letter to finding yourself and your person, even when you thought someone else might fill that space. Life takes us where it takes us but it's our job to embrace the journey and be brave. Loves yas. XO

About the Author

K.C. Lake writes angsty, realistic love stories packed with heart and heat. California Dreaming is her first romance series. An avid romance reader, her shelves are lined with trophies, and her TBR is out of control (then again, size matters). She lives with her grumpy, touch-her-and-die, non-billionaire husband and dog in the beautiful woods of Virginia. Find more info, subscribe, and connect at www. kclakebooks.com.

Your review on any book site or social media platform is greatly appreciated.

www.ingramcontent.com/pod-product-compliance
Lightning Source LLC
Chambersburg PA
CBHW021331310726
48971CB00001B/69